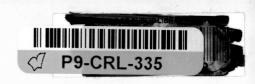

ISOLATION WARD

ISOLATION
WARD

JOSHUA SPANOGLE

DELACORTE PRESS

ISOLATION WARD
A Delacorte Press Book / March 2006

Published by
Bantam Dell
A Division of Random House, Inc.
New York, New York

Book design by Glen M. Edelstein

Delacorte Press is a registered trademark of Random House, Inc., and the colophon is a trademark of Random House, Inc.

Library of Congress Cataloging in Publication Data
Spanogle, Joshua.
Isolation ward / Joshua Spanogle.
p. cm.
ISBN-13: 978-0-385-33853-0
ISBN-10: 0-385-33853-8
1. Physicians—Fiction. 2. Group homes for people with mental disabilities—Fiction. 3. Women with mental disabilities—Fiction. 4. Virus diseases—Patients—Fiction. 5. Hospital patients—Fiction. 6. Baltimore (Md.)—Fiction. 7. Epidemics—Fiction. I. Title.
PS3619.P344I85   2006
813'.6—dc22
2005041743

Printed in the United States of America
Published simultaneously in Canada

www.bantamdell.com

10 9 8 7 6 5 4 3 2 1
BVG

The history of medical innovation has shown us unwilling to resist tangible individual benefit even in the face of unknown risks.
From "Uncertainty in xenotransplantation: Individual benefit versus collective risk," *Nature Medicine* 4, 141–144 (1998)

To the Spanogles, Waltemyers, Buffingtons, and Ureys

●

Acknowledgments

Many thanks to:

All those who read this book in its embryonic form, including Elisha Cooper, Austin Bunn, William Clifford, Alberto Molina, Michael Lee, and AJ Nadelson. For a guy who spends a lot of time in the hospital and in the lab, I've been blessed with a collection of highly lettered friends. I'd especially like to thank Jennifer Sim, who sacrificed countless hours and untold brainpower at the altar of *Isolation Ward,* and John L'Heureux, whose status as a teacher, writer, editor, and mentor is unparalleled.

My professors and colleagues at Stanford Medical School and elsewhere. Thanks particularly to Dr. Julie Parsonnet for her expertise in infectious disease and epidemiology. For their input about other things medical, I'm grateful to Dr. Art Reingold, Dr. Stephen Ruoss, Dr. Robert Chase, Dr. Sara Cody, and Martha McKee.

Alice Martell of the Martell Agency, who has been stunning through this whole process. I cannot imagine a more talented reader and advocate. I count the day I met Alice as one of the luckiest in my career.

Kate Miciak at Bantam Dell, editor extraordinaire. I—and all the characters in this book—are deeply indebted to Kate. Working with her has been like taking a master class with, well, the master. I've learned a tremendous amount through her, and still hold out hope that the bill for tuition will be negotiable.

Stanford Medical School, specifically the Stanford Medical Scholars Arts & Humanities Program and the donors who sustain it. Stanford's support of its students' endeavors, be they artistic or clinical or scientific, is without equal among medical schools. I am truly fortunate to be a student there.

Finally, my family, whose collective bookshelves groaned under the weight of so many pages. In an environment filled with such love of words and stories, how could I not grow up to write?

1. BALTIMORE

This is how it started. At least this is how it came to me over the telephone, 6:30 a.m. from a local health official trying to keep it together, fighting against little sleep and a ballooning fear that this might be The Big One.

A week and a half before, 4:15 p.m.: A thirty-one-year-old white woman presented to the Emergency Department with a sore throat, muscle pain in her legs and back, and a dry cough. She had a slight fever. The staff doctor thought it was garden variety flu, gave her some fluids and Tylenol, and sent her home.

Three days later, she was back at the hospital. The pain in her throat was worse; her tonsils were engorged and flaming red, flecked with pus. She'd added a good two degrees to the fever—this is Celsius now, so she's up to about 104 Fahrenheit—and a collection of new, disturbing symptoms: abdominal pain, diarrhea, bleeding gums, bloody nose. Rectal exam showed bright-red blood, indicating hemorrhage in the lower gastrointestinal tract. She had severe pain in the muscles of her neck and back. The guys in the ED tapped her spine, analyzed her blood, and started her on IV fluids. She was beyond emergency room help, so they admitted her to the hospital.

The docs upstairs swabbed the throat, took blood and tried to culture some bacteria, ran ELISAs to find viral antibodies. No luck. They kept pumping fluids, balancing her electrolytes, and generally giving her what we call in the trade "supportive therapy." It's what you do when you can't do anything else.

A day later, another young woman presented to the same ED with flulike symptoms: aches, fever, dry cough. Again, fluids and Tylenol, and the emergency medicine doc sent her home. The next day she was back: abdominal pain, muscle aches, high fever, vomiting, sore throat. Some bleeding in her gums. They admitted the woman and contacted the local health department. Still, though, no red flags went up.

Until the next day, when the skin of the first woman began to slough. It started as petechial hemorrhages—pinpricks of blood under the skin, a sign that tiny capillaries were leaking and bursting. But the pinpricks grew quickly into patches; the patches lifted off the underlying tissue, leaving raw, bloodied ulcers.

Then, early that morning, just after midnight, another young woman came into the emergency room. She, too, complained of flulike symptoms, and she was scared. It seemed that she lived with the woman who first presented, who was upstairs shedding her skin.

In the third case, the woman wasn't sent home but was immediately admitted. That was at 2:41 a.m. Four hours later, I was taking it all in from Dr. Herbert Verlach.

Verlach was rattled, and anything that rattled him, an ex–Army doc, rattled me. As he rambled on, I could almost hear his mind ratcheting through the possible diagnoses for these women: Lassa fever, Ebola, Marburg, or one of the myriad other nasties against which we're trying to protect the public. You tell yourself that the likelihood of its being anything really bad—or, worse, really bad and intentional—is pretty damned small. But that pretty damned small chance is what we're paid to watch for. And paid to stop if we can.

I wondered how Verlach slept at night.

Anyway, I sleep like shit, so I'd been up for two hours by the time his call came. Before I was off the mobile phone, I was in my car, speeding through Baltimore's morning rush, a tight feeling in my gut that this was not going to turn out well.

CHAPTER 1

St. Raphael's was an old Catholic hospital, struggling to maintain its independence in the face of overtures—friendly and outright aggressive—from Johns Hopkins and the University of Maryland. The hospital sat in the middle of a decayed neighborhood in the southwestern quadrant of the city, surrounded to the north and west by housing projects and to the south and east by a mix of old factories and abandoned row homes. The hospital served the needy in the immediate area, but extended its reach to the working-class neighborhoods of Pigtown and Locust Point. The last I heard, it was hemorrhaging money and talks with Hopkins and Maryland had started up again, this time at St. Raphe's behest. The former belle at the ball, now trying to dance with anyone who'd have her. Rumor had it the powers that be—admin at St. Raphe's, the Catholic archdiocese, the city, Hopkins, U of M—were just going to shutter the old girl. As the dirty pile of bricks, streaked black and dotted with a few forlorn statues of St. Raphael, came into view, I thought a mercy killing might not be the worst thing.

Still, there was a soft spot in my heart for the place. I'd just spent two weeks at St. Raphe's setting up a program to identify exactly the kinds of things that seemed to be happening. Outbreaks. Bioterror attacks. Bad things. St. Raphe's, in other words, needed me. Not like Hopkins, which basically taught my employers, the Epidemic Intelligence Service at CDC, how to play their game. If every employee at CDC were suddenly to die or, worse, to take a job in the private sector, Hopkins probably felt it could rebuild the Centers from scratch. No, St. Raphael's was a third-tier hospital in a city dominated by some of the best medicine in the world. My job was to get this old gal up to snuff.

Okay, my job. I am an officer in the Epidemic Intelligence Service, a branch of the Centers for Disease Control and Prevention. Apropos of my duties—to conduct surveillance for and investigations of outbreaks of disease—the title of *officer* is a fitting one. The cop jargon has been with us for a long time. *Medical detectives* was often used to describe officers in the service by those on the outside and on the inside, though the term long ago fell out of use, perhaps because it sounded a little too self-aggrandizing at the same time it sounded a little too trite. Anyway, that's what we do. We look for and hunt down diseases.

As with many things—fashion, say, or diet plans—there is some circularity to the history of the EIS. Originally conceived at the start of the Korean War as an early-warning system for biological attack, the EIS has spent decades searching for things to do. And it's done a pretty good job of finding them. The Service was instrumental in restoring public confidence after a polio vaccine scare in the fifties; it helped erase smallpox from the world; in the late nineties and early '00s it tracked down and set up surveillance for West Nile virus. And now the country is back to freaking out about bioterrorism. Which is why I was in Baltimore, helping to patch a hole in the country's disease-surveillance net. Normally, an old hospital wouldn't merit much attention, but St. Raphe's proximity to the nation's capital scared the public health gods, who wanted to ensure that any outbreak in the area was identified quickly. So, they sent me to set up a surveillance program.

Me. I'm part of the Special Pathogens Branch, which is in the Division of Viral and Rickettsial Diseases, which, in turn, is part of the National Center for Infectious Diseases, one of the Centers in the Centers for Disease C & P. My knowledge doesn't go too much deeper than that. Though I could spit out to you molecular biology of the family Arenaviridae, I couldn't sketch the organizational chart of the CDC. I leave that to the brilliant bureaucrats and technocrats in Georgia and

Washington. If there was a Nobel for institutional complexity, these guys would lock it up year after year.

I pulled my car into a no-parking zone near the Emergency Department and slapped the Baltimore City Health Department placard on the dashboard. I fished in the glove compartment and found my old CDC placard and put that out, too. Outbreak or no outbreak, the last thing I wanted to deal with was a towed car.

I ran through the automatic doors to the Emergency Department, pulling my ID around my neck as I went. The place was oddly serene; it was, after all, early morning, July, and a weekday. That was a good thing. Although Verlach was on edge, it seemed word hadn't filtered out to the rest of the hospital or, God forbid, the press. The past few years—the anthrax fiasco, SARS—had taught the public health world the finer points of a 24/7 media with an insatiable appetite for the new, new thing.

There was a beige phone on the wall behind the nurses' station. I grabbed it, pounded in the pager number for the hospital epidemiologist, and waited. Two minutes later, the phone rang. I picked it up before the first ring ended.

"Dr. Madison, it's Nathaniel McCormick. I'm in the ED," I said.

The voice that came over the phone was faint, muted. "And I'm up on M-2. What the hell are you doing down there?"

CHAPTER 2

M-2 was a single hallway flanked by double-occupancy rooms. The white linoleum floor was long ago scuffed to gray, the beige walls streaked with a grime that never quite vanished, despite the best efforts of housekeeping. It was the mirror image of M-1, the medicine unit directly below it, except that the end of M-2 was capped by a set of metal double doors.

A laser-printed sign was taped to the doors: ISOLATION AREA: CONTACT PRECAUTIONS MANDATORY. AUTHORIZED PERSONNEL ONLY. QUESTIONS? CALL BIOTERROR/OUTBREAK PREPAREDNESS AT x 2134. THANK YOU!

Now, no one's ever accused me of being understated, but I thought introducing a loaded word like *bioterror* might be a wee bit alarmist.

The isolation unit was split into two areas. I was in the first, a small vestibule with two sinks, a big red biohazard trash bag, and trays of gowns, goggles, gloves, and shoe covers. Three opened boxes of half-mask, negative-pressure respirators sat on a rolling cart. The respirators filtered down to five microns, about the size of, say, hantavirus. I was glad to see they were sufficiently worried.

This type of arrangement—a small, cordoned section of the hospital—was a holdover from the bad old days of tuberculosis. Not all hospitals had them anymore; most places just isolated the sick in private hospital rooms. But here was a short hallway flanked by four rooms, two on each side, cut off from the rest of the building, dedicated to keeping the infectious and infirm from the rest of us. A good little quarantine area.

After suiting up and finding my size respirator, I opened another set of doors at the back of the room. As the door cracked, I could hear a rush of air, felt a suck against the disposable gown. The negative-pressure system—pressure greater outside than inside, to prevent small particles from being blown into the rest of the hospital—was working. The air would be passed through a filter, then blown outdoors.

I made sure the respirator was fast against my face; then I pushed open the door and walked inside.

Three figures, looking like aliens in their protective getup, were talking in the middle of the hallway. Besides the people, there was nothing here but a crash cart, a large biohazard waste can, and a table with a fax machine, paper, and pens. The crash cart was filled with drugs, paraphernalia for placing a central line, basically anything we'd need if a patient's heart stopped or, in medical parlance, if they "crashed." The fax was directly connected to another machine at the nurses' station outside the biocontainment zone. Notes, orders, and the like would be sent from there to the other fax. It's how we planned to get around carting contaminated medical records back and forth into the hospital. St. Raphe's, like many places, was still in the dark ages of paper records.

Despite their masks, I recognized the female Dr. Madison and Dr. Verlach, who was black. The third man, an older white guy, I didn't recognize. I stepped up to the group, which made sort of an amoeboid shift to accommodate me.

"Antibodies?" Verlach asked, his speech raspy and tinny through the respirator.

"Not yet. Nothing specific," Dr. Madison said. "No idea what it is. . . ."

Finally, the three looked at me. Verlach said, "Dr. McCormick, you know Jean Madison. This is Gary Hammil—" He pointed at the man I didn't know. "He's the new Chief of Infectious Diseases at St. Raphael's."

Ah. The new Chief of ID. St. Raphe's had been casting around for someone for months; they must have netted Dr. Hammil in the past few days. Nice of them to tell me.

I looked at Hammil. "Nothing like diving in headfirst."

"Especially when the pool has no water," he said. We both forced a laugh.

"Dr. McCormick is on loan to us from CDC," Verlach explained.

"Okay, thanks for the introductions," Jean Madison said, annoyed. Then, to me, "Tissue, blood, saliva have all gone to the labs here."

"Here?" I asked.

"Baltimore City."

I looked at Verlach. He said, "Fastest turnaround. We sent samples to the state lab, too."

Hammil asked, "What do they have at the city labs?"

Verlach looked at the floor. "Um, we don't have much, mostly run-of-the-mill. But state is pretty stocked. Tests for the filoviruses, Marburg and Ebola. I think they have Lassa, Rift Valley, Rocky Mountain spotted fever, Q fever. More. They don't have everything, but they have a lot, actually."

"Well, CDC is there if you need us," I said. CDC had resources—modes of analysis, genetic libraries of pathogens—that far outstripped those of Baltimore City or Maryland State. We had, in fact, the largest repository of disease-specific tests in the world at our headquarters in Atlanta. We also had the largest repository of actual bugs. Not a place to take your kids when they're in the oral stage.

Madison spoke quickly. "Thank you, but I think we can handle this here."

Gary Hammil said, "Jean—"

"We have access to the state labs," she interrupted. "We don't need to call in the federal government."

A word about CDC's relationship with everybody else in medicine and public health: our jurisdiction is everywhere and nowhere. Really. We intervene only at the request of individual counties and states. If there's no request, CDC stays out of it. And though there are a million reasons why someone would want to ask for help from Atlanta, there are a million reasons why they wouldn't, most of them having to do with control.

During my training in Atlanta, they drummed into us, over and over again, the finer points of dealing with the locals. In general, we try to tread very softly. It's not something I'm particularly good at. In my evaluations over the previous year, "professional relations" was an area that consistently contained the phrase *needs improvement*.

Hammil looked at me. "Dr. McCormick, we appreciate your offer of support."

I nodded. I nod when I'm not exactly sure what to say.

Madison sighed. "Well, it looks like we have the lab situation worked out, for the time being, anyway. We'll use state." She turned to Verlach. "Baltimore City will head the outbreak investigation?"

"Yes," Verlach said. "I already spoke to the commissioner. We'll call state for more hands if we need to. Since Dr. McCormick is already here and familiar with the city, I'm going to ask that he stay on for the investigation."

Silence.

"I'd be happy to help," I said finally.

"I thought we agreed to rely on state," Dr. Madison said.

"For the labs, Jean, not for the investigation itself. Dr. McCormick is more familiar with this situation than—"

"Having CDC involved is going to signal the press—"

"He's already here, so we can downplay the request. Besides, not having him on board would seem like an oversight."

"I want to emphasize," I said, "CDC is here to help at your request. Just as it was with setting up the surveillance program, we can be as much or as little a presence as you want. The investigation and outbreak control will all be locally led, as well as contacts with the press. We'd also be happy to provide you with clinical expertise."

There was a long silence, and I knew I had just stepped into it somehow. Jean Madison—the Consistently Aggrieved—finally blew. "Oh, come off it. Clinical expertise?"

I stammered, "I'm merely offering assistance if you should need—"

"—if we should need clinical expertise. I know. Thank God you're there for us."

I looked at my shoes, covered in light blue paper booties. I sighed.

Jean Madison let out a sharp little laugh. "What do you think we do here, Dr. McCormick?"

"I—"

"We have some of the finest staff in the city to—"

"*Jean—*" Dr. Hammil said.

"—care for these women."

"I'm not commenting on the in-house expertise," I began.

"Of course you are! You seem to think you're in some backwoods clinic. Surprise, surprise, we have seen our share of sick people, and they *do* get better."

"I wanted you to know there are resources available to—"

"Thanks for your input, Doctor. We'll take it under advisement." With that, she turned to the door. Before opening it, however, she turned back. "I'm calling a staff meeting, gentlemen, in ten minutes. Dr. McCormick, since you seem to have expertise we don't possess in-house, I'd like you to present your differential for these women."

"But I haven't even seen the—"

She was already out the door.

Another door opened as a nurse, dressed in her moon suit, exited one of the patient's rooms. She said hello to us, then disappeared into another room. A hospital, even an isolation ward, is a place of constant activity, constant interruption, constant opening and closing of doors. Privacy for patients as well as for their caretakers is an alien concept.

After the nurse was gone, Hammil said, "How old are you, Dr. McCormick?"

"What? I'm thirty-three."

He nodded. "I guess that explains a lot. Grow up." He caught Verlach's eye, turned, and followed Jean Madison into the vestibule. The door closed with a hiss.

CHAPTER 3

Verlach and I were sharing a quiet moment, just the two of us in the hallway.

"I think she likes me, Herb."

Verlach said nothing. Even in the best of times, he didn't always know what to make of me.

"Yeah," I said, "you got it. I think she likes me in *that* way. It just comes across as pure, white-hot hatred."

"Well, things are a little tense here."

"Really? No."

Verlach regarded me through the respirator and face shield. "Gary Hammil I don't know. But I've known Jean Madison for years. She's a good doctor—damn good infectious disease doctor—good epidemiologist—"

"And she's still ticked that her surveillance program got slammed by Public Health. She's still annoyed they brought you and me in."

"That might be true."

"It is true. And this new guy, Hammil, says that I need to grow up? I'm an emotional Methuselah compared to her. Jesus."

"Okay, okay, you might be right, but try to see it from her side. She's been here for two decades. At this hospital. She's seen the assaults on its reputation, its finances, its medical staff. But it stays alive. To the point where the mere existence of this place irritates people. Everyone's on the sidelines waiting for a slipup."

"But dealing with this like it's a case of the sniffles is a slipup. Am I wrong here? Isn't hemorrhagic fever on the differential?"

"We don't know."

"Come on, purpuric rash? The bleeding? I haven't even seen these women and I'm thinking—"

"We don't know anything yet."

"But even if we're *thinking* about it, they—" I waved my hand toward the closed door. "This is bullshit."

"Don't sweat it."

"I am sweating it. *They* should be sweating it. This is crazy, Herb. They should shut down the wing. They should be kissing my ass—and your ass—asking for help. When do you think was the last time they saw Lassa fever here?"

"I don't—"

"Machupo? CCHR? Junin? Rift Valley—"

"I get the point."

"I know half a dozen people who've seen one of these in the last year." Gradually, I was able to get myself under control. "Come on. At least they should shut down the floor. Even with the isolation, I can't believe they still have patients up here. I can't believe it didn't even come up. You should shut down the floor if they don't."

"It's been five hours since we decided these cases might be related. All things considered, I think the hospital's doing an adequate job."

"Adequate? And that's enough?"

"Are you trying to tell me my job, Dr. McCormick?" Verlach glared at me until I looked away. "This isn't a textbook. And not everything happens as fast as you'd like." Even through the face mask, I could see he was very tired. Tired and anxious. "Still, you're right. You are correct." He sighed. "I've been in public health for seven years. Probably a hundred outbreaks in that time. I even handled a case in which a pissed-off waiter spread salmonella in the salad bar of the restaurant that fired him. But nothing quite like this," he said. "I'll suggest to Jean that she consider making an official request for help, though I can guarantee you she won't request it from you."

"Come on. I'm expecting to get it with a box of chocolates, maybe on the back of a boudoir photo—"

"Nate—"

"Look, I don't care whether she asks me or not. I care about keeping these girls alive. I care about nobody else getting sick."

"I know. But try to calm down about that."

We were silent for a moment. Then he said, "Look on the bright side: if you're going to get sick, Baltimore is the best place in the world to do it." That was a commonly held belief in this city and, indeed, elsewhere; I wondered what the folks in Boston would have to say about that. "Anyway," Verlach said, "I'm going to suggest they close down M-2."

" 'Suggest?' "

"Try to pick up on subtleties, Dr. McCormick. M-2 will be shut down."

Verlach walked into the vestibule, leaving me alone for a moment to contemplate what, exactly, was going on. Not to be arrogant, but I'm a smart guy. I understand the way the human body works, I understand the way microbes attack it, I'm even beginning to understand how bugs work their way through a population. But people, I do not understand. Their motivations and hidden agendas. The events of that day and the days following would show me just how severe a liability that is.

I walked into the vestibule, where Verlach was stripping off his protective gear.

"If we're investigating this thing," I said, "I thought we should begin by examining the women. Talking to them. I haven't even seen them yet."

"Work on that memory. You have a presentation in ten minutes."

Not wanting to touch the outside door handle with gloves that had been in the quarantine, I stripped off my gloves and put on a new pair.

"What are you doing?" Verlach asked.

"I'm going to look at the patients. I need to see what the hell I'm presenting."

"Your meeting, Dr. McCormick—"

"—can wait a few minutes," I said as I opened the door. "Tell them I'll be there when I get there."

CHAPTER 4

As a kid, I always wanted to be a bruiser, a tough, a real crusher, which made the verbal sparring with Jean Madison kind of ironic when you think about it. Or maybe it made perfect sense. Anyway, my ambitions as a twelve-year-old were more or less dashed by a delayed puberty and by a thrashing I got in the seventh grade from a budding sociopath named Chad Pershing. All those sit-ups and push-ups failed to help me against Chad, a hormone freak who had started to shave at age ten. The details aren't important; the upshot is: it was then that I decided the fate of Nathaniel McCormick lay less with the Joe Fraziers of the world and more with the Albert Schweitzers. If nothing else, I found it hard to believe that any member of the National Academy of Sciences would ever be able to kick my ass as thoroughly as Chad.

An uneventful but relatively productive high school career led me to Penn State for college. I took my degree in biochemistry, rode the coattails of some pretty important scientists doing some pretty boring research, and, by the end of my stint in State College, I had a broad range of medical schools from which to choose. Albert Schweitzer indeed. I ended up in California, at a university nicknamed The Farm, lodged in the bowels of Silicon Valley just south of San Francisco, in their

MD-PhD program. At the end of seven years, I would have my medical degree and my PhD. I chose to take a doctorate in microbiology.

But I never got either degree in California. In fact, I was just about halfway through when they kicked me out. Which is how I ended up at the University of Maryland to finish out my MD. Which may be one reason CDC put me back in Baltimore at St. Raphe's. Which is why I was in a grim cubicle of a room, looking down at the infirm Helen Jones.

She grunted when she noticed me, eyes rolling toward me for a moment, then back to the ceiling.

"Hello, Ms. Jones," I said. "I'm Dr. McCormick."

She didn't say anything.

I walked to the bed. "Hi," I said. Again she didn't respond. She just blinked a few times, tears dribbling slowly from the sides of her eyes.

One of the first things you learn when you start to see patients is how to identify the truly sick. Contrary to how it sounds, this is not always easy. Is the guy who just staggered into your emergency room having a heart attack, or is it a nasty case of gas? The distinctions are often surprisingly subtle. But after a few years with the unwell, you can ride on a subway and peg those fighting congestive heart failure, emphysema, whatever.

Helen Jones's current state was not subtle, and it didn't take a doctor to realize how much pain she was in. How much she hurt. Worn as it may sound, disease is terrible. Really. And it's not a fucking abstraction; screw those who try to put it in context with their "circle of life and death" platitudes. I got into this business to disrupt the damned circle.

I put my hand on Helen's shoulder. "It's going to be okay," I said, and hoped I wasn't lying to her.

The room was small, about ten by ten, and crammed full of monitors, IV stands. According to Verlach, Helen had been extubated earlier that day, but the medical team had left the ventilator in the room in case they needed it again.

This was probably a violation of some protocol—ventilators were normally used only in the intensive care units—but outbreaks of strange, hot diseases were protocol-busting events. To me, it was all very well and good that Helen Jones wasn't down in the ICU, sharing virus with the other super-sick.

I kept my hand on her shoulder for a moment, then gave a little squeeze before going to the foot of the bed to the medical charts there.

"Ms. Jones," I said, "I work for the Centers for Disease Control. We're going to try to find out what happened to you. We're going to make sure you get better." I waited for a response, but she just continued looking at the beige ceiling. "I'm going to examine you, okay? This will be quick."

The exam. Helen Jones, though supposedly recovering from her illness, looked like a person about to expire at any moment. Neck palpation revealed significant cervical lymphadenopathy. Hell, I didn't need to palpate to notice it; the lymph nodes in her neck were so swollen it looked as if someone had sewn a bunch of marbles under the skin. She was jaundiced—her skin a nasty yellow, the whites of her eyes the color of urine—either the result of the disease ripping through her liver, or from her body dealing with too much bleeding. There was a penlight on the cart next to the bed. I took it.

"Open your mouth." She didn't.

Gently, I put my fingers on the lower jaw and pulled down, shined the light inside.

The mucosa of her mouth was polka-dotted with brown blotches of different sizes, as if it had been blasted with a shotgun. Her gums themselves were almost completely discolored. But though it looked bad, it showed she was healing. If the sickness had been fulminant, the spots would have been bright red. As it was, the blood had clotted, turned brown, and her body had begun to reabsorb it.

"I'm going to pull down your gown, okay?" The tears still dribbled, but Helen Jones nodded, almost imperceptibly. "You're doing great, Helen," I told her.

I pulled her hospital gown to about midabdomen. There were patches of gauze everywhere—under her arms, on her breasts, on her belly. I took a corner of one of the bandages near her armpit and lifted it, revealing a large ulcerated area that had begun to scab. The skin, it appeared, had simply slipped away, leaving a denuded patch underneath. The amount of Helen's body that had suffered the insult—the surface area that had sloughed and scabbed—was impressive. As horrible as this thing was, as brightly drawn as the battle line was between me and it, I had to respect what it could do. Its power and its idiosyncrasies. I noted that the infection had spared much of her face.

As I reattached the bandage, Helen sighed, which launched a spasm of coughing, a heavy, gurgling sound. Something came into her mouth. Weakly, she tried to reach for the tissues next to the bed.

"Here," I said. I took a tissue and pressed it to her mouth. Into it, she spat a gob of phlegm the color and consistency of currant jelly. She'd been hemorrhaging in her lungs. Now, as her body began to win against the infection, the blood had coagulated and she was able to bring it up. I told her she was doing well.

I dropped the tissue into the wastebasket and noticed, as I did so, that the floor was littered with tissues, each one looking like a flower, a spot of red surrounded by a halo of white.

CHAPTER 5

I walked quickly toward the conference room on M-2, dodging gurneys—some filled, some empty—being wheeled to different parts of the hospital. I guessed Verlach had had his conversation with Madison and Hammil about shutting down the floor, and I guessed that conversation had gone well. Or, at least, it had gone quickly.

In any case, I was happy that patients were being kept from any chance encounter with our vicious little disease.

Fifteen heads swiveled when I opened the door to the conference room. Not Verlach's, though. He sat hunched over a sheaf of files, scratching absently at his balding head. Jean Madison made a show of looking at her watch and looking at me. I smiled at her, then glanced around the room to see who was there: all the internal medicine residents, most of the attendings, two nurses, and a couple of people who had the officious look of administrators.

The speaker, the chief resident in internal medicine, stood in front of a whiteboard, medical charts spread in front of her. She paused as I found a seat next to Verlach.

Jean Madison, whose short salt-and-pepper hair was gelled to the tensile strength of Kevlar, waved her hand at me and said, "For those of you who don't know him, Dr. McCormick of the CDC."

Normally, with such a fab intro as that, I'd launch into my soft-shoe routine. Considering the circumstance, I settled for a hello.

"Evidently, timeliness isn't taught in Atla—"

"Jean—" Gary Hammil touched Madison's arm.

"Go on, Dr. Singh," Madison said tartly.

The chief resident continued with her presentation of Helen Jones. The medical history was pretty much the same as I'd gotten from Verlach earlier that day—the flulike prodrome, the hemorrhaging a day later. Social history was a surprise, though. It seemed that Helen Jones never traveled—never out of the Baltimore area in her thirty-one years. This was something of a setback; Verlach and I would have loved to hear that Ms. Jones had just returned from Colombia or the Congo. This would have narrowed our list of potential nasties quite a bit.

But, as I said, Helen Jones had never been far from what was once officially dubbed, oddly, "The City That Reads." And, as it turned out, Helen Jones probably didn't.

"She lives in a group home for the mentally handicapped, a place called Open Arms," Dr. Singh said.

So Helen Jones is slow, I thought. Interesting.

Dr. Singh went on to describe Helen Jones's alcohol, drug, and tobacco history, which was negative. The history dragged on as Dr. Singh gave us enough detail to pack a Conan Doyle story. Though I had to admire her thoroughness, it was not serving us well at that point.

"Excuse the interruption," I said, "but where did Deborah Fillmore live?" Fillmore was the name of the second patient to present to the hospital. The third patient was Bethany Reginald.

Dr. Singh blinked. "I was planning to present Deborah Fillmore next."

I could feel the eyes on me. The presentation of patients follows relatively strict protocol, and I was breaking it by derailing us from Helen Jones to Deborah Fillmore. Where these women lived was important, though. All of us sitting through twenty minutes of presentation was not.

"Dr. Singh," I said, "where did Deborah Fillmore and Bethany Reginald live?"

Verlach's fingers were raking nervously through his mustache.

"Dr. McCormick," Jean Madison told me, "Dr. Singh will finish her case presentations—"

"With all due respect, Dr. Madison, we're trying to piece together an exposure history. The environment in which these women lived—"

"—can wait, Dr. McCormick," she said.

"Not really, it can't." I turned back to Dr. Singh. She looked at Dr. Madison and back at me. Finally, she said, "Bethany Reginald shared a room with Helen Jones at Open Arms. Deborah Fillmore lived in another group home, called Baltimore Haven."

"Thank you," I said.

Though I wanted to follow this line—environmental exposures—I didn't want to be lynched by a bunch of upset doctors. So I began to scribble notes in a small notebook I always carried with me. Dr. Singh finished up with the case presentation for Helen Jones. The group began to ask questions—about blood tests, cultures. All very good questions, but it was taking too long and it was driving me crazy.

I turned to Verlach. "You know the travel history of the other women?"

"No travel," he said, keeping his eyes straight ahead.

"You've been to the homes?"

"No, Nate." I could tell Verlach was also getting antsy with the pace of things.

"We need to get a move on. We need to talk to the other girls and get over to the homes—"

"Dr. McCormick," someone said sharply. I looked up. Gary Hammil was glaring at me now. Was I on everyone's shit list? "You'll be able to present us with a differential for Ms. Jones?"

"Yes."

"Good. Would you indulge us, then, with your wisdom?"

I glanced at Verlach, who seemed incredibly tense; I couldn't tell if he was annoyed with me or with the medical pissing match that was unfolding in front of him.

"Dr. Hammil, I believe that my time here is best spent in the field, trying to prevent any more transmissions from taking place. We have a geographic cluster, which affords us a starting place, a good one—"

"Dr. McCormick—"

"And your medical team is top-notch here. I don't know what I could add in terms of the care for these women."

"Dr. McCormick!" An angry flush crawled up Jean Madison's neck to her face. "You are here at the invitation of this hospital. Your behavior here risks jeopardizing the relationship between our hospital and your employer in Atlanta. You risk being uninvited by—"

"Actually, Jean, Dr. McCormick is now here at the invitation of Public Health. His role has changed." Verlach spoke quietly. "Dr. McCormick, why don't you give us a differential for Ms. Jones? Since we're assuming the cases are linked, your differential should suffice for the two other patients."

Jean Madison sniffed, "In the interest of thoroughness, Herb, I think we should treat the cases as individuals."

"We can't afford the time now," Verlach said. "You worry about the women. Public Health will worry about public health. Dr. McCormick?"

I stood and walked to the whiteboard. Dr. Singh took her seat.

The differential diagnosis, the crux of medical—as opposed to surgical—practice. The differential is basically your list of best guesses. For example, if someone comes to your office with diarrhea, your differential is very broad, ranging from amoebic infections to Crohn's disease to stress. Then, as new tests come in, you narrow it down. Eventually, you arrive at a diagnosis. That's how it's supposed to go, anyway.

"Okay," I said, taking a marker. "At the top of my differential . . ."

I wrote VHF in big red letters. "The viral hemorrhagic fevers," I said. I talked quickly as I wrote, trying to bring these guys—who may have known Ebola only from books and movies—up to speed on the dizzying number of viruses that make us bleed: Marburg, Junin, Congo-Crimean hemorrhagic fever, Lassa, dengue, and so on and so on.

"I hate this," Verlach said.

He and I walked quickly toward the isolation unit. Both of us had cut out of the meeting after my presentation.

"I hate this political bullshit," he continued.

"Thanks for running interference," I said. We pushed into the vestibule and began to suit up in the biohazard gear.

"You don't help things, you know. Your approach to this."

"You know what, Herb? I really don't give a shit."

Verlach paused in the midst of pulling on his gown; he looked as if he were about to pop me. Instead, he began to laugh.

"You're a piece of work, Dr. McCormick. You really are. You either got some balls on you or you're dumb as a post."

"Balls," I said.

"Well, we'll see which it is, won't we?" He was still laughing as he pulled on his respirator.

CHAPTER 6

Helen Jones was more alive than she had been an hour earlier, alive enough, at least, to talk to me.

Shoe-leather epidemiology—what I was doing that day—is not brain surgery. It's not even cardiology. It's police work. There are more questions like "Where were you Thursday night? What did you eat? Who were you with?" than there are like "What did the MRI say?"

So there I was, in my space suit, talking to our index case: Helen Jones, thirty-one, Caucasian, slightly overweight, lucid, mentally handicapped. She was very sweet, very tired, and—now that she was alert—very suspicious of me.

In fact, she said, "You are scary."

"I hope not."

"You are."

"Well, even if you think I'm scary, I want to help you. And so I can do that, Helen, you need to help me."

"You look like a monster," she objected.

"I'm not a monster, I'm a doctor." There was irony in there somewhere.

It went like this for forty minutes. But despite the suspicions and Helen's cognitive limitations, over the course of the interview, we were able to establish a few things: Helen lived in a group home for the mentally handicapped located on the edge of the gentrified neighborhood of Federal Hill. Eight other residents, all female, lived in the home, and all the residents ate their morning and evening meals together and "prayed together before each one." She made her lunch each day in the kitchen at the home—always peanut butter and jelly, some carrots, and a Coke. As Dr. Singh had mentioned earlier, Helen shared a room with Bethany Reginald, who was now in the room next door, talking to Herb Verlach.

I asked, and Helen said they weren't allowed to have any pets or animals. With other residents, she took the bus to work each morning; she worked in the laundry department of a nursing home outside the city. At the mention of her workplace, my stomach tightened a little; the last thing we wanted was some hemorrhagic fever ripping through the shoddy immune systems in a nursing home. She couldn't remember the name of the home.

I asked her if she *saw* any animals—mice or cats or dogs, ever, even once—at the group home or at the nursing home. She winced and said she saw a rat once where she worked and, she added, a couple of cats and dogs around her residence.

Had she ever been ill before? She couldn't remember. I asked if she had ever been in a hospital before. She didn't know what I meant. "A place like this," I said. Helen shook her head. We covered what we could of family, weekends off. We covered mail received and personal hygiene. Trying to pry something loose, I revisited food and animals. The clock on the wall crept toward ten o'clock. I needed to move.

"Do you have sex?"

Helen shook her head rapidly, which I took for misunderstanding.

"Has another man or woman ever touched you in your private parts?"

She shook her head.

"Have you touched them in their private parts?"

She blushed.

"These are weird questions, aren't they?" I asked, trying to re-connect.

"Yes."

"I don't like to ask them, Helen, but I have to. Sometimes doctors have to ask funny questions so they can help." I cleared my throat. "Okay, Helen, this one's really funny: has a man ever put his penis—his private parts—into your body?"

Helen didn't laugh. "God doesn't like that," she declared. Then she pulled the sheet around her neck and closed her eyes.

Unwisely, I took that for a no.

Verlach was in the hallway, sitting on a metal chair, scribbling notes. "Another meeting," he said without looking up.

"What meeting?"

"Administration this time, then that should about do it for St. Raphael's. For this morning, at least."

"No one told me."

"I'm telling you. I just found out myself. Just got paged."

I looked at the door, then back to Verlach in his space suit.

Climbing in and out of the gear was slightly less awkward than getting it on in a Yugo. Maybe not a Yugo. More like a Porsche Boxter, parked in a pull-off on a mountain road in the Alps, the sun setting, some yodeling in the background, Jennifer Garner ripping off her . . . But, I digress; threats of admin meetings drive me to fantasy.

"I just put this stuff on," I said.

He kept on writing. "They don't care."

I thought about that for a moment. "You go, Herb. Let me finish here. This thing isn't going to wait. Besides, I don't . . . Let's just say it might be better if I'm not there. I don't think they like me."

"Still, you should be there."

"Still, they don't like me."

Through the plastic shield, I could see the corners of Verlach's eyes wrinkle. He was smiling. "So that's why they teach you your attitude in Atlanta? To get out of admin meetings?"

"No, the attitude is all mine. Getting out of meetings is one of the perks."

Verlach stood and began to feed his notes into the fax machine. "They didn't page you?"

"No."

"Then you're off the hook. Even so, I don't think it was an accident you weren't called but are still expected to be there. They're going to give you hell for not showing up."

"Dealing with political bull is not one of my talents. Catching hell from Jean Madison seems to be."

The fax beeped, signaling the transmission had gone through. Verlach put his notes in a folder labeled *Fillmore, Deborah.* "All right," he said, "just do me a favor, Nate. Tread lightly, okay? I'm not going to keep shitting in my backyard, and I don't want you shitting in it either."

"Point taken. No pooping."

He chuckled, then left the room.

CHAPTER 7

Deborah Fillmore should have been in the intensive care unit. Why she wasn't I understood, but it was not medical judgment that had placed her on the medicine floor, far from the team that cares for the nearly dead.

A nurse was in the room, changing an IV bag. I introduced myself and asked how the patient was.

"You're the expert," she said. *So this is how it would be,* I thought. *Word* does *travel fast.*

Ms. Fillmore, a black woman, twenty-seven years old, pretty face, lay unconscious on her back. Two central IV lines—one in her upper chest and one in her groin—snaked from under the sheet to bags on a stand next to her. I had to hand it to the team at St. Raphael's. Getting lines into someone in Deborah Fillmore's state is difficult and, depending on the severity of the disease, unwise; the blood vessels keep collapsing and shredding each time a needle is stuck into them. But it seemed someone on the team was what we call in the business a "sniper," someone who can nail those difficult veins.

Debbie Fillmore had been intubated, and the ventilator filled the room with a hissing and clicking as it forced gas into her lungs. Three monitors bleeped, keeping track of heart rate, oxygen level in her blood, blood pressure, respiration rate, and oxygen delivery. A Foley catheter ran to a bag hung on the side of the bed, half-filled with urine. The medical team was worried about shock; the bags and the monitors were there to assess and maintain this young woman's blood pressure high enough to keep her alive.

I bent over the bed and looked at Deborah's lips and face. Even without moving the ventilator tube from her mouth, I could see the bloody spots of hemorrhage. I touched her forehead; she was blazing hot: 40.2 Celsius, according to the monitor. About 105 Fahrenheit.

I undid the tape that held the vent tube to her face and pushed the plastic to the side. I couldn't see much.

"Do you have a penlight?" I asked the nurse.

"No."

"Try to find me one, please," I said.

She glowered at me. "Nurse," I said, using the word in a way she'd hate but needing to reestablish the hierarchy. "There is a light in Helen Jones's room. I need that light. Now."

She huffed out of the room. I was quickly enlarging my list of enemies. But if there's one thing I've learned from life thus far, it's not making enemies that's the problem; it's making the wrong enemies.

I loosened the gown around Debbie's neck, careful not to disturb the central lines. Large, dark plaques spread down her chest, over her breasts, down her trunk. Her neck—with its spawn of huge lymph nodes—looked as if it had been crafted out of clay by a kindergartner with dexterity problems. Whatever had infected this young woman was attacking almost everything.

The nurse appeared with a penlight. She thrust it at me.

"Thank you," I said.

She didn't respond. Pulling the vent tube to the side, the penlight in my other hand, I peered into Debbie's throat. I almost dropped the light, jerking my hands back as if I had touched something hot, which, in a way, I had.

The mouth was alive with little hemorrhages. The tonsils, nearly the size of golf balls, were slicked in a thick gray-yellow pus, like they had been coated with mortar. They looked about to burst.

Seeing what these diseases do to a body always jangles me, makes me uneasy, makes me furious. Added to that unpleasant emotional mix was that I felt the victims here—the mentally handicapped—were cursed both with disease and a tragically hobbled understanding of it. I mean, try to put yourself in Debbie Fillmore's sloughing skin: You feel magnitudes worse than you've ever felt in your life and you *really* don't know what's going on. You don't fully understand why people in white are jamming needles into you, why everyone looks like an astronaut. You might not even understand what disease is, why your skin is lifting off in ugly patches.

That is terror, ladies and gentlemen, pain amped by a lack of comprehension.

Rage, not the most admirable quality in a physician, was, nevertheless, a reason I was in that room, a reason I became a doctor. Rage that Helen Jones and Debbie Fillmore lay bleeding, rage that the Blind Watchmaker of a God allowed such poison to evolve. Rage at my own impotence, at spending years of life working with pathogens and yet unable to lift a finger to help—

The nurse cleared her throat, and I realized I was sweating like a pig in the space suit, the muscles in my arm rigid.

Calm down, McCormick, I told myself.

I closed the mouth and reattached the tape on Deborah Fillmore's face, swore quietly.

I looked at the nurse, remembered our previous static, and offered her an olive branch of sorts. "What do you think?" I asked.

"What do I know?" she shot back. "I'm just a nurse."

This was not the time for her to bait me, and I tried to decide between an angry fusillade and a more conciliatory response. But I felt my pager vibrate. I never look a gift horse in the mouth, so I seized the opportunity and left the room and the stewing nurse.

CHAPTER 8

I undressed just enough to expose the pager. Verlach. I used the phone in the vestibule and called him.

"Congratulations, McCormick. You are now no longer the least popular person in this hospital," Verlach said.

"Great. My PR firm must have delivered."

"We're shutting the place down."

"The wing?"

"The whole hospital."

"Whoa." This was a surprise. I mean, it was a good thing—a very prudent thing—but still . . .

Anyway, I had to hand it to Verlach. The man moved fast. I told him that.

"We don't screw around here." He forced a laugh. "Still, it's too bad you weren't there to take the heat. I live in this town."

"Maybe not for long. They pull out the rope for you?"

"Just about. The hospital president said, and I quote, 'I'll have your balls in a jar if we're not open in five days.' He mentioned he'd have your balls, too."

"Well, tell him I sent mine back to Atlanta for safekeeping. Look, Herb, this thing is bad. Debbie Fillmore . . ." I paused.

"I know. That's why I'm shutting this place down."

"Okay. And with the tempo of this so far, we should be ready for more."

"Yes. We'll use the hospital as quarantine."

"Good." I thought for a moment. "Herb, the bug has hallmarks. We have hemorrhage in the mucous membranes; hemorrhage in the lungs and trunk. Nothing on the face. It looks like everything and nothing; I can't get a bead on exactly what it's attacking."

"Yeah, I know."

"Face sparing, but it gets the mouth. . . ." I contemplated how I was going to mention the unmentionable. Then I just went for it. "In the meeting, anybody mention bioterrorism?"

"Not these guys. But I put state on alert. You should call your people in Atlanta, just to give them the heads-up."

"Done. I wanted to talk to you first."

"Thanks for the thought." He seemed about to hang up, then said, "Nate, let's nip this thing in the bud. It could get nasty."

Nobody knew, I think, how right he was.

CHAPTER 9

When I landed in Baltimore to help out St. Raphe's and a few other hospitals in Maryland, I had just begun the second year of my two-year stint with EIS. So I guess you could say I was seasoned, at least as the Service goes. But I sure as hell wasn't seasoned enough.

I didn't know that, of course, as I dialed my way through the list of hospitals in the area, calling the infectious disease docs at each place to see if they'd come across anything like what we were seeing, to make sure they were on the lookout. Fortunately, the victims seemed to be confined to St. Raphe's. Fortunately, too, the doctors were spooked. Vigilance is one of the few things you have going for you at the beginning of an outbreak.

Nearly two hours later, after finishing the calls, I suited up to reenter the biocontainment area to interview Bethany Reginald.

We needed to talk, Bethany and I, before she got too sick to be of any help. Later, I would compare notes with Verlach, who, despite our worries about the situation, was the only other person on the case besides me. According to Verlach, the woman from state assured us we would have more help later in the day, tomorrow at the latest.

I looked down at Bethany Reginald, slant eyed and slightly fat, lying uncomfortably in the bed. Her genetic bad luck—an extra chromosome twenty-one, Down's syndrome—was not as severe as it might have been. A rose is not a rose is not a rose with Down's, and Bethany was relatively lucky. She could speak coherently and didn't have any of the heart or gastrointestinal abnormalities that one often sees with the syndrome. That day, despite the virus or whatever lighting through her system, she seemed to be in relatively good health. The calm before the storm. Just one IV perforated her arm—the St. Raphe's sniper had been at work again—taped heavily to prevent her from tearing it out.

But still I worried. Down's wreaked havoc with the immune system. Bethany, at twenty-five, had already lived a relatively long life for someone with her condition.

I took her small hand in mine and said hello. She responded with a "hi" and a squeeze, the hallmark single crease in her palm wrapping over my gloved fingers. The squeeze lasted a little too long.

"How are you feeling, Bethany?"

"I feel sick."

"Do you feel worse than you did yesterday?"

She thought about that for a moment. "Yes. I feel sick."

"Bethany, where do you live?"

"I like you," she responded.

And that's how we began.

We covered the same topics I'd tried to cover with Helen Jones. Fortunately, Bethany was in relatively good spirits and willing to talk. Unfortunately, she seemed to have an inability to remember many details of her life.

"Bethany, what did you eat for dinner last night?"

"Hmmmm. I don't know."

"Bethany, can you remember anything you ate yesterday?"

"You're cute."

She was lying, of course, considering my getup.

We tried food questions for a few more minutes, with negligible results. No matter. I could get the menu at her group home. We moved on to animals, for which she had a much better recollection. She'd seen rats at the home, as well as cats and dogs in the neighborhood. She'd seen dead birds. However, she wasn't able to tell me when she saw these things. I switched subjects from animals to what would prove to be one of Bethany's great passions: sex.

"Sex," she said almost wistfully. "I love it."

So we talked about it. I asked about partners. Lots, she said. Jerry, Douglas, Thomas, et al.—she couldn't remember them all, and she couldn't give me last names. I asked her about sex with women. She'd done that. I inquired about oral and anal sex, about other activities involving the exchange of body fluids. And let me tell you, describing anal sex and water sports to Bethany Reginald was a singular experience; I felt the heat rising in my face and was glad, for once, to have a mask on. Anyway, this girl had done quite a bit in her short life. Certainly more than I had, which isn't saying much.

"Bethany, do you have sex in your room where you live?"

Her eyes widened. Suddenly she was not tired; she was scared. "No, no, no, no—" The words came as a stream.

"Where do you have sex?"

"—no, no, no, no, no, no."

"Bethany, this is important. Listen to me, honey." I took her hand again. "I won't tell anyone. I promise."

Muttering her no-no-no, she tried to curl into a fetal ball. In doing so, she rolled away from the IV, which pulled tight, tipping its metal stand. I grabbed the stand before it fell; the motion scared Bethany and she began to scream, rolling toward me and ripping at the IV, yanking it out of her arm. Blood welled from the gash in her vein. When she saw the blood, she started to claw at her gown, spattering blood across her body, across my gown and mask.

I stepped back, watching Bethany roll back and forth and wail. That's the bitch of these diseases. Heroism—trying to restrain Bethany Reginald, for example, to prevent her from hurting herself—can get you killed. In stark terms, the diseases force you to look out for Number One. It's not something doctors do easily.

I hit the emergency call button and barked to the nurses to get into the room with some restraints. Because of the precautions, it would be a few minutes until anyone from outside the suite appeared.

Verlach pushed into the room, having heard the call from Helen Jones's room.

"What happened?" he asked. I didn't answer; it didn't matter anyway.

The two of us, two doctors whose lives were dedicated to saving the sick, stood impotently by while blood flowed from the hole in Bethany's arm. The blood wasn't clotting; it was flowing too fast. The virus or whatever had taken hold.

*   *   *

Forty minutes later, after Bethany had calmed down, after she had been restrained, and after a central line had been placed in her chest, I was standing outside St. Raphe's, leaning against my car, smoking a cigarette that I'd bummed from the intake nurse on the first floor. The security guard gave me some guff about smoking on hospital grounds, so I told him to shoot me if he wanted. He didn't want, and he left me alone.

My hand, I realized as I pulled the cigarette to my mouth, was shaking. One of the downsides of this job is that you spend a lot of time around things that have spent thousands of years evolving inventive ways to kill you. When some of those things actually splash on you, well, it's a pretty intense experience. It's kind of like being in a bad car accident and walking away, except you don't know whether you've really walked away: you feel fine for a week, then you're puking up your GI tract and getting last rites from the chaplain.

Verlach appeared, sweat already beading on his forehead in the ninety-plus-degree heat. He looked at me and the cigarette and frowned, thinking, I suppose, whether he should say something to the only public-health doc in the country who smoked. Good man that he is, he let it lie.

"Any contact with the blood, Nathaniel?"

"No."

"You sure?"

"I spent ten minutes in the mirror, Herb. I'm sure. No contact." I took a long drag on the smoke. "She okay?"

"She's sleeping now. What happened?"

Unfortunately, I was at the end of my cigarette. I stubbed it out on the bottom of my shoe and cupped the butt in my hand. I may pollute my lungs, but I don't litter. "I asked her about having sex in her room."

"That's it?"

"That's it."

"Well"—Verlach wiped his head with the back of his hand—"everybody's touchy about sex."

"Not Bethany. She was okay with the sex talk. She freaked when I asked about her doing it in her room."

Verlach got a confused look on his face. "Why would that be?"

I shrugged and walked to a trash can in front of the hospital and tossed the butt into it. "You ready to hit the streets?"

CHAPTER 10

An hour later, the transfer of patients out of St. Raphe's was in full swing. It seemed everyone knew who to blame for the shutdown, and Verlach and I suffered the sharp stares and mumbled comments. I was happy to be out of there.

Verlach and I were set to march into the community for our investigation. We were going in light, armed with specimen kits—swabs, labels, phlebotomy kits for taking blood samples—notebooks, and a few small-mammal traps. We were going out to look for reservoirs—animals or insects that served as hosts for the disease—and vectors—animals, insects, or people that served as conduits between the reservoirs and the sick women. We wanted to capture rodents and insects and send them to the labs for analysis. We also wanted to look at people, at their blood, their saliva. For diseases like the one we faced, the normal modes of transmission were rodent to man, insect to man, or man to man. Man-to-man transmission usually happened through body fluids. All very sloppy stuff.

Verlach went to the Baltimore Haven home, where Deborah Fillmore was a resident. I went to Open Arms, home to Bethany Reginald and Helen Jones.

I drove fast through the afternoon swelter. By that time, the city had soaked up most of the heat the sun poured in during the day, and radiated it back up at me. Flags lay limp on their poles, and fumes from cars and buses had little chance to disperse. Few people wandered outside. It wasn't a heat wave per se, but the ninety-three-degree days had been going on for over a week now, and a few unfortunate denizens of that city would be dead before the spell ended. Poverty means no air-conditioning. That and old age can kill you.

I pulled my car to the curb outside a brick row home that looked pretty much like the other brick row homes on the block. Maybe it had a few more flowers outside. Maybe it was a little better cared for than the others. But I'm splitting hairs here. On the whole, the block was nice, on the outskirts of the chichi Federal Hill neighborhood, the bleeding edge of gentrification.

An intercom box with a button sat to the right of the slate-blue door. I buzzed. A moment later, a voice cracked across the system, asking who I was. I answered, and the door opened.

Mary D'Angelo was a kind-looking woman in her fifties or sixties, dark hair just turning to gray, weight settling heavily on her hips. She embraced me, her arms wrapping lightly around my back. Those two limbs, I supposed, were the inspiration for the home's name. "Dr. McCormick, I hope we can help."

I told her I was sure she could. And I thanked her for the public service she was performing by allowing me to come.

"We're just so worried about Helen. Bethany, too, of course."

"I know. We're doing our best to help them and to make sure no one else gets sick. I know you're as concerned about this as we are." Always good to enlist support early on. "How many residents live here?"

"There are eight altogether."

"Are they here now?"

"No. All of our residents are able to function in society, Dr. McCormick. They're at work. The home is usually closed during the day. I'm here only to help you."

"What time do they return?"

"Everyone is home by six o'clock."

I looked at my watch. "Well, either I or someone else will be back then to take blood samples and talk to the other residents. Now I'd like to take swabs from the kitchen, from the bathrooms, also from Bethany's and Helen's rooms."

"They share a room."

I'd forgotten the two were roommates. A small mistake, but an amateurish one. Made it look like we had less information than we did. I played it lightly. "Well, that will make it easier."

"Well, that's good." I could sense Mary D'Angelo starting to dig in her heels. This happened more often than not, this reluctance to be probed and analyzed. Not to mention the threat of a PR catastrophe that can result from having a pathogen found at your place.

"I'd also like to set rodent and insect traps in the kitchen, the basement—"

"Dr. McCormick, we don't have rodents or insects."

"Then the traps will be much lighter when I take them away."

Mary D'Angelo crossed her arms.

"Would you mind giving me a tour?"

"Not at all, Dr. McCormick," she said flatly.

We started in the dining room, remarkably homey, with a large round table on which sat a lazy Susan. Framed images of Jesus, scriptural passages, and nature paintings covered the walls. Few of the paintings looked professional. Mary saw me looking at them.

"The Maryland Institute of Art has Saturday classes. Our residents often go."

"You seem to do a very good job of caring for them."

"We think so."

From there, we went to the kitchen. Now, I haven't investigated many group homes, but I've poked through quite a few restaurants. This kitchen was as clean as the best of them. Pots and pans, all washed, hung from hooks above an island counter. The drain in the spotless floor was unclogged and, well, spotless. Dishes were stacked in shelves above the sink. As for the smell, the kitchen at Open Arms didn't have the funk of an institutional kitchen.

Mary D'Angelo opened those ample arms as she presented the kitchen to me. She didn't say anything.

Back through the dining room to a living room with a piano, where, according to Mary, the residents sang and prayed before dinner. Then upstairs to the bedrooms.

There were four bedrooms, two bathrooms. Though all the beds were made and all the laundry in wicker hampers, there was a certain sloppiness to the second floor: dresser drawers not closed, food wrappers left on desks. The bathroom sinks had soap scum and toothpaste dried to the bowls; someone forgot to flush a toilet that morning. Mary flushed it.

"We try," she said.

She led me to a room at the end of the carpeted hallway. "Helen and Bethany are in here."

The room was like the others, perhaps brighter because of two large windows. The shag carpet was old but clean. One side of the room was decorated with religious-themed paintings and drawings, some from Saturday classes at the Maryland Institute, others clipped from magazines or books. The opposite side had a few religious pieces, but more nature pictures: animals, landscapes, and—perhaps I should have guessed this—a picture of Brad Pitt with his shirt off.

Mary walked to the movie star's photo, carefully removed the tack, and folded the picture into a pocket in her skirt.

"Will you be staying here this morning, Ms. D'Angelo? I'd like to get my samples and ask you some questions."

"Of course I will, Dr. McCormick. I wouldn't think of leaving you here all alone."

With that send-off, I walked back downstairs, took my specimen kit, and began in the kitchen.

The refrigerator, the sink, the floor, the drain in the floor, the drain in the sink. I daubed each with a swab and sealed it into a labeled plastic container. Food samples went into their own vials, as did squirts of dish soap and hand moisturizer. I checked under the sink, behind the refrigerator, in the cupboards for mouse feces. I didn't find any.

In the dining room, I took samples from the condiments on the lazy Susan. In the bathrooms, upstairs and downstairs, I took pieces of soggy soap, I took swabs from the moist ends of the faucets.

I rummaged through Helen's and Bethany's personal items. Sunscreen, Vaseline, moisturizer, all went into the specimen kit. In the bottom of one of Bethany's drawers—it had to be Bethany's—I found an old *Cheri* magazine. Hard-core pornography. It was under the loosened contact paper, difficult to find if you weren't sleuthing like I was. You had to hand it to the girl. I covered it back up with socks.

More quickly, I searched through the other residents' rooms. I pawed through the basement, into the backyard, through the living room, into the attic. I set up nine rodent traps; twenty traps for insects.

With Ms. D'Angelo's blessing, I rounded up all the mail dated within the past two weeks. We weren't looking for anthrax, but mail collection was de rigueur for anything that smacked of bioterrorism. Some days it felt as if we were moving as many pieces as the Postal Service.

Two hours later, my bag considerably heavier with sealed and labeled containers and J. Crew catalogs, I was finished. Mary D'Angelo sat in the living room, surrounded by religious tchotchkes, paging through a magazine.

"Finished?" she asked without looking up.

"Almost. I'll need your menu for the last month."

"Of course," she said, closing the magazine, an old copy of *Good Housekeeping.*

"Who makes the meals?"

"I do."

"Well, I'm sure they're very good, then." Mary looked at me with a frozen, impenetrable smile, totally unmoved by the compliment. I soldiered on. "Who makes the breakfasts and lunches?"

"The residents do. Breakfast here, lunch to go. I'm here until they leave for work."

"And what time do they leave for work?"

"Different times. Some of the girls work in the kitchens of nursing homes, so they have to be there early. Others work the laundry. They go in about an hour later."

"Helen said she worked at a nursing home."

"Yes. All of the girls do. We have an agreement with a company that runs a few homes in the area."

"Both Helen and Bethany worked in the kitchen?"

"Bethany worked in the kitchen, Helen in the laundry."

"Did they have any friends at work?"

"Friends?"

"I have some questions, Ms. D'Angelo, about the behavior of the residents here. You may not like them—the questions, I mean—but I need to ask anyway." Her smile stayed frozen. "I'll cut to the chase, then. Are you aware if any of the residents here are intimate? Sexually, I mean."

"Dr. McCormick, this is a religious home. All the women who live here are unmarried. It is one of the best-run group homes in the city."

"That didn't answer my question."

"No male visitors are allowed upstairs. In fact, the only male here with any frequency is my husband."

"Ms. D'Angelo—"

"Mrs. D'Angelo. I'm married."

"Mrs. D'Angelo, please help me out here."

She stood. "I am helping you, Dr. McCormick. I'll get that menu for you."

CHAPTER 11

"What do you have?" Verlach's voice was hushed. He was still at Baltimore Haven, the group home, bagging specimens.

"About twenty pounds of condiments, drain scum, and hand cream. How about you?"

"Got a mouse in the first ten minutes."

"At least no rats."

"Got one of them, too. This place is a cesspool. They tried to clean up—someone must have given them the heads-up—but even so . . . I'm calling somebody from Housing Services to look into this place. Poor girl."

The poor girl was Deborah Fillmore, unfortunate resident of Baltimore Haven. As Verlach described it, Baltimore Haven fit my prejudices of group homes for the mentally handicapped: a dirty, miserable dumping ground.

I was standing on the sidewalk outside Open Arms, already sweating through my shirt.

"You downtown?" Verlach asked.

"Going there now."

"I think we're going to use CDC labs, Nate. The guys downtown will box the specimens for you."

"Nice of you to tell me."

"We just made the decision. And just so you know, we're thinking about requesting more CDC on the ground as well."

That took me aback. Not a bad decision to call in reinforcements, but it suggested someone thought we couldn't handle this on our own. "So," I said, "this thing is getting big."

"Well," Verlach said, "we made it that way."

Which is true and, if you think about it, a little strange. We had three sick women who, if they had gone to separate hospitals, if they had not been picked up by sentinel surveillance, would have just been that: three sick women. They wouldn't have been the beginning of an outbreak. Now a hospital was being shut down, the federal government was being mobilized, and in a few hours the media piranhas would be feeding. Disease is odd this way. It's not like a murder or a bomb going off or a landslide. It's hard to know when something abnormal is happening, or when an illness is just part of the warp and woof of everyday life. But when somebody—us, your public health protectors—says something is wrong, well, it's like the explosion on the bus. It's real and it's frightening.

"Anything hit the news yet?" I asked.

"Not that I heard. It won't be long, though." Verlach paused, then asked, "What do you think?"

"I don't, Herb. That's why I'm so well liked."

"You keep on like you've been, I'll start to believe you."

"Funny." Which it wasn't. There was silence on the phone and I tried to divine what Verlach was thinking. I said, "You thinking it's a strike?" We don't really like to say *terrorism* too much, especially when other people are around. We use euphemisms. *Strike. Attack.*

More silence, which I filled. "Yeah. Strike at the retarded. Bring the country to its knees." I forced a laugh. Thought about it a little longer. "I can't rule it out."

"Neither can I. If you think about it, though, it's not a bad idea."

"Meaning . . . ?"

I heard some shuffling and assumed Verlach was removing himself to someplace quiet. His voice was hushed. "You hit slow folks—they might not be as vigilant as others, so you give them a gift or something— good start, right? They open the package, *poof,* the bug is in their system. So you got your first cases. But you're smart; you want to get the biggest bang for your bug. You know these folks work in nursing homes, a bunch of immunocompromised—"

"Where did Deb Fillmore work?"

"Nursing home in Bel Air. In the kitchen."

"Nobody told me that."

"You didn't ask, Grasshopper." Verlach cleared his throat. "So we see a bunch of parents and grandparents start to die, right? Hits us where it hurts."

"You're scaring me, Dr. Verlach."

"I've been scared for years."

"What's the name of Fillmore's employer?" Holding the steering wheel in my left hand, I flipped through my little notebook, found the name of the home where Bethany and Helen worked. "It's not Miller Grove?" I said, hoping it was. *Please,* I thought, *make this easy. Make it a contained, discrete cluster.* If all three women worked at the same nursing home, then we were getting somewhere.

"No. She was in a place called Oak Hills."

I found a pen sandwiched in the car seat; I wrote the name in the notebook. "After I drop this stuff off downtown, I'm heading out to Bel Air to check on the place where Helen and Bethany worked, a place called Miller Grove. I'll start working on Oak Hills as well."

"Okay," Verlach said. "I'll try to get out there as soon as I can. We may have some state people as well."

There was silence on the phone. I could almost hear Verlach scratching his head. "It would be nice to get a read on the agent. Even symptomatically. My kingdom for a nice, discrete collection of signs and symptoms."

"We got the hemorrhage on the trunk, in the mucous membranes, sparing the face. . . ."

"But taken together, it doesn't match anything."

"Or it matches too much—"

"That, too."

"Maybe we're dealing with a coinfection, maybe a variant." The conversation was worrying me a bit, and I wished I had a cigarette. "Okay, okay," I said. "What else? What else are you thinking for transmission?"

"After seeing the shithole I'm in, it could be a rodent or arthropod vector."

"But we have two cases at Open Arms. I tell you, Herb, the kitchen there is cleaner than the OR at St. Raphe's."

"Not saying much. Anyway, I'm operating on the assumption that we have a common vector. Maybe the homes have mixers or something. You know, dances where the residents share needles or swap transfusion products. . . ."

"Maybe. We'll see how close the ladies' workplaces are. How much the personnel interact, whether they share the same supplier, cleaning or groundskeeping services. Let's also be thinking of a human vector."

"Why?"

"Distinct subpopulation. Contact with the same people in the same circles. Remember those weird symptomic clusters in LA and New York? Gay men. Young." That was how AIDS first presented. And though neither Verlach nor I were in public health at that time—I was still spending my afternoons playing Dungeons & Dragons and fighting my way through puberty then—the story of how AIDS came to light was part of our profession's lore.

"You looking for Patient Zero now, Nate?" Verlach asked.

"I sure as hell hope not," I told him.

CHAPTER 12

I headed back downtown, to the Department of Health. A couple of techs waited with their packaging material and FedEx pouches. The airbills, I saw, already had CDC's Atlanta address on them. I gave them the samples from Open Arms, and they set to work, labeling, repackaging, sealing. Your public servants, when they want to, can move fast.

And we needed to move fast.

I drove from downtown to Miller Grove, the erstwhile employer of Helen and Bethany, located in the Baltimore suburb of Bel Air. I cut through the city to link up with I-95, and from there, north. I like hardcore urbanism, so I'd opened my windows to let in the heat and the smells and the sounds.

A red light stopped me at an intersection next to a housing project that was—apologies to Hobbes—nasty, brutish, and short, rising only two stories from packed-dirt yards. Young men in sports jerseys gathered on corners, shaved heads slicked in the heat, eye-fucking me as I waited for the light to change. As I said, I'd spent some time here—the last two years of medical school—and, the milling low-level threat outside the car notwithstanding, I missed the place. True, it had a murder rate that was among the highest in the nation, it had had an embarrassing and frightening syphilis problem a few years back. Race politics dominated. Summers were tropical, winters wet and gray. Compared to, say, dainty, boutique-laden San Francisco, Baltimore was hard to love.

Even so, the city was on the upswing. The downtown was being revitalized and gentrified in a way that was not without its critics. In an odd inversion, poverty was being pushed from center city to the inner suburbs as those with money realized the charms of an urban life with good restaurants, great bars, and an effervescent maritime vibe. I passed through the neighborhoods of Greektown and Butcher's Hill, through block after block of formstone rowhouses and white marble steps that residents scrubbed weekly and that gleamed like Roman statues. I found myself hoping that this outbreak or whatever would die quickly. I hoped this because I didn't want to see anyone else get sick. I hoped this, too, because this city didn't need another black eye just as it was crawling back to respectability.

But all good things come to an end, and after fifteen minutes, the city gave way to a nondescript swath of strip malls and housing developments that are the true hallmark of twenty-first-century America. Suburbs and exurbs had metastasized through the whole country, and I could have been on the outskirts of Minneapolis or Boston or anywhere in LA.

Off one of the major arteries in Bel Air—between a T.J. Maxx and a Circuit City—I found the turnoff for Miller Grove.

Dan Miller, senior administrator, put on his best game face—a pretty good one, actually, with capped teeth and dark tan—but I could tell he was sweating this one out. His head nurse, Gina Hatcher, was a thin black woman in crisp nurse's whites, which pegged her as someone from the old school. Both sat rigid as I told them about the biological meltdown of two of their employees. Actually, three employees. It seemed the Miller family owned four nursing homes in the area, including Oak Hills, where Deborah Fillmore worked. Oak Hills was just across the street.

Miller was savvy enough to know the shit through which we were wading was deep and getting deeper. Savvy enough, too, not to put up a fight, despite the fact that something like this could wreck him if he made poor choices or just had a run of bad luck.

"And you're acting with whose authority?" Miller asked nonconfrontationally.

"CDC and Baltimore City Department of Health."

"Ben Timmons?" Timmons was the health commissioner for Baltimore.

"And Herb Verlach. Dr. Verlach's heading up the investigation."

"Great. Know 'em both, both good men. Well, Dr. McCormick, you've succeeded in scaring the pants off us. What do you want us to do?"

"Answer some questions." I pulled out my notebook and fired: Any illnesses out of the ordinary? How many new admissions? New staff members? What kinds of contact did staff have with the patients? What were the details of laundry duty? Of kitchen duty? The answer to each question was either negative or not illustrative.

When I'd mined enough of Dan Miller and Gina Hatcher, I said, "I'd like to talk to the staff and I'd like to collect samples from Miller Grove and Oak Hills. Mr. Miller?"

"Yes?"

"I'd like you to put the word out that the kitchen staff shouldn't throw any food away. Have your people gather and hold the mail, too." I glanced at my watch; it was three thirty.

"Is everyone still here? The staff, I mean."

"Most everyone," Miller said. "We run three nursing shifts, so—"

"That's fine. We can get to any stragglers later if we need to. Can we gather everyone who's here?"

"Now?"

"No time like the present."

"Let's wait until after dinner, if we can. We can still serve dinner, can't we?"

I thought for a moment. I had—directly or indirectly—been responsible for the shutdown of a hospital earlier that day, and I didn't want to be responsible for delaying dinner for hundreds of elderly and infirm. "Sure. Just make sure the staff doesn't use any old food or condiments. Tell them to open everything new."

"I'll make the announcement," Gina Hatcher said.

I pushed up from my chair. "I'll begin collecting samples and setting rodent and insect traps." The nurse stood and started toward the door. I followed, but stopped at the doorway. "I want to thank both of you for this. You've been . . . well, you're making a difficult situation a lot easier."

Miller stood. "We know what you're dealing with—" He pointed proudly to a diploma on the wall. "Master's of Public Health. Hopkins, '78."

CHAPTER 13

At five o'clock, after swabbing and collecting in the kitchen at Miller Grove, I was standing in a small chapel, looking out over the gathered staff from two of the four Miller nursing homes. It was a motley collection, racially and developmentally. Just from the look of it, a quarter of the staff must have been "slow." I admired Dan Miller for his progressiveness; I also wondered what kinds of awesome tax breaks he was getting.

I introduced myself and explained why I was there. Though I cautioned against talking to reporters—"because we don't know much"—I was worried that the media had already caught wind of what had happened and were encamped downtown, outside St. Raphe's or outside the Department of Health. What we didn't need was forty more sources of information springing from the Miller homes.

Basically, what I wanted from these folks was: 1) whether they had seen anything unusual, like packages, rats in the kitchen, sicknesses; 2) what they knew about the three sick women; and 3) whether they knew the three sick women as more than just coworkers. Miller told them overtime would be paid to everyone, and cab fare given to anyone who needed a ride home. This was all the crowd needed to sit tight. Miller—fast becoming my favorite person in Baltimore—had pizzas trucked in from a local joint.

By the time I started to interview, fifty-plus people sat in the pews. It was going to be a long night.

I was into my third interview, stumbling through a give-and-take with a laundry worker named Rosa whose command of English was as bad as my command of Spanish, when the pizza arrived. Like any normal, hungry human, Rosa instantly lost interest in me and I let her go fight her way toward the food line. When she'd gotten her two pieces of pepperoni, she returned. We were about to continue the interview when I noticed a good-looking young white man stand up, muscle his way to the front of the line, and grab an entire box. He opened the box, took out a piece, and made his way to the back of the chapel. I'd kept an eye out for this sort of thing; you don't want someone who could help bolting before you had the chance to talk. Besides, the guy had just snatched an entire pie. Fairness, if nothing else, determined that I intervene.

"Who's that?" I asked Rosa. *"¿Quién es?"*

"Douglas," she said. *"El novio de Debbie."* El novio. Debbie's boyfriend.

I stood quickly. *"Esperar. Esper—"* I gave up and raced after him. "Excuse me, Douglas?"

He turned to me. He was big, black hair; his chiseled jaw was slightly slack.

"You must be hungry," I said.

He dropped the piece of pizza he was eating into the box, closed the lid.

"I'll get to you next. Five minutes. Can you wait? Can I talk to you in five minutes?"

"No, no. I—"

"You know, there are a lot of people to feed in there." I was trying to figure out if he was mentally handicapped or not. "Why don't we take it back inside, you take a couple slices, and we talk."

Nervously, his head switched left and right, as if he were looking for his wingman to get him out of the situation.

"Okay, I can talk to you now. You mind if I have a piece?" I reached for the box, and Douglas began to walk. Guess he did mind.

I followed him. "Someone told me you know Debbie Fillmore. Do you know Debbie?"

"No, no. I don't know her."

"Debbie Fillmore. Your girlfriend. Debbie."

"No. I don't know her."

Something was definitely wrong here. He was lying; that was obvious. And he was sweating like a marathoner.

"Why did you want to talk to me?"

"No I didn't."

"You waited for an hour to talk to me."

"No I didn't. I wanted . . ."

You wanted the pizza, didn't you, Douglas? I thought.

He was moving fast now, not toward the exit, but anywhere that was not near me. We turned down a long hallway. I powered through with the interview.

"Do you know if someone sent Debbie a package?"

"No."

"Did she get a package in the mail? Did she get a package from a friend?"

"I don't know," he said, looking straight ahead. "No!"

We clicked left, down another hallway. Douglas began to jog; I kept up.

"Was Debbie your girlfriend?" I was on his heels now; I could smell his sweat. "Did you ever kiss her?"

Frustrated with the running, wanting to slow this whole thing down, I put my hand on his shoulder. Mistake. Like a running back tossing a lineman, Douglas pivoted, swung his arms and the box of pizza at me, slamming his left arm into my trunk. I am not a small man, but it was enough to send me reeling. I bounced off the opposite wall, regained my footing, and he ran.

And then I stopped, realizing the futility—the near comedy—of the situation. There I was, racing down the hallway in a nursing home, chasing a retarded man who clutched a Papa John's box, being knocked around like a pinball, and, I noticed, being gawked at by a couple of nurses up the way.

My conversation with Douglas would have to wait.

CHAPTER 14

The next morning, five a.m., I drove to Open Arms to talk with the residents there. Mary and Mike D'Angelo, I found out, lived in the town house next door, and greeted me with coffee. I drained two cups to shake off the fog of four hours' sleep.

I sat in the living room as the residents came downstairs. Mary directed them to me, whereupon I asked them the usual questions. Nothing exceptional but for the obvious difference in how they felt about the two women. Helen, it seemed, was liked. Bethany was tolerated. Anyway, they were all worried about Bethany and Helen, and they were all petrified they would get sick. I tried to reassure them the best I could, which is to say I wasn't very convincing. Part of me wanted to quarantine all of the residents, make sure we kept this thing in its hole. But it was too soon for that: we didn't know modes of transmission or the chain of infection, we didn't know the reservoir, we didn't know the period of infectivity, we didn't really know anything. You can't keep a bunch of people locked in their homes if you don't know anything, so I reluctantly let the women get started with their day.

After morning prayers, the nine of us sat down to breakfast. Then, to the domestic music of breakfast cleanup, I interviewed Mike D'Angelo, a bear of a man with a full beard and belly. He was more cooperative than his wife had been. His answers weren't helpful—no packages or presents, no trips—but he wasn't holding back.

Then I asked about the women and sex. Mary, who was sitting next to her husband, tightened her crossed arms and pinched her mouth to a thin line.

"We don't allow that here," Mike said, looking into his coffee. He stole a glance at his watch.

"I understand that. But I'm wondering if you knew of anything. Maybe they talked about boyfriends?"

"Not to me," he said.

I let him have a moment to think; then I said, "I'm asking about this mostly because I'm wondering if they got any gifts. Sometimes lovers will use people to—well—deliver packages, things like that. Also, sex itself can transmit disease—" They were both looking intently at me. "Anyway, do you know anything?"

"No," he said.

I asked a few more questions, finished my coffee, and stepped toward the kitchen to check the traps I had set the day before.

Mike D'Angelo stood when I did. "Dr. McCormick."

Mary said sharply, "Michael—"

"Not now," he said to her. To me, "Would you follow me into the living room? More coffee?"

I declined the coffee and followed him. Mary D'Angelo stuck close behind us.

Mike settled his bulk on a stiff vinyl couch. Like his wife, he was in his fifties. Like her, he was a social worker. He continued to counsel with, he made sure to point out, a forgiving, Christian bent.

"Dr. McCormick, running a home for mentally handicapped women is not an easy task—"

"I can imagine—"

"Allow me to finish, please, Doctor. I don't want to spend more time with this than I need to." He sipped at his coffee. "Though we are well aware of different approaches to managing the mentally handicapped, we feel that a strict moral management—a Christian management—is best for our residents.

"Bethany has been with us since we opened this home, since she was eighteen. She's been with us through the ups and downs, learned with us as we learned how to manage a family like this. But, as in all families, there are problems, and problem children."

Three women stuck their heads into the living room and waved good-bye. "Lunch?" Mary asked. All held up their brown bags and, like a line of ants, marched out of the house. When Mary D'Angelo looked back to me, there was real pain in her face.

Mike continued, "Bethany is a problem. Please don't misunderstand me—we love her, and we are willing to forgive her. And we are worried sick about her. But she has tested us. Lord, has she tested us."

Mary looked away, but I glimpsed tears in her eyes.

"Well," Mike said, "you don't need to hear our sob story. And I don't believe that what I'm going to tell you will be of much help, but I don't profess to be an expert in disease. So I will say it. It is the right thing to do. I just ask that you be judicious with this—"

Another woman, a straggler, shouted a good-bye. Again, Mary asked about lunch, keeping her wet eyes turned away from the foyer.

"We ask that you be careful with this information, Doctor. It would be terrible if the other girls found out. It would be terrible for us in the community. We do have a reputation."

Mary said, "Michael—"

"Please, woman. A few weeks ago, I happened to have a cancellation during the day—a counseling session—and decided to come over and fix some lights that had been neglected. I often come over to do work when I have a cancellation, so I don't know what they were thinking—"

"They weren't thinking," Mary said.

"Mary." Mike cleared his throat. "I went to the second floor, where the lights were out, and I heard some noises coming from Bethany and Helen's room. I walked to the door to their room and opened it, and . . . and I opened the door, and I saw a man on the floor . . . kneeling behind a woman on all fours. They were naked. Bethany was there, on her back on the floor. But the woman on her knees was Helen."

CHAPTER 15

I drove fast to St. Raphael's, elements of this—what? outbreak?—gamboling in my head.

Sex, I thought. Three actors so far, two of them sick. It was by no means conclusive that we were dealing with anything at all like a sexually transmitted disease—the epidemiological lore is filled with red herrings and rabbit trails—but the idea was taking hold.

I built a chart of sexual contact in my head, a spiderweb of boxes and lines, each box with a name. Then it was small, only three boxes: Helen and Bethany and this unnamed, unknown man. Unfortunately, Mike D'Angelo didn't get the name of the man. He didn't even get a good look at him. After discovering the ménage à trois, he slammed the door and walked back downstairs to the living room. A minute later, he heard footsteps on the stairs, through the foyer, and out the door. He didn't press Bethany or Helen on the name. "Who it was wasn't important," he'd said. He hadn't spoken about it with Bethany or Helen, hoping, he said, that the shock of being discovered would cure them of any sexual desire. Hoping, I thought, that the whole nasty mess would just fade away.

Well, it didn't.

So, because she was a known quantity and promiscuous, I put Bethany in the center of my contact tree, drew lines connecting her to Helen and the unknown man with them. I drew lines to five other partners that Bethany might or might not have had. I drew a line from one of these partners to Deborah Fillmore. But Helen was the index case, the first patient, and not the promiscuous Bethany. Why?

Because these diseases don't follow a set script. For whatever genetic reason, perhaps Bethany was just a little more resistant. The contact tree began to look like a huge web, with Bethany at the center, a black widow surrounded by her victims.

The parking lot at St. Raphael's was nearly empty, the evacuation having been largely completed. The bigwigs at CDC, according to Verlach, had been contacted that morning by Ben Timmons, the Commissioner of Public Health for Baltimore. I thought for a moment about that call, about its repercussions. With it, Timmons was bringing in the cavalry. They'd help wipe out the enemy, sure, but they might trample me in the meantime.

Well, I'd been trampled plenty of times before, and I was still kicking. Timmons might have signaled his SOS, but the best he could probably do—trying to make it seem like Baltimore was in control while still asking for help—was to get another EIS officer or two. I was scared enough now that I wanted to bump this up a few notches. So I climbed out of my car and put in my own call to CDC, to the branch chief, Dr. Timothy Leary Lancaster. My boss.

"I think we need help, Tim," I said. Then I filled him in.

The old plan, as of yesterday, was to keep me in Baltimore and to use the local guys for everything but the lab work and what I could contribute. But for me, things changed with the possibility of sexual transmission. AIDS is still fresh in everyone's mind—how swiftly and silently it moved, not to mention its near-complete mortality—so I knew my story would resonate. My idea that the disease would burn itself out, that it was too hot, may well have been bullshit. We had no idea how long these girls had been sick. We had no idea how many others harbored the bug and may have been asymptomatic.

I wiped a trickle of sweat that trailed from my ear onto the phone. It was eight thirty a.m. and already in the mid-eighties with that Baltimore one hundred percent humidity. I might as well have been in Uganda.

"I'm worried," I told Tim.

"So am I." I heard him heave a breath through his nose. "I want to say it's not terrorism, but"—another long breath—"but you're giving me signs and symptoms we haven't seen before."

Giving me symptoms. Ha. Good one, Tim.

He went on. "Also, if you think about who it's striking first . . . You sow the seeds of this thing in a population that's not that sexually responsible, goes like wildfire through them, jumps to the larger population. . . ."

"We thought about that," I said, making sure he knew we were on the ball up here.

"Let me talk to the EPO"—the Epidemiology Program Office—"and see what we can spare. My plate is pretty clear. Talk to the Health Department, scare them, then call me back."

"They're already scared."

"Good. We should be able to get you another investigator, me probably, and a data hound."

Good little drummer that I am, I told him I'd do my best.

But I didn't tell him other things: that I'd no idea *he* would come, that I now regretted calling him, that I didn't want him within a hundred miles of Baltimore, that the local health department and EIS officer Nathaniel McCormick had it all under control. This mess could be a career-making event. And *I* was cracking it. Me. I sure as hell didn't want Tim Lancaster up there with me, stealing the spotlight.

My stomach churned. The bad ol' Nate McCormick was clawing his way out of the grave, worried about snatching his piece of the glory, the public be damned. I pushed him back into the dirt and, disgusted with myself, dialed Verlach's number.

Verlach seemed as jazzed as Tim, half with worry, half with joy that we were making some progress in the case. He was at Deborah Fillmore's home, talking to the residents there, and he'd started hitting the sex angle hard. In the meantime, he suggested I track down Bethany Reginald's and Helen Jones's lovers or lover.

I asked Verlach whether he'd heard anything from the lab about the samples sent from the sick women.

"I heard from them, and they found nothing."

"Our mystery bug," I said.

"Keeps things interesting."

"Unfortunately."

When he said this, I was at the entrance to St. Raphe's, fishing for my ID to show the security guard stationed outside.

CHAPTER 16

There are few things as spooky as a deserted hospital. Hospitals just don't close. Twenty-four hours a day, 365 days a year, decade after decade, snowstorms, Christmas, terrorist attacks, these places are open and alive. Most likely, St. Raphe's had not been this empty since its construction in 1915. When the human race finally does itself in, alien archeologists are going to find the hospitals much like I did that day. Except the elevators won't work for them.

I made my way up to M-2, where there were once again signs of life, or at least half-life: a couple of bleary-eyed residents and a skeleton crew of nurses. Gary Hammil was the attending on duty, looking as if he hadn't slept since medical school. I said a quick hello, danced around questions about how the investigation was going, and suited up. I went in to see the girls.

First, I went into Bethany's room. She was asleep, and she didn't look good. The disease was moving rapidly through her. Humanitarian that I am, I decided to let her rest. I went in to see Helen.

"Hi, Helen, I'm Dr. McCormick. Do you remember me from yesterday?"

She shook her head.

"I'm here to help find out what made you sick." Helen said nothing. "How are you feeling?"

"I want to go home." This was a good sign; she was well enough to want to go home. The disease seemed to be fading.

"Hey," I said. I pulled a chair to the side of the bed and sat, giving myself a moment to figure out how to approach this. "I need to ask you some more questions. Just like we did yesterday. Is that okay?"

Helen lolled her head toward me. The pinprick hemorrhages in her mouth were dark brown now as they clotted and were being reabsorbed. "Okay."

"I need you to answer these questions. With the truth, okay? Do you understand me?"

"Yes," she said weakly.

"It's very important." I took a couple of blank sheets from the folder I carried with me, which I'd feed into the fax machine after I was finished and pick up again on the outside.

Here goes, I thought. "Helen, has a man ever touched you in your private parts?"

"No—" she whined.

"Please. I need to know who has touched you."

She turned her head away from me; I wasn't able to ease into this as I'd hoped.

"Did you have sex with a man in your bedroom?"

The whining "no" again, which seemed not so much an answer to my question as a protest against it.

"Helen, who was the man with you and Bethany when Mike walked into your room?"

Her head turned away from me, she squeezed her eyes shut.

"Helen," I said. She was, I thought, pretending to sleep. I placed my hand on her arm. No response. *Do I deserve this?*

"Helen, listen to me. If you don't tell me . . . if you don't tell me the truth, I will talk to Mike and Mary about you. . . ." About what, I didn't know, and pushed on with a lie. "If you don't tell me, they will take you away from the home. You won't get in trouble if you *do* tell me. If you *don't* tell me, they will send you away. Do you want that?"

Her eyes were now open, her head shaking in quivering movements. Doing this to her was killing me, but desperate times, right?

I continued. "They'll take Bethany away, too. Do you want that, Helen?"

The shaking stopped. "Yes," she hissed.

Well, now, that was a surprise. "Why do you want Bethany to go away?"

"She brings them."

"Who?"

"Men. She brings them."

Aha. So Bethany and Helen's little daytime trysts were regular occurrences. The poor benighted D'Angelos, believing this was a single occurrence. Or pretending to believe.

"Were there many men, Helen?"

She was crying now. "Some."

"How many?"

"Some."

Okay, that was not so helpful.

"Do you remember their names? Please, Helen, this is really important. Do you remember their names?"

"No," she said. I tried not to let my exasperation show. After a moment, she said, "Jerry, Henry. More."

I wrote the names in my notebook; I was getting used to Helen's logical dips and turns. "Do you remember any of their last names?"

Confusion and crying. I tried to clarify. "Do these men work with you? Do they work with you and Bethany at Mr. Miller's?"

She nodded.

"Helen, do you remember who was with you when Mike saw you in your room? When Mike saw you and you and Bethany were naked?"

She started shaking her head violently. "No, no! Don't tell, don't tell."

"I won't tell." Then I added, "Mike and Mary love you," which was true. "What was the name of the man who was naked with you and Bethany?"

She clutched at my gown. Remembering what happened the day before, I pulled away, then thought *fuck it* and let her pull.

"Don't tell. Don't tell. Douglas. Please!"

"Douglas?"

"Don't tell!"

Okay. Bingo. We have a Casanova to Bethany's Catherine the Great.

"How many times were you with Douglas?" I asked. "Were you with Douglas one time?"

Painfully, she nodded.

"Were you with him two times?"

She nodded. "Please don't tell. Please don't tell," she warbled. She muttered something. Prayers, I think.

"I won't," I lied. "I promise you won't get in trouble," I said, trying to soften the lie. I'd pretty much do anything now not to get Helen Jones in trouble. Hell, if she got into hot water, I'd take her into my home. Brave girl.

Helen clutched my gown tighter. "Don't tell about Bethany. Don't tell."

"Bethany? Helen, I thought you—"

"I love her so much. Please. I love her *so much*."

I stayed with Helen for another ten minutes, stroking her hair as she wept. The pieces began to fall into place. Poor Helen. So smitten with Bethany she was willing to become a sexual addendum to her lover's powerful drives. I imagined the two of them in their room, together. What was it? Weeks? Months? Years, before Bethany got bored and began to bring others into the bedroom?

What was it like for Helen to see her girlfriend slipping away? What kind of heartbreak was it, not to be able to tell anyone?

Bethany was awake now, but her fever was creeping north, and she was a little delirious. She was, however, able to confirm the names given to me by Helen, as well as to contribute Mitchell to the list.

I asked her if she loved Helen. She said yes. I asked her if she loved Douglas and Jerry and Henry. She said she did.

In Bethany's mouth, I could see the spots of blood in that livid shotgun pattern.

My boss called to tell me he would be arriving in Baltimore that evening with a data guru called Sonjit Mehta. Tim Lancaster had been instrumental in setting up surveillance for West Nile in New York in '99 and then for the entire country as that disease spread west and south. He was a first responder to the attacks on 9/11, back when we feared that the terrorists might have attacked secondarily with germs. He knew most of the major players in public health in the Northeast. Because of his experience, his indefatigable energy, his ability to lead, and his political savvy, he was one of CDC's golden boys. He was someone I wouldn't mind being, but had a difficult time following. He was also thirty-five. Two years older than me.

I was happy he was coming. Really, I was relieved he was coming. And I might believe it if I said it enough.

I resigned myself to the imminent arrival of Herr Lancaster. Still, there were some things I wanted to do before he came and took over the city.

I tracked down the male members of this sordid love knot to their jobs at the Miller nursing homes. Henry and Jerry and Mitchell were there. Disturbingly, Douglas—whose full name was Douglas Buchanan—was not. The group home where he was a resident called to say he was sick. While I was there, I reinterviewed Henry, Jerry, and Mitchell. Though they had lied to me the night before about their relationships with the women, they were somewhat more forthcoming that afternoon.

Other than their trysts with Bethany and Helen, the three men's histories were uneventful. I drew blood and got semen samples. Next time you're trying to do something difficult—say, trying to teach your dog to recite Shakespeare—think about getting semen samples from a couple of mentally disabled men who don't really understand the reason for your wanting their seed. Dan Miller came down and pressured them, and I don't even want to think what kinds of legal boundaries we were crossing with his presence. Anyway, after a few minutes of cajoling, I sent them one by one into the men's room with a copy of *Hustler* and a condom. I'm happy to report that each man performed.

With my little bag of blood and sperm samples, I left Miller Grove, and drove to Douglas Buchanan's residence. I played the relationships through in my head over and over. Each time, the web got bigger. AIDS II—or the face-sparing hemorrhagic fever, or whatever the hell it was—might well be sliding out of control.

I called Verlach, who, at the moment, was off the street and in his office, having sent the poor state bastards out to interview the people we'd missed. The first twenty interviews in an outbreak are fun. The last one hundred are sheer, unforgiving hell. I didn't blame him for taking some cover in administration.

I gave him the download. "Making some headway," he said.

"Maybe." I told him I was headed to Baltimore Haven to talk to Douglas Buchanan.

"That's where Debbie Fillmore lives."

"Yes. Convenient for them."

"And for you. Enjoy yourself. The place is dank." He shuffled some papers. "I'd come with you, but I have to coordinate from here. Get ready for state and your CDC chums. And speaking of chums, it looks like your boss is coming up from Atlanta."

"I heard."

"I thought Timmons was going to request more guys like you, more EIS. I guess he wanted bigger guns."

"I called Tim Lancaster, Herb. I suggested he come."

"Oh," he said flatly. "I guess that's why Timmons looked like a grenade went off in his face."

I could imagine Tim Lancaster giving the full-court press to Timmons, scaring the hell out of him, not about a microbial blowup but about the commissioner's own career. Playing the old cover-your-ass. If things went wrong, CDC's shoulders were a lot stronger than Commissioner Ben Timmons's. Tim Lancaster knew it, Ben Timmons knew it. So did I, and so did Herb Verlach.

"Good luck with them," I said.

"Sure."

Verlach took a moment; I heard him flipping through more pages. "Douglas Buchanan. We missed him each time we were there."

"He's the guy who bolted from me at the nursing home."

"Right. Maybe you'll catch him at Baltimore Haven. Don't call ahead."

"I won't."

"And wait until you see the guy's room."

"What do you mean?"

"Just wait. You'll know what I mean when you see it." Verlach cleared his throat. "Hey, Nate, you're doing a great job."

I thanked him for the much-needed boost and said good-bye. But before I hung up, Verlach stopped me.

"Hey, check on the vermin for me, will you?"

"I thought the press was camped outside your office."

"Very funny, Doctor. Make sure the traps weren't tampered with. I have a little gray piece of tape on each trap. It'll be broken if anyone screwed with it."

CHAPTER 18

Jesus Christ, Verlach was right. Baltimore Haven was anything but a haven. Three stories of beige brick, housing thirty-six residents in a decayed neighborhood in northwest Baltimore. The top floor must have had a nice view of Druid Park. A pretty park, actually, if you didn't think about the murders and rapes that regularly occur there.

The door buzzed, and I walked down a hallway floored in cracked linoleum. A woman sat at what I guess was a receiving desk. Well, it was either that or a counseling station, since there was a small sign—faded now—with a bear and a dialogue bubble reading: Talk to me. I can help with ANYTHING. She seemed to be counseling a boyfriend now, cracking gum and giggling into the phone.

"Dr. Nathaniel McCormick, Baltimore City Health Department," I said, figuring the local Department of Health would carry more weight than some unknown national agency. I pulled out my Health Department credentials.

"Hold on," she said, and dropped the receiver from her mouth. "What do you want?"

To see this place shut down and you shoveling burgers at McDonald's. "I'm here to speak with one of your residents. Douglas Buchanan. I also need to check the rodent traps Dr. Verlach set yesterday."

"Call you back," she heaved wearily into the phone. She dropped it into its cradle. "Which do you want to do first?"

"I'd like to speak to Mr. Buchanan."

"Third floor, end of the hallway." She made no move to get up and lead me. *And this woman is in health* care? I thought. God.

"I'll find my own way."

"I'm sure you will."

To my left, there was a large recreation room cluttered with broken chairs, a couple of board games, and a television. Two slack-mouthed residents stared at the TV. If Open Arms was heaven for its inhabitants, Baltimore Haven was definitely some sort of hell.

Evidently, like Verlach said, there had been some effort to clean up since attention focused on this place. In fact, the effort was still going on. A man in filthy coveralls was mopping the stairs, and not doing a great job. Gray water cascaded over the steps. Fine for a fountain, not good for a means of egress. I held on to the railing and kept walking.

"Hi," I said. The man looked at me blankly, then slopped the filthy mop onto the stairs.

I walked out of the stairwell into a hallway about twenty feet long. Two doors lined each side of the hallway with another door—closed—at the end. From the stellar directions given me by my guide, I decided the door at the end of the hallway was Douglas's.

The first door on my right was open, or, more exactly, broken and open, hanging by a single hinge. In it, a man sat on one of two beds. He was hugging himself and mumbling. The only decoration in the room, besides a big poster for State Farm Insurance ("Like a Good Neighbor, State Farm Is There"), was a picture of a black Jesus surrounded by black apostles.

Through another open door, I saw a man lying on his bed, naked from the waist down, legs pulled up to his chest. Feces was newly smeared on the bed. In the next room, a man slumped in a chair, a tinny radio belching out fire-and-brimstone religion. He was, it looked like, trying to eat his shirt.

At the end of the hall, I knocked on the closed door.

"Who goes there?" I heard from inside.

"It's Dr. McCormick, Douglas. I saw you last night at the nursing home. I need to talk to you, please."

For a moment, there was nothing. Then I heard the sound of a lock being undone.

Verlach was right: Douglas's room was something else. Nothing to write home about, but in the context of Baltimore Haven, this was a suite at the Plaza.

The first thing I noticed was the lock—a nice Yale dead bolt—and that there was only one bed. In addition to being a single, the room was decked out in personal accoutrements: a large poster for the San Francisco 49ers, another for the SF Giants. There was a framed picture of the Golden Gate Bridge. No State Farm posters here.

Music played from a portable CD player. A window air conditioner hummed.

Dressed in blue jeans and a white T-shirt, Douglas Buchanan stood in front of me with his arms crossed. He avoided eye contact. "You have a nice place here, Douglas."

"Thank you," he said nervously.

I let the silence sink in for a moment; then I said, "You seem to like San Francisco." I gestured at the posters. "Have you ever been there?"

If there was one place *I* didn't need to see again, it was San Francisco, or anywhere in the Bay Area, for that matter. I'd rather spend a week in Baltimore Haven, bunking with the guy who chowed on his shirt, than one night in a four-star in downtown SF.

Well, maybe that's a stretch, but you get the idea.

I caught Douglas Buchanan staring hard-eyed at me; he quickly looked at his feet. "I ain't been there," he said.

"It's an interesting place," I said. Then, changing tack: "Are you feeling sick?"

"No." Quickly, he added, "Yes."

"Which is it? I just need to know. I'm not going to tell the people where you work."

After a long moment, he said, "No."

"I'm a doctor, Douglas. Would you mind if I felt your forehead? To see if you have a fever?"

I reached at him without giving him time to answer. He flinched, but let me touch his head. It was a little wet with perspiration, but despite the air-conditioning, it was July in Baltimore, after all. He felt fine to me.

I pulled back my hand and wiped it on my pants. "Douglas, I need to ask you some questions about your girlfriends. You have girlfriends, don't you?"

He hugged himself a little tighter. "No."

"Do you know Deborah Fillmore? She lives here."

He didn't answer.

"Do you know Helen Jones or Bethany Reginald? They work with you at Mr. Miller's nursing home."

"I don't know."

"Douglas, this is very important. Debbie, Bethany, and Helen are all very sick. They need your help."

He shot me a look. Afraid? Angry? I couldn't tell. "Douglas, I know you know them. They told me." Well, one of them, at least. "Douglas, do you know what sex is?"

"Yes, I know what sex is." He sounded annoyed. He sat on the bed and rubbed his strong, heavy jaw. If you didn't speak to him, you wouldn't know he was retarded. Even then, it might take a few sentences to realize he was, as they say, slow.

Okay, I thought, *one more try before I get tough.* "Have you had sex with Helen or Debbie or Bethany?" Douglas scooped up a small toy truck from a nightstand and began to spin its wheels. "When was the last time you had sex with any of them?"

Spin, spin, spin.

"Douglas, you have to talk to me."

Spin, spin, spin.

"Douglas, this is very important. I can call the police if you don't talk to me."

The spinning stopped. He looked up at me. Now there was fear in his face. Naked fear.

"No . . ." he whispered.

"I'll have to, Douglas, if you don't talk to me—"

"No!"

As his anger flared, a phone started to ring. I reached for mine, which was stupid, considering I always kept it on vibrate. My pager, too. It wasn't a phone in the room, either—there wasn't one. The noise was coming from Douglas's pocket. He looked at the pocket, then at me, then went back to spinning the wheels on the truck.

He said, "Two weeks or a week. I don't know." The phone continued ringing, then abruptly stopped.

"Who was it the last time?" He didn't answer. "Was it Bethany—?"

"Yeah."

"When?"

No response. I asked again.

"A week or two weeks ago."

"This is really important, Douglas. Besides Helen, Debbie, and Bethany, did you have sex with anybody else?"

He sighed. "Yes."

"Who?"

"You don't tell the police."

"I won't. What were their names?"

"You don't tell anyone."

In the interest of public health, I lied through my teeth. "I promise I won't," I told him.

Reluctantly, he ran through five names. I dutifully took each down into my notebook; some sounded familiar. "Do they work at Mr. Miller's nursing homes?"

"Who?"

"The women you had sex with."

"Yeah."

"All of them?"

"Yeah."

Good, I thought. *If this thing is sexually transmitted, we might be able to contain it.*

Douglas's cell phone squawked twice; someone had left a message on it. He didn't bother to silence it.

"Did you use condoms when you had sex with these women?"

He processed that for a moment, then said: "I forget."

Great. "Douglas, have you ever had sex with a man?"

"No!" he shouted. "Go. Go away now. Now it's time for you to go." He stood. "Go away. Go, go."

Douglas Buchanan was, as I said, a big man; he probably had two inches and forty pounds on me. My heart thudded and—I'm not going to shout this from the rooftops—I stepped back a pace or two. But I've taken a few blows in my time, including one from Douglas Buchanan the night before. However, that was before I thought he might be crawling with pathogens. I stood my ground anyway; Douglas came no closer.

"Douglas, I need something else. I need to take some blood from you."

"No." He shook his head violently and took a step toward me.

Violence, as was drilled into me through those first rotations in the ER and psych wards, is seldom spontaneous. There are signals: escalating agitation, threatening movements. The upsurge to violence is clear, what's not clear is the exact moment when the wave actually crests and the blows fly. Douglas Buchanan was definitely broadcasting to me he was about to crack.

This time, it was I who backed down. I said gently, "Okay, I think we're finished for now. But we'll need to talk later, okay?" The cell phone chirped again; I pointed at his pocket. "Could you give me your cell phone number so I could call you if I needed to?"

"What phone?"

"The cellular phone in your pocket."

A weird look came over his face. Douglas, it seemed, was pretty damned cunning for a retarded guy. He knew he was slow. More important, he knew people knew he was slow: he played on that.

I decided to let that one lie and moved to the door. I turned around just before I left.

"One more thing. If you have to have sex, use a condom. We're worried that the women you were with have a disease that is transmitted—it's contagious—through sex. Do you understand what I'm saying?"

"Yes." I might have been a lame public health appeal plastered to a city bus, for all he cared.

"Tell me what I just said."

"Sex can kill you."

Well put, Douglas. I said, "Will you use a condom when you have sex again? Can you do that for me?"

Douglas Buchanan, his eyes dead, nodded.

"Thank you, Douglas. You've done a very good thing." I forced a smile.

CHAPTER 19

On the way out of Baltimore Haven-cum-Hell, I stopped at the counseling desk, where, if you can believe it, the woman was still chatting it up. I tapped on her desk, which had the desired effects of making her stop the conversation and deeply annoying her.

"Are the residents permitted to have cellular phones?"

"There's a pay phone in the hall behind you," she said nastily. I looked. Indeed, there was a pay phone in the hallway.

"Not what I asked."

She got off the telephone and rummaged in her desk, finally producing a beat-up sheaf of photocopied papers. She leafed through them, stopped on one, and read: " 'No resident shall be permitted to possess personal communication devices (pagers, cellular telephones) while residing at Baltimore Haven.' " She reassembled the papers. "To keep them from dealing drugs," she explained.

I didn't see why they couldn't use the pay phone to deal drugs, and I almost said something about it. I didn't, though, when I looked closer at the phone. The thing was missing its mouthpiece and earpiece. Wires sprang from the gutted ends of the handset.

I turned back to her. "Can you show me to the kitchen and the basement?"

"Why?"

"I need to check the rat traps."

She looked pointedly at her watch, then looked at me with a practiced fuck-you stare. "You can wait here for Dr. Jefferson. He wants to talk to you." Then she picked up the phone and began to dial.

I took that as my cue.

I walked past the desk down a small hallway to where I hoped the kitchen would be.

"Hey!" she yelled after me. "Hey, you can't go back there."

I saw a grungy dining room on my right, plates of half-eaten breakfast still on the tables.

"You'll be in deep shit, you keep going!" If she was right about that, we might actually have the reservoir for our disease. "What's your name?" she screeched.

Well, if she didn't remember, I wasn't going to help her. "Dr. Faustus," I shouted back. By that time, I had my phone out and was dialing Verlach's number.

"Where are the traps?" I asked.

Verlach gave me the rough locations of ten rodent traps. I took out my notebook and sketched a quick map of the kitchen, in which I was standing, and the pantry and basement. Two of the kitchen staff were lazily assembling sandwiches while a Latino radio station jangled in the background.

"I have a feeling things are going to heat up here," I told Verlach.

"Better you than me. Listen, get what you can, then get out of there. When I was there, Jefferson sent a couple of his associates to help me out. Scary-looking guys making life hard. That's why it took me so goddamned long."

I looked around. The place stank, that much was true, but there were no piles of rotting garbage, no foul sludge bubbling up from the drain in the floor, nothing like that. "Herb, I think they cleaned up since you were here."

"I guess we could have expected that." He paused. "I'll have the judge work on a court order to give you emergency access to the place."

"Right. The judge."

"Well, tell them that, anyway. Should get them off your back for a little. It worked yesterday."

"If they hassle me, we'll rip this place apart. We have the authority."

"Come on, man, don't go running roughshod. This guy has powerful friends—"

"Gotta go," I said, and hung up the phone.

In the kitchen, there was nary a rodent to be found, although I did see some mouse droppings in a few corners that the mop must have missed. I double-checked Verlach's little pieces of gray duct tape, and sure enough, they had been broken on three of the traps. So at least we knew there were rodents. What unholy diseases they were carrying would remain a mystery for a little while longer.

I refilled the bait caches and went into the pantry.

Normal institutional fare—a few cloudy bottles of oil—going rancid, probably—flour, oatmeal, et cetera, et cetera. More mouse shit. Again, nothing in the traps. One trap with broken tape.

To the basement I went. Or tried to go. The door was locked.

"Do you have keys?" I called to the kitchen workers, both heavyset Latinas. They looked at each other. *"¿Tienen llaves?"* Neither moved. *"Soy un doctor, de la officina de salud."* I was mangling their mother tongue here, but I hoped I got my point across. I produced my CDC badge. *"Necesitan abrir la puerta,"* I said. *You need to open the door.* Now frightened looks. I was about to use my trump card—ICE threats— but one of the women pulled a key chain from her apron and opened the door.

"Muchas gracias," I told her, and flicked on the lights and headed down the steps.

Hercules' Augean stables must have looked antiseptic compared to the basement at Baltimore Haven. Piles of institutional crap were everywhere. Old carpet rolls here, broken chairs and tables there. There were a few bags of rice that lay in the corner, split and spilling their contents onto the floor. In the midst of all this, I saw how pathetic my drawing had been. I reoriented it and made my way around the cluttered, dank cellar, trying to key the little Xs on the paper with the location of the traps.

Behind a clutch of broken light stands, I found one. Empty. I moved along the damp wall, past cardboard boxes disintegrating in the moisture. Piles of clothes tumbled from one, broken picture frames and torn photos from another. The personal possessions of the residents? If so, I wondered why they weren't upstairs in the rooms. Probably had something to do with stripping the residents of any last vestige of identity. The management probably called it "therapy."

I heard a scurrying in the shadows. Another trap, with a big mother of a rat running in mindless circles inside it. I lifted the trap and put it on a broken table in the center of the room. Quickly, I found the other cages, one of which housed another member of the class Rodentia.

Then I heard footsteps coming down the stairs.

Dr. Randall Jefferson stood at the bottom of the steps; behind him stood a much larger man who would most aptly be described by the term *thug*. Jefferson was black, his henchman white. I knew the doctor by reputation—a prominent psychiatrist and businessman in the city who, by the looks of his fifteen-hundred-dollar suit, was doing quite well for himself—and from stock newspaper photos Verlach had showed me. Last I heard, the city was paying out about three hundred dollars per day to folks like Randall Jefferson to care for the mentally disabled. Supposedly, care involved decent housing and food and, importantly, vocational training and psychotherapy. I wondered about the quality of therapy given to the man upstairs who was eating his shirt. I looked at Jefferson's shoes, which probably cost as much as I make in a week. Hmmmmm. Let's see: Baltimore Haven had thirty-five residents. At three hundred dollars per day per resident . . .

"Dr. McCormick," he said in a faux patrician accent. He knew my name. Evidently, the owner of Baltimore Haven was a bit concerned about yours truly. He continued. "You've gotten yourself in quite a spot."

I looked at the mounds of junk around me. "Don't I know it. I have no idea how I'm going to navigate around that settee there."

He shook his head, a humorless, shit-eating smile on his face. "That's very funny."

"I try." There was a rat trap with rat in my hand, and I set it down on a chair with three legs.

Jefferson said, "You spoke with one of our residents without notifying us first."

"I didn't know I needed to notify you."

"I'd like to know the content of that conversation."

"I'm afraid it's confidential. Doctor-patient privilege."

"Tsk, tsk, Dr. McCormick. We both know that's not true. You're not Douglas's doctor, nor does an investigation like this confer on you doctor-patient privilege." He was half-right; Douglas Buchanan wasn't my patient. He was, in all likelihood, Dr. Jefferson's patient.

"But an investigation like this does allow me to enter the premises and talk to whomever I'd like."

"Not without a court order."

"I have one," I lied. I should have had one, Verlach should have gotten one, and Randall Jefferson shouldn't have been giving me such grief. Unfortunately, no one thought there would be problems like this.

"Then let me see it, the court order."

"It's with Dr. Verlach."

"Ah. I'm sure it is." Jefferson finally let the grin fall from his face;

I was amazed at how long he'd sustained it. This guy had the makings of a great politician. "Dr. McCormick, you seem like a well-intentioned man. And let me assure you that we are well intentioned, too. We want to cooperate with the public health authorities in your investigation of this terrible illness. We don't, however, appreciate being taken for granted. We only wish that you'd call before you descend on our facilities and interrogate our residents. That way, we might help make the process easier."

Or hide what you need to hide, I thought. I said, "I'm sure we'll be contacting you soon. Today, probably. And we'll need to have another conversation with Douglas Buchanan. Again, probably today."

"Then I can probably help you. If you tell me the content of the conversation you just had with him."

I said, "Great, why don't we go speak with Mr. Buchanan now? I still need to get a blood sample from him. And semen. Perhaps you can help with that."

Neither Jefferson nor his thug seemed to care for this suggestion. Coolly, Jefferson said, "Unfortunately, I think Douglas stepped out."

"Why am I not surprised?"

I looked around the basement. There was perhaps one more trap to check, but I was willing to skip it. I had two in my hands already, and I didn't expect Jefferson or his henchman to help me out with a third. I picked up the rat traps, which the rodents didn't seem to like. They were bounding around, squeaking.

"You'll be kind enough to leave those here." Jefferson pointed at the traps. "You can come back for them when you have a court order. We'll keep them safe for you."

"These?" I held up my hands. "I brought these with me. I keep these little guys as pets. For company."

"You're a very funny man, Dr. McCormick."

The thug, a bullet-headed gent of professional-wrestler dimensions, shifted his stance. I saw the overwhelming wisdom of getting out of there.

"I suggest you put those traps down and contact your lawyer. You are, I believe, going to need him."

"Or her," I told Jefferson. "I could be wrong, but I think they let girls study the law in this country."

Why do I say these things?

"Dr. McCormick, the cages."

"Excuse me," I said, as if I hadn't heard him, and took a step toward the basement stairs. The two men stood their ground in front of me. In the cages, the rats were freaking out.

The thug reached out to grab one of the traps. Without thinking—and I really should have thought about this—I headed for the steps. The man wrapped his thick fingers around the cage mesh and pulled. I didn't let go. The shaking back and forth excited the rat even more. The thing started to scream and literally bounce from side to side in its prison. Again, I thought of the man eating his shirt upstairs.

"Ah!" the thug screamed, and jerked back his hand. He pressed it to his lips. "It bit me! The fucking thing bit me!"

Both rats were shrieking now, and I swung a cage at the henchman to knock him back a little. I ran up the steps. Jefferson was yelling something behind me.

Even as I jogged through the hallway to the front doors, I began cursing myself: stupid, stupid, stupid, stupid. I looked at the cages in my hands, at the rats inside them. It would be a sick irony indeed if my little friends were our vector and if I, Dr. Nathaniel McCormick, had infected someone else.

I hoped—I prayed, actually—that my buddy had not broken the thug's skin.

I needed to calm down before I went back to Guilford Avenue and the Baltimore City Health Department to drop off the vermin and confer with Verlach about what I'd found. The most direct route would have been to hop the Jones Falls Expressway straight to downtown. Instead, I went through the city, toward the Baltimore campus of the University of Maryland and toward one of my favorite places for lunch. Even a medical detective on an outbreak investigation has to eat. Especially if he was just assaulted. Especially if he was worried about infecting someone with a disease.

A few words about me and University of Maryland, Baltimore campus. First and foremost, good old Maryland is my alma mater. The latter half of my medical school training was there, which means I went through my clerkships in the university hospital, which means I learned how to be a doctor there. My preclinical training, those moderately important first two years of basic science, had been spent on the West Coast, at that famous university smack in the middle of Silicon Valley. The Farm: all sun and fun and outstanding national reputation. But I hated Northern California. For reasons that had more to do with character flaws in yours truly than anything else, I'd beaten a hasty retreat from the Golden State.

Maryland, to their undying credit, gave me a second chance at medicine and I'd graduated. With honors. After that, I went to the University of North Carolina for an internal medicine residency and, finally, ended up at CDC in Atlanta. All in all, my life had been pretty good since I'd fled California, though I spent far too many years south of the Mason-Dixon Line for someone who breaks out in the heat and humidity.

Anyway, there I was, back on Redwood Street at Mary's Diner, sitting at a Formica table, chomping a two-dollar burger. The car was illegally parked out front, the windows were cracked open, and the rats were basking in their cages on the floor of the backseat. I chatted up the waitress, whom I remembered perfectly and who had no idea who I was. I stopped chatting when my cell phone vibrated.

"Nathaniel, it's Jean Madison." She sounded exhausted. No formal "Dr. McCormick" now. "I have some bad news."

"What is it?"

"Well . . . Whatever it is, it looks like it's lethal." She heaved a sigh into the phone.

"What?"

"Deborah Fillmore is dead."

CHAPTER 20

The burger I'd eaten thirty minutes before was bubbling unpleasantly in my stomach. Perhaps it wasn't the burger per se; perhaps it was the ambiance. I was in the path labs at St. Raphe's.

Hopkins and Maryland had both offered to let St. Raphael's use their pathology labs—everyone wanted a little piece of the glory—but nobody thought it wise to transport a pathogenically hot item like Deborah Fillmore's body any further than it had to go. The thing was, as

Dr. Madison said, lethal. This changed the equation somewhat, and everyone was skittish. Consequently, we were decked out in the best protective gear the Health Department had to offer: full biohazard suits with respirators. And it still didn't feel safe.

At the first cut, I almost lost my hamburger, which would have been a real mess, considering the respirator over my face. As the pathology tech pushed the big knife into the abdomen, blood began to run. And run. A bolus of blood surged from the abdomen, splashing the tech's gowned arms. Everyone jumped back and yelped; then it was silent. All you could hear was the water running on the path table and the regular inhalations through the respirators.

I heard a whisper: "Oh my God . . ."

"It's all right—Juan, is it?—it's all right," someone said to the tech. "I'll take care of it." A man stepped forward. Jack Dowd, a pathologist from Hopkins who had an interest in things viral—we were ninety percent sure it was viral now—walked to the table. A pathology resident followed, as did the chief pathologist from St. Raphe's. This was an important moment for them. Pathology isn't surgery, and it's not every day that a pathologist gets a chance to show how big his balls—her balls, too, excuse me—are. After a pause, Dowd began to cut, speaking low into the microphone that hung from the ceiling.

"Patient name: Deborah Fillmore. MR number: 7716321. Time of death: thirteen ten, July fifteenth. Patient is an African-American woman. . . ."

And we watched as steel-balled Jack Dowd cut. Technically, what killed Debbie Fillmore was multiple organ failure, which is pretty much what it sounds like. The kidneys can't filter the blood, and the balance of fluid and electrolytes in the system goes haywire. Other organs starve for blood. Finally, the lungs go, the heart goes, the brain goes.

What caused the multiple organ failure is what we call shock— Debbie couldn't generate enough blood pressure to perfuse all her organs. And what caused the shock was her internal bleeding, secondary to the rupture of capillaries and larger vessels. All the blood that now poured from her body cavity should have been in her arteries and veins.

Each organ was carefully removed and weighed, then sliced apart. *Carefully* is the operative word here; no one wanted to slip with the knife and end up like Debbie Fillmore.

After a half hour, I'd learned what I needed, basically that this thing killed like a viral hemorrhagic fever. I showered in the path lab showers, now makeshift decontamination showers. Smelling of disinfectant, I left.

"Goddamn it, Nate, why didn't you just let him take the cage?"

"They're trying to stymie an outbreak investigation."

"Well, this sure isn't helping. It could, in fact, be a real problem." Verlach drummed a pen against his desktop. "Tell me again: he tried to grab the trap . . . ?"

I recounted the story again.

"This sure as hell isn't helping anything. Are you sure the bite didn't break the skin?"

"No," I said.

"Damn it. I'll call Jefferson, make sure his friend got cleaned up."

"You know him?"

"Somewhat. You're black, you're a doc, you're in Baltimore, you know each other." Verlach looked at me and I dropped my gaze. "Aw, shit, Nate, why'd you have to . . ." He trailed off, and his hand ran back and forth over his bald head. "Listen—Jefferson—whatever else he is— is a doctor. He should know what to do. He should also know what the hell we're dealing with. The shit he pulled was . . . He's a freaking sleaze, that's all."

We were sitting in Herb Verlach's tiny office, which had barely enough room for the metal desk and all the medical journals stuffed into it, much less two grown men; my foot was pressed against a trash can. Verlach sighed. "Okay, until we know more, we'll assume the gentleman just got a little pinch."

"Fine."

"What are your thoughts on human vectors?"

A word on the incident with the rat. Though Verlach was being kind—very kind, actually—in giving me no more than a light chastisement, the situation was not looking good for yours truly. Whether or not the rat bite broke the skin, there would be hell to pay. Public health officials should not be caught up in things like this. And though I felt justified in what I'd done, and though the bite itself was a product of Jefferson's man's stupidity more than anything else, and though, in the end, I would be cleared of any wrongdoing, it was not, as they say, good form. Jefferson and his lawyers could make trouble. That's why Verlach was pissed.

Anyway, back to human vectors. I said, "Sure looks like there's something there. One man had contact with three sick women. Douglas Buchanan."

"If Buchanan's the source, why hasn't he been ill?"

"Some sort of immunity, perhaps." Diseases have different effects in different people. To wit: West Nile virus causes encephalitis in only about one percent of people who pick it up. Only a subset of those die. "Might be that the disease only strikes a certain genetic subpopulation. Maybe it just strikes women, has something to do with estrogen or testosterone levels."

"Could be."

"Or he's dormant now and soon will come down with something. We don't know there's not someone else out there who's been playing in the same ballparks."

"The odds are against it," Verlach said.

"Not really. The whole community seems to be sexually charged."

"And you know this for a fact."

"Yeah, Herb, I've been screwing the mentally handicapped for years. Seriously, though, I've been talking to these people for two days now. It seems like everybody's been sleeping with everybody. Has surveillance turned up anything at the other hospitals?"

"We have the word out, but still nothing. If it showed up, I think we'd see it. Symptomatologically, it's pretty shocking."

"We don't know that it always manifests that way. It could just be a flu in some people." I paused. "Douglas Buchanan may be an asymptomatic carrier."

"Or he might not have the disease."

"Yes, that's true."

At that moment, my phone vibrated. It was Tim Lancaster. He and Sonjit Mehta had just arrived at BWI and would be at the Health Department within the hour.

Verlach was tapping the pen against his thin mustache now. "Let me call Jefferson, try to straighten that up."

He paged through a directory, looking for Jefferson's number, I assumed, when his pager went off. He glanced at the little device and swore quietly. While he dialed, I sat there, feeling sorry for myself, sorry that Tim Lancaster was now in Baltimore. Though he didn't know it, Herr Lancaster was about to tear into me like a lion into a newly killed gazelle. Or something like that.

Having no idea what to do before the ax fell, I watched Verlach as his face went from mildly displeased to incredibly displeased.

"It's out," he said, hanging up the phone. "Maryland just got cases four and five. They're en route to St. Raphe's right now."

He bolted from the office. I followed.

CHAPTER 21

We moved fast.

The two cases were named Bryan Tinings and Maggie Phelps. Both were residents at two of Jefferson's other houses—Bryan at a place called Baltimore Gardens, Maggie at Baltimore Lawn. It was relatively quiet outside St. Raphe's; evidently the press hadn't yet caught wind of the two patients being moved from Maryland.

On a bench outside the hospital, smoking quietly, sat a woman in a nurse's uniform. Rarely have I wanted to bum a smoke so badly. It didn't hurt that she was attractive.

Verlach intercepted a resident at the hospital entrance and began to question him. I heard Verlach ask who had accompanied the two new patients.

The resident pointed to the smoking woman. "That's Tabitha Kinard," he said. "She brought them in."

I looked back at her calmly exhaling a cloud.

"We'll need to talk to her," Verlach said.

"I told her to stay."

"Good job," Verlach said.

"Thank you, sir," the resident said, beaming. *God,* I thought, *how brutal medical training is that such a weak compliment can go so far.*

Verlach and I put on masks and followed the resident inside.

Maggie and Bryan, both midthirties, were pretty much following the script for this thing. Maggie was further along: she had pain in her chest and abdomen, slight hemorrhaging in her mouth. Bryan was just beginning. With his aches and low fever, he might have just had the flu. However, as he told it, Nurse Kinard insisted he come into the hospital. *Way to go, Nurse Kinard.*

The two patients lived in separate residences, one all male, the other all female. The residences were in adjacent row homes. Neither of them worked at the Miller nursing homes: Bryan was a janitor at a movie theater downtown; Maggie cleaned rooms at a motel. We took down the names of their employers.

Also, cases four and five were an item. We plunged through the sex questions: with whom, how often, with or without protection. Bryan denied involvement with any woman other than Maggie, and I believed him. Maggie also denied any "sexing," as she called it, with anyone other than Bryan. But her eyes shifted on the denial.

"Maggie," I said. "You have to tell us if you were, uh, 'sexing' with anyone besides Bryan."

"No. I love Bryan."

"If you love Bryan, then you have to tell us. He's sick, and we might be able to help him if you tell us the truth."

"I love Bryan."

She and I went on like that for another ten minutes, with Verlach standing next to me, getting increasingly agitated. Finally, he broke in. "Maggie, do you want to kill people?"

That took her by surprise. It took me by surprise, and I was wondering if the strain had finally gotten to him.

"No," she said.

"Do you want to kill Bryan?"

"No. I love—"

"Well, that's exactly what you're going to do if you don't tell us the truth. If you don't tell us who you were sexing with, you'll kill Bryan."

"I love—"

"We know you love him. But you're going to kill him if you don't talk to me."

"No—" she whispered.

"Who else were you sexing with?"

"I don't—"

"Who else were you sexing with?" She didn't respond. "Who else were you sexing with?" he asked with a sharper tone.

Maggie began to weep.

"Herb—" I said. This new Herb Verlach was making me a little uncomfortable.

"Who else were you sexing with? Do you want to kill Bryan? Who else were you sexing with?" His gloved fingers gripped her arm.

"I don't know. I don't know. He was—"

Verlach pressed on. "What was his name?"

Maggie shook her head, sobbing.

"Was he a white man or a black man?" Not wanting to neglect anyone, I added, "Was he a brown man?"

"A white man," Maggie, who was black, said.

"Was it Bryan?" Bryan was white, and I wanted to make sure she wasn't confused.

"No. He was big. A big white man."

"When were you sexing with this man?" Verlach asked.

"I don't know," she whined.

"Maggie, where did you sex . . . were sexing . . ." Verlach was getting frustrated. "Where did you have sex with this man?"

"Mr. Jefferson's birthday party." She looked at us, afraid. "I don't kill anyone. I don't want to kill Bryan. Please."

"You're not going to kill Bryan," I assured her. "You're doing great, Maggie."

Verlach hammered her, trying to pry loose a name that might never have been there. Because he was my ad hoc boss, because I had fucked up royally so far, and because he seemed to be getting results, I said nothing as she wept and protested her innocence. But I couldn't watch this anymore. "I'm going to talk to the nurse," I said, and walked out of the room.

I found the resident who'd ushered us into the hospital and asked him where Nurse Kinard was. He thought she was in the waiting area for M-2.

Tabitha Kinard, RN, was, upon close inspection, even better-looking than she had been from afar, with long, braided hair and cheekbones that would cut glass. She paged through an old copy of *Newsweek*. I introduced myself, extended my hand. She shook it.

Desperate to get a nicotine fix as well as to question the nurse, I asked, "May I bum a cigarette?"

"There are reporters down there now."

"We're not going down there."

Two minutes later, we stood on the roof of the hospital, looking over the blighted neighborhoods of South Baltimore, both of us puffing away. Normally, I would have made a stupid comment about the cigarettes, about how they'll kill you, but it didn't seem appropriate.

"I'm going to lose my job," Kinard said matter-of-factly.

"Why do you say that?" I asked.

"Because I am. Because it's important to answer the questions you're going to ask me." She took a drag on the cigarette, blew out a cloud of smoke. "But it's okay. Easy to get a job if you're a nurse. Ask away, Doc."

So I did. She gave me the story of caring for Maggie, then hearing the news about the outbreak in a short blurb on the radio. She was worried, but didn't act until Bryan—whom she knew to be involved with Maggie—had a fever the night before. When nothing improved by morning, she brought them in.

"I thought it was flu," she said.

"It might be," I said unconvincingly. "Let's hope. When did you first determine Maggie was ill?"

"Three days ago."

"And her condition steadily worsened?"

"Yes."

"Why did you wait to bring her in? You knew she was sick with more than the flu."

"Debbie Fillmore died."

"Then why did you wait?"

She held my gaze for a long moment. Her eyes were an incredible honey gold. "I waited because we weren't to tell anyone if there were signs of illness. No doctors, no hospitals. Maggie was isolated in her room yesterday. We were supposed to take care of her at Baltimore Lawn."

This was odd. "Why?"

"Orders from Dr. Jefferson. God—" She leaned against the concrete cornice. "I really am going to need a job now. What are the benefits like at the Health Department?"

"I'm with CDC."

"Oh. Well, I have some family in Atlanta." She smiled. "I don't know why we were to do it. All I know is that a couple of days ago, Dr. Jefferson called the three of us—the three nurses who take care of the residents—and told us we were to take care of all medical problems in-house. He never gave us any reasons. But then, with Dr. Jefferson, you never really ask for reasons. You met him."

"Yes."

"He said to watch out for you and the black doctor and anyone else who was asking questions. He said he'd provide all the necessary equipment to care for the residents, and that we shouldn't worry."

"Did he? Provide the equipment, I mean."

"It's supposed to arrive today." She looked at her watch. "I'm supposed to be meeting them now." She smiled. "Oh, Randall is going to be pissed off." I noticed a little tremor in her hand. She saw me notice, and placed her hands on the concrete, looked out over the city.

"Is anyone else you know sick?"

"Not that I know of. They'd be here if that was the case."

I took a long drag on my cigarette. "Ms. Kinard, I'm going to ask you not to talk to the press about this. We don't know what's causing this outbreak."

"The press seems to know that already."

"Right. But we do have some theories. Again, not for the press. Especially in light of Maggie and Bryan, we're worried that the source of the pathogen—the reservoir—may be in one of Dr. Jefferson's homes—"

"I wouldn't be surprised."

I, however, *was* surprised by her answer, by the fact that she already knew or suspected something. "Do you know what's causing the disease?"

"No, no, Doctor. I didn't mean that. It's just . . . well, you saw Baltimore Haven, didn't you?"

I nodded. After a moment, I asked, "If you'll forgive me for prying, why do you work there?"

She laughed. "The short story is that I have two kids, and Dr. Jefferson pays better than anyone else in town. The long story is, well, long. And probably not important for you to hear."

"I should be the judge of that."

"I'm telling you it's not important."

Touchy, touchy. "Okay, well, we're also worried that the disease may be transmitted sexually. We don't know that for sure, of course, but—"

"If it is, Dr. McCormick, you have something to worry about.

There is a lot of sex going on in the homes. Many of our residents have a drive that's through the roof. A rape a week, at least. More, much more, consensual sex."

"Anyone try to control it?"

"Not really. Dr. Jefferson thinks it's therapeutic."

"Why doesn't anyone get pregnant?"

"Dr. Jefferson puts a lot of trust in Depo shots." Depo-Provera is the one-shot-three-months-no-pregnancy contraception.

My stomach churned as I pictured St. Raphe's filling up with more and more cases of the "flu."

I stubbed out the end of my cigarette and put the butt into my pocket. "Were you at Dr. Jefferson's birthday party?"

"Goes with the job. Yes, I was there. Dr. Jefferson wasn't."

"Maggie Phelps implied she had sexual relations with a man at the party."

"Maggie Phelps is in love with Bryan Tinings, the other—"

"Even so, she said she had something to do with another man at the party. A white man. Tall."

"Dr. McCormick, there are a lot of tall white men in the homes we oversee."

Kinard extinguished her cigarette and dropped it on the roof. I took out a card and handed it to her. "If you remember anything, please call me. In the meantime, we're going to get hold of the rosters for Dr. Jefferson's homes. I'd like to see you later today. Maybe we can piece together some of the relationships between these folks."

I bent down and picked up her cigarette butt and dropped it into my pocket. Tabitha smiled at me. "You some kind of goody-goody, Dr. McCormick?"

"Probably not," I said, and then walked toward the door. Kinard didn't move.

"Wait a second, Doctor. . . . There is a tall white man in the homes who seems to be quite active sexually. Well, to be perfectly honest, he's a sexual predator. We deal with a lot of his . . . conquests. I didn't see him with Maggie, but it's possible. He's over at Baltimore Haven. His name is Douglas Buchanan."

Sexual predator, possibly sexually transmitted disease. Douglas Buchanan, already in the middle of three cases.

"Thanks, Ms. Kinard." I reached for the door handle. "Oh, one more question. Why is Douglas Buchanan's room nicer than anyone else's? He's the only one I saw in a single occupancy."

"I don't work at Baltimore Haven."

"Why might his room be nicer than anyone else's? Any suspicions?"

"I don't know."

"Why isn't he disciplined for his, well, for his proclivities?"

"Might be the same reason I get—did get, sorry—special treatment."

"Which is?"

"Dr. Jefferson liked me. Maybe he liked Douglas, too."

"Wait, you mean he—?"

"No, no." She laughed. "Dr. Jefferson and I had that kind of relationship. But with Douglas Buchanan, well, there is some other reason he gets good treatment. No idea what it is."

Just before I closed the door, I heard Nurse Kinard say, "But all good things come to an end, don't they?"

CHAPTER 22

Faster.

The longer a case goes unsolved, the less likely it is to be solved. As with a murder, the more time goes by, the more people forget where they were and what they did. The more they have a chance to rethink their stories and cover their asses.

Maggie Phelps's and Tabitha Kinard's fingering of Douglas Buchanan clinched it for us. It also seemed to clinch it for the judge, because thirty minutes after I was on the roof of St. Raphe's, chatting it up with Nurse Kinard, we had a court order to enter Baltimore Haven.

Verlach, for his part, smelled blood or victory or whatever it is ex–Army docs smell. This was fine, except that I was riding in the car with the man, and he was doing sixty through streets designed for speeds half that. I snapped on my seat belt.

My pager vibrated and I looked at the little LED number that came up, not easy to do when vaulting through potholes. I recognized the digits, the same ones that had shown up on my cell phone a half hour before and on my pager three times in the last half hour. Tim Lancaster, it seemed, really wanted to talk to me. The feeling was not mutual, and I put the pager back on my belt.

We screeched to a halt outside Douglas Buchanan's home. Baltimore PD was supposed to be there as an escort, and I'd imagined this as a major action, with the boys in blue—guns drawn, shouting threats—running interference for us. But the BPD wasn't there yet. It looked like the storming of the beach would involve just Verlach and me.

Actually, not quite.

"What the hell?" Verlach said.

A large man was walking toward us. A thinner man in a suit was at his heels.

"That's Dr. McCormick," the large man said, pointing to me as I stepped from the car. He seemed to be holding a grudge from our little encounter with the rat the day before.

The thin man approached us. "I'm Drew Mizursky, one of Dr. Jefferson's attorneys."

They knew me, so I didn't make an introduction, though Mizursky seemed to be waiting for one. Finally, the lawyer said, "I want to inform you both that we are currently in the process of obtaining an injunction against any further harassment of Dr. Jefferson or the residents in his facilities."

"Good luck," I said.

"Dr. McCormick, you should know that we have filed the necessary papers for a protection from harassment order against you in particular for your assaults on Dr. Jefferson and Mr. Dunnigan here. Any trespass into the property will be seen by the court as further evidence—"

"Get out of the way," Verlach said, and walked up the steps.

"Dr. McCormick, you should also know that we have filed assault charges against you for the attack yesterday on Mr. Dunnigan. The police will be—"

"The attack?"

"Yes. You attacked Mr. Dunnigan here with a rodent—"

"Come on," I said.

"Tell him to fuck off, Nate." Verlach was buzzing away at the call box outside the door.

"Fuck off. It didn't break the skin," I said.

"Untrue," the lawyer said. On cue, Dunnigan held up a bandaged finger.

"Did you do that yourself? Or did the rat next to you give the bite?" I pointed at Mizursky.

"I resent your insinuations," Dunnigan said, but he couldn't help smiling.

Verlach stopped buzzing the call box and pulled the court order out of his pocket. "Why don't you look this over?"

The lawyer stepped quickly to Verlach, grabbed the paper, speed-read it, and handed it back. "That'll be invalid in an hour."

"An hour's all we need."

I climbed the stoop and began knocking at the door. No one answered. "This is unbelievable." I turned. "Let us in."

Dunnigan smiled. The lawyer did not. "We don't have the key," Dunnigan said.

"Get one," I told him.

"Hmmm," Dunnigan said, "I think we lost it." Neither man moved.

Verlach pulled out his cell phone. "I'm going to get the police down here." He put the phone up to his ear and pointed at Mizursky with his other hand. "You, lawyer shithead, are going to have to explain to your client why his front doors have been ripped off their hinges. And explain to a district judge why you obstructed an outbreak investigation—"

"And *you* and the city are going to be liable for any damages both to the property and the reputation of—" Mizursky looked as tense as Verlach.

And they went on like that while I banged away at the door. I thought Verlach was going to pull out some of his basic training moves and break the attorney's neck. Instead, he turned away and said something to the police functionary on the other end of the line. I continued to beat the hell out of the door. Bang, bang, bang.

Verlach said, "This really is the most fucked-up political mess—"

Just then, the knob on the door turned, and it swung open a crack.

"Close the door!" Dunnigan yelled from the bottom of the steps. He ran toward us. Too late. I had my foot in the door and was pushing hard to open it. Inside, a woman screamed, "Close the door! Close the goddamned door!"

A slack-jawed man in dirty sweatpants and a T-shirt stumbled back into the hallway when I pushed the door open. The counselor/ receptionist—whatever she was—beelined toward us.

"Get back to the rec room!" the woman screamed at the man in the sweatpants, who seemed dazed by the sudden explosion of activity. As she passed him, she gripped his shirt and tried to pull him out of her way. He cowered and made little whimpering sounds. "Get back to the fucking rec room!" she snarled, and slapped him, and he skittered down the hall. To us, she said, "You can't come in here."

I looked at Verlach, who had the court order out and was already walking past the woman toward the stairs. I followed. As I moved past the woman, I said, "If you touch him again . . ." I let the sentence hang, gave her two seconds of hard-assed staring, and trotted after Verlach.

Douglas Buchanan's door was locked.

"It doesn't end, does it?" Verlach asked, and knocked on the door. "Mr. Buchanan? It's Doctors McCormick and Verlach. We need to talk to you."

Not necessarily the way to get someone to open the door, Herb, I thought. But, as I said, Verlach was on a mission. In fact, I liked him better this way. It made me think that if it had been Verlach in that basement the day before, he'd have done the same thing I did, pushing his way through Jefferson and Dunnigan. I liked that.

Meanwhile, I had my PalmPilot out, scrolling through the address book for the Miller Nursing Homes. I found the number, got my phone, and dialed. Dunnigan, Mizursky, and the receptionist stood in a phalanx behind us. Two dead-eyed men popped their heads out of their rooms.

"Call the police," Mizursky told the receptionist. "Tell them we have some men trying to break into a private room here. Tell them they are threatening to assault the residents and staff."

I couldn't believe this. I mean, I was getting really furious; I wasn't thinking clearly. "Tell them there's going to be a lawyer with a broken neck."

The receptionist took off down the hall. Mizursky called after her, "Threats of imminent harm."

Verlach began to pound on the door again. Miller's secretary finally picked up the phone. I said, "It's Nathaniel McCormick of CDC again. Is Dan Miller there?"

He was in a meeting, the secretary said.

"Hold on," I said to Verlach; he stopped banging. Into the phone, I said, "It doesn't matter. Can you just check if Douglas Buchanan showed up to work today?"

There was silence on the phone and silence in the hallway. Mizursky pulled out his telephone and dialed. "Bill," he said, "we have that goddamned injunction yet?"

The secretary came back on the line. "He hasn't shown up yet."

"What time does he usually arrive?" I asked.

"The shift starts at eight," the secretary said. It was nearly four o'clock. I thanked her and clicked off.

"He's not at work," I said, and Verlach began banging again. I joined in. "Douglas," I called, "please open the door. We need to talk to you. We can help you."

I had a vision of Douglas Buchanan lying in his bed, safe behind that good Yale dead bolt, listening to the banging on his door. Maybe a pair of headphones snaking from his little stereo to his head, doing his damnedest to shut out the racket at his door. Doing his best to crawl into his shell and forget the world.

At times, I felt that way. Hell, I felt that way now. To be in my bed, disengaged from—

"Fuck this," Verlach said.

Far off, I could hear the wail of a siren.

I turned around. Mizursky was still on the phone, presumably trying to get the goddamned injunction. Verlach pushed by him and the others, making his way down the hall to wait for the cops. The dreary residents of the place retreated into their rooms.

Wait for the cops. Why the hell should we wait for the cops? We were the good guys, and the stupid bastards in the hallway behind me were trying to tangle us in injunctions and phone calls and outright harassment. I mean, this was not a complex issue.

There was eight feet between the door and me, no one between. The door was cheap laminate. And we had a court order, which might not be valid after we'd had a little discussion with the police downstairs, with Ben Mizursky confusing the situation the best he could.

Fuck them. And, frankly, fuck Herb Verlach if he needed the police to back him up.

"Douglas, stand away from the door!" And I ran. My shoulder bit into the flimsy laminate, which bowed and cracked around the dead bolt.

"Stop—" Mizursky shouted. I think he said something about breaking and entering. I stepped back about five feet, glanced toward them. Verlach cracked a smile. Dunnigan came at me, fast.

I ran at the door again.

This time I tore the dead bolt through the cheap wood, cracking the door open an inch. Dunnigan slammed into me, and the two of us fell through the broken door and stumbled into the room together.

The first thing I saw was the mess—there were clothes and belongings strewn about, drawers overturned on the floor, the small closet's contents lying in a heap. But something was definitely missing.

There was no Douglas Buchanan lying on his bed. There was no Douglas Buchanan cowering in a corner, or waiting for me with fists raised. Douglas, it seemed, had disappeared.

The two representatives of Baltimore's finest—hats off to them—were measured, thoughtful, and definitely on our side in the little dispute. Since September 2001, law enforcement and public health had generally fallen into bed with each other and were pretty comfortable there. Protecting the public safety, that's what we did.

So there we were, Verlach and I and Mizursky and the two cops. Dunnigan had left, presumably to torture cats or whatever he did for fun.

Mizursky was busily taking down badge numbers and making threats about disciplinary action. One of the cops was trying halfheartedly to placate him.

"What about that?" The other cop, a black man in his thirties whose badge said C. Blakely, pointed to the broken door.

"I thought I heard someone in distress," I said. "I guess I was wrong."

The officer noted this in a small pad. "Understandable."

Verlach and I finished off the initial report and then asked permission to search the room, looking for, well, whatever we could get. Mouse shit, used condoms. Anything. But this had become a police matter now; we were instructed to wait for the detective and the forensics tech.

Mizursky, mercifully, had better billing waiting for him at the office. He left. But by that time, Dunnigan, unfortunately, had returned.

"I want to press charges for assault," he informed Officer Blakely. "Dr. McCormick attacked me with a rat."

Blakely said, "You mean he came at you with the lawyer who just left?" Ah, well, we all had a good laugh over that. One of the perks of being a physician is that you're not a lawyer. I prayed the jokes would never die; they gave me constant affirmation about my career choice.

"You see that address there?" Blakely handed Dunnigan a card. "That's the address of the Baltimore City Police Department. I'm sure if you went downtown, the caring officers there would be happy to take your complaint."

Dunnigan proved himself to be smart for a Cro-Magnon, taking the hint that his help wasn't needed at that time. He turned and moved down the hallway, knuckles dragging along the floorboards.

Usually, missing-persons cases don't elicit a lot of get-up-and-go in any police department, but Verlach and I put the fear of God and mass contagion into Officer Blakely, and he passed that on through the ranks. Within a half hour, we had our detective and our tech.

So, all four of us—the guys from the BPD, Verlach, and I—pulled on our rubber gloves. When the tech, who was doing the grunt work, came across anything she thought was interesting, she'd let us know, and either Verlach or I would take a swab or a sample and bag it. In the first twenty minutes, she called us over for every hair or odd fiber she found. Eventually, Verlach told her we were interested only in animal crap and wet things: semen, mucus, blood. She got the picture.

By that time, I was standing outside the room, taking questions from a detective called John Myers. Myers seemed to be the old-school type of detective, by which I mean his style hadn't changed from the late seventies, when I assumed he'd joined the force. He wore an Ultrasuede blazer with a narrow tie. A sparse salt-and-pepper mustache sprouted from his lip. At about five six, one forty, he looked like an intense Chihuahua.

Myers looked to Douglas's room, then back to me. "You said he was agitated the last time you saw him."

"That's true."

"You know why?"

"Sure. I was making him agitated. I was questioning him."

"What kinds of questions?"

"Ones regarding his sexual habits."

"Do you feel he had any reason to run away?"

I looked down the hall. One of the sad souls who lived there watched us. Myers followed my gaze. I said, "You mean besides the obvious reasons?"

I told Detective Myers, "There is some suspicion that Douglas may have been a sexual predator."

"That might have been a compelling reason for him to leave."

"But I don't know if he knew we knew. I don't even know if he knew there was anything wrong with what he was doing. All things considered."

"Who told you about Mr. Buchanan's, ah, proclivities?"

"Tabitha Kinard. She's a nurse over at the other homes."

Myers took another look through the shattered door to the room, caught sight of the 49ers and Giants posters, and said, "We don't have enough good teams in this city for him? We won the goddamned Super Bowl, for Chrissake. He from San Francisco?"

"Said he'd never been there. Could have been lying, I suppose."

"I've been to Frisco before," he said, using that annoying appellation. "Nice city. They got the gays, though. Question: This guy go for that? Was he a predator for men? Did he predate ass?"

Probably not, I thought, *nor did he hack nouns into incorrect verbs.* "I don't know. He said he'd never had sex with men."

"Okay." Myers closed his notebook. "Guess we're finished for now. I'm going to talk to the other guys up here . . . *try* to talk to them, if they can get me any info through the drool." Unfortunately, Myers seemed to be loosening up, making jokes. I gave him my best blank stare. "Anyhow, is there anything else you can think of that struck you as odd about Mr. Buchanan, Doctor?"

Where to start? "This room is a hell of a lot nicer than the others."

"So?"

"I don't know. You're the detective. Ask Dr. Jefferson why Douglas Buchanan got special treatment."

"I *am* the detective, and I'll ask what I think is relational."

Relational? It seemed I was getting under Detective Myers's skin, too. I didn't need that. "Sorry, Detective. It's been a long day."

"It's always a long day, Doc. Anything else?"

"Yeah. Douglas had a cell phone."

"So?"

"Residents here aren't allowed to have phones."

"Okay, then. You have the number?"

"No."

"We'll get in touch with the phone company, get the calls to and from the phone if we need."

"Could you let me know when you do? I'm interested in who he talked to. It would be easiest and fastest if you just contact me directly. Avoid the bureaucratic logjam." I handed him a card and let him chew over that for a moment; he nodded. "We want to talk to everyone he's had contact with. They could be at risk."

"For what?"

"That, Detective, is what we're trying to find out."

CHAPTER 23

Boy Wonder had his arms crossed, his skinny ass on the edge of the desk. The two of us were in a tiny office at the Department of Health. For the time being, it was to be CDC's Baltimore headquarters.

Tim Lancaster let the silence drag out, taking me in through his geek-chic glasses. The man looked like a bird, a crane, maybe—those specs, the beaky hooked nose, the high forehead, the six-four frame. He perched there for a good half minute before he said, "Four times, Nate."

"Five," I said, "if you count the cell phone call."

More silence.

"You can't do this," Herr Lancaster said. "You can't ignore my pages."

"I was sort of in hot pursuit, Tim."

"You can't do this, because if I had known you were in hot pursuit to the place where this assault with the rat—"

"Alleged assault."

"Whatever. I would have told you to back off."

"I was with Herb Verlach, who's my boss here. He didn't tell me to back off."

"I'm your boss. I'm the trump card boss, okay? I page you four times, you sure as heck better get back to me. End of discussion." He scratched at his neck. The scratching thing is one of Tim's tics. Stress-induced pruritis. "Besides, these guys haven't been through this before. They don't know how easy BS can screw everything up."

"They're not a bunch of rubes. I think we're doing a pretty good job."

"Okay, but somehow somebody's taking a leak in somebody else's pool, and somebody's really ticked about it. It's not just the rat thing. Those guys—this Jefferson guy—shouldn't have been hassling you in the first place. So we have to assume something's going on here. You can see that."

"Sure." And it was true. For whatever reason, someone—and it seemed like that someone was Dr. Randall Jefferson—was trying his best to impede our investigation.

Tim pushed himself off the desk and circled around to a chair. He sat. "All right. You need to respond to my pages. Are we clear on this?"

"Crystal."

"So, give me the situation. A to Z."

And I did, beginning with Helen Jones's arrival at St. Raphe's ED and ending with Tim's and my disagreement. Tim alternated between scratching notes and scratching his chest.

"All right," he said.

"I'm not quite done yet. Then you said, 'I'm the trump card boss. If I page you, you have to get—'"

"Why do I put up with this?"

"Because without me you'd have no one to page a hundred times."

"Right." Tim looked back over the pages of notes he'd taken. "Though it pains me to say it, you've done a very nice job here. Despite the obvious F-ups. It's not easy. As you probably know, state is sending a few more people. You're more familiar with this thing than anyone else. So, I'm gonna ask you: you think I should counsel that local or state take the lead on this?"

"Let it be local. They know it the best. Verlach's a good man."

"Right. Former military, family doc, trustworthy." I could almost hear his political brain chugging away. "Maybe we should counsel that he talk to the press."

"For the details, sure. But Dr. Timmons will want—"

"Timmons's too slick. A politician. We need a real doctor up there."

"Tell Verlach what to say," I suggested. "Prep him. He'll be fine." Apropos of nothing more than my sour grapes, I added, "You know we aren't always so good at dealing with the media."

"At least we have experience. Hopefully we can avoid some of the F-ups of Boca."

October 2001 was an excellent, if brutal, education for public-health officials. The anthrax attacks at the Boca Raton offices of American Media, in which a sixty-three-year-old photo editor died, were handled expertly in some respects, foolishly in others. The major mistakes were not made in the investigation itself—the response was, in fact, thought to be a success in that respect—but in the handling of information. Physicians and epidemiologists and others with scientific training aren't the most forthcoming bunch in the best of times. The culture tries to be one based on fact, not supposition; on data, not guesses. Fact and data take a long time to collect and analyze. As people got sick, a panicked public wanted to know what to do *now*.

This culture clash played out under the glare of TV lights. The docs and public officials didn't answer the media's questions. "We don't have enough information." "We don't know." "No comment." These phrases became the mantra of the poor bastards in Florida. Meanwhile, the employees of AMI continued to work for four days, until health officials shut the place down. That the authorities let people work in such a hot zone was, according to the employees and to many observers, a betrayal bordering on criminal negligence.

Tim said, "The FBI wants to send some people up from Quantico."

"Jesus," I said. "We don't even know if it's an attack. It doesn't look like an attack, it doesn't walk like an attack—"

"We don't know what these attacks look like."

"The hell we don't, Tim. I've been talking to these people. We have no boxes or mailings. Nothing saying 'Death to the Great Satan' or 'Death to Big Brother.' Nobody's claiming responsibility here. And we're talking the retarded as a target here. Not Tom Brokaw. If you want to sow fear into the population, you hit powerful people. Or at least people others can identify with. This is like AIDS and homosexuals. It's too easy just to say 'That's their problem.' "

"Nobody ever gave terrorists an A for appropriate targeting."

"Bullshit," I said, and it was. Still, Tim looked nonplussed. I stormed on. "If there's anything criminal, it's that Randall Jefferson has those people living in a shitpile."

"I know. I'm trying to hold the FBI off. I am. But the longer this thing goes, the harder it's going to be for me and Chief O'Donnel to hold them off." He leaned back in the chair.

The fastest way to communicate that a public health issue had become a terrorist issue would be to involve the FBI. Their presence screams bioterrorism. Tim Lancaster and Division Chief Pat O'Donnel knew this in their bones.

Tim said, "We already have two people from the Army's bio-weapons lab at Fort Dietrich."

"They're here now?"

"Coming down later today."

"Thanks for letting me know."

"I don't even know everything that's going on here, Nate."

"Great. Does Baltimore Public Health know about the Dietrich folks?"

"Sure they do. Ben Timmons requested them. I just hope he doesn't let it drop to the press just yet. This whole thing's threatening to become an F-ing mess."

I should say something about Tim Lancaster's language. The man doesn't swear, though not for religious conviction or delicate upbringing. It has to do with a wife who doesn't let him, out of concern for their four-year-old at home. Rumor has it that Tim used to be able to make sailors blush. But now everything is "Heck" and "F this" and "Holy S." Way to go, Mrs. Lancaster.

"Well, then," I said, "I'd better get back out there."

"Nate—"

Just then, as if on cue, there was a knock at the door. Verlach poked his head in. "Dr. Verlach," Tim said. "Dr. McCormick was just singing your praises."

"Nothing too good, I hope," Verlach said. "Don't want to ruin my image. Not to interrupt, but Jefferson called off the dogs. He's opening all his facilities to inspection."

"What changed?" I asked.

"Got religion, I guess. And the fear of more bad press. Our lawyers called, Nate. They're dropping the assault charges."

"No more rat attack?"

"No more rat attack."

"Freedom," I said, half-joking. I moved toward the door.

Tim said, "Where are you going?"

"Hitting the streets, boss. We've got an outbreak, you know."

"Wait," Tim said, then was quiet. It was an uncomfortable moment, Verlach hanging in the doorway, me standing in the middle of the room. "Dr. Verlach, will you excuse us for a moment?"

Verlach nodded and closed the door. Tim motioned me back to my chair.

"Nathaniel, I told you we have a couple of people from the state department of health here to help out. I don't need you on the street."

"What are you talking about?"

"I want you to file a full report with me this afternoon."

"I can do that—"

"And I want you to work with Sonjit on a database of everyone you and the other health officials have talked to. Construct a spot map and chart the contacts so we can narrow our list—"

"We have narrowed our list."

"And when Beth and Andy arrive, I want you to brief them on what you've been doing—"

"Beth and Andy? Why are they coming up?"

"Because I want them to. They'll be here tomorrow morning."

"You can't do this, Tim."

"It's a promotion, Nate. You're being vaulted to the Mount Olympus of administration. I want you to get all the data work finished; then I'll want you to direct the feet on the street."

"Tim, look, I'm much more useful out there—"

"No, Nate, you look. You've done a great job to this point—"

"So let me continue to do a great job."

"You want me to spell it out? Being involved in an altercation with a member of the community? With a rodent that may be harboring a pathogen? Breaking down doors? By the way, how's your shoulder?"

"I needed—"

"You needed to reel it in, Doctor. You're not the FBI. There's a reason we want to keep these guys in their nest at Quantico, and there's a reason I want you here, in this office."

Fucking Tim Lancaster. I should have seen this. I should have known I'd gotten off too lightly before. I should have known the compliments were just a way of preparing me for the blow. And really, when Tim told me to wait, I should have bolted past Verlach into the hallway and then to the street.

Instead, all I said was a pathetic "Why are you doing this?"

"I already told you. Sonjit's set up in a cubicle outside. Go find her and get started."

Perhaps I should elaborate on CDC here, its culture, its mores, its history, and the stifling of Dr. Nathaniel McCormick.

The "Communicable Disease Center" was established in the late forties—five years or so before the Epidemic Intelligence Service was created—in order to combat malaria in the U.S. Then, as now, we were part of the Public Health Service, which itself was born of the Navy. Though the PHS split from the Navy decades ago, we still have uniforms—Dress Blues, Dress Whites, Working Khaki—which look a lot like their military counterparts. Some folks really dig the uniform thing—former director Satcher always sported his medal- and ribbon-laden armor—but I don't. Can't get into the formality; can't get into the scratchy material. One of the perks of being far from the home office is that I don't have to don the stodgy duds all that often.

CDC changed a lot from the early days. For starters, the name became the "Center for Disease Control"; the s was added later as one center begat others. "Prevention" came in '92 to emphasize an expanded mission. By the last century's close, there were twelve centers, a budget north of six billion dollars. But the goddamned uniform code was still in place, as well as a quasi-military hierarchy. I was a commissioned officer, if you can believe it. And that—the rigid martial structure—really got under my skin. Though not as restrictive as, say, Mother Navy, it still meant that orders were orders. As much as I complained to Tim Lancaster about not wanting to take a desk job, he was my commanding officer and, at the end of the day, his word was law. If he told me to drop and give him twenty, I could bitch about it for ten minutes, but by the end, I'd be huffing through a bunch of push-ups. This was a slight problem for a lot of us at CDC. We were a bunch of strong-willed and independent docs and epidemiologists who, if the situation called for it, could be ordered around like Army grunts. Luckily, I hadn't shipped out to

Iraq, but friends of mine had. Five days' notice and you were bound for exotic Baghdad.

Anyway, CDC wasn't the military, so I had some wiggle room vis-à-vis the Commandant. Apologies to Tim, but I didn't find Sonjit and I didn't get started. Instead, I walked to the front desk and bummed a cigarette from one of the security guards. The guy caught the "MD" on my badge and said, "Those things will kill you, Doc."

"I don't inhale," I said. What a card I am.

It was in the mid-nineties that afternoon, with humidity just as high. I walked away from the entrance of the building, which was definitely a no-smoking area. I half-hoped Tim Lancaster would look out his window and see me. That would throw him into a fit.

With the heat, it was pretty unpleasant to be standing on the concrete, puffing away. But I sure didn't want to be back in the air-conditioned hellhole I'd been assigned to, helping Sonjit crunch numbers, or typing up reports, or administering whatever else I was supposed to be administering.

So, I smoked my way through one cigarette, then bummed another one from a guy sauntering past me. He gave me one without saying a word. What a great country.

Two individuals in Army uniforms, a man and a woman, walked by. The folks from Fort Dietrich, I guessed. They gave me sideways glances that said: Individual smoking outside public health building. *Suspicious. Make note.*

You'd think I had the plague.

Anyway, as I stubbed out number two and resigned myself to going back inside and seeing Tim Lancaster again, my pager vibrated.

"Goddamn it, Tim," I grumbled. Though I didn't want to call him back, I wasn't stupid. I was already playing fast and loose with my career, and I didn't need to be petty anymore. I checked the number. It wasn't Tim's.

I called the number. A gravelly voice said, "John Myers."

"It's Dr. McCormick."

"Oh, hey. Listen, Doc, we have something you might be interested in."

"What is it, Detective?"

"Why don't you come down to the station?"

"You want to put me under arrest?"

"Would if I could." He laughed. "No, I got something else. Bring that other doc, too."

"Herb Verlach?"

"Yeah."

I thought about that for a second. Now, what I should have done was tell Verlach the cops had called, then tell Tim. Dr. Lancaster could then make the decision about whether or not I should go. But I knew what his decision would be and I knew I wouldn't agree. So, no call to Tim. And there was no reason to involve Verlach, who'd be put in an awkward position by the call.

"Dr. Verlach's out of the office," I told Myers. "But I'll be there in a few minutes."

I called Sonjit, told her I was going out for some food and that she could start without me.

CHAPTER 24

Having spent some formative years in Baltimore, I knew exactly where to find the police station and I arrived there less than ten minutes after John Myers called.

So there I was, sitting across a table from the detective himself and some sort of technician in a nondescript, windowless room.

"We got Mr. Buchanan's number from Cingular," Detective Myers said. "Thought we'd give him a call, make our job easy. But his phone service had been disconnected."

I said, "That must have happened recently. He got a call on it when I was talking to him yesterday. There was a voice mail, too. The phone kept beeping after he didn't pick up the call."

"We checked that. Any messages he had were cleared out when the phone service was disconnected."

"Who disconnected it?"

"We got to assume it was Mr. Buchanan. We dug into the details of the phone use. First off, he had some prepaid plan, so he never had to go through credit checks or anything like that. Makes sense, we figured. He didn't want to be getting bills at the home if he wasn't supposed to have the phone. And I don't know what kind of credit he had, considering.

We're checking on that. Anyway, there was a lot of time he paid for. And he used it."

"He had a lot of girlfriends."

"That's what you would think."

"What do you mean?"

"We got Cingular to give us the phone records. Your Mr. Buchanan blew through at least five hundred minutes a month calling one number. One number only. Nothing else. No calls for pizza. No calls to Mom and Dad, but that's another story. No calls other than to one number in San Jose, California."

"Who's at the number?"

"That's why we wanted you to come down." Myers nodded to the technician, who had a small tape recorder in front of him. The tech hit a button.

A few rings, then a voice: *"Casey! You bad man. Why didn't you call me?"*

Another voice: *"Ma'am, this is Detective John Myers with the Baltimore City Police—"*

Then the line went dead.

"That's it?" I asked.

"That's it."

"Who's the woman? Who's Casey?"

"I was hoping you might be able to help us with that."

"I'm hoping, too, but I don't know anything about it."

"Mr. Buchanan didn't say anything at all about a woman on the West Coast or someone named Casey?"

"No. But it makes some sense, I suppose."

"What does?"

"All the San Francisco stuff in his room. I guess he had ties out West after all. Did you find anything interesting there? In his room?"

"Besides the posters, no. No pictures, no letters, nothing. I'll be questioning Randall Jefferson later this afternoon, but he's already tried to put me off. Tells me he doesn't know individual residents that well."

"I was told that Randall Jefferson was cooperating now."

"Not with us."

"He opened all his properties to the Health Department."

"Maybe that's all he's doing. He's not talking to us." Myers leaned back in his chair. "Cocksucker's playing games."

"Did you call the San Jose number again?"

"Yeah, about ten times. It just rings and rings until a recording picks up. You know, 'The blah-blah subscriber is unavailable.' Seems our mystery woman doesn't keep voice mail. We're talking to her phone company to try to get her name, but they're not playing ball with us. Say it's a matter of privacy and since she's not the one missing . . . That kind of crap."

I ran through what I could remember of the conversation I had with Douglas Buchanan. Definitely no mention of a woman in California, no mention of anyone called Casey. And nothing whatsoever that might clue us in to where Douglas Buchanan went. Well, nothing except this number and the woman who owned it. I said, "You told me he never called his parents."

"That's right."

"Still, they might have some idea where he is."

"The story is they were in York, PA—just up the road—until '97. They're probably still there, for all we know."

"Well, talk to them, Detective."

"Don't think they can talk to us. They're six feet under. Both of them. Father kicked off in the beginning of that year, '97; mother followed a few months later."

"Where was Douglas before he came to Baltimore?"

"We'd like to ask Douglas that. Nobody knows. We're checking state institution records now, and we'll try to get more from Dr. Jefferson. Jefferson's administrative folks claim they don't know where Douglas Buchanan came from. They assumed it was from his parents' home in York."

This was definitely not adding up. And the fact that it wasn't adding up with this particular guy at this particular time was disconcerting.

"When did he get to Baltimore Haven?"

"According to their records, he arrived in '97. Right after his parents died."

"So, Detective, you're telling me that we have a possible sexual predator on the loose, a sexual predator who might be carrying some deadly disease, and not only do we not know where he is, we don't know anyone who might have any idea where he is?"

He was getting a little annoyed. "I'm sure as hell not happy about it."

"What about his friends? Any other social ties?"

"Guy seemed to be a loner."

"Except when he was sticking it into anything with a hole. How can he have nobody?"

"Happens more often than you think, Doctor."

Visions of Douglas Buchanan pumping poison into an unsuspecting population were making me sweat. "Your missing persons stay missing for long, Detective?"

"It's been years, but I had a good track record."

"Great, so you're over the hill. That's just great."

He laughed. "Now I look for the ones who make people go missing. I'm homicide. They wanted to bring out the big guns for this."

"You're big guns?"

"What? You don't expect a prick like me has the second-highest close rate in the department?"

"Where's the guy with the highest?"

He smiled. "How'd a guy as young as you, and a doctor to boot, get to be such an asshole?" He looked at me, deadeye. "You scared us good, Doctor. We're not taking chances. I volunteered for this. I got a family here."

CHAPTER 25

As per Herr Lancaster's dictate, I drove back to the Department of Health to work on the database of names with Sonjit, a homely woman with a knack for numbers and the work ethic of an early Protestant. The report I was to file for Tim could wait; he'd already gotten all the important information from me. He knew filing the report was busywork, and he knew I knew, which is why he didn't ride me about getting it done. And so grind the delicately nuanced gears of bureaucracy.

By eleven p.m., Sonjit and I had about thirty people in the database: name, sex, age, all of the identifiers. We also had fields for all the notes we'd taken on the individuals. The names themselves would be dumped into a geographic software program—for the spot map—and into the flowchart program. Together, these would allow us to see graphically who'd had contact with whom and where they lived and worked. It's amazing what the graphics can make clear—little boxes with lines spreading out connecting those who'd had contact with one another. Amazing how much information notebooks and lists of names can hide.

But any more clarification would have to wait. Sonjit was on her fourth cup of coffee, and I'd been up since four that morning.

"Time to wrap up for the night," I said.

She looked at me, bleary-eyed. "I'm going to stay a little longer," she said.

"Get some sleep," I said, smiling. "Tomorrow's a big day."

"Aren't they all?"

I nodded, wondering if she was going to pull an all-nighter. And they call government employees lazy.

I drove to my apartment in Mount Vernon Place, a nice little residential neighborhood on a rise west of the Inner Harbor. There was a park here, lush and long, cascading downhill to the north. Periodically, the city would put public art throughout the grounds. Years before, when I first arrived for medical school, the place was dotted with brightly colored sculptures of fish. That exhibit stayed until vandals made off with one of the pieces, entitled, aptly, *Rogue Grouper.* The irony made headlines.

At the top of the park stood Baltimore's tribute to George Washington: an immense marble pillar topped with a bronze statue of the president. I stood looking at the monument through the gauzy, humid air, wondering if the great man ever envisioned a world where men like me worked for the government he created, for a part of that government that had a bankroll eight hundred times what the entire U.S. government had in 1790. I assume he never envisioned a world where a single retarded guy, sowing his poison seed, would ever be such a threat.

I turned from the monument and walked to my building, an old granite mansion that had been split into tiny units. CDC normally puts us up in hotels, but I'd wanted to be in Mount Vernon Place, relatively close to where I lived during med school. So, I'd found the flat myself: small, furnished, perfect. CDC obliged me, as did the landlord, who gave me a week-to-week rental. But any ideas of personalizing the apartment never materialized. I'd done virtually no nesting since I arrived in Baltimore, except for the three beers and the pack of American cheese in the refrigerator. And the box of granola in the cupboard. I ate the cheese and washed down a few handfuls of granola with a beer. Life was good.

In bed, I did my best to sleep but could not. My mind locked on

Douglas Buchanan and wouldn't budge. Where was the guy? Had Randall Jefferson moved him to another of his homes to keep him from talking to us? Had he relocated Douglas to a motel somewhere? Had Douglas simply had enough and run? And if any of these ruminations were true, then why the ransacked room? What had been removed? Why the discontinued phone service?

Where are you, Douglas? What have you done?

CHAPTER 26

Sonjit was already in the office, typing away, when I arrived the next morning around seven.

"Not here all night," I said.

"I slept." She nodded toward the break room down the hall. "The couch is very comfortable."

"Taking one for the team."

"Dr. Verlach came in last night with more names and data. From him and the state epidemiologists."

"How many?"

"Nearly one hundred—"

"They've been busy."

"I've been busy. I've entered about forty so far," she said.

"And?"

Sonjit's hands flew over the keyboard.

I walked behind her and looked at the screen. There was a web of boxes and lines, much too large for the small computer screen. Later, we'd use a special printer to put the whole thing on large pieces of paper. In the middle of the tangle, like a fat spider, sat Douglas Buchanan's name.

"Our man," I said. As if there were any doubt. "This should be enough to convince them."

"Who?" Sonjit asked.

"Whoever needs convincing."

"I don't have all the information yet," she said.

"We don't need any more information. This is—"

Just then, Verlach craned his head around the flimsy wall of the cubicle. "Dr. McCormick—"

"Did you see this?" I asked him.

He looked at the graph on the screen. "Whoa. Any word on Buchanan's whereabouts?"

I told him I hadn't heard anything. I didn't tell him about my meeting the day before with John Myers, about the telephone calls to San Jose. That was my little piece of the action. "I'll touch base with the detective on the case."

"Okay," he said. "I think it's time we involved the state police and the departments of surrounding counties to keep an eye open for this guy. We need to talk to him."

"That might already be under way. The cops seem pretty worried."

"Good." He ran a hand over his pate. "Did you find anything out . . ."

"I've been stuck in the office," I said. "You heard about my promotion."

"Yeah. Forgot about that. Sorry." Verlach looked at his watch. "Press conference is starting in an hour."

And he left.

To calm a jittery public, the bosses wanted to get something official out before the morning news programs ended. I had a fantasy of sorts: whipping up some fake blood, then bolting in front of the cameras and coughing up gobs of the stuff. I'd have sent half of Baltimore fleeing to the hills.

My mood notwithstanding, I went down to watch the press conference. It was decided that Ben Timmons would make the speech and take most of the questions. Verlach would be introduced at the end to fill in any holes. Looks like politics won out over presentation, which wasn't a surprise. Besides, it would have raised some questions if Verlach, relatively low on the totem pole, had presented everything while Ben Timmons waited silently in the wings.

Still, the Wonder Boy was right. Timmons did look like a politico. Some moron had even let the man go in front of the cameras with his hair slicked. Jesus.

The conference began. Timmons acknowledged CDC both for

setting up the surveillance program and for their help in the first days of the outbreak. Tim, from the sidelines, caught my eye and gave me a thumbs-up. I pretended not to see him.

The first questions were, predictably, about the what and who of the pathogen. There was a question about terrorism, which Timmons handled admirably, saying simply that there was no evidence to support the claim. Things began to get good when a reporter from one of the television stations asked about harassment of community members during the investigation. Everyone there knew who the community member in question was.

"We are working hand in hand with members of the community to identify the cause and the source of this outbreak, and we trust that they will give their full cooperation in this matter. We cannot conduct an effective investigation without the cooperation of community members. We need their help."

Ouch. Randall Jefferson must have felt the heat crank up about a hundred degrees. Timmons, it turned out, was pretty damn good in front of the cameras.

About ten minutes into the Q and A, my pager vibrated. Detective John Myers's number was on the little LED screen. I silenced it and clipped it back to my belt.

A minute later, the pager vibrated again. This time, I called back.

CHAPTER 27

"We found him."

"What?" I asked.

"We found him. Douglas Buchanan." Myers's voice was steady, though he might have been forcing it.

"Where?"

"In the woods in Carroll County up near Westminster."

"What the hell is he doing—"

"He's dead."

The noise of the press conference filtered into the hallway where I stood. I pushed the telephone harder into my right ear and jammed my finger into my left. "What happened?"

"We don't know. But it sure as hell wasn't suicide and it wasn't an accident."

"Is Douglas—is the body with you?"

"No."

"How do you know it wasn't an accident?"

"Believe me. Look, your friend's twenty minutes north. It's a Carroll Sheriff and Maryland State Police case now. They share jurisdiction up there, but we'll be working with them. You want to get some guys over to the station?"

I looked down the hall to the press conference, to the frenzy of shouted questions and camera lights. Verlach, Tim, and everyone else would be so involved, I wouldn't want to intrude. Or at least that's what I'd tell them.

"Everyone else is tied up right now." I walked through the hallway toward the exit. "I'll be there in five minutes."

We were in the car, John Myers and I, speeding north along I-795 into Maryland farm country.

"How did they identify the body?" I asked.

"When we put the word out to all PDs in the region yesterday, we faxed them a picture and gave them the heads-up on how urgent it was."

"You were one step ahead of us."

"We do this for a living, Doctor. Anyway, Carroll called us about thirty minutes ago. Seems a farmer was out with his dogs at dawn this morning and came across the grave."

"How did he die?"

"We're going to have to wait to determine that. Looks like it might be hard."

"Why?"

"The body was mutilated pretty bad."

"Then how'd they ID him?"

"I guess the face was still there, Doc."

We pulled off the highway to one of the rural roads that cut through the farmland, and if I had been driving through for almost any other purpose, it would have been pleasant. Ample spring and summer rain meant the corn was already waist-high and verdant. The sun was clearing the mist that hung over the fields. It was a picturesque scene, truly, except for the blue and red emergency lights glinting ahead of us.

And except for the heat. "Jesus," Myers muttered when he opened the door and the humid air rolled in.

We were off to the side of the road, hoofing it along the cornfield to the hubbub. A coroner's van had maneuvered its back end to the edge of the wood, flattening a semicircle of corn as it ground forward and back to get flush against the trees. Three other vehicles—a state police crime scene investigation truck and two Carroll County Sheriff's trucks—were parked in the short strip of grass between the field and the tree line. I caught the blue-white flash of a photographer's camera. The vegetation absorbed the voices; it was weirdly quiet.

A uniformed officer saw us coming and intercepted. Myers flashed his badge, and the uniform waved us toward a fat man in the woods twenty feet away. The man was squatting, looking at something below him. He wore shirtsleeves, large wet circles blooming from the armpits. A shoulder holster hung below his left arm.

From the edge of the wood, Myers called out, "O'Leary." The fat man stood and crunched the dried leaves as he walked over to us. Like everyone else in the woods, he wore a surgical mask. Unlike everyone else, he wore aviator sunglasses.

"Dee-tec-tive Myers," he said, pulling off the mask. "How goes it battling the dregs of humanity?"

"Shouldn't talk that way about my chief."

O'Leary laughed richly. "Hell, he never liked me anyway."

Myers told me, "O'Leary here used to work for the Baltimore PD. But he got soft and moved to the burbs."

"I moved to avoid just the kind of sick shit we're dealing with here. You never can quite escape, can you?"

"That's real philosophical, O."

O'Leary looked at me. "This a new recruit?"

"Nathaniel McCormick, the Centers for Disease Control," I said. O'Leary was gloved, so we dispensed with handshakes.

"Dr. Nathaniel McCormick," Myers added.

"Pete O'Leary. *Detective* Pete O'Leary." O'Leary gave a pinched smile that quickly faded. "John told me you're the guy that put the fear of God into us, Doc. We're all going to get hit with the plague, we don't find your friend. That's what John said." O'Leary moved to scratch his face and paused two inches from the skin. He stripped off a latex glove, threw the glove on the ground, and scratched.

"Detective Myers said you found him," I said.

"What's left of him. Jesus Christ, it's pretty fucking— Let's put it this way. I almost puked. And I never puke." O'Leary twisted his head and gave his neck a crack. "The Broken Man. That's what the boys are calling him."

" 'The Broken Man'?" I asked.

"Yeah. Humpty-Dumpty, the Eggman, Hollow Man. I liked the Broken Man, 'cause it sounds more . . . you know." I didn't know. O'Leary, I guess, sensed it and sensed I didn't really groove on the gallows humor. He said, "Anyway, why don't you guys grab some gear. We'll take a look at your friend."

Myers and I went to the coroner's van, grabbed gloves and masks with face shields, but didn't put them on. O'Leary led us into the woods.

"Try to follow me close, would you?" O'Leary said. "The state crime scene guys been here all morning, got casts of a couple footprints, a few treads. They may want to take more."

The mood darkened as we crossed the tree line. No more jokes here, not much speaking. Police tape had been woven through the trees, marking off an area about twenty feet square; streamers of the yellow tape also ran into a different part of the woods. A couple of men stood in a hole up to their shoulders. Masks and gloves only.

"The body's in there?" I asked.

"Yeah," O'Leary said, looking ahead.

"They're in the hole with the body?"

O'Leary glanced at me. "The grave was real deep. We excavated around it so we wouldn't have to jump in there with him."

We covered a few more feet before the smell hit me.

It was incongruous, the smell, not the organic stench of rotten leaves or even of decaying flesh. It was a pungent chemical scent. I knew it instantly.

"Bleach," I said.

"Yeah," O'Leary said. "Fucking weird."

Earth had been removed in a rough semicircle about ten feet in radius. The hole sloped from its edge downward; the crime scene guys were standing on a lower level, looking into the bottom of the crater. Though I was only five feet away, I still couldn't see the body.

In a line near the edge of the grave sat a number of thick plastic bags.

"What's in those?" I asked.

"Fast-set concrete. Your guy was covered in it."

"For what?"

"Hell if I know. Cut down on the stink. Keep us from getting to him. Maybe make him into a mother of a paperweight." O'Leary grinned. I didn't. "Anyway, looks like they just poured some bags of Sakrete down the hole, then threw in some water. Only a couple inches covering the body. Still, it took five guys three hours to dig the hole and chip out the concrete."

I moved to the lip of the excavation.

Even from that vantage, I couldn't see much. But what I could see was, simply, a fucking mess. Liquid slicked one of the tech's hands. And these guys had on masks and gloves only, mucking through the gore as if this were just another death.

"Wait, wait, wait," I snapped. "Get out of there. Get away from the body."

The techs looked up.

"Hey," O'Leary said. "What the hell are—"

"Get out of there!" I yelled.

The techs looked at me curiously. I might as well have been flapping my arms and clucking for the reaction I got. "Step out of the hole," I said slowly.

"Who the hell is this?" one of the crime scene guys said.

"Guys. Everyone." I was trying to calm down, realizing that my reaction could have been a bit more diplomatic. Diplomacy was hard, though, considering I saw these poor bastards in the hole, protected by next to nothing, smeared with blood and God knows what other bodily juices, picking up some bug, spraying it into their girlfriends or wives. "This body may be hot. You know what that means? It might be crawling with virus or something else. And if you catch this virus, it can kill you."

"We got masks. O'Leary—?"

"Get out of there, fellas."

"Why the hell didn't somebody tell us? Jesus, O'Leary, they said the guy might be sick, but . . ."

As the techs scrambled themselves out of the hole, I became aware of everyone around watching us. Myers looked at me like I'd just pulled a gun. O'Leary stared as if he wanted to pull a gun. On me.

"Okay, everyone, my name's Nathaniel McCormick. I'm a doctor with the Centers for Disease Control. You know why I'm here?" No one ventured a guess. I pointed to the crater. "I'm here because this guy—or the guy we think this is, or who it probably is—" I was getting a lot of blank stares. *Great work, McCormick,* I thought, *getting up on your soapbox before you're even sure it's Douglas Buchanan in the hole.* I powered on. "The man whose body this is might have had a disease. A pretty bad one. So I have just two questions to determine whether we have to worry. First, did anyone get any blood or secretions on their skin? Any bodily contact with any fluids?" Mumbled nos. "Good. That's great. Two, does everyone know what universal precautions are?" A couple of mumbled yeses. "Great. Do it. Take universal precautions. From now on, anyone touching the body needs to have on goggles and a gown in addition to the mask and gloves. We just want to be as careful as we can."

The crime scene techs walked slowly past me. "Hey," I said to them. "If you took the precautions, you're okay. I just wanted to scare everyone."

"Well, you did it, Doc," one of the techs groused.

I said, "You'll be fine." Then, to O'Leary, "You have a list of everyone who's been in contact with the body?"

"Sure, Doc. Anything you want." He shook his head. "Anything you want."

"I just want to make sure everyone's safe."

"Sure you do."

O'Leary was still eye-fucking me. I'd basically cut off his balls and handed them to him in front of his crew. And I'm sure the detective was also thinking about—God forbid—the lawsuits that would open up if anyone here actually got sick. *Screw it,* I thought. *These guys should be better than that.*

My public health duty finished for the hour, I put on my face mask and gloves and stepped to the edge of the crater. Gingerly, I crept-slid down the slope toward the body. The smell of bleach got stronger and I felt like a doughboy on the Western Front, in a trench recently knocked by chlorine gas. Myers was behind me. At the bottom, I stopped.

John Myers coughed. "Holy Jesus," he said.

*   *   *

It was Douglas Buchanan, all right. He lay on his back, six feet of dirt rising in a wall on one side of him. The body bag that encased him had been unzipped. Chips of damp concrete clung to the outside of the thick black plastic. The grave, if it could be called that, had an uneven floor, so that Douglas's hips sank lower than the rest of him. Liquid, which I assumed to be bleach, pooled there. His shirt had been removed, and his pants were pulled down to his knees.

John Myers pivoted and made his way up the dirt slope. "I gotta breathe," he said. I looked back to the body.

A jagged cut ran in a large Y from each of Douglas's shoulders to his sternum and down to his pubis. It was the same type of cut pathologists use when conducting autopsies. The left side of his rib cage was pulled back and lay over the lip of the body bag like an open door revealing his chest and abdominal cavities. The scene reminded me of the work of the great Renaissance anatomist Vesalius. Figures in his etchings were often placed in pastoral settings, reclining peacefully as they retracted their chest walls to give the viewer an eyeful of viscera. They were beautiful pieces, really. A world apart from what was below me now.

And there was another difference between the anatomist's drawing and Douglas Buchanan: Vesalius's figures had their organs.

Without disturbing the body, I could see that Douglas Buchanan's heart and lungs were gone. He was also missing his pancreas, his liver and gallbladder, and his spleen. The neck was flayed and the thyroid removed. *The Broken Man?* O'Leary took too much literary license with his moniker. This body wasn't broken, it was *stripped*.

"You ever seen anything like this, Doc?" O'Leary asked.

I ignored the comment. "Can I open the other side of the body?"

"Sure." O'Leary threw up his hands. "What the hell? You seem hell-bent on scaring everyone else away from the investigation. You the boss now."

"Cool it, O," Myers said quietly.

I climbed out of the crater, went to the coroner's van, and got a paper gown and some goggles, two pairs of gloves to double-glove, then returned to Douglas Buchanan's body. O'Leary and Myers weren't talking. Nobody was talking, in fact, and the silence made the awful scene even more awful.

Squatting at the edge of the body, I reached to Douglas's right side and used my hand to retract his chest and abdominal walls. The ribs had already been broken from a previous, violent retraction, so the flap fell open easily. No kidneys, it looked like. The stomach was gone. So were sections of small bowel. There were, I noticed, no flies. Nothing could live here.

I dropped the flaps of muscle, rib, and skin back into place.

I noticed the penis and scrotum had been pulled up so they rested on top of the dead man's closed thighs. The flesh of the scrotum had been sliced open and the testicles removed.

"My God," I said.

The head. It rested on a small pillow of soil, so that Douglas seemed to be looking down the length of his body. The top of the skull had been sawed through, and it had shifted from the rest of the cranium. The brain was missing.

I stood, climbed up the dirt slope, stripped off my gloves and mask, and breathed deeply. Bile rose in my throat, but I forced it down. I'd be goddamned if I was going to let these guys see me puke.

I turned to O'Leary. "Is the medical examiner in Carroll going to handle this?"

He looked at Detective Myers, then back to me. He sighed. "That's the plan."

"All right," I said, "I'm going to suggest that the body be moved to St. Raphael's Hospital in Baltimore. That's where we've quarantined the people who are sick already. Your forensics team can work there if they need to."

O'Leary looked at Myers, then back to me. He nodded.

I asked, "Will there be any jurisdictional trouble?"

"There won't be. I'll make the calls."

"John," I asked Myers, "any problem on the part of Baltimore City?"

"Shouldn't be."

O'Leary spoke up. "It's still our investigation, though—"

"Of course," I said.

"—the body was found here. Looks like he was killed here, too."

"How do you know he was killed here?"

"Not here here, here over there." O'Leary pointed to another cordoned area, about ten yards away. "We found some disturbed leaves. We got a positive for blood."

"Blood?"

"Just a trace."

"A trace . . ." I looked around. "How the hell did the farmer find this? I mean, I'm no expert on dogs, but . . . there was concrete all over it. And the body bag was filled with bleach."

O'Leary shrugged. "We got real lucky. The guy who found it has hounds, which was a break. We got a light trail of blood from over there to this. The dogs must have got the scent from the blood, then started digging at the grave site." He looked around. "Yeah, we got real lucky. Another day or two, a good rain maybe, and even hounds wouldn't find anything."

I followed O'Leary to the second cordoned spot. The tangle of police tape actually formed a lane, of sorts, between the two boxed areas. He said, "We have three sets of footprints headed toward this site, two headed from this site toward the grave, two headed away from the grave. All of it's pretty incomplete, though." He lifted up the police tape and stepped into an area where a man on his hands and knees was pawing through the downed foliage. "The best we figure it is that whoever did this cut your guy up here, then transported the body to the grave, which was already dug."

"Why do you say that?" I asked stupidly.

" 'Cause you don't mutilate someone in a six-foot grave. Plus we got the blood traces. Maybe they punctured the body bag when they cut him."

I took a deep breath, finally felt my head begin to clear. "These people were thorough."

"Yeah." He looked blankly at the crime scene tech moving through the leaves. "Goddamned lucky," he repeated.

CHAPTER 28

Il Duce was not pleased.

"Was I that vague?" Tim Lancaster asked. "Was I unclear when I said I wanted you to be working here, in this office? Was it that unclear that I wanted you on a short leash?"

We were sitting in a conference room at the Department of Health,

Herr Lancaster, Herb Verlach, and I. The doors were closed. I hoped they were thick.

"It was clear," I said. "But the service gives EIS officers the freedom to follow hunches and—"

"But not for something like this. Not when we have the press crawling up our butts, lawyers rumbling about civil suits, assault charges against you—"

"The charges were dropped—"

"Quiet. And I specifically told you to stay put. I don't have to tell you, Nate, that this kind of behavior could put you back in Atlanta, doing literature searches on every outbreak of flu for the past five hundred years."

Which was true and it wasn't. EIS isn't so well staffed that they could afford to relegate me to weeks of busywork. Besides, because my infraction had been relatively slight, Tim would have had to answer questions about my banishment. Notwithstanding the previous few days, my evaluations had been generally stellar. Add to that, despite what Dr. Lancaster said now, the guy liked me. Don't ask me why.

He said, "We can't go gallivanting to murder scenes."

"It was a damn good thing I was gallivanting. They were mucking around with only gloves and masks."

"So you run in, screaming and yelling, telling them they're going to die?"

"I didn't say they would die."

"That's how they heard it."

"That's not my responsibility."

"Don't be obtuse. Of course it's your responsibility."

Verlach chimed in. "My people are fielding calls from half the municipal staff in Carroll County. You scared them good, Nate."

Thanks, Herb. "I wanted to."

"Dr. McCormick," Tim said, "most of your instincts are good. Most of them. But you are *out of control* here. Are you so fucking concerned— yes, *fucking* concerned—with solving this case that you don't care what kind of problems you're creating for the rest of us? For CDC? For the health departments here? For the goddamned city itself? Are you so damned blind that you can't see the bigger picture? Come *on.*"

My face flushed and I could feel the sweat pricking through my scalp. Under the table, my hands were knotted together.

"And this call from Douglas Buchanan's phone. How long were you planning to keep that to yourself? I have to find out about that from Dr. Verlach, who finds out about it only because he happened to talk to the detective on the case?"

Tim was up and about, pacing and scratching like a chimpanzee. Though I'd seen him annoyed, I'd never seen him this annoyed. "You piss off everyone you come in contact with. The state police up in Carroll said you marched in like a freaking general and screwed up their crime scene—"

"They said they were finished—"

"I don't care. What they're saying now is that you screwed things up royally. They're saying you took the body from them and sent it to Baltimore. Think about that for a second, will you, Doctor? They're not bitching about these things because what you did was wrong, they're bitching because they don't like you. Even your contact in the Baltimore PD is hightailing it from you. Because he knows he has to work with all his friends up north again."

Tim's fingernails dug into his scalp. "And what are you doing spending so much time on one person?"

"He's the vector, Tim." I was whining.

"Is he, now?"

"Look at the spot map. Look at the graph of contacts. He's at the center—"

"I can't look at them because they're not finished. And they're not finished because you were running around with the cops."

Touché.

Tim sighed. "Okay. Okay, let's just assume he's at the center of this. If that's so, if he's the first one, why wasn't he sick?"

"Different incubation times."

"Wrong. With a disease that seems to be moving this fast—infection to full-blown in two weeks—he is unlikely to be the vector."

"He could be resistant. He could just be a carrier."

"Unlikely, Nate. What's the carrier rate in humans for hemorrhagic fever?"

"Low."

"Right. We're playing an odds game here. And we're allocating resources. Hours spent on some detective chase is not the best use of your time, is it?"

I didn't answer.

"Is it, Dr. McCormick?" His tone was scathing.

"No. I guess it's not."

"Learn how to sink time into things that are more likely to matter. Bethany Reginald, for example." Now he spoke in an incredibly annoying kindergarten-teacher voice. He took a large piece of paper from the top of the table and held it out. "You see this?"

I looked at the paper, boxes and lines of the contact chart. "Yes."

"What do you see?"

"I thought you said this wasn't finished."

"What do you see here, Doctor?"

Tim was really being an asshole about this. "I see Bethany Reginald."

Indeed, Bethany Reginald—not Douglas Buchanan—seemed to be at the center of this particular graphic. He pulled out the spot map; the two places where Bethany spent most of her time—Open Arms and Miller Grove—had the highest concentration of sick people.

"Now, Bethany is sick, right?" Tim continued. "There's obviously something wrong in that young woman. If you had stayed around this morning, you would have found out that she did indeed have intercourse with a man called Roger Epstein, who had intercourse with Deborah Fillmore."

On the contact chart, Tim traced a circuitous line from Bethany Reginald to Deborah Fillmore, bypassing Douglas Buchanan and landing on Roger Epstein. Then his fingers went to his neck, raking away.

"I got the division chief breathing down my neck on this. The director herself is asking questions. This is getting hot, Nathaniel. Really hot. Too hot to have this kind of recklessness. We are here at the invitation of the local authorities, and I'm worried we're wearing out our welcome."

I looked at Verlach, whose eyes were glued to the Formica table. "Herb, am I screwing up that badly?"

His eyes met mine and the fucking Army officer said, flatly and directly, "It's a tough environment, Nate. It takes experience to learn how to deal with the politics of everyone involved."

"More people will get sick if I'm not in the field, Tim," I insisted.

"More people will get sick if you are, Nate." He scratched at his neck. "That's why I'm pulling you out. Completely."

*   *   *

Tim didn't actually remove me completely. Instead, he decided to send me to California to follow up on the woman who'd received calls from Douglas Buchanan, since, as he put it, "you like this detective work so much."

I, of course, protested, both because I felt I was more needed in the East and because CDC already had EIS presence in Berkeley and a fresh EIS graduate, a woman named Brooke Michaels, in San Jose. I also protested because I thought—we all thought—the woman in San Jose was a dead end.

After Tim left the room, Verlach and I had a quiet moment in which he couldn't meet my eyes. I guess my former comrade-in-arms knew he was abandoning me to the political machine. Eventually, he moved toward the door and said simply, "Enjoy sunny California for me."

He didn't know how impossible that would be.

CHAPTER 29

It took me less than an hour to pack up my things. I left a message for the landlord that I would be leaving early the next morning and that other people from CDC would be moving in. Two new EIS officers, Andy and Beth, had arrived that day and were camping out at a Holiday Inn or wherever CDC saw fit to put them. Anyway, their early arrival led me to believe that my transfer had been decided long before that afternoon's meeting.

While the sheets churned in the washing machine, I pulled out an old address book. I had all my relevant addresses in my PalmPilot, so why I kept this ratty thing—held together by two rubber bands—I didn't know. Well, actually, I did know.

I flipped to the Cs and there she was: Alaine Chen. About six numbers and half as many e-mail addresses scratched out and rewritten, although I don't think I'd ever used half of the numbers or addresses. They were there just to keep track.

The last number I had for her was in Northern California, for a Redwood City apartment. I was sure she'd moved, that her location, phone number, and e-mail had changed about five times since the last time I put in a change. She could be anywhere. On second thought: no, she was still in California. Born, raised, educated in the Golden State, there would be no reason for her to leave.

"Alaine Chen," I said aloud, and tried to summon up the mental image of her—the glossy black hair, the beautiful face, the legs that would launch a thousand ships. There was more pain than pleasure in that picture. I closed my little beaten leather address book and tossed it into the trash. Then I gathered all the other odds and ends of refuse from the apartment, threw it on top of the book, and carried the whole thing to the garbage chute.

I folded the sheets and blankets onto the bed and generally readied my pied-à-terre for return to the landlord. Then, at four thirty that morning, I went for a long run. I did this—I ran—to clear my head and clear my body of the cigarettes I'd had in the past few days. I also ran to punish myself. That morning, I had a lot to punish myself for, so by the end of my five-mile loop, I was heaving bile into the gutter outside my apartment. But I finished in record time.

Anyway, I figured I was done with the cigarettes. I'd let that be a hallmark of my time in Baltimore. Dirty habit for a dirty city, and I was on my way out of both of them. My career had taken a good punch in this city, and its sights and sounds—the very things that I used to enjoy—were beginning to annoy me. It was good I was getting out, I guessed.

But maybe that was rationalization. I spit a last gob onto the sidewalk and went into the apartment.

At six, I was showered and ready to go, leaving an apologetic note about the dirty towels. At six thirty, I was at the Health Department. This would be my final briefing of the team about the situation in Baltimore, the final transfer of information. My flight was early, so I hauled my luggage along with me. As I sat it in the corner of the conference room, Tim stuck his head in.

"Bethany Reginald died," he said.

"God. When?"

"Last night around ten."

It always happens, these small connections physicians—even a non-clinical doc such as me—make with sick people. The stereotype of the unfeeling doctor aside, we get into this profession to help people. Whether as a thoracic surgeon or a family doc or an epidemiologist, we get into this to make people well. So, as corny as it sounds, Bethany meant something to me. She'd taught me that the mentally handicapped have lives, sex lives and love lives, as complex and nuanced as the rest of us. And now poor, retarded, sexually adventurous Bethany Reginald was dead.

"Has anyone told Helen Jones?"

Tim looked at me blankly. "Bethany's friend," I said. "The index case. She and Bethany were lovers."

"I don't know. I'll make sure someone does. At least no one else has gotten sick in the last twelve hours. We have pretty extensive surveillance going on, and nothing. Each hour with nothing new is another victory." He looked at his watch. "Briefing in seven minutes."

It was a roundup of the usual suspects plus Beth and Andy—the new EIS officers—and John Myers and Pete O'Leary. Douglas Buchanan, Helen Jones, Bethany Reginald, and the web of sexual contacts was the subject of the meeting. Tim let me run the meeting. My swan song.

I stood in front of a projection of the contact chart that Sonjit— God bless her—had finished the night before. The image covered an entire wall.

I ran through the webs of sexual involvement, drawing attention to the fact that Bethany and Douglas sat in the center of those webs. Both of the boxes representing them had large dark slashes through them indicating they were dead.

I moved on to my theories.

"Though we still haven't found a reservoir, there is some reason to believe that a rat may have transferred the disease to humans. The Jefferson properties, where Case Number Two, Deborah Fillmore, lived, may be the source, since we found ample evidence of rodent infestation. The disease symptoms bear some resemblance to the hemorrhagic fevers, and, I don't have to tell most of you, Lassa, Machupo, and the other arenaviruses are found in rodent hosts. Baltimore is a major port, so it's not unthinkable that some exotic rodents infected the local population. We might also be dealing with an indigenous, but previously unknown, arena-like virus. And until we find some indication this was intentional—mail or anything else—I think it's best to assume the source is natural."

I saw Tim nodding.

"Okay, so, a possible scenario: Bethany Reginald, or Bethany and Helen Jones, visit Douglas Buchanan at the Jefferson home. Or the women are infected at Open Arms, their home. Purely based on hygiene, it looks more likely that the Jefferson properties would harbor something."

Okay, considering the interest in Bethany Reginald as the source of the disease, I was about to skate onto thin theoretical ice. Douglas Buchanan was my man, he was the key; I was convinced of it. Let everyone cut me up behind my back after I was gone.

"So let's assume the bug is at Jefferson's Baltimore Haven. Bethany prods Helen into going over to visit Douglas for a little tryst. There, Helen is infected with the disease, and she's able to pass it on to Bethany and Douglas. Douglas, for whatever reason, does not get sick. Perhaps he has some natural immunity, perhaps its latency is longer in males. Anyway, he is, by some accounts, a sexual predator. He infects Deborah Fillmore, his reputed girlfriend, as well as Case Number Four. Case Number Four may have been infected in a possible rape at Mr. Jefferson's birthday party two weeks ago. Case Number Four goes on to infect her boyfriend, giving us Case Number Five."

I looked at the new EIS officers. "I would check whether Bethany and/or Helen ever visited Douglas at Baltimore Haven."

"It doesn't make sense that Douglas would show no symptoms," Beth said. She was a petite woman with a blunt cut and a Harvard MD. She always seemed to wear something like a scowl, or maybe it was just when she spoke to me.

"Sure it does," I said confidently, knowing full well that everyone would doubt it. "If we assume that Douglas is a sexual predator—*was* a sexual predator—then we might assume he had sex with many more people than we now know. I'd check on that. Tim said we've had no other cases. It could be that, as with West Nile, only a subset of the population is vulnerable to the disease. But Douglas's perceived immunity brings me to scenario number two: Douglas Buchanan is actually the first one infected. He's our index case. He's living in Dr. Jefferson's home and has contact with vermin and their feces, urine, other excreta. If that's true, we might be dealing with some kind of mutation."

Verlach mouthed "Good point" and jotted something down.

Mutation is a characteristic of all living things. Because viruses have such a high rate of replication—and because some viruses, like HIV, have poor genetic editing mechanisms—mutation is frequent. It's possible, then, that viruses will become more virulent with successive transmissions—i.e., potency is amplified. If mutation was at work here, and Douglas was the first one to be infected, his "immunity" would actually be due to the virus's relative harmlessness in him.

Tim spoke. "What we could salvage from Douglas is being flown down to Atlanta today. If—when—we get a bead on what bug we're dealing with, we'll see whether it's in him."

"Unless it was hiding out in the missing organs," I said.

"Sure."

"Okay, last one, scenario number three: Douglas is still our vector, but he brought the bug from somewhere else."

There was silence in the room, which I took to mean everyone thought this theory was bunk. Still, I had to mention it, if only to justify why the hell I was being sent to California to chase it down. "I know it's unlikely, but we should entertain all possibilities. I'm just throwing these theories out. You guys"—I pointed to Andy and Beth—"have all the files and interviews. I hope the picture will become a lot clearer. If you have any questions, call or page me." I wrote my pager and mobile number on the whiteboard. I looked at Detectives Myers and O'Leary. "Okay, so what's the fuzz doing here?"

There was forced laughter. I continued. "Because Douglas Buchanan was clearly murdered, the police are an active part of this investigation. Detectives O'Leary and Myers will be working closely with whoever ends up following the Douglas Buchanan angle."

Beth raised her hand. "I'll be working on that."

"Great," I said. "Detectives, you want to tell us what you've found out?"

"Well," Myers finally said, "O'Leary—Detective O'Leary—and the County Sheriff's Office are going to head the investigation along with help from the state police. I'm going to help out, since a lot of this is cross-jurisdictional." He fidgeted. It wasn't the cops' turf, I guessed, and they weren't gung ho about addressing this group. "We don't have much so far. Dr. Jefferson says he doesn't know anything about Douglas Buchanan, and he didn't know he had a rapis—a sexual predator on his hands. We're meeting with him this morning, and we'll apply a little pressure. So far, it seems that no one knows for sure where Mr. Buchanan came from. It's like he just became etherealized out of nowhere."

Became etherealized, John? I thought.

Beth asked, "What about the murder itself? Any clues?"

"Well, in consideration of Mr. Buchanan's alleged habits, and the nature of the murder—I mean, we thought it might be someone who was extremely angry at Mr. Buchanan and was trying to send a message—it might be that one of his victims or his victims' relatives took care of the problem. They were so pissed at Mr. Buchanan that they mutilated the guy."

There was silence at this, and Myers stammered on. "The coroner said it looked like the organs were taken by someone who knew what he was doing. He said the procedures were kind of sloppy but were probably by someone who had knowledge of anatomy."

"A doctor?" Beth asked.

"Or a vet, or a butcher. But it wasn't done by some random nut job who was angry the guy raped his daughter."

"Unless the nut job was a pathologist," Beth shot back.

"All pathologists are nut jobs," Tim said.

There was some laughter.

I asked, "But we don't know why they took the organs or what they did with them, right?"

"No." Myers scrunched around in his chair. "We've seen some pretty bad things, but this . . . It's not the kind of mutilation we'd expect. I mean, most of the mutilations we've seen are different, things cut up and off, not cut out, right, O'Leary?"

O'Leary shrugged.

Myers cleared his throat. "Anyway, we're still trying to figure it. We'll be talking with Dr. Jefferson about all of this."

"What about the bleach?" Beth asked.

"The concrete was to cover the scent, we think. The bleach could be used for that."

"Infection," I said.

I felt eyes shift to me.

"If someone was worried Douglas was sick, maybe they wanted to reduce the chance of infection."

"So, our nut job pathologist is a humanitarian," Tim said dismissively.

He glanced at his watch. "Okay, Dr. McCormick, you need to be on a plane and we need to get back to the field."

Asshole.

To the sound of closing notebooks, I apprised everyone of my plans—California to follow up on Douglas's contact, then back to Atlanta—and wrapped up the meeting.

After my last words, Tim collared me, saying he'd called the California and Santa Clara public health departments to give them the heads-up I was coming. Brooke Michaels would be showing me the ropes, he said.

Wonderful, I thought.

Tim clapped me on the shoulder and bolted from the room, presumably to make one of his billion daily phone calls.

"Nice job, Nathaniel. Very thorough," Verlach said. He shook my hand warmly. "You'll be missed. Tim probably told you, but I'm managing the transmission and surveillance. Keep me informed."

"You do the same," I replied. He nodded and left.

I stopped by Beth's cubicle and interrupted a discussion between her and the detectives. I made sure she knew she could contact me anytime. Time was getting short, and I grabbed my luggage and headed for the exit. John Myers caught up with me.

"They're giving you the boot, huh?"

"No thanks to you, John."

"What can I say, Doc? You're a prick, and you fucked up yesterday. But I'm a prick, too. I like pricks."

"Maybe we should date."

He seemed to like that one; he slapped me on the shoulder. "Already got a wife and kids."

"Too bad."

"Listen, I'll get your back here, but you keep us informed, you find anything out there."

"As long as it's quid pro quo."

"You gotta cut the medical jargon."

I wasn't going to explain. "As long as you keep me in the loop," I said.

"Okay. Deal. If you're three thousand miles away and not a pain in my ass, I'll keep you posted." The elevator stopped on the ground floor and we stepped off together. "The woman's name is Gladys Thomas, the one Douglas Buchanan called. Here's the address we have for her."

He handed a piece of paper to me. San Jose, all right. The city, not one of the ritzy suburbs.

I said, "So, what if you hadn't found me just now?"

"What do you mean?"

"I would have left without this." I held up the paper with Gladys Thomas's name and address. "You wanted me to figure it all out on my own? Thanks, John. You're a fine human being."

"Don't mention it. Take this, too."

He thrust something into my hand: it was a photo of Douglas Buchanan, a big, grainy blowup.

I said, "You have a picture of yourself, too? So I can remember this fantastic trip?"

I don't know exactly why I was giving Myers such shit; probably because I couldn't dish it to Tim.

"You'll thank me for that, Doc. Important for identifying the deceased to people who may have seen him but may not know his name. You don't watch cop shows?"

"I would if it didn't mean I had to watch cops."

Myers was smiling at me. "Doc, I got a soft spot for you, you know? You're a lot like me. You piss people off, but it looks like you get the job done."

Great, I thought. *I'm a lot like Detective John Myers.* I was elated.

I stepped through the glass doors to a waiting taxi, leaving the detective, Baltimore, and this entire sorry chapter in my life behind.

I grew up in a small town in southern Pennsylvania, not far, in fact, from where Douglas Buchanan had lived before coming to Baltimore. Anyway, that being the case, Baltimore/Washington International was the closest major airport, and I knew it well. By instinct I found my way through the gauntlet of security to the gate. Long ago, when I was still in medical school on the West Coast, I would have taken Southwest Airlines, transferred in Phoenix or Las Vegas, then continued on to San Jose. But it was a different year, a different circumstance. I had travel orders this time, and was able to hop the first direct flight to San Francisco.

The flight was packed, so I assumed some poor bastard had been bumped to make room for yours truly. Like the military, CDC might send you into the nastiest hot zones, and like the military, they didn't want you to wait to get there.

On the plane, I ordered a double Scotch, downed both bottles, and ordered another. I tried to think about what I was leaving behind, what I was going to. But that mostly depressed me, and I fell asleep.

2. CALIFORNIA

CHAPTER 30

Ah, San Francisco.

Through the jet's window, I could see the peninsula slide into view, stretching like a great finger toward Marin County to the north. The Golden Gate Bridge looked electric against the blue, blue ocean. The Transamerica building was there, the office towers along the Embarcadero. The bay was dotted with sailboats. It was just as I'd left it.

I felt like I was about to throw up.

Though I'd ruminated entirely too long on it, I was not going to see Alaine Chen. I'd done my best to erect a bulwark against thoughts of her, but in the line for the rental car, I got a pang about having thrown out her telephone number. Not that I would have called her, not that she would have seen me. Not that the number was even close to correct anymore. Still, those scratches in my book were the last tawdry threads to a previous life. Let old acquaintances be forgot, easier said than done.

The line for the rental was too long, too slow, and I was thinking too much about things that shouldn't matter to me. To get my mind off the complicated Dr. Chen, I blazed up my Palm and found the number of the only person in California I was sure I wanted to see. Scratch that: the only person I *had* to see. If I was on the West Coast and she found out I hadn't visited . . . well, I wouldn't be surprised if the earth opened up and swallowed me whole.

And lo and behold, she answered. The old voice crackled into the phone.

"Nathaniel McCormick," she said.

"Dr. Tobel." I felt a smile stretch my face.

We chitchatted for a few minutes, bringing each other up-to-date. It had been a while since I'd spoken to her, but we glossed over the intervening years in the time it took the rental line to move forward five feet.

"And what brings you to San Francisco?" she asked.

"I need to attend to some business."

"Business? You're not going to tell me you left CDC for a job in industry, are you?"

"On days like this, I wish I had. But no. It's CDC business."

"Nothing serious?"

"It is serious, actually. You heard about the outbreak in Baltimore?"

"Yes, I did read something. . . ."

"Well, it has to do with that. I'll fill you in when I see you."

We set up a lunch appointment for the following day.

Dr. Tobel said, "I hope it's no trouble, but can you come to the lab? I have a very tight schedule tomorrow, unfortunately. We'll go to lunch from there. You don't mind, I hope."

"You're still at The Farm?" I asked.

"I am. Same building, same lab."

Well, in that case, yes, of course I minded. "No, of course not," I said.

CHAPTER 31

I got a car with a GPS navigation system. It was Silicon Valley, after all, so when in Rome . . . More important, I told myself, I was responding to an emergency and didn't need to waste time getting lost. First thing, I programmed in the address for the Santa Clara County Public Health Department.

It was still early afternoon, early enough to avoid the nightmare of Bay Area traffic, so I was able to take the 101 south to San Jose. The highway was one of the Ugly Ones, a big, nasty gash through the landscape that clotted with traffic every morning, every evening. Like so much else, I didn't miss the roads here.

Thirty minutes into the trip, I passed green signs marking the exits for my former university. In the four years I lived in the area, I'd made this drive countless times, shuttling back to school from dinner or dancing in San Francisco. Having spent so much time trying to forget this place, I was surprised how familiar I still was with the roads, the hills, the little cities that hung off the freeway like baubles off a necklace. But I sure as hell didn't recognize the big-box superstores, the massive office buildings, the unending swath of development that bracketed the 101.

I turned on the radio and found an old favorite station. It was now called, I think, La Música, and played some hip-hop Latin stuff. Not my cup of tea. I settled for the local NPR station and felt old.

San Jose. The female voice on the navigation system guided me gently off the sunbaked 101 to the 880 to the city's sunbaked streets. For all the money and fame that San Jose attracted in the 1990s, it was still, at its core, a cow town. A commercial vacancy rate near twenty-five percent left the downtown looking ghostly and sad, with *For Lease* grafted on to the buildings and amoeboid clumps of young men gathered on the sidewalks in the middle of the day. The party was definitely over.

I parked in the garage across from a midsized gray building that housed the Santa Clara County Public Health Department, Disease Prevention and Control Program. I walked into the building, which had about as much security as a video game arcade. I found a receptionist of sorts, and asked him to page Brooke Michaels. Then I sat on a hard plastic chair next to a stand filled with public health brochures. I read one on genital warts.

Just as the brochure was really getting good, I heard a voice above me. "Dr. McCormick. You don't look any worse for the wear. You could use a tan, though."

"Brooke." I looked up to see Dr. Brooke Michaels in all her blond, bronzed glory. "And you should watch yours. We're supposed to set an example, you know. Wouldn't be good if you knocked off at thirty with melanoma."

We shook hands. "Twenty-nine," she whispered, and turned

toward the hallway behind the guard's desk. I followed her through double doors to a warren of offices, fighting to keep my eyes off her well-toned rump. I'd forgotten how good-looking she was. Or maybe I'd just tried to forget. Anyway, she was well muscled, with fantastic lips, azure eyes, and to-die-for posture. She had the whole California surfer girl package going for her, though she was originally from about two thousand miles east.

The offices looked a little strange—long white hallways with tiny offices pasted onto either side. I asked Brooke, "What was this space before you guys invaded?"

"The sexually transmitted disease clinic. The exam rooms are our offices."

I made a note to watch where I sat.

Brooke turned back toward me, flipping the golden hair. "Tim Lancaster told me briefly why you were coming. I told him I'd be happy to check it out, that they didn't need to send you, but he declined."

She was asking for some sort of answer, but I didn't indulge her. Brooke being Brooke, she asked anyway. "Why did they send you all the way out here? State didn't bite on this?"

"No."

"But they have EIS officers in Berkeley and LA—"

"They didn't want to touch it either. Besides, Tim wanted someone familiar with the situation back east."

"Oh," she said, unsatisfied, but letting it lie for now. She opened the door to a small, cluttered office. "My kingdom." Medical journals and files occupied every available surface. I could have been in Verlach's office back in Baltimore. *What is it,* I wondered, *that makes all public health docs' offices look the same?*

"Sorry it's a mess," she said, clearing magazines from a chair.

I said, "Not a reflection of your mind, I hope."

"My mind is organized better than the Library of Congress. It's only my office and my life that are disasters."

"Sorry to hear that."

"Not at all. I'm in perfect Zen harmony with the chaos." She took a seat behind her desk. "So," she said, "what's going on?"

I gave her the précis, omitting, of course, any negative assessment of my own performance.

"They booted you, hunh?"

Shut up, Brooke.

Brooke, I should mention, was in Atlanta when I did my training the year before. She was in her second year at EIS, stationed at CDC's home offices, and ran one of the workshops for the new recruits. The training felt like a heady boot camp, five grueling weeks in the heat of a Georgia summer. There was a certain amount of bonding that went on in the ranks of the EIS, and Dr. Michaels and I bonded especially well on more than one occasion. We were, as they say, an item, for a couple of weeks anyway. But Brooke put in for an assignment in California, worked at CDC in Berkeley for a while, then took a public health job with Santa Clara County. Ostensibly, she came out here to follow a fiancé who had just taken a junior faculty position at the university. One might also argue that she wanted to be as far away from me as she could. I should write a book: *How to Alienate Women.*

I glanced at my watch. "I need to get into the field, Brooke."

"So why did you stop by here?"

"To show my face, let the Health Department know I arrived safely. Everything's copacetic with me being here?"

"I called the state health department in Berkeley. They said hell no; then I went down the line to the guys here. They threw up when they heard you were coming."

"Thanks."

She smiled softly, like she knew she'd crossed the line. "Everything's perfect. We're all glad you're here. Tim made the calls and— Here." She handed me a piece of paper. It was a memo extending an invitation to me to follow up on the cases in Baltimore. It consisted of exactly three sentences.

"We're glad to have you."

"I'm sure."

"Seriously. It's good to see you."

I scanned her face to see if she was telling the truth, but couldn't figure it. To work, then. I dug into my folder and pulled out Gladys Thomas's address. "I have the address of the woman I'm supposed to talk to out here. I have reason to believe she might be in an institution or a home affiliated with the state or county."

She concentrated on the paper for a moment. "I think it's a home on the edge of town. A nice one."

"Group home for the mentally handicapped?"

"Yes, Nathaniel. For the mentally handicapped."

"Just making sure. How did you know from this address?"

She reached to a shelf above her desk and pulled down a red accordion folder stuffed to the gills with paper. "One of my jobs here was to evaluate the effectiveness of health education programs in homeless shelters, group homes, things like that." She began to leaf through the pages, stopped, pulled out a page, and gave it to me. "Plus, I have a photographic memory. You don't remember that?"

"I don't have a photographic memory, so no, I don't remember." The form was a long xeroxed thing with various lines filled in with pen. The address, when I finally found it, matched the one John Myers had given me. Santa Ana Services. "Great, Brooke. Thanks."

I jotted down the phone number and name of the place. I handed Brooke her page and stood to leave.

"You don't want to call first?"

"No," I said, "I think I'll just drop in. I found it's better to catch them with their pants down."

"The mentally handicapped? Same old Nathaniel, still pursuing the low-hanging fruit."

"I did it in Atlanta." Chalk one up for me and the snappy comeback.

"Be nice. I was lonely and confused. The humidity made me horny."

"I could tell. Listen, I'll call you with what I find. Thanks."

"I'll come along."

"You don't need to."

"I know I don't. I'd like to."

I sighed. "Brooke, just lend me a parking permit."

CHAPTER 32

The afternoon commute was in full swing, and it took nearly forty minutes to cross town. Brooke sat in the passenger seat flipping the edge of the parking permit.

"How does it feel to be back?" she asked.

"I'm not back. I'm here for two days."

"That bad, hunh?"

"No. I love it here. Who could hate this—" I pointed to the scorching fireball of a sun. "I thought it was supposed to be cooler out here."

"It's a dry heat."

I looked at her. She was smiling. "Right," I said.

The glorious South Bay, ground zero for all the transgressions, mistakes, rejections, and whatever other depressing acts, impressions, and thoughts I'd had in my life. I looked up at the sky, cast gold by the sun. Another shitty day in paradise.

Brooke directed me to a residential area in the outer ring of the city. The neighborhood was a nice one, and we drove through a corridor of massive oaks and large Victorian houses. I pulled to the curb in front of Santa Ana Services, though there were no markers or signs to tell us this was the place. Generally, the natives are restless about having group homes in their midst, and advertising the presence of one invites too much attention and the occasional rock through the window.

"This is it," Brooke said.

I double-checked the address. It matched.

Though the car was parked in a perfectly legal spot, I held out my hand for the dearly won parking permit.

"You don't need this," Brooke said.

"Habit," I said. "Besides, it reminds me why I let you come along."

I took the laminated card from her and hung it from the rearview mirror.

A petite woman—early middle age, with a nice, round face—opened the door. She wore jeans and a sweatshirt with a sequined bear on it. Brooke and I introduced ourselves.

"I hope nothing's wrong." She had a slight accent. She introduced herself as Rosalinda Lopez, one of the staffers who worked at Santa Ana.

I told her we needed to talk to Gladys Thomas.

"Oh, Gladys. *Pobrecita . . .*" Rosalinda trailed off. "Is something wrong?"

"I hope not. To make sure, we need to speak with Ms. Thomas. Just ask her a few questions."

As if following a script written by her counterparts in Baltimore, Rosalinda began to get suspicious. "What do you need to ask her?"

"These are questions for Ms. Thomas. Since they involve medical issues, both what I'm going to ask and what she answers is confidential."

"What medical issues? I am a nurse, Doctor, and I know about the health of the residents—"

"Good. Tell me, is Gladys Thomas sick?"

Rosalinda paused, as if deciding whether to answer that one. "Not for a while, for six months, maybe."

"What was the illness six months ago?"

"Just a bad cold. She was in bed for—"

"Is she sexually active?"

A blush started at Rosalinda's neck. "No, I wouldn't think she is."

"I need to speak with her, Ms. Lopez."

"And I would like to know why."

We faced off for a moment—a little battle of will between Rosalinda and Nathaniel. Eventually, the nurse caved. "Come in. I'll get her."

She led us into a carpeted foyer, which gave out to a hallway flanked by a living room and a small office. I could smell dinner being cooked somewhere in back.

The place was nice. Really. Not as homey as Open Arms in Baltimore, but comfortable. Kind of like a grandmother's house, with its ticking clocks and oil paintings of fruit. It even had that musty sweet smell. As in Open Arms, Christian paintings and icons dotted the walls. Say what you want about hard-core Christians, but they sure care for a lot of people the rest of society would just as soon forget.

"Wait here, please." Rosalinda pointed to the living room.

"Again," I said, "because of the nature of the questions, is there a place I can speak with Gladys in private?"

"Wait here." She pointed to the other side of the hallway.

Brooke and I took our seats in the small office, which must have been the nerve center of Santa Ana: filing cabinets, psychology books, a computer sporting a screen saver that said *One Day at a Time* in gyrating 3-D letters.

"You're being kind of brusque with her, aren't you?" Brooke asked me.

"I've dealt with these people before."

" 'These people'? What does *that* mean?"

I didn't answer, because it probably didn't mean anything other than that I wanted to get the hell out of there, get back in the car, and get on a plane to the East Coast as fast as I could.

There was a heavy creaking on the steps.

*   *   *

Rosalinda and a woman I assumed to be Gladys Thomas stepped to the office doorway. Gladys was taller than Rosalinda, and she tried awkwardly and unsuccessfully to hide behind the shorter woman. Her head drooped and she sort of shuffled this way and that. Very shy, maybe.

Both Brooke and I stood.

"Gladys, this is—"

She'd obviously forgotten our names.

"I'm Dr. McCormick, and this is Dr. Michaels. We want to ask you a few questions."

Gladys didn't respond, just gave a big, world-weary sigh.

"Go on, honey. Sit in that chair. Answer the doctors' questions." Rosalinda pointed Gladys toward an old cloth-upholstered chair, then took a seat herself. She gave me a look and said, "He won't bite you, will you, Doctor?"

"I gave up biting years ago." I smiled, then realized no one else was smiling. I said, "No, Gladys, I don't bite. Neither does Dr. Michaels." I smiled again.

Reluctantly, Gladys Thomas slouched into the office.

Gladys was tall, five eleven maybe, which probably accounted for her stoop. I'd put her at twenty-seven or twenty-eight. Dark hair, blue eyes. She was pretty. Very pretty, actually, except for the hunch and the facial slackness. I could see why Douglas Buchanan would have been interested.

I looked at Rosalinda, hoping she'd get the hint and leave. She didn't. "You don't mind if I stay," she said.

"Yes—"

Brooke cut in. "In our experience these interviews go much better without family or friends around. If there's a problem, we'll be sure to come get you, Nurse Lopez."

Rosalinda glared, then stood. "I'll be across the hall in the living room if you need me." *Good work, Brooke.*

Gladys Thomas stared at the floor and heaved another sigh. I realized then what had set me off when she walked into the room—the slow, lugubrious movements, the frown. I'd seen a lot of this through my med school rotations and through residency. Simply put, the woman was depressed.

Gladys Thomas sighed again. God, she really did look miserable.

She snuck a look at me, and our eyes met.

"Is something wrong, Gladys?" I asked.

"Hunh? No."

"You seem upset."

She fidgeted. "No."

I scrawled in my notebook, just lines to act like I was writing. I watched Gladys watch my hand.

"You know, you can tell us if anything is wrong. We're doctors. We help people."

Gladys said nothing, just frowned and didn't meet my eyes. Brooke frowned, too, though for different reasons. She said, "It's okay, honey. You can tell us."

Gladys scuffed her feet.

"Gladys," I said. "Do you have a telephone? A cellular phone that you carry with you?"

Her eyes cut to the ground and she said, "No."

"Do you have a telephone like this one?" I pulled the phone from my pocket and held it for Gladys to see. She shook her head.

"Do you know someone named Douglas Buchanan?"

She looked quickly from the floor to me, then back to the floor.

"Douglas Buchanan," I said again.

"I don't know him."

"I think you might know Douglas."

"I don't."

"You left a message on his telephone, Gladys."

She began to cry softly.

"Gladys, how did you know Douglas?" She was quiet except for the weeping. "Gladys, who is Casey?" She turned away from me and brought her knees up into the chair. The chair was too small to hold all of her, so the legs kept slipping out and she kept retracting them.

"Who is Casey?"

I glanced at Brooke, who shot me a look. She was getting the same vibe I was: this girl was holding a lot inside.

"Who is Casey?" I said again.

Gladys looked quickly at me, then back to the floor.

"Gladys, that's good. Look at me. Are Casey and Douglas Buchanan the same person?"

Nothing.

"Have you ever been to Baltimore? It's a city on the East Coast. Gladys, have you ever been there?"

Nothing.

I reached into my folder and pulled out the picture of Douglas Buchanan—the big black-and-white reproduction that must have been a copy of a copy of something the Baltimore PD got from Jefferson's files. I stood and held the photo in front of Gladys.

"Do you know this person?"

She looked at the picture for a beat, then snatched it from me. Lightly, she ran her fingers across the glossy paper.

"That's Douglas," I said. "You know him, don't you?"

Recovering quickly, she said, "I don't know him." But she didn't hand the picture back.

"He's dead. The man in the picture is dead."

For Gladys Thomas, this was the bomb drop. My words seemed to stun her; her bottom lip quivered.

"He died two days ago." I let that sink in. "He's dead. Do you know what dead is? He's gone. He's never coming back." I don't think Gladys was listening to me; she just sat there with her mouth open.

Brooke touched my arm. "Dr. McCormick—"

I said again, "He's dead, Gladys."

Something in her eyes flickered, and she pulled the picture to her lips and began to sob. "No!"

"Yes."

Brooke gave me a hard look.

So I let Gladys sob for a moment, then said, "He was hurt, and we want to find who hurt him. We need your help."

Mucus and tears flowed over her face, spattering the picture, which was now pressed to her chest and neck. "I love you. I love you," she sobbed. "Casey, Casey, Casey."

I waited for the sobs to subside. They didn't. Brooke stood up and put her arms around Gladys, who sank into them; the sobs turned to a wail.

"Shhhh," Brooke said. Gladys, still gripping the picture, threw her arms around Brooke. I watched, touched. Some primal female bond cutting across IQ points. Gladys howled.

The door swung open. "Oh my God," Rosalinda said. "What are you doing?" she shouted.

"It's okay," I said.

"It is certainly *not* okay." Another scream ripped from Gladys's lungs. "You have to leave," Rosalinda said. "Go. Now. Go!"

"We need to finish this," I said as Brooke rocked Gladys, trying to console the inconsolable.

"You cannot come in here and upset—"

"Frankly, I can." I walked to the door of the office. Rosalinda shot a look toward Gladys and Brooke, seemed to size up the situation, and decided to leave her charge in the hands of the nice doctor. She turned toward me.

I opened the door to the hallway and heard a shuffling of feet moving toward the back of the house. So much for confidentiality.

After the door to the office was closed, Rosalinda asked, "What?"

"As I said, I work for the Centers for Disease Control—"

"I know that—"

"We believe that Gladys was involved somehow with a man in Baltimore who may have been sick with a disease. A very bad disease. The federal government—me—wouldn't be involved if we weren't very concerned about this. We're worried that he may have transmitted the disease—"

"What do you mean, she was *involved* with this man?"

"Romantically."

"Who is he?"

"All we know is that he was from Pennsylvania, lived in Baltimore, and was murdered this week."

"What?" Rosalinda's face froze, and she said something in Spanish. Then she recovered, and began to shake her head. "Doctor, I don't care about a murdered man in Baltimore. I care about these girls. And that one in there"—she stabbed her finger toward the office—"she's never been outside of the Bay Area, much less California. Baltimore?"

"We don't know how she's involved, but we called her from back east, and it sounded as if she knew him."

"It could have just been a mistake. You could have had the wrong number—"

"She's still clutching the picture of him. Look, Ms. Lopez, this disease is dangerous. We wouldn't be here if it weren't. Two people are dead from it already. All of the sick people so far have been mentally handicapped, and most have had a connection somehow with this man. We're worried that Gladys might be sick, and that whatever disease is in Baltimore might be here."

"I don't believe this."

"Believe it," I told her. "What is she so upset about?"

"What do you mean?"

"She's walking around like the living dead. How long has she been like that?"

"What? I don't know. A few days, maybe."

"All right, then. This guy back east was killed a few days ago." I let Rosalinda process that. "Look, she was upset her boyfriend wasn't calling her back. Now she's upset that he's dead."

Rosalinda's mouth moved, but nothing emerged. At the top of the stairs, a huddle of concerned faces were looking down at us, doing a poor job of hiding around a corner. "God forbid what's killing those girls in Baltimore is working its way through here," I told Rosalinda. "Or is threatening to. We really could use your help."

"I thought you needed this to be confidential."

"Well, you know what?" I looked at the faces at the top of the stairs. "I think it's beyond that now."

CHAPTER 33

After the worst of Gladys's grief had burned itself out, the four of us sat in the living room, cups of tea in front of us on a low table.

Rosalinda was eyeing the wet photo of Douglas Buchanan, laid out next to her teacup. I asked her, "Do you recognize him?"

The way she looked at it, I thought she was going to tell me she knew him, that he'd been around Santa Ana many times before. Instead, she surprised me. "No," she said.

"Are you sure?"

"Yes, I'm sure."

"You're positive—"

"I said I don't know who he is, Doctor."

I pointed to the picture. "Gladys, what's this man's name?"

Gladys shifted her puffy eyes to the photo. "Casey," she said.

Rosalinda said, "She may be confused about who—"

"Casey," Gladys said.

Rosalinda pursed her lips.

"Do you know his last name?" I asked Gladys.

She looked at me as if she didn't understand.

"Casey who?" I said.

Gladys shook her head.

"How do you know him?"

"He was my husband."

Glances shot between Brooke and me. Rosalinda's face was stony.

"You were married to him?"

"He said we would get married. When he came back."

"When he came back from where?"

"He was going to a place near New York. Where the planes crashed."

"Did he say he was going to Baltimore?"

"I don't know. I love him." She turned on the faucet and began to weep again.

I asked, "Did you ever have sex with Casey?"

Rosalinda glowered at me. Perhaps I was too blunt, but it did shock Gladys out of her crying. Way to go for the insensitive male. John Myers would have been proud, I think.

"No. I loved him. We were getting married."

I was on a roll, so I fired again. "Did Casey ever live here?"

"No. He lived in another place."

"Did he live here in San Jose?"

"He lived somewhere else."

"Did he live in this city?"

Gladys looked confused.

"He may have lived somewhere else in the area," Rosalinda told me. " 'Here' means this house, I think."

"But you never saw him?" I asked her.

"No," she said. Sheepishly, it seemed to me.

Rosalinda seemed to be doing a fine job of interpreting what Gladys told us or didn't tell us, depending. I said to her, "Ask her when Casey left."

"A long time ago," Gladys said.

I asked, "Where did you get the telephone?"

Rosalinda answered, "Her parents got her the phone."

"Ask her," I said.

"Honey, who gave you your telephone, the one you carry with you?"

"Mom and Dad."

Rosalinda gave me a look that said "See?"

"Then why was the billing address here?" I got no response from either woman. "Would Gladys's parents trust her to pay for the phone bill on her own?"

Both Gladys and Rosalinda stayed quiet. The two had to be in cahoots somehow. Perhaps Rosalinda took care of the bills.

"Why'd they cut off the service? The service to the telephone was cut off two days ago. Why?"

Gladys stole a glance at Rosalinda. Scratch that; she was staring full-bore at the nurse, as if pleading for help. Brooke cut in. "Gladys, I'm going to ask your parents about the telephone. I want to know why they stopped service on the phone."

Gladys's eyes widened. "No. No! Don't tell!"

Good going, Brooke, I thought. I looked at her. She was frowning. No doubt she was learning what I'd learned recently myself: People lie, and not just about their health habits, not just about sex and drugs, not just about how many drinks per week they ingest. They lie about big things and small things. They lie if they're smart, they lie if they're slow.

"Did you have anything to do with paying for the cellular phone?" I asked Rosalinda.

"No."

"Did you ever see a bill?"

"No! Doctor, you are not the police, right?"

"I am not the police. I told you in the hallway what I'm doing." And: *I don't believe you for one moment about not seeing a bill, Nurse.* "Gladys, I'm going to ask you a question, and it's very important that you tell me the truth. Did Casey get the telephone for you?"

"I-I love him so much," Gladys stammered. Her face contorted, her mouth pulling open like the figure from Munch's *Scream.* Spittle dribbled down her chin. She made no sound.

Brooke tried. "Gladys, please tell us: Did Casey get the phone for you so that you two could talk to each other?"

But she fared about as well as I had; Gladys closed her mouth and began to sob again. The interview was over—I could see that as plain as the tears on Gladys Thomas's bewildered face and the worried-angry look on Rosalinda Lopez's.

We made an appointment for eight the next morning and left.

CHAPTER 34

Brooke and I walked to the car. The sun was low over the mountains, the sky painted an imperial purple. Pretty, really, despite the circumstances.

Brooke interrupted my California dreamin'. "They're lying, aren't they? They're both lying."

"That's what I think."

"Why?"

"Why is that what I think?"

"Come on, Nathaniel. Why are they lying?"

I slipped into the driver's seat and started the engine. "If I knew that, I'd be on a plane tonight."

My stomach growled loud enough that Brooke looked over. I realized I hadn't had anything to eat since I'd forced down a club sandwich on the flight.

"I'll drop you downtown. Then I need to grab some food and think these things out."

Brooke said brightly, "Thanks, Nathaniel, I'd love to have dinner with you."

"You don't need to get home to your husband?"

"No," she said simply. *Interesting,* I thought, but I didn't press. She added, "There's a great Japanese place near work."

We rode in relative silence for a while, only Brooke's directions— "Left here," "Right at the next block"—interrupting.

Finally, Brooke said, "Maybe he *was* in love with her, even though he was sleeping with all these other women. That would account for the phone and might even account for why they hadn't slept together."

"Gladys never actually said they didn't sleep together. But yes, I was thinking the same thing. It's like he got his rocks off with all these women in Baltimore but strung the good girl along in California. Wanted to have his cake and eat it, too." I thought for a second. "I don't like it."

"What?"

"The lies here. Why are Gladys *and* Rosalinda lying? What's in it for them? What's in it for Rosalinda?"

"Maybe having a relationship like this is against the house rules. Maybe Rosalinda knew about Douglas and Gladys. If that's the case, then she'd want to keep it quiet, right? To save her own skin."

"Maybe. I'll ask about that tomorrow." But there was more at work than just keeping an illicit affair under the rug; I was sure of that. Well, I wasn't sure, but I had a feeling about it.

"Why do you think Casey got her the phone?" Brooke asked.

"So they could talk, keep the lovers' lines of communication open."

"No. Why do you think it was Casey who got her the phone and not someone else?"

"Like I said, it was for long-distance pillow talk. Remember, the phone was immediately cut off after the Baltimore police made contact. It was almost as if they had a contingency plan. You know, 'If anyone ever gets this number, make sure you cut off the phone service.' "

"And you think Gladys could have done that?"

"I don't know. But I think Gladys could have told Rosalinda about it, and *she* might have cut it off. She knew about the phone; that was for sure."

"But why would Casey go through all the trouble of getting her the phone? Why risk sending money to Gladys and have her pay for the phone?"

"Maybe he was being watched."

"By who?"

I shrugged.

"We'll have to press her on that tomorrow." Brooke stared out through the windshield. "I'll take her aside and try—"

"Brooke—"

"—to work it out of her. I think we had something of a connection—"

"Brooke," I said more sharply. She looked at me. "I don't need any help with this investigation. Thanks for coming today, but I'm the one who's been assigned here."

She frowned and sat back in the seat. "But you're here at the invitation of the Santa Clara Department of Health. That's who invited you. That's who *I* work for."

"So?"

"So I'm running a couple of TB and HIV surveillance programs, but they're running themselves. And I can help you."

"But like you said, you don't work for CDC anymore—"

"So?"

"So this isn't your job. Besides, at CDC you were, what? Epidemiology Division? This is a Special Pathogens investigation—"

"Oh, don't get all departmental and bureaucratic on me."

"Seriously. I'm here for a few days to wrap this up and get the hell back east. It's a dead end anyway. I'll be done by tomorrow morning at eleven."

"What about the phone and the secret affair? What about 'I don't like the lies'?"

"What about it? They had a relationship. They got a phone, and now Gladys and her nurse are lying about it. A little weird, sure, but I'm convinced it's irrelevant to what's happening in Baltimore."

"No, you're not."

"Yes, I am. This guy—Casey or Douglas or whoever—was probably killed by the brother of someone he poked. He was a sexual predator, remember? He pissed people off."

"You're not convinced this is irrelevant. You're just trying to get rid of me."

"You're right, Brooke. And just because we slept together half a dozen times means you've got the window to my soul."

She grinned at me. "That's right," she said, and kept on smiling.

<hr/>

CHAPTER 35

By the end of the sushi dinner, I was exhausted—loaded with fish and a beer, jet-lagged and coming off a week's insomnia—and Brooke had worn me down. Despite my best efforts, we were talking about Douglas/Casey and Gladys Thomas again.

"Why did she say New York?" Brooke asked.

"Because New York is famous, Baltimore's not. Maybe that's all she could remember. Maybe that's what Douglas said—Casey. He was from York, PA, after all. Maybe she got confused."

"I think this is all very strange. And the way she said 'New York, where the planes crashed,' that was like adding a time stamp to it. It's as if when she learned about the city, at least when it was important to her, New York was still identified by nine-eleven. It seems to say that Douglas Buchanan became affiliated with New York sometime *after* the attacks."

I finished off my beer. "There are too many jumps between York and New York and 'where the planes crashed.' It didn't seem like he was much of a presence here recently." I thought for a moment. "A situation like this would make it easy for him to keep two separate lives."

"You said his parents died. Maybe that's where he got the money for phones and for traveling."

"And maybe that's for the police to figure out. Look, we're getting off track here. All we need to deal with is whether she banged Casey or not. And, if she did, whether she's hiding some nasty bug." I signaled the waiter for the check.

"Where are you staying?" Brooke asked.

"I'll find a motel out by the airport."

"I have an extra bedroom. You're welcome to—"

"A motel is fine. Besides, what would hubby say?"

"He wouldn't say anything."

"You have him that whipped, hunh?"

"For that to happen, he'd have to exist."

I had the awful feeling of having just jammed my foot deep into my mouth. "He's not dead, is he?"

She laughed. "Not remotely. Last I heard, he was balling one of his graduate students. The perks of being a professor, I guess."

The check came and we both reached. I snatched it away from her. She stared at me. I asked, "Did you just say *balling*?"

"I did."

"The vocabulary of a liberated woman."

"Learn to deal with it, Dr. McCormick." She finished off her beer. "You get dinner, I'll provide the lodging."

The waiter returned with a credit card slip, which I signed. I gave the guy a twenty-five-percent tip, courtesy of the U.S. taxpayer.

"We called off the engagement six months ago," Brooke said.

It took me a second to pick up the thread of conversation. When I did, I said, "I plead innocent."

"You shouldn't. You're a big reason why it didn't work."

"Me?"

"You were so much of a man in bed, Nathaniel, I could never be satisfied by anyone else." I was being made fun of, and I felt myself beginning to blush. "After I finished that first year in Atlanta, I took the assignment at the state department of health in San Francisco to be with Jeff, stayed there for a few months before leaving EIS and coming down to Santa Clara. He and I tried to make it work for a while. Boy, did we try. But really, how could I think of getting married when I'm away from this guy for three months and can't keep my hands out of another man's pants? It told me it just wasn't right."

"Or that you're a nympho."

She didn't seem to like that one—I guess, in the case of broken engagements, you could dish it out and not take it—and excused herself to the bathroom. There went my invitation to stay the night.

"The bed is just a futon and full of cat hair," she said when she returned. "I hope you don't mind."

I did, in fact, mind the cat hair. But all things considered, accepting a little kindness from Brooke Michaels seemed like just the right thing to do.

CHAPTER 36

Brooke's apartment was a nice two-bedroom affair that looked like it had a lot of light in the daytime. Plants everywhere. A cat—Buddy was his name—lounged on a chair. On the walls, there were a few Ansel Adams prints, pictures of Brooke on mountaintops, on a boat in scuba regalia, in a forest, lugging an immense backpack. A road bicycle hung from hooks on one wall; below it rested a mountain bike.

Brooke, who'd called in to her office to check messages, scrawled notes onto a pad. When she finished, I pointed to the bikes.

"I saw this piece at the MoMA once. I think it was called *Bikes in Repose*. How'd you afford it on your salary?"

"Daddy owns an oil company. He bought it for his princess." She smiled, but the smile faded to a look I didn't like.

"What? Your dad doesn't really own an oil company?"

"Tim Lancaster left me a message. He was making sure you arrived safely."

"That's it?"

"And he said to keep an eye on things, let him know if there are any problems."

So, Tim was enlisting Dr. Michaels to spy on me. Fantastic. "Do you have any beer?" I asked.

"Help yourself."

I pulled a bottle out of the refrigerator, twisted the cap, swallowed a gulp. I said, "You don't work for EIS anymore. Tim's not your boss. He never was your boss."

"No."

"So you don't owe him anything."

"No, I don't. But it's not good politics, Nathaniel."

"You gotta be kidding me. You're going to give him updates on me?"

"No. But it does put me in an awkward position."

"Why? Just tell him everything is terrific. Tell him we discovered the cure to AIDS written on a napkin under Gladys Thomas's pillow."

"Don't worry," she said. I drained half my beer before she added, "It was a little slimy of him to ask me to keep tabs on you."

"Tim is slimy. He's not actually human, you know; he's a filovirus. That's why he does so well in Special Pathogens."

She laughed.

"Okay, so maybe I am on his shit list," I said.

"No. You? I thought you were next in line for director."

Everyone's a comedian.

"Anyway," she said, "I'll cover for you, Nathaniel. You know I will."

I pulled a long draft of beer. "I don't need that."

Brooke smiled and said nothing.

Brooke retired and I, despite a grinding exhaustion, hopped on the computer in Brooke's office/guest room and checked my e-mail. A message from Tim, asking me how things were going. After his call to Brooke, I figured he didn't need to know how things were going, so I deleted the message without responding. Not good politics, maybe, but good for my soul.

I cruised around the Web for a while, checking the newspapers for what they were saying about the outbreak in Baltimore. Nothing much. The baseball season was halfway over, and a bomb had just macerated a dozen people in Jerusalem, so the sick retarded folks were squeezed down to a few lines. On the whole, this wasn't a bad thing.

On a whim, I went to a national phone directory site and typed in *Alaine Chen* with the Northern California town I last knew her to inhabit. Okay, it wasn't really a whim; I'd been thinking about doing it all day. Anyway, I got no hits. So I went to the Web site for my old university and clicked on the "Search for People" tab. I entered her name in the field and . . . eureka, I got a hit: campus address, with home and campus phone numbers.

This was the type of information I didn't need. More exactly, the emotions it dredged up were the type I didn't need.

I logged out of my account and shut off the computer without writing the numbers down. But I remembered them. Unlike Brooke Michaels, I sure as hell don't have a photographic memory, not for anything useful, anyway. But for numbers of old girlfriends who can do little more than torture me, I'm an ace.

My cell phone sat next to the computer with its charging cord snaking like a flagellum from its rear end. It was after eleven o'clock, two a.m. Eastern time, and I should have been tired enough to fall asleep standing upright. That is, if I didn't have those ten digits ricocheting around in my brain, knocking other thoughts out of the way, chipping away at the wall between me and a flood of painful memories.

And damn it if that wall didn't collapse.

I pictured her face, her eyes drilling into me across a restaurant table, her foot snaking up my leg underneath. I remembered the way she sometimes held my hand, squeezing so hard it felt like we'd fused. Her laughing at my stupid jokes. The morning she brought breakfast to my apartment at five a.m., before having to be at the hospital at six to pre-round. I was dull with sleep, balancing the plate on my bed, when I found the note cooked into the salmon-and-goat-cheese omelet. *I love you,* it said in blurred blue pen, the first time either of us ever spoke or wrote those words to each other. . . .

I picked up the cell and, without thinking, dialed.

Somewhere around the third ring, I got an inkling of how crazy it was, what I was doing. Then, when the female voice I knew so well said "Hello," I knew it was insane. I hit End on the cell.

I lay on my back on the stiff futon, running that word—*hello*—over and over in my head.

How long had it been since she'd said that to me? When was the last time I'd heard that voice?

I remember the first time I heard it, or at least the first time I heard it when it wasn't answering some question about the Krebs Cycle or the pathogenicity of epidermolysis bullosa in a crowded lecture hall, the first time I heard her say my name. We were at some medical school function, a party at a bowling alley. She was slightly drunk, I was really drunk, and we bowled in adjacent lanes. I don't remember exactly what was first said, but I think it had something to do with her dynamite bowling shoes. Before I knew it, we were talking, an actual conversation about how it was possible for someone—me—to gutter-ball six times in a row. The repartee lasted for forty glorious seconds or so, before I realized I was talking to the unapproachable Alaine Chen. Then adrenaline dumped into my system, cutting through the beer, drying out my mouth, shooting my blood pressure up to the high triple digits, fogging my thoughts, slaying my wit. I needed to escape but, somehow, managed to ask her to dinner before I did.

She said, "Sure, Nathaniel."

That night, despite the alcohol, I tried to figure out why. Why she said "Sure." Why she would go for a guy from central Pennsylvania who had never been out of the country, who was autodidact enough to have read Goethe but pronounced the name as if it rhymed with "growth," who drove a twenty-year-old car so pocked with Bondo it looked like it had come straight from a leper colony. She drove a Mercedes, had gone to Yale, had studied for a year in Paris. So why the hell did she say "Sure"? Was she slumming? We were too country boy/city girl. Too state school/Ivy League. Too white/Asian. Choose your opposites.

I expected it to end even before that first date, for her to call me and beg off with some excuse about having to plant-sit for a friend or something. But she didn't beg off, at least not for a couple of years. By then I was in too deep. And how I got in too deep with someone who, despite the good façade, turned out to be as shallow, as comfort- and status-obsessed as Alaine Chen, I don't know.

Actually, I do know, since I was focused on some of the same things for a while. But why I was fixating on her nearly a decade after our parting . . . well, chalk it up to being back in fucking California.

Really, this wasn't the best use of my time. I should have been working the angles of Douglas-cum-Casey and figuring a strategy for when I talked with Gladys Thomas and Rosalinda Lopez in the morning. But I was tired and lonely and heartsick, and that little word seemed to offer just enough comfort to get me to sleep. Hello, hello, hello.

CHAPTER 37

I was awake at dawn, draining fluid from my eyes and nose. The cat's dander had worked its magic, and the little parasite itself was curled on my pants, which I'd left on the floor. I hissed at the thing and it skittered away through a crack in the doorway.

Needless to say, I hadn't slept well, though if it was because of the cat or dreams of Alaine, I couldn't be sure. Thankfully, the cat was gone and Alaine was just a dull pulse in the background.

I grabbed the pants, trying to shake off whatever feline detritus still clung to the fabric, and pulled them on. Then I went into the living room to make some telephone calls. Brooke's apartment seemed to be located in the only wireless hole in all Silicon Valley, so I had to sit in the chair in front of the computer to connect my calls. If I shifted ten inches, I dropped the call. I'd dropped one to John Myers already.

"John, sorry about that," I said once I got him back on the line.

"You on a cell?"

"Yeah."

"Those things sure aren't ready for prime time. And what's wrong with your voice? Sounds like you got a mother of a cold."

"Must be the connection. So, anyway, it seems our guy went by Casey for his girlfriend out here—"

"Makes sense."

"Makes sense?"

"I'll get to it in a second. Go on."

I got back into the story. "So he had some connection—a significant connection—to California, which would explain the San Fran posters in his room."

"Okay," Myers said.

"You should check how much money his parents left him. The guy had to have some funds to keep that room at Baltimore Haven and to jet-set with his girlfriend out here. Takes money to lead a double life."

"He visited her out there? When?"

"I don't know, actually. Though I suspect he wasn't a stranger here. The nurse at Gladys Thomas's home was holding back, but I'm sure she recognized him." I waited for Myers to say something. He didn't, so I asked, "What were you going to tell me?"

"We talked to Jefferson yesterday. The guy's a fucking pain in the ass. We might actually have to indict him, if you can believe it. Anyway, he was real concerned about where you were."

"Why?"

"We don't know. We assumed he wanted to make sure you actually left town. You got under his skin."

"Like scabies."

"What?"

"Nothing. Bad joke. So, you told him where I was?"

"Sure."

"Did he shout for joy?"

"No. Was as pissed off as before. Anyway, we tried to get the word on why Mr. Buchanan was treated like royalty, and he said he didn't know anything about it. He gave us his admissions papers and some other shit that didn't produce nada."

"When was his admission?"

"December '97. Just after his mom died."

"So, you got nothing? I give you all this great shit, John, and you give me squat?"

"I thought you were a doctor, Doctor. You wanna play detective? You trying to step on my turf?"

"I'm trying to stop an epidemic."

I heard him chuckle. "Don't get your panties in a bunch. You never asked why we think we might be able to indict Jefferson."

"Okay, John, why do you think you might be able to indict Dr. Jefferson?"

"Fraud."

"Great. We knew the guy was doing something fishy. How does that help me?"

"Jefferson was taking state money for a dead man. It seems your friend Douglas died—"

"I know. I saw the body, remember?"

"Twice."

Neither of us spoke for a few seconds. Finally, Myers said, "I had a guy I know up in PA do some digging for me. The deceased is from there, right? And I thought some poking around might turn something up. Well, it did. Let's see: Douglas Buchanan died October 1998. Cause: congestive heart failure."

My head felt full; it was having trouble digesting what the detective was saying. "So, what you're saying is that Douglas Buchanan—or who we thought was Douglas Buchanan—"

"—wasn't him. Looks like your friend Casey decided to steal a dead man's identity."

"That he picked up sometime after '98."

"That's what it looks like."

I was thinking fast, trying to put the pieces together. "There are a couple of possibilities here," I said.

"Right," Myers replied. I had the feeling he'd already worked the possibilities out but was going to let me discover them for myself.

"Casey could be from back east, could have taken Douglas Buchanan's identity, then traveled out here and met Gladys Thomas."

"Or she could have met him on the East Coast."

"Could be, but I don't think so. She talked about him leaving—she said that, 'leaving'—so I assume he was out here for at least some time. He had to be here for him to leave here."

"Okay."

"Or he could have lived in California, met Gladys, started this affair, then gone east." There was silence on the phone. "Or," I said, "it could be none of the above."

"Now you're talking," Myers said, laughing.

"In any case, we got some sketchy information that indicates Casey didn't go east until about a year ago."

"We have quite a gap, then. Jefferson's records say he's been there since '97."

"Did you check with the state? Make sure they've been making payments since then?"

"Yeah. This is the basis for the fraud case. Payments from the state have been continuous since '97."

"So . . ." I said.

"So, Jefferson was taking payments from Social Services for a guy who died out of state in 1998. Sometime between October of 1998 and earlier this year, your friend Casey came in and took over the spot."

If Jefferson was trying to . . . well, maximize profits, he probably would have double-billed the state for both the dead Buchanan and the new arrival. Unless maximizing income wasn't the only reason.

I said, "This would be a pretty convenient arrangement if you were trying to hide out."

"What do you mean?"

"If Casey was running from something or someone, then taking over Douglas Buchanan's identity would be a pretty easy way to escape, right? Who could trace it? The parents are dead; Buchanan died out of state."

"Good. The only way to trace it would be to find the death certificate."

"Which you did."

"Right. And only because we were looking."

Both of us took a moment to process the information. Casey's death was looking less and less like the result of some pissed-off relative taking revenge. Something bigger was at work here.

"What can you do to make Jefferson talk?" I asked.

"I got the rubber hoses and the thumbscrews ready."

"That's how they do it in Baltimore?"

"I wish. The guy's talking through his lawyer. Not a good sign, for him or for us."

I asked Myers to keep the information about Douglas Buchanan's two deaths to himself. I was off my turf here. This was more detective work, less epidemiology. But I was convinced this detective work might lead us to the cause of our disease. I was convinced that I knew more of the angles than anyone else and was, at that point, the best man for the job. And I sure as hell didn't need Tim Lancaster sticking his nose into my business.

Myers was reluctant to stay mum at first—"I don't like stopping information flow in an investigation," he said—but eventually gave in.

"Work fast" were the last words I heard before the line went dead.

"Good," I said aloud, my arms crossed in front of me, the cell phone still in my hand. "Good, good, good."

But apart from having some freedom from Tim Lancaster, things were not good. In fact, they were very bad. Sinister clouds were gathering; who or what was behind them, I didn't know. What I did know was that they stretched across the country, from California to Maryland and God only knew where else.

I sat in the chair, brooding, until there was a knock at the door. "Come in," I said.

Brooke stood there, framed in the doorway, a big Penn T-shirt dropping to the tops of her thighs, revealing quite a lot of those well-formed legs. I was too agitated to take any pleasure in the eyeful.

"Breakfast?" she asked.

Again, I looked at my watch. "I gotta go."

"It's not even seven."

"It's late." I stood. "And I have to talk to Gladys Thomas."

Brooke turned and walked to her bedroom. Before she was out of earshot, she said, "*We,* Dr. McCormick. *We* have to talk with her."

CHAPTER 38

We didn't leave right away for Santa Ana, Gladys Thomas's home. I wanted to shower and wash off the cat and lack of sleep. Feeling somewhat more human, I was still sneezing as I pulled on clean underwear and soiled trousers.

When I walked into the living room, Brooke asked, "You're not allergic to my cat, are you?"

"That little bastard? No way. I think I'm allergic to you."

"Funny. I'm still coming with you."

And she did. Actually, I went with her, since we took her car instead of my Buick rental. We walked to a line of cars under an awning, and Brooke made for a red BMW convertible. I said, "Daddy?"

Brooke unlocked the door, my side first, and walked to the driver's side.

"No. Daddy is actually a high school teacher in Virginia. This is from the bank." After a moment, she said, "It's three years old, okay?"

"I didn't say anything."

She looked at me over the cloth roof, biting her lip just a little.

Then she climbed into the car, hit a button on the console, and the roof folded into the back. We drove.

As we pulled into traffic, Brooke said, "I got it for a song. The car. Some business student at the university was leaving for a job in Tokyo and had to get rid of it in a hurry."

"Good for you."

"Look, I need to drive. I'm in California."

"I wholly agree."

"And I've been through four years of med school, four years of residency. Eight years of hell. I deserve a decent car."

"You do."

She slammed into third gear. "Oh, stop with the holier-than-thou attitude."

"Brooke, you deserve this car."

"What kind of car do you drive?" she demanded furiously.

"1986 Corolla—"

"Jesus Christ, Nathaniel. You wear hair shirts, too? Jesus."

"It's a dependable car."

"I'm sure it is."

"I just don't care that much about cars is all."

She drove in silence. Then she said, "I'm selling this next week."

"Really?"

"No, but you're a bastard for making me feel guilty about it."

Whether I liked it or not, Brooke Michaels was getting on my good side, which, to tell the truth, was not a place I was prepared for her to be. It was . . . well, let's just say that Alaine Chen was not the only emotional quagmire in Northern California. Maybe the stickiest and deepest, but not the only one.

Anyway, I was feeling pretty kindly toward Brooke. And though *partner* would be too strong a word, I brought her a little more into the fold by telling her what John Myers had told me earlier that morning about Douglas Buchanan.

"It's really weird, Nathaniel."

"I think so, too."

But before we could mine the hows and whats of Buchanan's double demise, we were turning onto the block for Santa Ana.

"Uh-oh," Brooke said. She was looking forward; I followed her gaze.

Ahead of us, parked in front of the home, facing traffic, was a police slickback, unmarked, the emergency light still sitting on the dash. Behind it was a black-and-white cruiser.

As we walked toward the front door of Santa Ana, it passed through my mind that John Myers might have called his counterparts in the San Jose PD to help him out. The thought made me furious. Not only did it mean we'd have the police out here mucking things up, it meant Detective Myers didn't trust me worth a damn.

Was Myers that fast? Were the cops already talking to Gladys Thomas?

I checked my watch. *Damn it,* I thought, *I shouldn't have taken the time for a shower.*

At the door, after ringing the bell, Brooke looked at me and asked, "What do you think—"

The door swung open, and a mountain of uniformed cop stood in front of us.

"What's going on here?" I asked.

I suppose he thought he ought to be asking the questions, so he tried to stare me down for a few seconds—which he did pretty well—before asking, "Who are you?"

I sighed and fished my ID out of my pocket. Brooke did the same. He looked at them. "Thought you were reporters," he said. "Don't know why you'd be interested in this."

"We're not reporters and we are interested."

"You're doctors."

Great work, Sherlock. "Yes," I said. "We're here to speak with Gladys Thomas."

The cop looked up at mention of the name and handed back our IDs. "Can't do that."

"This is part of a public health investigation, Officer," Brooke said.

The cop crossed his arms and looked at Brooke, then at me. "You can't talk to her because she's dead."

CHAPTER 39

I couldn't put together a thought. Nor, evidently, could Brooke. Eventually, I managed to ask, stupidly, "When?"

"Last night or this morning."

I tried to push past the officer. "Hold on there," he said, easily blocking the way. "You can't go back there. It's a crime scene."

"I'm a doctor. We're both doctors."

"Unless you're the coroner, she don't need you anymore."

"Look," I said desperately. "We need to talk to someone—"

"You are."

"Jesus Christ—"

We stood there for a moment, facing off. Two servants of the public involved in a little turf war. Perhaps the warmth enjoyed between cops and public health was an East Coast thing. I looked over at Brooke. She was pulling out a pad and a pen.

I said, "Officer, we're concerned that Ms. Thomas may have had some information concerning a public health emergency."

"Like I said, Ms. Thomas is not going to be able to help you."

"Who's investigating the case?" I asked.

"The San Jose Police Department. What are you doing?" the cop asked Brooke.

"Taking down your badge number. I'm with the Santa Clara Public Health Department, Officer"—she looked pointedly at the name badge and wrote down the name—"Sutter, and I think they might be interested—"

"Okay, okay," he said. "I don't give a rat's ass. The lady is dead. She's not going to be able to tell you anything."

We moved inside. He called after us, "They're in the back, in the garage. The detective's name is Walker."

Out of earshot of the cop, I said to Brooke, "You really charmed him."

"The sensitivity training paid off," she said flatly.

As we walked into the hallway, past the small office, I apologized silently to John Myers for doubting his motives. The events of the last week were getting to me, and my paranoia was revved up. Not a bad thing, on balance, as long as I kept it in check.

Voices drifted down the hallway. To our left, in the living room, there was a gaggle of eight or so women, huddled on couches. Two staff members there: one talking to the group, the other—Rosalinda—trying to console a seemingly inconsolable woman. She glowered at me as I walked by.

The hallway ended in a swinging door. I pushed through it to a modest kitchen backed by a paned-glass door. Through the glass, I could see an outbuilding, a garage perhaps, and a person standing in an open doorway. Brooke and I walked outside and down the wooden steps to a small yard. The person in the door—a tall black woman, tightly braided hair—had her back toward us, looking into the garage. She was taking notes.

I said, "Detective Walker?"

She turned. "Yes?" She eyed us, chewing on a piece of gum. "Who are you?"

We pulled out our IDs.

Walker looked at them briefly. "What are you doing here?" she asked.

"Gladys Thomas was part of an investigation we're working on." I explained the outbreak in Baltimore and Gladys Thomas's possible connection to an infected individual. Walker took in the information silently and made a couple of notes in her notebook. After I finished my spiel, I asked Walker what had happened.

"Cut-and-dry," she said, grinding away at the gum. "At least for the time being it is. We got a call this morning around seven. Seems Ms. Thomas went out last evening. Nobody knew she was gone except for her roommate, but . . ."

"What?" I asked.

"The roommate. A piece of work. Anyway, this morning the roommate finally decided to raise the alarm. Staff gets involved and looks all over the house. They called the local ERs and got nothing. Eventually, someone thought to check the garage." She motioned for us to follow her. "Just inside the doorway, please. This scene has been contaminated enough."

Brooke shuffled into the garage in front of me and stopped abruptly. I heard her gasp.

I squeezed past Brooke into the building.

The scene before us was surreal, like the set for a performance-art piece. There were no cars in the garage, and the floor space was clear except for a few lawn chairs, boxes, a barbecue set that had been pushed to the wall. Clear but for those things and a single chair that lay on its side in the middle of the room, underneath Gladys Thomas's hanging body. A short rope ran around her neck to one of the broad crossbeams that supported the building's roof. The beam was only seven feet off the ground, and Gladys's feet nearly brushed the concrete floor.

A photographer circled the body, his camera clicking and strobing.

I stood for a moment, taking it in. Eventually I said, "May I?" and pointed to the body.

Walker sighed. "Just don't touch anything."

I nodded and walked to the center of the room. Brooke followed.

Gladys Thomas's eyes bulged and her swollen tongue protruded from the mouth. The previously pretty face was puffed and contorted. She'd bitten deep into her tongue, and dried blood cracked on her lips and over her chin. Even in the dim light, I could make out the small hemorrhages in the thin skin around her eyes, a sign of strangulation. The bruises and contusions around her neck were broad and dark. Though we'd have to wait for the pathologist's report, it didn't look as if Gladys had died quickly, from a broken neck. She'd had a messy, painful death.

"Too bad," Walker said to herself. "A real shame."

"The officer outside said this was a suicide," I said, looking closely at the distorted face.

"That's what we're calling it," Walker replied.

" 'We'?"

"I'm ruling a suicide. It'll be checked out by the medical examiner, but . . . I've seen a lot of these. It's a suicide."

"Was there a note?" Brooke asked.

"There's never a note."

I pulled out the small pad from my jacket and began jotting observations. I moved around the back of the body. At Gladys's buttocks, a wide, faint stain spread across her light-blue cotton pants. For a minute at least, I focused on the stain.

"Did you see this?" I asked Walker. She came over and looked at the discolored fabric.

"Urine," she said.

"Right."

"They always void—"

"I know. But look at the pattern. It's spread out along her buttocks. I'm not a detective, but if she died hanging like this, you would think the urine would run down her legs, right?"

Walker looked as if she was about to say something, then stopped herself. She glanced at the photographer. "Get this," she said frostily.

"I already did," he replied.

Walker nodded and began writing in her notebook. "You like that CSI show, hunh, Doctor?"

I looked at her. "No, I just—"

"Get out."

The words came from behind us, from the doorway to the garage. I turned. It was Rosalinda. "Get the hell out of here," she yelled.

Everyone—Walker, the photographer, Brooke, me—looked back at the figure in the doorway. "They killed her." Rosalinda pointed at me.

"What?" I asked. Walker's head had swiveled toward me.

"They pushed her to this. She was fine until yesterday when they made her so upset—"

"Ma'am?" Walker said, moving closer.

"They killed her!"

"Ma'am—"

"She would have been fine if they never came!"

"Ma'am, why don't we step outside?" Walker placed a hand on Rosalinda's shoulder.

Rosalinda jerked her arm back and screamed: "Don't touch me!"

Walker turned to Brooke and me and snapped, "Stay here." Then, gently, she took Rosalinda's elbow and led her outside to the small yard. I looked back to the body.

"You about done?" the photographer asked. He made a big deal of checking his watch. No, I wasn't done, but without touching the body, I couldn't do much more there. I didn't want to give in that easily, so I turned to Brooke and asked, "Do you have anything else?"

"Not right now," she replied.

I stepped back from the body, and the skinny man began to shoot again, flashing a couple close-ups at the urine stain on the pants. Contrary to what he said to the detective, it looked like he hadn't really gotten it on the first pass.

Outside, I could hear Walker's and Rosalinda's voices. I didn't want to walk into the hornets' nest, so I hung out in the garage for a few more minutes. Eventually, the voices stopped and Detective Walker walked into the building.

"She's upset," Walker said.

"I could tell."

"With you two. She thinks you—"

"We heard her."

Walker flipped to a clean page of her notebook. "What happened yesterday?"

I saw no reason to hold back. So, I told Walker about the lies, the relationship with dead Douglas/Casey. I told her about Gladys Thomas's shock and despair when she found out her beau was dead.

I noticed the photographer had stopped taking pictures. "She's sick?" he asked anxiously.

"She's dead," I said. "You'll be fine. Just glove before you touch her. Wash your hands. Use a mask if you're going to be moving her around a lot. Treat her as if she has AIDS."

"We treat everyone as if they have AIDS," Walker said.

"Good." The photographer was staring at the body. "You'll be fine," I told him again.

"How upset did she seem?" the detective asked.

"Extremely so."

"Upset enough to kill herself?"

It was a simple question, but a vexing one. *Kill herself. Was Gladys Thomas upset enough to kill herself?* Until that day, I had never met someone who'd killed herself. Sure, I'd seen the aftershock of successful and unsuccessful suicide attempts in my rotation through the emergency room and through the path labs. But I'd never spoken to someone hours before she pulled the proverbial trigger. On the surface, it made sense: an upset woman, distraught over the loss of her lover, kills herself. Neat, tidy, even romantic. But there were too many things wrong with it.

"Doctor?" Walker insisted. "Was she upset enough that she would have killed herself?"

Brooke answered, "We're not psychiatrists. We don't know."

"Maybe Dr. McCormick does."

"I'm not a psychiatrist," I said.

Walker seemed perturbed by the answer; it was obvious we were getting off on the wrong foot. But I—and I sensed Brooke, too—was irked. The police seemed to be doing a slipshod job here. Retarded lady kills herself. Not a major deal by big-city-police standards.

Walker said, "I may have more questions for you. So, your information, please."

"I'm only in the area for another day."

"Your contact information."

I gave her my cell phone number and my office number at CDC. Brooke coughed up her digits. Walker turned away from us toward the body, which I assumed to be our dismissal. But I wasn't done. "Have you questioned Ms. Lopez?"

Walker turned around. "What business is that of yours?"

"I told you. We're investigating an outbreak." I really did not want to get into some interjurisdictional spitting match; I softened my tone. "Detective Walker, anything you can tell would be greatly appreciated."

"I questioned her earlier. What do you want to know?"

"Did she say anything about a boyfriend? About the Casey we mentioned?"

"No."

I pulled the black-and-white picture from my folder and showed it to her. "This is the murdered boyfriend. The best we can figure it is that he called himself Douglas Buchanan on the East Coast, and Casey—we don't have a last name—out here. Like I said, Douglas Buchanan was an assumed name, from a person who died years ago."

"This is being investigated—?"

"By the Baltimore PD and Carroll County Sheriff's office. Maryland State Police are involved as well. I'll make a copy of the photo and fax it to your office."

"Thanks," Walker said. "But I'm still going to treat this as a suicide, subject to change depending on what the ME says. The investigation of this"—she pointed at the picture—"Casey isn't our problem."

"No," I agreed. "Not yet it's not."

CHAPTER 41

Walker and the photographer stayed with the body as Brooke and I stepped into the backyard. Under a large oak, there was a picnic table. We sat down and waited quietly for the guys from the ME's office to arrive. I was thinking about a cigarette. Brooke wasn't. "I think I'm worried about all of this," she said.

"I am, too."

"No, I mean worried. I'm frightened. . . ."

"What?"

"I'm worried it might be an attack."

It was, in fact, something I'd always been worried about. But I wanted to hear what she was thinking. "So tell me," I said.

"Think about it. You have some man who's carrying a disease. For argument's sake, let's say it's a virulent strain of HIV. So this guy, he's a suicide bioterrorist, and he's copulating his way through a vulnerable population."

"Okay," I said.

"You said his room in the home in Baltimore was nice, right? Well, he's keeping himself in style; he's got his own little room in a sleazy home for the retarded, because he's taking this enormous chance. He's got a cell phone, stereo, all the stuff that no one else in the home has. After he's done his dirty work, his handlers knock him off to keep it quiet."

"Why do his handlers knock him off? I thought he was a suicide—I don't know—a suicide fucker—"

"I'm serious, Nathaniel."

"So am I."

She looked away from me. "I don't know. Maybe it wasn't a suicide deal. Maybe he thought he would be cured. Maybe that's what his handlers told him. He probably thought he'd do his work in Baltimore, come back here, get cured, then go on and marry Gladys Thomas."

"It doesn't add up, Brooke."

"I'm just thinking here, okay? I'm just thinking."

"All right, sorry. Let's just think. What's the agenda?"

"What agenda?"

"If it's a terrorist attack, where are the letters, the demands? The claims of responsibility?"

"Maybe they're waiting for it to get really bad, for it to blow up in the press. Think about it, Nate. Think about how terrifying it is. No mail, no crop dusters, no aerosol cans. This guy himself is the bomb. Think about that."

I did. It still didn't add up.

"And Gladys Thomas is a loose end, right? Maybe—"

"Brooke—"

"Maybe they found out about her when Casey died. Maybe they killed her because they were worried—"

"Brooke—"

"What?" she said, too loud. "Don't yell at me," she said softly.

"I didn't yell at you."

"You did."

"Well, you were getting carried away."

"Somebody has to. You should. It's your job."

"Look," I said. "I *got* carried away. That's why they kicked me out of Baltimore."

"Oh, I see. Since when did Nathaniel McCormick start caring so much what other people thought?"

"Since he heard the swishing sound of his career going down the toilet. Brooke, this sky-is-falling scenario is good thinking. It's the kind of thinking we should be doing—"

"It's what I am doing—"

"—but we need to keep it in context. Right now this thing is just a disease. With some weird elements, that's true. I'm out here to follow up on one of those elements." There was some commotion from inside the house. "The medical examiner's guys are here," I said, standing. "And I need to head up to the university and visit an old friend."

"An old friend."

"An old professor. And unless you want to drive me up there and risk seeing, uh . . ."

"Jeff."

"Unless you want to see Jeff again, I need to get back to your place and get my car."

She pushed herself up. "I don't want to see Jeff."

"Okay," I said.

We walked into the house and introduced ourselves to the two techs from the ME's office, made sure they knew the safety precautions they were to take. One of the guys, a thick white guy with a shaved head, tried to pump us for information. I told him the bug didn't look airborne, but that he should be careful and not worry. Way to go for paradoxical directions; I felt like a spokesman from Homeland Security, telling everyone to be vigilant but to live a normal life.

As we got to the main hallway, I could hear weeping from the living room. I said to Brooke, "We should talk to the other residents and staff. See if they recognized Douglas, see if any of them had contact with him."

"Have a little compassion, Nathaniel. Wait until tomorrow."

"My plane leaves tomorrow."

"Do a rash thing," she snapped as she beelined toward the front door. "Change the flight."

CHAPTER 42

At Brooke's place, I faxed Douglas Buchanan's photo to Detective Walker, then drove north to a rendezvous with my old mentor, my old university, and, probably, a swarm of unpleasant memories. Truthfully, though I'd played my return to the place over and over in my head—usually a high-octane fantasy in which I was coming back to deliver a commencement speech or accept an honorary degree—I had no idea what I'd feel.

I left the highway at University Avenue, which cut straight through a town that had come to be synonymous with the dot-com excesses of the 1990s. Though the boom times were over, this particular hamlet seemed not to have noticed. I waited in a line of traffic that moved at a slug's pace and was composed almost entirely of German and Japanese luxury vehicles and SUVs. Ken Kesey, back in the liquid sky days, used to live in this area. I wondered what he'd think about the glistening train of BMWs that snaked through the boutiques and restaurants hawking eighteen-dollar salads. He'd probably think it was a bad trip.

Eventually, traffic began to move and my speed got well into the teens. The road passed under train tracks, then rose again to meet The Farm.

Whatever my feelings about the university where I'd spent four grinding years of medical and scientific training, I had to admit it: I love the grandeur of the place. It isn't grandeur in the East Coast sense; it lacks the Gothic and Georgian gravitas of Yale or Harvard. But it is grand nevertheless. The entrance to the university grounds—which are, by sheer acreage, the largest of any university in the country—is marked by two large sandstone arches that give way to a half-mile-long thoroughfare lined with palm trees. The trees, the gift of some rich alumnus with an eye for spectacle, rise like massive pillars with broad green Corinthian capitals. Rumor has it the trees were thirty thousand a pop.

The medical school itself was barely recognizable. Two massive science buildings bulged from where there had only been patches of green years before. The buildings were impressive and impassive, hewn from what looked like solid blocks of buff-colored sandstone. My entrance made me think of a quote I once read by a famous art historian: Coming into New York City through Grand Central Station, "one entered the city like a god"; coming in via Penn Station, "one scuttled in like a rat." Well, if sandstone arches and palm-lined boulevards make you feel like a god, giant medical buildings make you feel like a rat. Especially if you're the rat they kicked out years before.

Anyway, I suppose there was more here at play than an architecture-induced inferiority complex. There was, too, that feeling that institutions do not change; they remain the same as when you'd left them. Especially true for schools and colleges. So it's jarring when you find that the doorway where you pissed after that party is now a security door with a security guard behind it; the bushes where you got that dynamite blow job after the fall formal is now a student center. Universities do not remember their children. And this university definitely did not remember me. At least that's what I hoped.

Fifteen minutes before the appointment with Dr. Tobel. Figuring I might as well face my demons, I locked the car, pumped the meter with quarters, and walked toward the school.

Once inside, I recognized exactly nothing. Gone were the banks of beige lockers in which we'd stashed books and stethoscopes. Gone was the refrigerator in which lunches sat for weeks and which smelled like a landfill. Gone were the cramped, ammoniac bathrooms.

I stopped a girl who looked to be about thirteen and asked her where the med school was.

"It's over there"—she pointed through the wall—"near the admin buildings."

So they finally gave the students the long-promised new classrooms. I had a pang of nostalgia for the old place, but my reverie was cut short by a screechy voice behind me.

"Nathaniel? Nathaniel McCormick?" I turned my head to see a short, dark-haired woman in a long white coat, the pockets filled with stethoscope, pens, pocket charts. *Oh, God,* I thought, *not now. Not ever.*

My stomach churned and I ratcheted through the faces of every white woman I knew from my early years.

"Jenna Nathanson," she said, sticking out her hand, saving me from having to stumble through a conversation in which I never once said her name. On the downside, if I remembered Jenna Nathanson correctly, this was going to be a less-than-pleasant tête-à-tête. I wondered why the hell I hadn't stayed in the car.

"Hi, Jenna," I said. "Long time."

"It sure has been. Wow. It really has been a long time. What have you been up to? Why are you back here?"

I told her about working for CDC, about being here for a job and wanting to visit the old school.

"Great. That's great. It's good to see you're finally back on your feet after such a rough time." *The good old backhanded compliment,* I thought. "You got an MPH, then?" she asked. Evidently, she didn't think I could get back into an MD program and had opted for a master of public health. All things considered, it wasn't a bad assumption.

"No. MD."

"That's awesome. Where?"

The conversation was killing me. "At the University of Maryland," I said.

"Fine school," she said disingenuously. "Well, I stuck around here for neurosurgery. They asked me to stay on for faculty. I'm an assistant professor now."

Jenna seemed not to have noticed I didn't ask. "Good for you," I said.

"Yeah. Brain surgery's tough, though."

"Well, it's not rocket science." I smiled; Jenna didn't.

"But it's brain surgery."

"Yes, it is," I said. How did I get ambushed into this conversation again?

"The work's not too bad, but being a woman . . . it's hard."

About ten quips came to mind, but I steered toward safer shores. "I imagine it is."

"Anyway, somebody has to crack the boys' club," she said, giving me the weird feeling that I wasn't even there, that she was talking to a wall or a shrink. But then she touched my arm. "How is it being back after—well, you know?"

That was my cue. I looked at my watch. "Gosh, Jenna, I'm going to be late for a meeting. Congratulations on everything. Sounds like things are really falling in place for you."

I backed up as I spoke, not allowing opportunity for a coffee invitation or other social trap Jenna Nathanson might spring on me.

Outside, I walked a good distance from the old building before looking around to make sure Jenna was gone. All was clear, and I sat on a bench. Only when I looked up did I realize I was sitting across from the Heilmann Building, where Harriet Tobel had her lab. Unlike everything else here, it looked the same as it always had: a blasted sandstone structure where I had spent many hours, where I had broken down in front of Dr. Tobel and asked—begged—her to help me. I looked to my right and saw the gray Dunner Building, the place that housed the lab in which I did my PhD work. In the corner, third floor, that's where I'd been cocky, happy, ambitious, feeling like a Master of the Universe, where I'd flamed out. "Flamed out." That's what my classmates called it. I began to sweat.

CHAPTER 43

My flameout. In the career of an MD-PhD, the first two years of education are spent with the normal MD students, twenty months dedicated to basic science, the so-called preclinical classes: anatomy, biochemistry, physiology. But when the normal med students went off to the clinics to learn how to be doctors, the MD-PhDs went to the labs to learn how to be scientists. One's choice of labs was excruciatingly important. Not only were you choosing your environment for the next four years, you were choosing a mentor and a field that would—it was hoped—produce for you a surfeit of publications, grant money, and contacts. Choose well and do good work and the world was your oyster. Choose poorly and, well, you could always be a doctor.

In short, you wanted clout and respect, which shed like a virus from your respected and powerful principal investigator, your PI, and infected you. The end goal for most of us was the same, that grail of grails: your own faculty appointment and your own lab.

After a year of searching, I settled on the cancer biology lab of Mark Jurgen, a transplant from Germany who was interested in the effects of viruses on human DNA. Dr. Jurgen worked with human papillomavirus, which causes warts and, in a subset of unlucky women, cervical cancer. Specifically, Jurgen was looking at the role of the virus in cell signaling. How, he wondered, did the virus cause the cells to divide crazily in some people? Though he worked with HPV, there was no reason to stop at warts. The idea of infectious causes for cancer was in vogue then, and Jurgen's work was thought to apply across the board. I was hooked.

The Jurgen Lab had the reputation as a pressure cooker. Jurgen expected results, and he expected his team to know how to get them. There wasn't a lot of hand-holding, and his lab meetings were famous for sending people away in tears. But the man got results, and published them in the choice places: *Nature, Cell, Science, Cancer,* basically the A-list of scientific journals. And though the whole endeavor was young—Jurgen had been around for only eight years—his doctoral students and postdocs were going on to places like Duke, Penn, Harvard. It was the place to be for young, smart, self-directed grinds like me. With my advisor Harriet Tobel's blessing, I hitched myself to Jurgen's coattails. And it went wonderfully. For a while.

I carved out a niche working with the hepatitis C virus, which can cause liver cancer in some people. Hepatitis B and liver cancer had been getting a lot of attention then, but hep C was relatively untouched in this regard. My work with the virus was a big switch for the lab, though, since the papillomavirus is double-stranded DNA and hep C is single-stranded RNA. Anyway, enough of the nitty-gritty science. Suffice it to say that my work was new for the lab and no one there truly understood what I was doing. This gave me a lot of freedom, which, at the time, seemed great. In the end, though, it let me slide deeper into a scientific grave.

Anyway, I thought I'd hit on a novel way the viruses spurred tumor growth, and I set about designing experiments to prove it. And, after two short years, I did prove it, and my results would have added significantly to the body of knowledge. With Jurgen salivating over the results, I readied the papers to be sent to top journals. I was a rising star in the lab, the medical school, and—dare I say it?—the field of cancer biology. There was only one problem: my results weren't exactly valid.

Let me flesh out the scene a bit more: compared to academic medicine, Wall Street and Hollywood are for candy-asses. If you want real pressure—and the promise of riches of the mind as well as of the world, the envy of your colleagues—try working in a powerful lab with a brilliant and driven principal investigator. With all due respect to Jenna Nathanson, it is brain surgery. Hell, scratch that; it's a lot harder than brain surgery. Neurosurgery is for mechanics; neuroscience and cancer biology and molecular biology are for geniuses. As for money . . . the biotech revolution was seeing that the top dogs got paid and got paid well.

Let me also flesh out my culpability here: I didn't start by fudging data. My initial results were promising. So promising, in fact, that Jurgen was offering me the world. I was his golden boy and I basked in the sunshine of his admiration. When things began to go south, when the data I knew should say one thing said another, I started to massage the numbers a bit. I was right and I knew I was right; I just couldn't get the goddamned numbers to fall in line. There it was: my path to fame and glory, threatened by a few stupid digits. I massaged and massaged until there was no way in hell I would ever be able to go back.

My strategy wasn't as misguided, naïve, or malicious as it sounds. Science is often a race, and I was running against a number of other labs working on similar problems. To the victor, all spoils. To the losers, years of work lost. Literally. I mean, you might be able to publish something in a third-tier journal, but even that might be a stretch. Feeling the heat, I wanted to take advantage of a quality in the submissions game. The time course of publication is a long one. I had every intention of running my experiments again while the papers wended their way through the submission and editorial process. I told myself that if, God forbid, the results didn't pan out, I would pull the papers. And I believe, to this day, I would have. But it never got to that.

A month or so before I was to submit the papers, Jurgen called me into his office. He'd been at a conference earlier in the year and had been chilly toward me since his return. I chalked it up to his peripatetic Aryan nature. Anyway, I was in the middle of writing the methods section of my paper and I asked him to wait.

"Now, Nathaniel," he rasped. From his tone, I knew something was up. I went into the small office ten paces from my lab bench.

Jurgen folded his long Teutonic frame behind his desk and leaned back in his seven-hundred-dollar office chair. "Close the door." I did. He said, "What's going on?"

I felt myself begin to flush. "What do you mean?"

He tented his fingers and leaned forward. He spoke each word distinctly. "What is going on with your work?"

Sweat prickled in my scalp. "It's going fine. I'm just—"

"You're blushing."

"I know."

"And you're sweating."

A good scientist never misses anything.

"I know," I said.

He cleared his throat. "At the conference, I ran into Don Applegate." Applegate was a researcher at the University of Chicago whose lab had been working on the same problem I was. "We talked about the research. He seemed surprised that we'd gotten the data we did."

I didn't say anything; Jurgen continued. "*Very* surprised. So surprised, in fact, that he told others at the conference, and they, too, were surprised."

So, more than for the sin of fabricating data, I was being crucified for the sin of embarrassing my PI. Of course, Jurgen would never say this.

"Since the conference, I have had the opportunity to monitor a few discussion boards. It seems as though there is much doubt about what we've been doing. I imagine after the paper is published, there will be others who will try to replicate the experiments."

But I knew then, as Jurgen did, that the paper would never be published. My face burned.

"I have been spending the past few weeks with your data. A lot of time, Nathaniel. And I am having some trouble understanding how you came up with it."

"I explained it all to you. And it's all in the methods. You have access to my lab notebook—"

"And I have seen you have blacked-out some numbers."

Lab notebooks are the crumb trails of scientists. They record everything, or at least that's how it's supposed to be. You never erase or blacken something. You just cross it out. I should have known that, but I was sloppy. What I did was akin to shooting a man and leaving the gun with fingerprints at the scene.

"I—"

"Don't speak." His tic was to clear his throat. He did it again. "Last month, I had Karen run some of the assays—"

"Last month? You had her run the experiment without telling me? You don't trust—?"

"No. Not now I don't. But I want you to be quiet now, and then I want you to tell me I am wrong. If I am." The guttural throat clearing again. "Karen ran the assays and did not get your results. She ran them again. She still did not."

I said nothing, just stood in his office and burned.

"So, I ask you the question: Did you fabricate your data, Nathaniel?"

My options blazed through my head. I had known from the beginning this was a possibility, but as the months and years went by, the possibility seemed more and more remote.

I started slowly. "I may have rounded some numbers—"

"Goddamn it!" he shouted. "Thank God I caught this. Goddamn it. This, I can't believe."

"I can explain."

"Explain what, exactly? What can you explain?"

"I just need more time. I'm right, Mark. I'll run the assays again and—"

"You can't do that. Not now. *You* can't do that."

"But I—"

"Get the hell out of here. Leave now. Do not stop at your bench. I will send someone to you with your belongings." He stood and cleared his throat. "Someone from the academic affairs office will contact you."

Later that day, in fact, someone from the academic affairs office did contact me. At the hearing, I was asked to leave the PhD program. After a year's probation, they would let me finish out my MD, with the restriction that I conduct no more research—in the basic sciences or the clinical sciences—while at the university. I agreed to all the demands, including attending a two-day conference on research ethics. I also agreed to meet with members of Jurgen's lab and walk them through my work for the previous two years.

It is famously hard to get kicked out of medical school, the theory being that it is so difficult to get in, everyone admitted should have the chance to be a doctor. On a more cynical note, there is such an investment in making a doctor that no school wants to lose out on that investment. Anyway, as hard as it is to get kicked out, I managed it.

During my probationary year, I volunteered at a local clinic. If I wasn't going to be a physician-scientist, I'd take a shot at being a good doctor. For two months, I took histories and blood pressures and temperatures. I became adept, I was part of the team, I had the admiration of the staff. I was also bored out of my skull. Since I hadn't been to the clinics as a medical student, and since I'd spent the past two years in a lab, I wasn't permitted to practice much medicine. So it was blood pressure and history, day after day. My fantasy time was split between wishing that I'd never fabricated the data and wishing that I'd fabricated better. By the end of eight long weeks, I was getting more than bored; I was getting bitter. So I quit.

To make some money, I got a job at the coffee shop on campus. That's when the love trouble began. No longer the promising young MD-PhD student, my relationship with the beautiful Alaine Chen was rotting away before my eyes. I struggled to keep it—man, did I struggle—but no bright, young, superficial woman wants to be with a sullen barista if she can help it. And she could help it. So she left.

In the tradition of my father and my father's father, I began to drink. A few nips to get to sleep at night turned into a few nips before work and half a bottle of bourbon to get to sleep. After a month with no Alaine, I managed to finagle a fellow coffeehouse peon—an undergrad majoring in religious studies—to sleep with me a few times. This took some of the sting out of my desperation, but she dropped me after a particularly inebriated evening during which I pounded on her dorm door loud and long enough to draw the police.

Those were the days.

The climax of my self-destruction walked in with three former classmates who, at that time, were just finishing their final year in the clinics. They had already matched in their residencies, their MDs were just on the horizon. For them, life was good. They were drunk. I was pretty looped myself.

The first guy up to the counter recognized me. "Hey, man, heard about what happened. Bummer."

"Yeah," I said. "What can I get you?"

"How about some data? Can you cook some of that back there?" It was the kid behind him. A thick surgeon type named Pablo.

"What did you say?" I asked, a broad fake grin on my face.

"You heard me," Pablo shot back, the soul of wit.

"Don't mind him," the first guy told me. "He's got his drink on. He's heading to UCLA for orthopedics. You know the type."

"Sure," I said.

But Pablo wasn't giving up. "He's the guy who faked the data. Got caught and booted from school. Fucking lied and then gets caught."

The first guy turned to Pablo, but by then it was too late. I was already leaning over the counter with a good right hook that landed square in the surgeon-to-be's face. Pain shot through my hand, and I heard a crunch as the nasal bones cracked beneath it. Pablo grabbed at his face. He kept yelping "Ah, ah, ah" over and over again as I tried to land another one. Blood streamed in a web over his fingers.

The first guy pushed me back over the counter. "What the—"

But it was over. Pablo was slumped on the floor as people gathered. A few fraternity types sidled up as if there was something to do at that point. I jammed a crooked finger at the jerk moaning on the floor, checking his nose. "Fucking cocksucker. Get them to fix it at UCLA, you cunt. You fucking cunt."

So it was in that moment, filth pouring from my mouth, hand jabbing at the air, that my engines finally flamed out. The police came; Pablo went to the emergency room. The first guy, now an oncologist in Philadelphia, convinced kindly Pablo and the police that Pablo had been the instigator, and no one pressed charges. The rulers of the medical school were not pleased, however. They demanded I leave.

I did. I was twenty-five.

The good old Dunner Building. Fuck it. I looked at my watch, got up from the bench, and walked.

CHAPTER 44

I trudged the well-worn stairs of the Heilmann Building to the third floor. Eight years since I'd last made that climb, and the stairwell, at least, hadn't changed. I thought I recognized some of the dirt.

As I said, Harriet Tobel's lab was the first one in which I worked, and I would have stayed there if she hadn't convinced me that I should broaden my experience. In those early years, I wondered if she didn't see something wrong with me, and convinced me to go elsewhere to avoid having such a liability around. But over time she proved her loyalty to me.

I passed the Microbiology Department's administrative offices, then stepped up the pace, hoping to avoid another Jenna Nathanson–like encounter. Labs ran along both sides of the hallway. Each was marked with a little placard that had on it the name of the PI and the postdoctoral and grad students who worked in the lab. In the corner—actually, in the corner and running for yards in either direction—was the Tobel lab. I walked inside.

Through the maze of black lab benches, I saw a thirty-something guy who was probably a postdoc and a young woman who had to be an undergrad. The postdoc was at a computer; the undergrad, gloved, was running gels, some of the most tedious grunt work in a lab.

At the far end was a wooden door with a small brass engraved plate on it: Harriet Tobel, MD, PhD. I knocked and opened the door.

"Dr. Tobel," I said. She sat behind a desk awash in papers. Most docs' offices are like this; no scientist or doctor worth his or her salt would be caught dead with a clean office. Tidy offices bespeak misplaced priorities.

"Nathaniel," she said. She didn't stand, so I walked over to her and embraced her. Her frame was small, frailer than the last time I'd seen her, it seemed. Still, age had been kind to her, and she looked very robust for a woman in her early seventies who'd been knocked into disability by a childhood bout with polio. "So good to see you," she said. "So very, very good."

Damn it if I wasn't thrilled to see this woman. Sure, I hated California, but seeing Harriet Tobel almost made the trip to the dark side worth it. Almost.

I yammered on for a while about stupid stuff—CDC, the recent droughts on the East Coast and in my romantic life. But the words were like comfort food for me, pabulum that Dr. Tobel and I could share. I—and she, it seemed—savored the moment.

Eventually, Dr. Tobel said, "So, Dr. McCormick, tell me what brings you here."

In two minutes I did, omitting too much.

"Well," she said, "we'll have time for more discussion over lunch. Many things have changed since you were gone. Have you seen the lab?"

"Just what's between here and the hallway."

"Well, Nathaniel, it's grown. I took over the Kopelman lab next door when Henry moved on to UNC. Let me show you."

She struggled from her chair and grabbed the two canes that sat propped against the desk. She unfolded her crooked legs, the legacy of polio, and I followed her out of her office.

In the lab, she pointed her chin at the postdoc and the undergrad and the three rows of benches. "Some of the work is the same as when you were here. HIV mutation and drug resistance. Things are going well with it. Yonnick"—she indicated the bearded postdoc—"is working on a paper we will submit to the *New England Journal of Medicine* in the next few months. Yonnick, Leyla, this is Nathaniel McCormick, an old student of mine. Nathaniel's a mover and shaker at CDC now."

Despite all the derailments in my life, Dr. Tobel's sentence made me sound impressive. And I loved her for it.

Yonnick and Leyla muttered hellos. Somewhere in the background, a centrifuge whirred. *God,* I thought, *it has been so long since I've been in a place like this.* The sounds, the smells . . . it was like coming home.

"But this, Nathaniel, I think you'll love."

She moved to the next room, her canes padding on the tiled floor. The room was smaller than the first one, but far better equipped: new high-pressure chromatographs, a computer at every workstation, a PCR machine in the corner. New, expensive stuff.

"The pleasures of working with private industry." Her wrinkles pulled into a smile. "We are well funded here."

I heard someone tapping away at a computer across the room.

"Private industry?" I asked, but something seemed to have distracted Dr. Tobel. "You're working for the Empire now?" I asked.

She smiled as she came back to the moment. "Have you heard of Chimeragen? The company?"

"I think so. Has something to do with xenotransplantation."

"Still keeping up on your reading, I see."

"Some of it."

Xenotransplantation and xenografts are the cross-species transplantation of organs and tissues. There's a certain amount of xenotransplantation that's found its way into everyday medicine: heart valves from pigs, skin from pigs. But Chimeragen was going for the big stuff: solid organs, like kidneys and hearts. Experiments with this sort of thing had been going on for decades, without great results. The first recorded experiment happened in Germany in the early 1900s—a physician by the name of Unger sewed a primate kidney into a human. The recipient died immediately when his immune system revved up and blood clotted in his vessels. Then, in the twenties, an American doctor transplanted lamb kidneys into a human. The patient survived for nine days. Better, but still not standard practice. Considering that even the concept of blood typing was still new in the early part of the century, the experiments were impressive.

Primate kidneys, lamb kidneys, dead patients: this is where my knowledge stopped, basically because that's all I could remember from a transplantation lecture I attended a decade before.

"You're working for Chimeragen?" I asked.

"With them, yes. They got a large grant from the NIH and significant investment from Spanna Pharmaceuticals to conduct their work. The NIH money was earmarked to study the risks of cross-species infection—viruses, prions, all those nasty things you work with. They needed someone independent to monitor their work. They called me and I jumped at the chance."

"Congratulations," I said, though I wasn't exactly sure how independent Dr. Tobel could be, all things considered. "What stage are the trials? Are they clinical yet?"

"They should be moving into Phase Three"—the stage just before FDA approval for the process—"in the next year or so. It's extremely exciting. We've scratched over every tissue of the current recipients and have found nothing. The patients are totally clean."

"Who are the recipients?"

"Do you know Otto Falk?" she asked, ignoring my question.

I knew the name, and he was definitely not one of the recipients. Falk was a big transplant surgeon who came over from Johns Hopkins fifteen or sixteen years before. He was famous as an advocate for xeno-transplantation. It was from his lecture, in fact, that I learned about the early experiments.

"He lectured me once," I said. "So you're working with pigs? Falk loved pigs, if I remember."

"Yes. Closest in size and morphology to human organs. Yes. The noble pig."

I heard the person across the lab swear quietly.

"How big is your Chimeragen team?" I asked, trying to get a better glimpse of the woman—from the voice, I was sure it was a woman—through the shelves of catalogs and bottles of reagents.

Dr. Tobel didn't answer me. "Why don't we head to lunch? It's nearly two and I haven't had a bite all day. I'll give you the full tour afterwards."

The woman swore again, and I heard her push out her chair and begin walking around the bench toward us. She rounded the corner and stopped cold when she saw me. And I, for a moment, thought I'd died.

"Hello, Nathaniel," she said.

"Alaine," I said.

There was a thick silence. Finally, Dr. Tobel said, "Dr. Chen is one of our team members."

Unable to think of anything at all, I nodded.

"How have you been?" Alaine asked.

"Okay," I said. My voice quivered.

"Lunch, Nathaniel. The café closes in a few minutes."

"Good to see you," Alaine said as we left the lab.

I nodded.

In the elevator, Harriet Tobel touched my arm. "I'm sorry, Nathaniel. Alaine wasn't to be here today. And she wasn't at her usual bench. If I had known—"

"That's okay. It was a long time ago." Not long enough, though. Forever wouldn't be long enough.

CHAPTER 45

We went to a small café in another lab building, presumably in the interest of preventing another chance encounter with the woman who'd broken my heart. The medical school is filled with these—small sandwich shops and cafés—each building seeming to have one with a different theme. A captive clientele meant good margins for the outfits lucky enough to get the concessions contracts.

To keep up appearances, I ordered a sandwich, but was unable to make much of a dent in it. Though I didn't want to talk about the outbreak or Douglas Buchanan or Gladys Thomas, I sure as hell didn't want to talk about Alaine Chen. So I began to weave the tale for Dr. Tobel. Besides, I thought, she was a microbiologist. She'd worked for CDC back when they were called the Communicable Disease Center; she'd done some early work with viral hemorrhagic fevers before HIV strode into town attracting much of the funding and many of the best minds. She might be able to shed some light.

As I talked, Dr. Tobel became quieter. For a woman who'd spent much of her life investigating AIDS, any talk of sex and death would be sobering. I finished up with the facts and went on to the theory of bioterrorists sowing a disease into the population through sex. "Does it sound far-fetched?" I asked.

"I'm not an expert in that."

"But what do you think?"

"I think it sounds quite sinister."

"Yes. And the patient population it's attacking is unexpected. I'm worried about what's going on, Dr. Tobel. Have to say I'm pretty worried."

"You're trying too hard, Nathaniel. The unexpected does not necessarily make for efficacy. You're not writing a Tom Clancy novel, you know."

No, I wasn't writing a Tom Clancy novel. No, bioterrorism wasn't the most likely scenario. But it might have been the worst, and something very wrong *was* going on here. I guess my discomfort must have showed, because Dr. Tobel's face softened. "It's good that you're thinking this way, though. I'm glad the government has you working for them." She smiled. "You said a doctor named Randall Jefferson was involved in all of this?"

"Yes."

"Well, I will call him. I'm sure he's told you everything he knows, even if he didn't tell you in the most pleasant way."

"You know him?"

"We were acquaintances—not friends, really—when I was at Johns Hopkins." She looked across the room. "He's a good man, Nathaniel. You just got on his wrong side."

"Doesn't seem hard to do."

"Well, he has a lot to protect."

"Including cesspool group homes?"

Her face remained impassive. "I know you're concerned. I am, too." Her mouth drew to a sad smile. "I know you hate having been taken off the investigation, but it's probably for the best."

I laughed, then stopped when I saw she wasn't joking. "I can't believe you're saying that. You just said it was good the government has me working for them."

"And it is." She paused, uncomfortable. "But, Nathaniel, you're still young. You're a little too ambitious, even for a field populated with ambitious people. The shortest direct route is not always the best."

It wasn't hard to read between the lines of what she was saying: the same character flaws that had me bolting from medical school got me kicked out of Baltimore. But there was one major difference. "I didn't do anything wrong this time," I said.

"Except alienate those who could help you. This club we're in is a small one, Nathaniel. Everyone knows everyone, and everyone protects everyone. Especially from the prying eyes of a public that doesn't take the time to understand what we're doing. It's all black-and-white to them." She took a small bite of her sandwich. "Otto Falk plasters one side of his office wall with the hate mail he's gotten and the other side with letters from people who are dying as they wait for their kidneys. 'Burn in hell, you Nazi bastard' or 'Please hurry, my brother is going to die without the kidney.' He's a devil or an angel in their eyes. But really, he's just a man. And you—" She looked directly at me. "You don't understand why everyone doesn't roll over when you, in a self-righteous fog, browbeat them for information. Dr. Jefferson, for example. You serve two masters, Nathaniel, and I thought they would have told you this in your training. You need to protect the health of a society, sure, but you also need to protect society: its laws and its grant of individual rights—"

"What about the right of people not to be infected?"

"Oh, it would be wonderful if we lived in a police state where any home could be searched and swabbed. Where anybody could be compelled to divulge all the dirty secrets of his or her life to stop an outbreak that may or may not be relevant to the dirty secrets. Have there been any new cases?"

"I don't know."

"Well, you should." She picked up half her sandwich, considered it, and put it down. "Perhaps this is an isolated incident. Perhaps one of the sick women picked it up from someone who traveled in South America and who brought back a new strain of Machupo different enough from the known virus to be missed by your assays. Perhaps this strain is transmitted only through sex and blood. If it is, and if it moves as fast as you say, then thank God. It will burn itself out. But if you had your way, we would quarantine all of Baltimore, throw Randall Jefferson in prison, and be done with it."

I was annoyed now, so I said, "Maybe that's what we should do."

"And maybe *you* see everything in black-and-white. Not a good trait in a scientist or an epidemiologist."

We ate in silence, me nibbling halfheartedly at my sandwich, getting angrier with each bite. Of all the people who I thought might understand, Harriet Tobel would be the one. "You can't have everything, Dr. Tobel. And I'm willing to sacrifice some individual rights for the greater good. Forced quarantines work. So damn me if you want. But if we had found Douglas and locked him away for a while, none of this might have happened."

"But you don't even know if this Douglas is the key," she said sharply. I flinched at the vehemence in her tone. "Nathaniel, Nathaniel, Nathaniel." She smiled, reached across the table, and patted my forearm. "You are such a work in progress, young man. It has been—and is, I must say—beautiful to watch you develop."

"I think I'm sick of developing. Someone put me in the stop bath, pull me out, let me dry."

"But that wouldn't be half as interesting, would it? And you wouldn't be half the man you will be."

"I'm glad you have faith."

"I've always had faith. And with you I always will." She leaned back in her chair. "Well, I will place a call to Randall Jefferson. I imagine there's not much I can do, but I can try to calm him down. Maybe he'll tell me something about this young man in whom you're interested." She pulled out a PDA and scratched something into the screen. "You said the man's name was David Buchanan?"

"Douglas. Or Casey. I forgot to tell you that. It's what he was called out here. It's pretty damned confusing—" I stopped because of an odd look on Dr. Tobel's face. "What?"

"Casey? You're sure it was Casey?"

"Yes. Why?"

"Nothing. Casey what?"

"We don't have a last name. What's wrong?"

"Nothing's wrong, Nathaniel. What did this man look like?"

"He was— Wait, I have a picture." I fished in my notebook for the photograph of Douglas Buchanan—Casey—and slid it across the table. When she saw it, her face changed: it could have been surprise, it could have been straining to see the picture clearly. I thought she might say something, but instead she glanced at me and handed back the picture.

"I really need to be on my way, my dear. So wonderful to see you." She reached for her canes. I stood, gave her my arm, and helped her up.

"Dr. Tobel," I said, "if you can think of anything, *anything*—"

"It was wonderful to see you, Nathaniel."

And with that, she left me, her canes thumping along the polished stone floor.

CHAPTER 46

Baffled but heartened that at least someone seemed to know something, perhaps, about what was happening in Baltimore, I walked back to the car. As I passed the Heilmann Building, I paused. Although women should have been the last thing on my mind, I couldn't shake seeing Alaine. I toyed with the idea of racing up to the third floor, sticking my head in the Tobel lab, and indulging in some witty repartee with Alaine Chen.

But I was kidding myself. I made toward the parking lot and pulled out my cell phone. I had a case to crack.

I paged Tim. Twenty minutes later, as I exited the highway into San Jose, the epidemiological wunderkind called me back.

"I found the woman, Gladys Thomas," I told him.

"And?"

"She's dead. Hung herself early this morning." A few long beats passed.

"Okay," he said. "Okay, that's weird. Hung herself?"

"Yes. I saw the body." It was, as Tim said, weird. Not just the sui-cide itself, but the method. Though hanging is a relatively popular way of offing oneself, the stats say that women prefer swallowing pills.

Tim asked, "Did you, ah, meet with her before that happened?"

"Yes." I told him about the love affair between Douglas Buchanan and Gladys Thomas, and explained the connection to Casey, Mr. Buchanan's West Coast alias.

"Weird."

"Well, here's the really weird part." I told him about Douglas Buchanan's demise, resurrection, and demise. "So the way I figure it, it means that Casey, or Douglas, had two identities, one of which he stole from a dead man in Pennsylvania. Either he lived out here as Casey and moved east or he visited here as Casey. It's the same guy, Tim. We con-firmed it with a photo."

"Do you have a last name for Casey?"

"No."

There was silence on the phone. "I don't know what the heck to do with this. When did you find this out, by the way? About Douglas's dy-ing twice."

I lied. "Twenty minutes ago."

"Okay. You're not sneaking around behind my back, are you? Still trying to keep your fingers in Baltimore?"

"I'd never think of it," I said. "I just happened to call Myers to say hello. Find out how his hemorrhoids were treating him."

"Right." I heard his car stop and the door open. "Look, to keep you in the loop: we're focusing on a rodent or arthropod reservoir. Baltimore's a port town, so it's not inconceivable that some insect or rat jumped ship and imported our bug. A few men in one of Jefferson's homes actually work at the shipyard, so it's not inconceivable. But . . ." He breathed loudly through his nose. "But with what you are telling me now, I have to talk to Detective Myers, tell him information should come to me first, not to you."

Tim took the phone away from his mouth and spoke to someone. A big shot has no time for phone etiquette. He came back without break-ing tempo. "What we've discovered is creeping me out, Nate. It's getting really oddball. I don't like the way this thing walks, talks, or smells. We still don't know thing one about Douglas Buchanan's murder...." He seemed to be thinking something over. "I'm not a cop. We're not cops. The FBI has really been pushing to get involved—"

"The FBI?" This was not good news. I could see the headlines: FBI INVESTIGATES POSSIBLE BIOTERRORIST ATTACK.

"Yeah. I've been trying to hold them back, because we were sure this was a natural situation. But with what's come to light in the last few hours, it can't hurt—"

"Tim, not yet. I'm making progress here. If you bring them in, they're going to muck everything—"

"What did I say about us not being cops? This ain't our strength, Gunga Din. We deal with the disease, let the Bureau guys deal with the murder and the stolen identities." There were sounds of people talking in the background; Tim lowered his voice. "Look, I know you're ticked about this. You feel like glory's been snatched from you every time you do some good work. But you know what, Nate? S happens. This isn't about you—"

Right, I thought. *It's about you, Tim.*

"—it's about dealing with the situation—politics and everything—in the most effective way." He paused. "Did they have sex?"

"Who?"

"Your girl out there, Gladys whatever, and Buchanan."

"She said they didn't."

"You believe her?"

"Yes. It seems she was really just in love with him."

"Right," he said, his voice thick with sarcasm. "Whatever. Get tissue samples and send them. You'll be back in Atlanta tomorrow?"

I answered the question that wasn't really a question. "Yes," I told him. The sweat beaded on my forehead and dribbled down my cheek. I was pissed off. I pulled up to the no-parking zone in front of the Health Department. A security guard wandered over to the car. I stabbed a finger at the placard on the dash and he moved on.

I changed the subject and asked whether there had been any new developments in Baltimore.

"No new cases. But it's only been thirty-six hours."

"That's good."

"Yeah, but I'm worried. I wonder when the floodgates will open."

"Well, if they do, and you need more manpower—"

"Then it'll be good to have you in Atlanta to coordinate. Look, I have to go. I have a press conference to deal with. Question, though: you're not ticking everybody off out there, are you?"

"No, Tim."

"Are you ticking *anybody* off?"

"I don't think so."

"I don't mean whether *you* think you're ticking them off. Would *I* think you're ticking them off?"

Bastard. "No, Tim. You wouldn't."

"Good. Anyway, you won't have much time to. I want you in Atlanta tomorrow." I wanted to thank him for reminding me when I was to be in Atlanta. I'd almost forgotten in the past two minutes. "All right, I need to go. Try to keep the natives from rioting."

"Tim?" I said. "There's something else."

But the line was already dead.

"You're a real asshole, you know that?"

Brooke called me two minutes later.

"Where are you?" she asked straightaway.

"Outside your offices. I need to—"

"You need to get down here. I'm at the medical examiner's."

"That's what I was calling about. What are you doing there? This isn't your respons—"

"I told you, work is slow. You have to get down here."

"What's wrong?"

"Just come over," she snapped, and hung up the phone.

CHAPTER 47

By the time I'd walked to the building that housed the county medical examiner's offices, cleared myself through security, and made my way through the tangle of hallways to the basement, it was past three o'clock. I assumed by that time the pathologists would have been well into Gladys Thomas's autopsy.

And indeed they were; I could see that from the other side of a large glass window that separated the administrative offices from the suite. There were three figures in the room, all of them gowned and gloved and masked: two bent over the body, one looking over their shoulder. The observer, who looked vaguely female, waved me over to my right. Brooke. I made my way around the desks—only one of which was occupied, by a middle-aged secretarial type who looked half-dead herself—and pushed through a door emblazoned with *Autopsy Suite*. I entered into a vestibule stocked with gowns, gloves, et cetera, and suited up. A door marked with all kinds of warnings about contamination led to the autopsy room itself.

Brooke was waiting for me.

"Took you long enough," she said.

"Daedalus couldn't have designed a more confusing labyrinth."

"Who?"

"Never mind."

She led me past two stainless steel autopsy tables, one with a covered body on it, one without. On the third table lay Gladys Thomas, looking, well, nothing like Gladys Thomas: her chest cavity had been opened; her viscera lay on a table two feet away from the rest of her.

Brooke introduced me to the doctor. Luis Gonzales was in the final year of a two-year forensic pathology fellowship. The tech was a guy named Peter, who didn't look too happy to be there. After introductions, the first thing Dr. Gonzales asked was "Is it really Ebola? What's happening in Baltimore, I mean." I saw Peter, up to his elbows in gore, pause for my answer.

Brooke looked at me. "I already told them it's not, Nate."

"We just want all the information we can get," Gonzales said as he weighed the liver and jotted something down.

I told him we didn't know what it was, but it was unlikely his current body had been infected with . . . well, whatever it was.

"That's what I told them," Brooke said.

Gonzales looked at her. "You scared the hell out of us when you called. Nobody wanted this one, after the word came down. Except me and Peter."

"I didn't want it," Peter said.

"But you're a brave man and will go far in life," Gonzales replied.

Brooke stepped up to the table. "Dr. Gonzales, tell Dr. McCormick what you told me."

Gonzales hesitated. "This is not official," he said. "This is just my opinion, right?"

"Absolutely," I said.

"Well," he said, looking down into the corpse, "she died of asphyxiation, that's for sure. You saw her, right?"

"Yes."

"You take a good look at the contusions?"

"No. The detective wouldn't let me touch."

Gonzales began to paw over Gladys's body, and I, for the first time, got a good look at the deceased.

Anyone who thinks death is peaceful has not seen enough death. Gladys Thomas's swollen lips jutted out so that it looked almost as if she were about to blow a raspberry at us. Her eyes were open, and if she'd been alive, I'd say she looked frightened. A great jagged Y ran from each shoulder and down her abdomen, and the flaps of flesh around the Y had fallen inward toward the chest and abdominal cavities. It was grotesque.

Gonzales moved his hands to the head and turned it to the side, exposing the neck. "We got about a thousand pics of the neck and head, but let me see. . . ." Gonzales rinsed the area with a hose. "We got all the scrapings and fiber samples this morning. That stuff just went to the lab. We won't hear back for a few days."

He played with the neck, taking his time. The flesh had been opened around the trachea, and he was working his way through layers of tissue, peeling muscles back so they flapped down over the chest like a bib. "You saw her hanging, right?"

"Yes."

"Did you see the noose?"

"I did."

"Then you saw it wasn't the best knot. Not a surprise, considering no one knows how to tie a good knot anymore. Especially a vic like . . ." He didn't finish the sentence. "What I'm saying is that she didn't die from a broken neck. She strangled."

"I figured."

"But look at this. See?" He carefully reassembled the neck and ran his finger along the line of the bruises. "There are two sets of abrasions here." He pointed to an area that ran around the neck like an ugly, smudged necklace. There was another, fainter abrasion slightly above it, angled upward. You really had to look to see the difference.

"So?" I asked.

"From the damage to the carotids and to the hyoid bone, it looks like this lower one did her in. This wasn't done by this upper abrasion. See? The carotids don't spasm that high."

I looked at the mess of flesh on the table in front of me and saw in a flash the woman. Alive, twenty-four hours ago. Crying, walking, clutching at Brooke. Now she was split like an animal carcass in front of me. The contrast was too jarring: I closed my eyes and removed images of the living Gladys Thomas from my brain.

She's dead, McCormick. Simple as that.

"Dr. McCormick?" Gonzales was staring at me.

"Yeah. I'm looking." I focused and ran through my anatomy and pathology and tried to see the difference between a spasmed and non-spasmed carotid. It was a lost cause. Nevertheless, I said, "Yes. I see."

Gonzales continued. "Now, our victim didn't tie the best knot. And I'm assuming that she didn't jump off the chair, find out the rope wasn't quite tight enough, readjust, and try it again."

"What are you saying?"

"What I'm saying is that whatever made this lower mark killed her."

Things began to click for me. "Go on, Doctor."

"Somehow, a ligature pulled more horizontally and caused most of the damage. That's this lower one. After the lower injury—the one that did her in—another ligature made this upper mark. See how the abrasion isn't nearly as bad and blends into the lower bruise? That's because she was almost dead when this was made. We'll have to look at the crime scene photos, but I'll bet the rope she was hanging by matched the position of this upper mark."

"Which means she was killed by something pulling horizontally on her neck."

"Exactly. It's not totally inconsistent with her hanging herself. But she would have had to lean very far out on the chair to get the horizontal mark."

"So let's be frank: it looks as if someone stood behind her and pulled a rope horizontally, and that's the injury that killed her. That's what you're saying?" I asked.

Gonzales backed up from the body. "Whoa. I'm not a cop. I'm not saying any of this is true. I'm just saying what it looks like to me."

"And I'm just asking you to say what you think."

There was a nasty silence. Finally, Brooke interrupted. "Luis, you already told me."

"But you are one person. I tell you, then I tell him, then I get a call from my boss asking me what the hell I'm doing making these conclusions." He let out a sigh. "Okay, but I'm speaking unofficially now."

"Hey," I said, "I'm the king of unofficial. In terms of criminal investigation, I'm the furthest thing from official. I'm just a lowly public servant trying to keep people from getting sick."

Gonzales sighed again. "Okay. What I think is that whoever did this didn't do the best job of covering up a strangulation."

"So you think that she was murdered."

"Going out on a limb, I'd say so. But like I said, it's not the best job. It would have been easy enough to line up the marks. These don't." He looked up at me. "Whoever did this was sloppy."

"Or they didn't care about us finding it," I said.

CHAPTER 48

After filling out the FedEx information, preparing the biohazard containers for transporting samples of Gladys Thomas's tissue to CDC, I left the ME's. Outside, I called Detective Walker, asked her about the investigation on the dead woman.

"We're making progress," she said.

"Can you give me any details?"

"Dr. McCormick, the San Jose Police Department is doing its job."

"You can't tell me any more than that?" I asked, maybe a little too sharply.

She shot back, "I have a question for you, Doctor. Just what, exactly, is your jurisdiction?"

That was a stumper. The California and Santa Clara health departments had invited me in. The San Jose PD had not. And unless I proved a significant public health concern to someone, any jurisdictional argument I'd make was certain to be a dog. But beggars can't be choosers.

"I told you," I said. "Gladys Thomas is tied to a case concerning an outbreak in Baltimore." Even as I said it, I realized how weak it sounded. "Her murder—"

"Murder? Now we're calling it a murder? Isn't that funny—we're the police and we deal in this stuff every day, and the best we've managed so far is to call it a suspicious death. What makes you so sure it was murder?"

I saw no reason to involve Luis Gonzales at that point, so I said, "I'm inquiring, Detective."

"We'll take care of the inquiries, Doctor. I have your number. I will contact you as soon as we have any information that bears on your investigation."

"I'm leaving for Atlanta tomorrow."

"Well, you'll be missed in San Jose."

"Listen, would you do me the favor of calling me when you find anything out? Whatever you may think, it does have a bearing—"

"I have your number," she repeated, and hung up. I wondered if the double entendre was intentional.

It was dinnertime when I reached Santa Ana; the smell of food drifted over the front porch through open windows. I hit the doorbell.

A woman who was not Rosalinda Lopez answered the door. She looked vaguely official, so I introduced myself and told her that I needed to talk to everyone in the home.

"The police already talked to everyone here," the staffer informed me.

"I know. I'm not the police. I'm a doctor."

I flashed her my ID and told her it was federal government business—whatever that meant—which seemed to do the trick.

She led me to the dining room, where seven women sat around the table, eating. There wasn't much conversation, not surprising considering the empty place setting that looked like a missing tooth. Why they'd laid out a plate and utensils, I didn't know. Honoring the dead, I guess.

The only sounds were the clicking of metal on porcelain.

"I'd like to start with you, if you don't mind," I told the staffer who'd let me into the house.

She mumbled something about setting an example; then we retired to the living room. She slid the pocket doors closed.

First things first, I got her vitals: Her name was Velma Tharp, she was originally from Stockton, but came down after junior college to look for work. She'd been at the home for about eight months.

Enough of that. I pulled out the picture. "Do you recognize this man?"

"No," she said.

"Were you aware of any relationship Gladys had with any man?"

"What kind of relationship?"

"Romantic, friendship, whatever. Doesn't matter."

"No," she said. "Not really."

And that's how it went for the next fifteen minutes. I did the cop-type questions—Did you see anything unusual last night? Any odd phone calls? But Velma Tharp seemed to have had her head in the proverbial sand; when I told her we were finished, she promptly stood.

"Oh, one more thing," I said. "What's your shift here?"

"Usually, eight to eight. I do the overnight Sunday through Thursday."

"Those are normal shifts? Twelve hours?"

"Yes."

"And you say you didn't hear or see anything unusual last night?"

"No."

"It's not eight o'clock. Why are you here now?"

"With all that's happened and with Rosalinda leaving . . ."

"She left?"

"Quit today. Just like that. Really left us in the lurch."

I made a note of it, thanked her, and asked her to send in the next woman.

Through the pocket doors, I heard Velma say something to a woman she called Stacey. By the time she sat on the couch across from me, Stacey was already in tears. After getting name and age, I asked her how long she'd been at the home. She didn't know. I pulled out the picture of Douglas.

"Do you know this man?"

"Yeah."

Bingo. "Do you know his name?"

"No. He was Gladys's boyfriend, though."

"Did he come here?"

"Sometimes."

"Did he ever stay here?"

"No." She said it emphatically. "We're not allowed."

"Do you know how often Gladys met with this man?"

"Sometimes."

"When was the last time he was here?"

"Long time."

We went on like that for another ten minutes, me lobbing the simplest questions I could think of, Stacey bunting back monosyllabic answers.

The next girl came in, then the next. Each interview followed the same script. All knew Casey, some by name, others only by his picture. If nothing else, Casey had done a hell of a job keeping a tight rein on his girlfriend.

It was pushing past eight o'clock, and I heard a television go on in the room across the hall. Some of the women went upstairs.

Around nine o'clock I got to my last woman. As luck would have it, the woman had gone upstairs to her bedroom and Velma had to retrieve her. Ten minutes later, Mary Jacobson situated her ample rear in the couch. She settled her hands in her lap and leveled her blue eyes at me. She was, she informed me, Gladys's roommate.

I went through questions that had by that time become routine. As I probed, I quickly sensed that all had not been dandy between the roomies. So I asked about it: "Did you like Gladys?"

"No," she said without hesitation.

Okay, I thought. "Why?"

"Gladys talked all the time on the phone. Nah, nah, nah. All the time. Gladys—" She faltered.

"What? Mary?"

She struggled with the words, then spoke. "Gladys would be touching herself. Down there." She pointed to her lap. "It was gross."

"While she was on the phone?"

"Yeah. It was really gross."

I found myself sizing Mary against Gladys and wondering if the woman sitting across from me had the strength—and the cunning—to murder her roommate and string her up in the garage.

I asked, "Did Casey ever sleep over?"

"No way."

"Did he ever visit Gladys in her room?"

"My room."

"Right. Your room."

"No way."

"Do you think they ever had sex?"

She thought about that for a moment, then asked, "Put his thing in Gladys?"

"Yes."

"No."

"Are you sure?"

"Gladys would have told me about it."

"Why would she tell you?"

"Gladys told me everything."

"How do you know that?"

"Gladys thought I liked her. Gladys thought I was her friend."

Chalk one up for the universality of human misperceptions. The last time I thought someone really liked me was a year before, and that someone was Brooke Michaels shortly before she left for California to be with her fiancé; and that was just after I found out she even had a fiancé. Gladys and I had both been duped.

"Was there anything different about Gladys in the past few days? Was she acting funny?"

"Gladys was acting weird, all sad."

"Did she talk into the phone?"

"No."

"Did you hear her go outside last night or this morning?"

"The lady already asked me that."

"The lady? Detective Walker?"

"The police lady."

"Tell me. Did you hear Gladys leave the room last night or this morning?"

"No."

"You heard other things, though."

"I had these." She dug into a pocket in her robe and pulled out a pair of earplugs. Why, Mary, you little snoop. So the talk, talk, talk didn't bother her unless she left out the earplugs. She probably got off listening to the steamy phone conversations between her roommate and Casey, then stuffed in the earplugs when she wanted to sleep. Last night, she'd said, she wanted to sleep. I believed her.

No more questions for Mary Jacobson came to mind, so I ended the interview and walked to the front hallway. I imagined her alone up there, sleeping like a rock without her earplugs for the first time in years and loving it.

Velma was in the small office, playing solitaire on the computer. I asked her who was winning. She seemed a little confused by the question, but finally said the computer.

"Can you give me Rosalinda Lopez's telephone number?"

"I can't give that out."

"Why?"

"Because we can't give out employees' home phone numbers. And she's not even an employee anymore."

I saw a sheet of contact numbers pinned to a corkboard on the wall. I'd bet the rental car outside that Rosalinda's number was there. I walked to the corkboard, found the number next to *Lopez,* and wrote it down.

Velma glowered at me as I left.

CHAPTER 49

It was nearly ten o'clock. I hadn't eaten since lunch, hadn't slept well in a week, and I still had reports to file with Tim and Herb Verlach. I also had a bunch of messages waiting for me on the cell phone, which I listened to as I started the car.

The first message was from John Myers, saying he had gotten a call from Tim Lancaster, but not to call him because he was fucking exhausted and he was going to bed. He'd call me in the morning. The second was from Brooke, saying she was home and to call her. The next message was from Harriet Tobel. The time stamp was an hour before.

"Nathaniel, please call me when you get this message. I don't care what time you call; it's very important. Call me at home. I'll be here." She left the number.

The final message, too, was from Dr. Tobel. This time her voice sounded taut and she said tersely, "Ivory Coast, Nathaniel."

Strange, I thought. *Very strange.* It seemed that Dr. Tobel was finally going to tell me what she was thinking, that whatever she'd been holding back earlier in the day was going to be revealed to me. Fine. But "Ivory Coast"?

The phrase—the place, Ivory Coast—was not quite as random as it seemed. Years before, after the disciplinary committee (of which Harriet Tobel was a member) suggested I leave school, I was sitting in her office, crying like a jilted teen. She hadn't fought for me to stay in school. I told her I felt betrayed. She shook her head and said, "Your time is finished here, Nathaniel. For better or worse, you'll never be able to crawl out of the hole you've dug for yourself. But this doesn't mean your life is over. Far from it."

She was the person who suggested I leave California. She suggested I apply for the Peace Corps. Unable to see any path now that the narrow road of medicine had been barricaded, I realized it was either that or . . . what? I was assigned to a rural area in Ivory Coast, a tragic country in West Africa. For two years, I helped local and foreign doctors set up clinics to battle the explosion of AIDS in that country. It was there, in the wilds of Africa, that I stopped regretting what had happened to me and started regretting who I had been. The only contact with my previous life was through rare e-mails to Dr. Tobel.

Watching hundreds die alone, rolling around on mattresses soaked in their own diarrhea, flesh bursting in bedsores and cancer, fired my robust anger at disease. Having given up on medicine, I felt an MPH and a degree in foreign relations might be the best way for me to continue the fight. I wrote to Dr. Tobel about this, and she suggested I not entirely give up on being a doctor. She might be able to do something for me. As I said, she had come to California from Baltimore, from a faculty position at Hopkins. She was unable to persuade her former colleagues there to give me a chance; the stature of that place meant they would never have to take a risk on someone like me. She gave up on Hopkins— "Their arrogance is unbelievable," she'd said—but pushed like hell at the University of Maryland. Why? I wondered.

She told me on a call the day before my interview at Maryland. "Because, Nathaniel, you have purpose. Unlike so many students who blow in and out of my office, you have purpose for good."

Purpose.

I should mention something here. Despite Dr. Tobel's lauding of my newfound purpose, the fact any medical school in the country even considered my overtures—after I'd been booted from another school— was astonishing. Normally, my application would have found its way, very quickly, into the recycling bin. CDC, Boy and Girl Scouts that they are, would have incinerated the app lest they be contaminated by any grime adhering to it or to me. Nobody in medicine wants tainted goods.

So, how did a liar and a fighter like my former self worm his way back into med school and into squeaky-clean CDC?

During the deliberations at school about how, exactly, they could best rid themselves of me, Dr. Tobel intervened. As I said, she was on the disciplinary committee, and wielded an extraordinary amount of influence there and in the school as a whole. She prevailed upon her colleagues, who probably wished the rack were still a legal form of punishment, to expunge my record of its nastier elements. To wit: *Expulsion* was changed to *Indefinite leave of absence as per student's request*. When CDC called my reference from my former med school—Harriet Tobel, of course—she told them I'd left school to serve the underserved in Africa. Her little manipulations, her application of muscle on my behalf, saved my career in medicine—literally.

When I was in my residency at UNC, after a particularly grueling month during which I doubted my mettle as a physician, I called her and asked why she'd done so much for me. I asked why she'd helped me remain in a profession that seemed too complicated, too demanding, for someone as flawed as I was.

She listened to my griping, then said, "Nathaniel, I think you have the potential to be a truly great doctor. There's a problem in medicine when physicians feel they are different from those for whom they care. When they feel they're more capable, not just at doctoring, but at the rest of life as well. Ours is not a path that allows for an honest appraisal of our own weaknesses, so we come to believe we don't have them. You have been forced to face your failings. And this brings you and your patients to the same level. You are human, they are human. It would be a great loss to this profession if, after all you've learned, you were to choose another path."

I wondered then if she didn't see some parallel between herself and me. Her crippled body, my crippled character.

So, back to Ivory Coast. After a nice bout of soul-searching and a few more e-mail exchanges with Dr. Tobel, I pursued medicine once again. I spent a week in the big city Abidjan, making hundreds of dollars' worth of international phone calls, gathering the necessary documents from my undergrad and medical school days, faxing my transfer application materials from a tiny, cramped travel office in the center of

town. Three months later, Maryland admitted me as a third-year medical student.

That was Ivory Coast. But what the hell did it have to do with anything? Why was Harriet Tobel saying the name into my voice mail? It
was odd; I was worried.

I dialed her number and the answering machine picked up. I hung
up, waited a few minutes, and dialed again. Still the machine.

"Dr. Tobel, it's Nathaniel McCormick." I waited. Nothing. "Please
give me a call on my cell phone when you get this message. I was inter-
viewing, so I didn't have the phone on, but it's on now. Call me as late as
you like."

I fished out the number for Tobel's lab. After a few rings, the call
rolled over to another line. A woman answered. In fifty years, after my
brain is riddled with Alzheimer's plaques and I've forgotten my own
name, I will remember that voice.

"Hi," I said.

There was a pause, then "Nathaniel."

"The one and only." *Lame,* Nathaniel.

"That's true."

It was my turn to talk but, damn it, I came up with nothing.
Finally, Alaine said, "What's up?"

"Not much." I didn't want to ask for Dr. Tobel yet; I wanted to
keep Alaine talking, spend a little more time with that voice. "Just working on some things."

"Harriet said you're out here on an outbreak investigation. How's
it going?"

"Brilliantly. The bugs are gone, the bad guy's in jail, and I finished
it all before lunch."

"Really?"

"No. The bugs are still out there, we don't know if there are any
bad guys, and it's well past my dinnertime."

She laughed and I think said my name. I guess I was getting my
groove back.

"Harriet's not here," she said.

"Oh," I said. That was disturbing, but while I still had Alaine on
the line . . . "How are you?"

"Working. Always working."

"All work and no play, Alaine . . ."

"I've always been dull."

"Right. Just like Mata Hari."

"What?"

"Bad choice of exciting historical female."

"Truly. Okay, Nathaniel. I'll tell Harriet you called."

"Do you know where she is?"

"I don't. She left early."

"She still lives in Atherton? Same place?"

"Yes."

There was a pause in which the conversation was supposed to end. Instead of ending it, I said, "I'm heading back east tomorrow."

"Well, have a safe flight."

"I'd love to catch up."

"I thought we just did."

"Come on, Alaine."

"I'm sorry," she said. She exhaled a soft breath. "Nathaniel, I'm engaged."

For a moment, I thought she meant she was engaged in some other activity the next morning. Then I realized she meant *engaged* engaged.

"Oh," I said. "Oh . . . I'm, ah . . . I'm very happy for you."

"Thank you."

"Who's the lucky man?"

"You wouldn't know him."

"Try me."

"His name's Ian Carrington."

"I don't know him."

"See?"

"What does he do?"

"He's a venture capitalist."

"He still has a job after the bubble?"

"Yes, he does—"

"I thought all those guys were driving taxis now."

"He's very smart."

"I'm sure he is." There were about a dozen other things I thought Ian Carrington was, but I kept them to myself. I said, "All right. Tell Dr. Tobel I called."

"I will." I was about to hang up when Alaine said, "Nathaniel."

"What?"

"It was good to talk to you."

"Yeah," I said, and hit End on the cell.

CHAPTER 50

By the time I reached Dr. Tobel's Atherton neighborhood, I managed to calm down a little. By a little, I mean I wasn't thinking homicidal thoughts about Alaine's beau anymore. But I was still pissed off.

I wound the car slowly through the dark streets. Unlike many of the nouveau riche hamlets on the Peninsula, Atherton had been dripping in money since the beginning of the last century. Immense houses were closed in by even bigger oak and palm trees, so that the houses seemed to shrink back from the road behind their walls of vegetation. It was not a welcoming neighborhood; it was the kind of place where driving around aimlessly might generate the interest of the police.

I drove around aimlessly for a few minutes until I got my bearings; I wasn't stopped by the police. In fact, I didn't see another car until I pulled into the semicircular driveway in front of Dr. Tobel's house. There was a big Lexus in the carport—Dr. Tobel's, I assumed. The other bay was packed with gardening paraphernalia.

The house was a bit smaller than its neighbors, but still too large for one person; Dr. Tobel's husband had passed away a number of years before, and I guess she never got around to moving to a smaller place. White stucco walls and a low-slung roof gave the place a welcoming, Spanish feel.

There was a light on upstairs—the bedroom, I assumed. I got out of the car, walked up the flagstone steps to the front door, and rang the bell. I heard it chime and waited for a light to click on. No light, but from somewhere in the house a couple of dogs began yapping wildly. I rang the bell again. Nothing but the dogs. My heart was thumping, and I pulled out my cell phone. I punched the callback number for Tobel and heard the telephones ringing in the house. Five rings and the answering machine picked up. I snapped the phone shut, leaned on the doorbell for a good five seconds, then gave up.

I sat on the steps and called the lab again. The call rolled over and rolled over again until voice mail picked up. So even Alaine had left the lab, hurrying home, no doubt, to make passionate love to her Igor, or Ivan, or whatever the hell his name was.

The dogs continued their frenzied barking. Perhaps Dr. Tobel had gone out for a walk or for coffee or for anything and would be back presently. It was a bit of a stretch for a seventy-year-old crippled lady, but it was better than, well, better than the alternatives.

Twenty minutes later, I hit the bell again and tried the door. The bell rang and the doorknob didn't turn, and nothing moved inside but the dogs. I made my way along the front of the house. A broad deck extended from the front door along the outer wall and ended in a hedgerow. Double French doors separated the deck from the dining room. I peered through the doors. The dogs, two dachshunds, had tracked me through the house and were bouncing off the glass in the French doors, barking furiously. No one, I was convinced, could sleep through that racket. No one.

Goddamn it.

"Dr. Tobel!" I pounded on the glass. I dialed her number again, and again heard the phone in the house ring until the answering machine picked up: *"You've reached . . ."*

I tried the French doors. They, too, were locked. I moved around the entire perimeter of the house, through the jungle of hyacinths and laurel. The dogs followed me through the house, their barking fading in and fading out as they backtracked to intercept me at each door. All the doors were locked.

The car in the carport, the dogs running loose in the house, the light upstairs . . .

I picked up a cobblestone from the garden and ran to the French doors. Holding the back of the stone, I pushed it into the glass pane nearest the doorknob. It didn't break, so I stood back and threw it. The glass shattered and the dogs went crazy and the stone bounced off the carpet inside. I reached my hand inside and undid the lock. As I withdrew my hand, a piece of glass sliced my wrist; blood beaded along the two-inch cut.

Inside. The house was alive now with barking, spastic dachshunds. One peed on the floor as he backed up and yipped and growled. There was a dog cage, opened, next to the dining room table. I called Dr. Tobel's name, but my voice quickly died out in the carpet and books and barks. I had been to the house a few times before and remembered the layout: kitchen to the right, stairway and large living room to the left, bedrooms and studies upstairs.

No sound came from the kitchen; I went there anyway, hoping not to see Dr. Tobel splayed out on the floor, a pot of tea boiling. But the kitchen was serene. I took a paper towel and pressed it to the cut on my hand. I moved to the living room and then to the stairs.

"Dr. Tobel? It's Nate McCormick. Are you all right?"

Up the stairs to the carpeted upper hallway. I saw a slightly opened door and a light burning. I pushed the door open.

"Dr. Tobel?"

A bed sat against the far wall, the bedspread rumpled as if someone had been lying there. The reading lamp was on, but there was no open book, no sheaf of files on the bed or on the nightstand. Next to the bed was a large dresser covered thickly with photographs in silver frames. To my right, another door was open and a fluorescent light shone from inside. The bathroom.

"Dr. Tobel?"

A cane lay half on the carpet of the bedroom, half on the bathroom's pink-tiled floor. The body of my mentor was twisted on the floor, one cane at her side, one at her feet, her arms and legs akimbo. An amber bottle lay opened beside her; tiny white pills dotted Dr. Tobel's body, the sink, the floor.

She lay there, her eyes half-opened and her mouth stretched back in a grimace. Quickly, without thinking, I moved to Dr. Tobel and pressed my fingers to her neck: no pulse. I pulled a makeup mirror from the counter near the sink and put it close to her mouth and nose. No fogging, no breath. Her skin was cold to the touch.

I stumbled out of the bathroom.

CHAPTER 51

Often, I have noticed, it is possible to distill the entire experience of another person into one memory, a memory that becomes shorthand for everything you felt. It might be the last time you saw them, the fading waving figure through the rearview mirror of your car. A fishing trip, perhaps, or a gesture. When I think of my father, for example, I first see the red face of a drunkard, furious and a little scared because he'd just hit his son across the face with a belt. Thence, everything else flows, the good and the bad.

Oddly, my boldest memory of Harriet Tobel is not my own. It was not even communicated to me by her. It came through the oral tradition of the medical school, the one that perpetuates the mythos of the institution, its faculty, its famous and infamous students. To put it more crassly, I got it through the med school rumor mill.

Dr. Tobel, we all knew from the first weeks of school, was the crippled professor we saw lurching from the lab to the dean's office to the classrooms. Other than the fact that she seemed to be *able* to get from A to B without help, I never understood why she chose the canes instead of the wheelchair. And though she was my advisor, and I had met with her a handful of times in those first few weeks, I never had the courage to ask.

But that's not the memory, the memory that is not mine. The memory is this, told to me by a gangly fourth-year medical student in that first week: Harriet Tobel on the golf course with her canes. She hobbles to the tee; someone gives her a club. In a single, swift motion, she raises the club, drops the canes, swings at the ball, and falls to the ground. She does this for nine holes, eighteen if the more ambitious rumors are to be believed. Swing, hit, fall. Swing, hit, fall. That story was shorthand for a life: like Washington and the cherry tree, like Teddy Roosevelt and the charge up San Juan Hill.

There she now lay, this woman who'd observed all the nastiness I could summon, who'd risked some of her considerable reputation to help me in California and again in Baltimore. She'd seen all the warts, carbuncles, festering sores on the character of Nathaniel McCormick, and she hadn't run from me. Not like Alaine. Not even like Brooke Michaels. For me, her support was as fundamental as those canes were for her.

And now I was alone, sitting on the carpet of the bedroom, gazing down into bathroom, blood from my hand slowly soaking the paper towel. I was afraid I would not be able to get up again.

When the initial shock had finally burned itself out, I stood, blew my nose, wiped my eyes. Though my brain was still pounding with emotion,

I made a stab at objectivity. I tried to be a doctor, or an epidemiologist, or a medical detective, or whatever the hell I was. I tried to be what Dr. Tobel believed I could be.

On the nightstand, there was a telephone. I picked up the receiver and dialed information for the medical examiner's office. I hung up before the operator gave me the number. I needed to think.

"Nathaniel, please call me when you get this message." Dr. Tobel's last words kept looping through my brain. *"Ivory Coast."*

Now, two feet away from me, she lay dead.

It wasn't right.

I went back to the bathroom and tried to take in the scene. The medicine cabinet door was open; pill bottles had been pulled from the shelves and had fallen into the sink. A soap dish was overturned on the floor as if Dr. Tobel had grabbed at anything to stop her fall.

I took a tissue and picked up the small amber bottle that was opened and empty on the floor: nitroglycerin, which matched up with the tiny tablets spread all over the room.

Dr. Tobel, it seemed, had died of a heart attack, a myocardial infarction in medicalspeak.

I looked in the medicine cabinet. The top shelf was filled with white and amber vials of prescription medications—Digoxin, Lasix, Ramipril, Losartan, Lipitor—and a smattering of over-the-counter laxatives and stomach medications. The drugs read like a medical chart for heart disease.

In that case, I guess it was a heart attack.

I played the scene over in my head: She's in bed waiting for my call. The chest pain starts. At first she thinks it's angina, but she's worried because she was resting and angina shouldn't hit when you're at rest. Or maybe she knows then it's a big one. She's a doctor and familiar with the symptoms—the sweating, the pressure on the chest, the pain radiating to the jaw or down the arm. She heads for the tablets, hoping to pop a couple under her tongue, relieve the pain. But she knows.

She barely pops the top off the vial before her oxygen-starved heart goes into an arrhythmia. It arrests. She dies.

She dies, just before she was to tell me something "very important."
Ivory Coast.

I went to the telephone, dialed information again, and this time got the number for the medical examiner's office. Because the death had been unattended, the person at the ME's said, they'd send over the police to ask a few questions.

Good, I thought. Then I sat on the floor outside the bathroom door, looked at Dr. Tobel's body, and tried to think.

I didn't hear the car until it stopped. Quickly, I moved to the window that looked over the drive and the garden. Nothing. The car must have been in front of the big hedgerow that ran between the property and the road. The engine ran, a faint rumble that barely perturbed the silence outside. I waited for a car door to slam, for whoever was inside to make an appearance. But nothing happened. After a full minute, I decided to go downstairs and see who it was. If it was the police—and who else would it be?—I'd be able to get things started. This death bothered me, and I wanted an autopsy to get underway quickly.

I could still hear the engine when I stepped onto the front stoop. As I rounded the end of the hedgerow, I heard the car slide into gear and begin to move. I got the first letter of the license plate—P—and saw it was a dark-blue or black sedan, with only one person, the driver, inside.

The car moved steadily through a stop sign at the end of the block.

"Shit," I said.

The police, two of Atherton's finest, were not happy to be there. Both seemed bored, which left me wondering what Atherton cops would normally be doing on a Wednesday night. I mean, this wasn't Oakland or San Jose.

So, the three of us sat at the dining room table while, upstairs, the medical examiner's men packaged Dr. Tobel's body for transport. The dogs ran around our feet.

The female half of the team, an Officer Bein, looked at me across the table. "And why do you think there's something wrong here?"

"I just don't think she was that sick."

Bein glanced at her partner. "Well, you're the doctor, but isn't that why they call heart attacks the silent killer?"

"That's high blood pressure," I corrected automatically.

"Whatever."

"Why didn't she get to the phone?" I demanded. "Heart attacks rarely kill you immediately."

"It didn't kill her immediately," Bein said. "What about the pills? She tried to get them into her mouth."

"Someone could have put them there."

Bein rolled her eyes.

I said, "And what about the car parked outside? What about it taking off as soon as I came outside?"

"Dr. McCormick, we've been through this. We have the first letter of the plate and that it's a dark sedan. You know how many matches we'll get on this? It's not like it's a crime to park your car here. . . ."

"You know of anyone who harbored grudges against Dr. Tobel?" This was from Officer Mackey, Bein's partner.

"No," I said.

"You know anything about lovers?"

"No."

"Was she a gambler, Dr. McCormick?"

"Come on, are you serious?"

"I should ask you the same thing, Doctor. You see, the scene here, this is not a police matter. Your friend died of a heart attack."

There were sounds on the steps, and I heard one of the ME's men swear loudly. The dogs heard it, too, began to bark, and scuttled into the foyer.

Mackey told me, "Put them in the cage, will you? They're going to trip up the guys on the stairs."

I gave the officer a good fuck-you gaze, then went to the kitchen for some dog treats. In the foyer, a gurney was parked near the front door. The ME's men made their way awkwardly down the stairs, a black body bag slung between them.

"Cute dogs," one of them said, nodding toward the two dachshunds, who sat solemnly underneath the gurney as if they were looking for protection.

I couldn't take my eyes off the black, zippered plastic.

"Come on, guys," I said to the dogs. Once they spotted the treats, they followed me back into the dining room to their cage, where I closed them inside.

As I sat down at the table, Officer Bein said, "I have some questions for you now. What happened to your hand?"

I'd forgotten about the hand. "I cut it breaking that window." I pointed to the French doors with the missing pane.

"Why'd you break the window?"

In the foyer, I could see the ME's men drop the body onto the gurney. I turned away.

I said to Bein, "Because she wasn't answering the door. I was worried."

"If you were worried, why didn't you call the police?"

"Because I'm a doctor. I could have helped her if she needed it."

"So you broke in?"

"Yes."

"Why were you coming to the house, anyway?"

"We had plans to meet."

"This late?"

"Yes. No. We didn't have plans to meet. I was supposed to call her. When she didn't answer, I got worried. I came over." Dr. Tobel's body was wheeled through the front door. One of the ME's men was quietly whistling a Broadway tune I've always hated. "Look, this is a waste of time. Don't you guys need to dust the place for fingerprints or something?"

Detective Bein cracked a smile. So did her partner. "And whose would we find besides yours and hers?"

"I don't know—that's why you check for them, right? You're the police."

"Maybe we *should* dust, Jack," Bein told her partner. "And we'll get a forensics team in here to comb for fibers, and—hey—maybe this is too big for us. I'll put in a call to the FBI. We can dragnet the whole neighborhood." Both cops were grinning. Bein said to me, "Yes, we are the police, and my professional opinion is that I see nothing strange here. We could run you down to the station and interrogate you if that would make you feel better."

It wouldn't make me feel better. I didn't say that. Instead, I told her, "You guys are really a bunch of pricks, aren't you?"

That got some reaction. Bein said, "Listen, you arrogant—"

"Look, Doctor." Mackey shot a warning glance at his partner. "We appreciate that you're upset, but there isn't anything here. And we're busy." He pulled out a card. "The body's going to the medical examiner's. They'll do an autopsy. That should make you happy—"

"It will."

"But I got to tell you, Doctor, I'm with Officer Bein here. This is an elderly lady who died of natural causes. Still, if you find anything, give us a call."

Mackey stood and handed his card to me; then the two officers left. I can't say I was disappointed they were gone, but as the sound of the vehicles faded, loneliness enveloped me. I went back into the dining room, opened the dogs' cage, and sat on the floor as they jumped in and out of my lap, trying, as dogs will, to get me to smile. I didn't.

CHAPTER 52

"Please come back."

"I can't, Brooke."

"What do you mean you can't?"

"I need to call her children."

"You can call them tomorrow."

"I can't do that."

"You need to sleep," Brooke said. "Look, I'll come pick you up; then I'll bring you back tomorrow morning. You can—"

"Thanks," I said. It was after two a.m. I'd called Brooke to unload. But after waking her up, I couldn't think of anything to say. Any words I could think of—hollow, cored-out, sad, miserable—would sound too trite, too unimportant. "You go back to bed. I'll be there sometime soon."

"Nathaniel—"

"Good night, Brooke. Thanks."

I hit End on the cell phone. Thirty seconds later it rang.

I answered. "Brooke—"

"You shouldn't be alone."

"I have the dogs."

"Nathaniel."

"I appreciate the concern, but I really have to go. Good night." I ended the call. It began to ring again. I silenced the ringer.

*   *   *

Dr. Tobel had two children, two boys. Oddly, I knew nothing else about them. Though their pictures were prominent on the bureau in Dr. Tobel's bedroom, she'd never spoken of them to me.

After looking around the kitchen for the children's telephone numbers and finding nothing, I went upstairs. The dogs trotted after me into the study. They lay next to one another on the floor. I sat in the worn leather chair behind the big oak desk and switched on the green banker's light. The room looked like something plucked from the middle of the last century: the old desk was topped with a battered leather blotter; textbooks and old reference books lined the walls. Pictures—none more recent than the 1970s—hung on the walls. There was a fireplace set into the wall, with a long mantel stretching above it. On the mantel was clustered a motley collection of objects: antique ice tongs, masks I had sent Dr. Tobel from Africa, an Incan or Mayan pot. All in all, the room was almost a museum piece.

Except for the technology. The computer, on a stand next to the desk, must have been purchased recently. The flat-screen monitor looked new. There was also a scanner, a fax machine, a DSL hub, a port for a PDA. Dr. Tobel's aesthetic tastes might have stalled out decades before, but her facility with technology had not.

Why was I up here again? To find the numbers for her children. The two boys.

Please call me when you get this message. It's very important.
Ivory Coast.

I looked through the drawers in the ancient desk, hoping to find an address book. Paper, envelopes, staples, office supplies. Personal financial records. I flipped through them, enough to find out that Dr. Tobel's salary from the university was in the low six figures. A few odd consulting jobs added fifty thousand or so to last year's income. Interesting, sure, but important?

Ivory Coast.

Forget the kids, I thought. I moved to the book-lined shelves and started to scan for atlases, books on Africa, anything. I found a few, pulled them out, and began leafing through. Nothing. After fifteen minutes, I'd been through all the books I could find and was about to head downstairs to look for more when my eyes rested on the mantel, on the masks I'd sent from Africa.

After I'd been admitted to the University of Maryland, I sent Dr. Tobel two wooden masks carved from ebony to thank her for her help. They were expensive pieces, even in American money, the equivalent of one month's Peace Corps pay. And they were beautiful. One: a lion's head, flames spraying out of its mouth across its cheeks. The other: a ferocious-looking goat.

Now, the combo of lion and goat wasn't totally random; it was kind of a joke. In Greek mythology, the chimera is a two-headed—guess which two heads—she-monster with a serpent's tail. In biology, a chimera is a mix of different biological components into a single organism. Technically, for example, someone who gets a transplant organ is a chimera. Dr. Tobel had done some work with chimeric cells. I'd actually helped with the transfections when I was in her lab, putting genes from one organism into another. Not to get too metaphorical here, but a chimera is also how I thought of Harriet Tobel. I mean, she didn't terrorize Greek cities or anything like that, but she was ferocious in her own way. Despite her broken body, despite being a woman in a field ruled for so long by men, despite mentoring a problem like me, she'd prevailed.

Pretty clever joke, hunh?

The pieces, I'd forgotten, were heavy. And they really were gorgeous, I thought: heavy, dark, terrible. I took the goat mask in my hand and held it like I was about to put it on. And that's when I saw the words, lightly scratched in pencil, gray against the black wood: *Marine Bank of CA #12.*

"What the hell?" I whispered.

I began turning the mask over in my hands, looking for something else, some new bit of information. Deep inside the nose of the mask, I saw a glint. A key, attached with a small piece of tape.

Ivory Coast.

The room exploded in barking and the dogs tore from the room. I heard the sound of a car door slamming.

From the landing, I couldn't see the door, but I did hear footsteps on the outside stairs. My hand still gripped the ebony mask. It was unwieldy, but felt heavy and effective enough. I hooked my finger in its eye and gave it a few short swings.

There was a sharp rap at the door, and the dogs, who had been on the steps, bolted down to the foyer, yapping madly and running in small circles on the carpet. I bent down behind the balustrade to get a look at the door. There was another knock.

I steeled myself, gripped the mask tighter, and walked down the steps.

The lights on the porch were out, so that the figure outside stood in darkness. I could see he had on a sweatshirt or something, the hood pulled over his head. He was holding something in his hand. He shifted on to one leg, cocking a hip.

I'd know that hip-cock anywhere, so I stepped to the door and unlocked it.

"What are you doing here?" I asked.

"You shouldn't be alone," Brooke said. A surreal moment passed where I didn't know whether to hug her or step aside to let her pass. So I stood there, an uncomfortable grin pasted to my face. Meanwhile, the dogs jumped against Brooke's shins.

She pushed a travel mug into my hand. "Tea," she said, then bent to pet the dachshunds. "What are their names?" she asked.

"I never found out."

"Well, it looks like a safety-deposit box key," Brooke said.

"Sure does."

"And Marine Bank of California is a bank."

"Sure is."

"Number twelve is probably a branch number."

"Yup."

Brooke and I sat at the dining room table with the tea, the ebony mask, and the key between us.

"It's weird, Nate. It's almost as if she knew something might happen to her, so she called you to get this . . ." She trailed off.

"I know," I said.

"So, what do we do now?"

That was the question, wasn't it? Contact the cops? No. Call the FBI or Tim Lancaster? No way.

"Well," I said, looking at my watch, "in five hours, we find Marine Bank of California, branch number twelve—"

"Nate, I don't know if we should—"

"She left this for me. Not for the police. Not for her kids."

We sat in silence for a while. Finally, Brooke said, "You're right."

I took a sip of the tea.

"But what do we do now?"

"You should sleep," I said.

"While you do what, Nathaniel?"

I took another sip of the tea, then looked square at Brooke. "We're not going to have access to this house after tomorrow, after her sons get here."

"And . . . ?"

"I think we need to find out everything we can about what Dr. Tobel was doing."

"What are you saying?"

"I'm saying we should search through Dr. Tobel's files. Find what—"

"Oh, good God, Nathaniel. No way. This is like breaking and entering."

I wanted to tell her that the breaking and entering had already been taken care of earlier by yours truly. Instead, I said, "Look, Dr. Tobel was very important to me, okay? She's dead, it's weird, and I want to find out what the hell went on."

"You have the key."

"It's not enough. Go home if you want. Call the police on me if you want." I stood up from the table. "But I'm going upstairs."

After I walked out of the room, I heard a quiet "Jesus Christ, Nathaniel"; then I heard Brooke on the stairs behind me, the two dogs scrabbling behind her.

*   *   *

As luck would have it, searching through the files in Harriet Tobel's study took very little time.

"There's nothing here," I said.

I stood in front of a large wooden credenza that ran under the windows on one side of the room. Keys had been easy enough to find—in a coffee mug on the desk—and I'd opened the top drawer to find it only half-full. I rifled.

"There's nothing here," I said again.

Well, it wasn't actually nothing, but it wasn't interesting to me that evening. Though I didn't know what, exactly, I was looking for, I knew it wasn't copies of Dr. Tobel's old journal articles, as impressive as they were—many of them A-list: *Science, Nature, Biochemistry,* etc.

I closed the top drawer, opened the bottom. More research, the recent projects. This was more exciting, but as I made my way through the hanging green folders, I realized all the recent projects weren't here, only Dr. Tobel's HIV work. Odd. She had an entire lab devoted to the work she was doing with Chimeragen, and yet there was nothing on that work here. On second thought, knowing how paranoid biotech companies can be, maybe it wasn't surprising there was no information at her home. Not secure enough, perhaps. Still . . .

"There's nothing here, either." Brooke was fooling with the computer.

"What do you mean?"

"I mean *nothing* nothing. I can't even boot up. The hard drive's been reformatted."

"You're kidding." True enough, the screen was black but for a pulsing white bar. "Let's try again."

Brooke held down the power key for a hard boot and the machine began to whir. After thirty seconds, we got nothing but the damned white bar. There was a drawer under the computer stand, which I opened. I found a Windows boot disk and put it into the computer. Finally something happened, and, after a few minutes, I got the familiar Windows screen. But there were no files. Nothing, nothing, nothing.

Brooke was right: the computer had been reformatted.

I flipped through the disks and saw there was only program software—the Microsoft Office suite, some data-analysis programs, her PDA installation software—but no data files. We searched around for the PDA, for any CDs, any floppy disks, but found nothing.

For kicks, I shut down the computer and booted it up again. Same old Windows desktop with nothing interesting on it.

Brooke yawned.

"You're dragging," I said.

"It's almost five," she said, stretching. "This reminds me of residency."

I went over to the bookshelf, started looking across the spines of the books as if there might be a folder sandwiched in there.

"Nathaniel, you're right. This is really off somehow."

"I know it is."

"So let's think about it—"

I started pulling books off the shelves, letting them fall to the floor. The dogs, who were sleeping in a corner of the room, jolted awake.

"That's not helping," Brooke said.

"I'm pissed off and I'm tired."

"Like I said, that's not helping." Brooke yawned again. "Okay, did Harriet Tobel have a company office or just the university?"

"I don't know."

"So, we don't know that. Back to what we do know: You tell her about Casey and about the situation in Baltimore; you say she seems very disturbed, doesn't want to talk with you. But later that day, she calls you, sounds desperate to talk. You can't get in touch with her, you come over here, and she's dead."

"Yes. She's dead."

"So, maybe she wanted to get you the key and wanted you to find her, you know, upstairs."

"For Christ's sake, Brooke, Harriet Tobel did not kill herself."

"I'm just brainstorming here, okay?" Brooke said stubbornly. "Maybe she was involved in this whole Casey thing somehow. How, we don't know. Maybe she wanted to get rid of everything having to do with it. That's why we find all these holes in the files, why the computer's been tampered with. Except, well, there is the key. But maybe the stress gets to her or she—"

"Don't you listen to me? She. Didn't. Fucking. Kill. Herself."

Brooke looked at me, shocked. I softened my tone a little. "Look, I know Harriet Tobel. And she did not commit suicide. Case closed." I began to put the books back on the shelves. "Another scenario. She wants to tell me something—say, something about this Casey thing—and someone comes into the house and kills her. That person cleans out the files and erases the computer."

Brooke sat up. "I think we're very tired. She was an old lady, Nathaniel. You said she had a medicine cabinet full of heart medication. Most likely, she had an MI. Maybe she'd reformatted her computer, maybe she just got the computer and was transferring the files—"

"Then where are the disks? Where's the backup? Where are the paper files?"

"I don't know." Brooke stretched her arms out on the desk and put her head down on the blotter. "It's five o'clock in the morning and I don't know."

No rest for the weary.

We didn't find a damned PDA, we didn't find a goddamned address book, or any list of friends, colleagues, kids. Wrong, wrong, wrong.

I went into the living room to look for something, and the next thing I knew, I was emerging painfully from a deep sleep. It—the pain of waking—reminded me of residency, of sleeping for an hour in the call room, of having a pager jar me awake. It wasn't a pager this time, thank God; it was Brooke Michaels, sitting next to me, gently shaking my shoulder.

"Hey," she said.

"Hey yourself," I said. There was a blanket on me. "I fell asleep."

Brooke nodded. I tried to blink the sleep away, tried to sit up even though it was the last thing I wanted. More than anything, I wanted to pull her to me, bring that body next to mine, feel its warmth. Forget everything that's happened.

"How long?" I asked.

"Half hour."

I sagged down on the sofa. "I feel like shit."

Brooke smiled at me. "Oh, Nathaniel. Are you okay?"

"Sure," I said. "No. I'm not okay."

She reached over and lightly stroked my hair.

"She was always there, you know. Always, always there. I don't talk to her in a year and I know I can call or write and she'd . . ." I closed my eyes, felt the fingers moving gently across my scalp. "Get this, Brooke. When we were in Atlanta, I e-mailed her. I said I met this fantastic woman and she's engaged and what should I do?"

"Wow. Who'd you meet?"

"Funny. She wrote back, 'Well, Nathaniel, you should probably pursue it. God forbid you look back on it in five years and think, If only . . . The last thing you want in life is regret.' "

Brooke was quiet. I opened my eyes and saw she wasn't looking at me.

"So, stupidly, I took her advice."

"Nate . . ."

"What?"

She just shook her head.

"It's amazing how fast you can fall for someone, Brooke. You know, when you let things go, when you try to will things to happen." I don't think I would have been saying these things if I hadn't been a little drunk on melancholy and lack of sleep. Or maybe I would have. Who knows?

She said bleakly, "I was confused—"

"I don't care."

"I *told* you I was confused."

"I told *you* I was falling for you."

"So why do you think I ended things?"

How was it, I wondered, that three days ago I was alone in Baltimore and relatively happy about it, and now I was in Northern California, enveloped by three of the biggest female forces of my life? Perhaps it was best that I strap on my armor, shield myself, go back to that lonelier, safer time.

"You know what else is amazing?" I said. "How quickly you can kill something off when you want to. How completely you can do it if you want."

Brooke glanced down at me, surprise or hurt or whatever on her face. Then she stood and left the room, giving me the chance to contemplate one of the biggest lies I ever told.

Five minutes later, Brooke handed me a telephone. "Larry and Don," she said.

"What?"

"The children." She handed me a piece of paper with some scrawl on it.

"Where did you—?"

"Their numbers were programmed into the kitchen telephone. The first two to come up on the screen when I scrolled through were Larry and Don."

"How do you know these are the kids?"

"Come on. The first two numbers on the phone? My mother does the same thing. Jeff's mother . . ." She trailed off.

"Jeff."

"The ex-betrothed, Nate. Look, I don't want to talk about him, or last summer, or anything like that, okay? Your friend just died; we just rummaged through all her stuff. . . . Anyway, trust me. With the numbers." She pointed to the phone in my lap. "It's time to call."

"Thanks. Seriously." I looked at a clock across the room; almost six. "Brooke, I didn't mean to get too heavy. I'm tired and sad, that's all. And I got to say I was a little pissed about how things ended in—"

"It's okay. Really," she said, cutting me off. "Why don't we just focus on what we need to do? I'm going to get a cup of tea."

The phone seemed very heavy in my hand. I held it for a second, then scrolled to the first name in the memory. Larry. I dialed.

CHAPTER 54

After breaking the unpleasant news to Larry Tobel—corporate lawyer, denizen of Chicago, asshole—I taped cardboard over the windowpane that I'd smashed. Then I walked through the house once more to make sure I hadn't missed anything or left something out of place. Brooke was already gone; we'd agreed to head back to her apartment to catch some winks and clean up.

On my way out, I noticed, hanging on a coatrack to the right of the front door, a clutch of ID badges. On top was a thick plastic card for Chimeragen. Dr. Tobel's computer-generated picture decorated the lower right corner. Below it was a hospital badge, also with her picture. Under these hung older ID cards, long past their expirations.

I pushed the Chimeragen and hospital IDs into my pocket. Then I left the house.

Larry Tobel. He was shocked, of course. But he was also pissed at me—wondering who I was, wondering why I'd found his mother, wondering what I was going to do with the damn dogs. I told him I was a former student and a friend of his mother's, told him I'd had a meeting with her, which is why I'd had the opportunity to find her dead. As for the dogs? Well, they were *en route à chez* Brooke, going insane in the backseat of my car. I smelled urine, which I was reasonably sure wasn't mine.

Thankfully, Larry said he would call and inform his brother, Don, about their mother's death. I sure as hell didn't want to talk to another distraught, gruff Tobel kid.

By the time I'd arrived at Brooke's place, she'd already surfed the Web and found the address for Branch #12 of Marine Bank of California. It wasn't far—in a town called Redwood City—and it opened at ten, which gave us a few hours to sleep.

"Where's the cat?" I asked as I set the dogs' cage down in the living room.

She pointed to the top of the refrigerator. "It's where he goes when he's scared. You can let them out."

I did. The smaller of the two dachshunds poked his nose tentatively out of the cage, then took his first steps. The other followed. The cat stared down from the refrigerator, and if looks could kill, there would have been two smoldering piles of ash in the middle of the room.

"Is that water on their feet?" Brooke asked as the two creatures padded around, sniffing everything, leaving wet pawprints behind them.

Shit. "Oh," I said casually, "maybe."

Brooke bent down and dabbed her finger in the liquid, then put it to her nose. "Brooke—" I warned.

"It's urine." She glanced at the two brown creatures making their way around the apartment. "Damn it, guys." She went to the kitchen area and brought back a spray bottle and paper towels. "I'll get the floor," she said, handing me a clump of Bounty. "You can take care of the cage."

Cleaning dog pee out of a dog cage: not my idea of a good time after pulling an all-nighter. But I did it. Then I showered. Then, thank God, I slept.

CHAPTER 55

Marine Bank of California, Number 12, Redwood City Branch, stood alone in an old commercial strip near the train tracks. It was a big building, but as with most places in this part of California, the look of it was almost purposely nondescript.

As we made our way across the parking lot, Brooke said, "You know they're not going to let us into the box."

"Of course they are," I replied. "We have the key."

"This isn't Switzerland, Nate. You need ID to get into these things. ID and the key."

Oh. I hadn't counted on that. In fact, I didn't have the first clue about safety-deposit boxes. No one in my family—no one that I ever knew of, at least—had a safety-deposit box.

"Why didn't you tell me that earlier?" I pushed through the doors and was blasted by air-conditioning.

"I was sleep deprived and didn't think of it."

"I'll sweet-talk them."

"Good luck," Brooke said.

In the bank, the teller stations stretched out to the left, while a few lonely desks were situated along the right side of the room. I spotted a pleasant-looking matron sitting behind a desk, bundled in a thick cardigan against the Nordic microclimate. Marnie Gill, Customer Service.

She smiled and asked how she could help.

"I need to get into this safety-deposit box," I said, fishing the key out of my pocket. Brooke rolled her eyes.

Marnie took the key and laid it on the desk. "Your account number?"

"I, ah, don't really have an account here. This is a friend's box. She gave the key to me."

Marnie hammered away impassively at the keys on the computer in front of her. "I'm sorry, but without express permission, we can't give you access to the security boxes here. The name on the account?"

"Harriet Tobel."

More typing; she stopped for a second and fished a small manila envelope from her desk drawer. She took the key and dropped it inside.

"Ah, that's my key," I protested.

"It's not," she said tartly. "It's the bank's key. And our policy in situations like this is to retain it for the proper account holder."

Brooke was smirking. She mouthed: Sweet sweet-talk. I wanted to wrap my hands around her neck.

Marnie said, "Could you spell the last name?"

I did.

The computer chugged and Marnie slipped the envelope and the key into her top desk drawer. She typed a few more characters into the computer. "Yes. Harriet Tobel." She looked at me. "What's your name?"

Great, I thought. *She's going to call security, they'll call the police, then I'll spend the rest of the day explaining to the cops why I'd stolen Dr. Tobel's personal effects. . . .*

"Nathaniel McCormick," I said. "Look, maybe we should just leave. We can take care of all this later—"

"Wait, please." Marnie's nails clicked on the plastic keys.

Brooke wasn't smiling anymore. She actually looked a little worried.

"Could I see a picture ID?" Marnie asked.

I gave her my Georgia driver's license. She studied it for a beat, looked at me, then handed it back.

Marnie opened the top drawer of her desk and removed the envelope with the key. I braced myself for her call to security to bust us. Instead, she slid the envelope across the desk to me. "I'm sorry for any inconvenience, Mr. McCormick. We must be careful, you understand."

She must have seen the confusion on my face. "The account holder changed access privileges for this account yesterday, adding your name. It's why your name didn't come up right away. Again, I apologize for any inconvenience." She stood.

"Yesterday? Can you tell me what time she came in to change the access?"

"Sure." Marnie bent back over her keyboard. "Five forty-five. Just before we closed."

And just a few hours after we'd met for lunch, a few hours before Dr. Tobel died.

* * *

While Brooke sat at the customer service desk, flipping through a really interesting brochure on mortgage rates, Marnie led me to the bank's vault. Outside of it, a desultory guy in a uniform sat at a desk, reading the *San Francisco Chronicle*. The guy pointed to a sign-in sheet on the desk, which I guess was Marnie's signal to scram.

"A pleasure serving you, Mr. McCormick," she said.

I thanked her and initialed the sheet.

The thick vault door was open flat against the bank's wall; a metal grate covered the opening to the vault itself. The guard put down his paper, asked for ID. I showed him my license. After a longer look than was needed, he pushed himself out of the chair and unlocked the grate.

"Follow me," he said.

I did, down a short hallway to a long room faced with hundreds of small doors. He went to one of them, opened the little door, exposing the locked metal box inside. He jutted his chin toward the box, which I assumed meant I was to take it. I pulled it out and followed him across the hall to a room with a small table and a single chair. The guard closed the door as he left.

It was just me and the box.

Nathaniel, please call me when you get this message. It's very important. Ivory Coast.

I held the key in my sweaty hand, Harriet Tobel's last words to me whirling in my brain. Before I knew it, I'd slid the key into the small lock and turned it. I pulled open the top of the box.

Inside, a single item sat on the gray metal. It was a videotape.

CHAPTER 56

The day was beautiful—not too hot—and it should have been nice to be riding in a BMW convertible with a beautiful blonde. But both Brooke and I were freaking out a little about what we might see on that tape. And then there was that question pounding in my head like an ominous drumbeat: *Did Harriet Tobel die because of this?*

At the apartment, all was peaceful. The dogs were asleep, the cat wide-awake, scheming, no doubt, a painful murder for the dogs.

"Shall we?" I asked.

Brooke nodded.

I pushed the tape into the VCR and grabbed the remote. "We should get some popcorn," I said.

"Funny."

I fell back onto the couch next to Brooke. As I did so, my pager went off. A familiar cell phone number popped up on the LED screen. "Tim," I said.

"Are you going to call him back?"

"Later."

"Are you going to call him before we see what's on the tape?" Brooke asked.

"No."

"Okay, Nathaniel, we need to watch this."

"Okay."

Still, I didn't move.

"Come on." And with that, Brooke reached over my hand and pushed Play on the controller. The screen scrambled for a second. Brooke didn't move her hand.

An image appeared: grainy, black-and-white. An image from a surveillance camera set high in a room. A bed filled most of the field, the bottom of the bed at the bottom of the screen. There was a figure in the bed—a woman—with a few monitors surrounding her. An IV ran from her chest to a stand hung with bags of fluid. *Okay,* I thought, *we're in a hospital.* The woman looked like she was sleeping.

The time stamp on the bottom of the screen dated the scene almost two years before. Above the time stamp, I recognized three block capitals that designated the university medical center where Dr. Tobel had her lab. That meant the security tape had been taken somewhere in the hospital.

Brooke said, "A hospital room."

"Strong work, Doctor."

"Shut up."

Nothing in the room moved except the flashing digits on one of the monitors.

"This is it?" Brooke asked, sounding disappointed.

"I assume it's not. I hope it's not."

"Number three, it says." Brooke pointed to the blocky white digit next to a two-letter abbreviation. "Room three."

We watched for five more minutes. Nothing changed but the numbers.

"Time to fast-forward," I decided, and hit the button.

But for the speeding time in the bottom of the screen, nothing changed—the woman didn't move, no one entered, until—

"Look—" Brooke said as a figure sped into the field of view. I rewound the tape and played it at normal speed.

It was a man. The camera was high and to his back; his face was covered in a face shield and surgical mask, so we couldn't see his features. He wore a gown and gloves. He pushed a cart in front of him.

"What's on the cart?" Brooke asked.

"Basin, maybe."

The man began to undo the woman's gown, exposing her breasts, torso, and the blue plastic diaper around her hips. A large scar ran across her right side, from under the arm to the midline about four inches below the breast.

The man put a couple of towels underneath the woman's buttocks, unfastened the diaper, removed it. Dropped the soiled thing into a biohazard bag. Throughout, the woman didn't move.

"Well," I said, "she appears to be comatose."

"Strong work, Doctor."

He brought the cart closer to the bed.

"He's bathing her," Brooke said. "He's going to bathe her."

Indeed he was, moving a sponge underneath and between the buttocks. It was disturbing, the way he'd wash, then pat dry. Too loving almost. A catheter snaked from between the woman's legs to a bag of urine attached to the side of the bed; the man moved the catheter to one side, then the other, cleaning around it. Wash, pat dry. Wash, pat dry. The sequence moved up the belly to the breasts, armpits, neck, face.

"What is this, Nathaniel?" Brooke asked. "He's bathing her. Big deal. Fast-forward."

"Wait," I said.

The man toweled off the naked body, then fished around in the cart. He moved to the woman's hands and began filing.

"He's just an orderly, Nate. Let's move on."

As the man moved from filing fingernails to toenails, I caught a glimpse of the eyes through the face shield, above the mask. I froze the picture. "Can you make out a face?"

"No," Brooke said.

I pushed Play. The man finished with the toenails and stood at the foot of the bed. I thought he would return to the cart, but he just stood there, his back to us, looking the length of the nude body.

Then he stepped to the cart, I guess to put the nail file down, and grabbed a tube of something. Then he stepped back to the foot of the bed. He kept staring at the body. I saw his right hand move to the front of his hips, lift his gown.

"Oh, no—" Brooke said beside me.

The hand began to move slowly and rhythmically. After a moment of that, he undid his pants from beneath the gown. He undid the cap to the tube and squirted something into his right hand.

Brooke said, "He's whacking off? This is what we're supposed to see? Oh—"

Just then, the man put down the tube and climbed onto the bed. "I can't watch this," Brooke moaned. And she didn't. She turned her head.

I, however, did watch as the orderly maneuvered between the legs of the comatose woman, moving the catheter to the side. He thrust into her a few times; his body went stiff when he came. The whole thing was over in two minutes. Finished, he climbed off her, cinched his pants. He took the sponge and cleaned up his mess, put a new diaper on her, redid the gown, smoothed back the woman's dark hair. For a long moment, he looked at her. Then, slowly, he lifted his face shield and pulled down his surgical mask. He bent and kissed the woman on the lips.

The man replaced the surgical mask and face shield, so when he turned toward the door, I still couldn't get a good look at him. Then he began to pull the cart out of the room. Then he was gone.

CHAPTER 57

"Is it over?"

"Yes."

"He raped her."

"Yes."

The tape continued to play, but it looked as it had in the beginning: a woman lying in a bed, nothing moving. It was sickening—she didn't look like she'd just been raped.

"This is awful," Brooke said. "Please turn it off."

"I need to see if there's anything else."

Brooke was silent. A thousand things were flying through my mind. Who was the man? Who was the woman? Why had Dr. Tobel wanted me to see this? The tape, of course, was just the beginning. It was only the opening to a conversation Dr. Tobel and I would never have.

And this—the tape itself, the circumstances of how it had come to me—spawned other questions. I let the ideas churn for a while. Finally, I said, "They killed her."

"Who killed who?"

"Dr. Tobel. Somebody killed her. So she wouldn't say anything about this." I gestured toward the television.

"How do you know that?"

"I don't, okay? It's just what I think, Brooke. Somebody didn't want this thing to get out."

"Who?"

"I don't know. I guess whoever would be affected most by a fuckup like this."

We stared at the screen. "Oh, Nate," Brooke said. "If that's true, we need to find out who the man is. And who that poor woman is."

Very astute questions, Sherlock, I thought. Then, unwisely, I said it.

Brooke glowered at me, but didn't say anything. Eventually, she spoke. She said what I was thinking but what I sure as hell didn't want to hear. "You know, your Dr. Tobel must have been involved in this somehow."

Your Dr. Tobel? "What do you mean *involved*?"

"She had the tape. She saved the tape."

"Meaning what?"

"Meaning she didn't just stumble across it. This is a rape, and last time I checked, it was highly illegal. There's got to be some reason she didn't turn it over to the police."

"Maybe she did turn it over to the cops."

"I don't think so. She wouldn't have had any reason to keep it, then. She wouldn't have hidden it away in a safety-deposit box. This is secret, Nate. And there's got to be a reason why Harriet Tobel kept the secret."

"Until now," I said glumly.

"Right. Until now."

Just then, the tape went black. "That's it," I said, and hit Rewind.
My pager vibrated. Tim.

"Still no more new cases," Herr Lancaster said.

"That's great."

"Great and not great. Bryan Tinings died last night. Same way as
the Fillmore woman. Multiple organ failure."

"Jesus. Maggie Phelps's boyfriend."

"Yes. She's pulling out of it, but she's not taking the news about her
beau's death real well. We've locked down all the group homes where
we've had cases—"

"Is that wise?" I interrupted. "I mean, they're going to be stuck in
the homes, screwing each other's brains out."

"That's a risk I'm willing to take. It's only five homes at this point.
We've narrowed the incubation time to seven to ten days."

"So we're in a holding pattern."

"Holding our breath, if that's what you mean."

Okay, I thought, *time to drop the bomb.* "Tim, I'm delaying the
flight." Brooke sat cross-legged on the couch next to me. She'd been lost
in thought, but her head shot toward me with "delaying the flight."

"Why—?" Tim Lancaster asked, annoyed.

"A friend of mine out here died. . . ."

"I'm sorry to hear that."

"I want to stay around until her funeral."

Tim chewed that one over. "When's that?"

"Today's Thursday. She's—she was—Jewish. She needs to be
buried by Friday sundown. Shabbat."

"You're a Jew?"

"With a name like McCormick? No."

"Well, your mother could have been. . . . Anyway, I need you in
Atlanta. Tomorrow latest."

Even for Tim, this was a little too much. "Tim, you said we're in a
holding pattern."

"No, *you* said that. And I'd like someone familiar with the
Baltimore situation down there. We need to coordinate the lab work be-

tween Atlanta and the locals up here. I need you to ride them down there."

"This was one of the most important people—"

"This is growing beyond us now. The FBI's involved—"

"And you're the one who brought them in," I pointed out. To Brooke, I mouthed: F-B-I.

"No, Nate, my bosses brought them in. Goes the whole way to the top."

"Great."

"Besides, it's for the best. Takes some of the heat off us. But we need to keep up appearances. It would be good for you to be down there as point man."

"If it's so important for me to be point man, then bring me back to Baltimore. Maybe you should go to Atlanta. That's your turf. I'm a field officer, not a—"

"You know I can't do that."

"I know that you don't want to do that." Icy silence. I'd gone too far. "At least let me stay out here to follow up on Gladys Thomas." I was going to tell him about the tape, about the weird circumstances of Harriet Tobel's death, but decided not to. Tim was ambivalent enough with my performance on this case so far; I didn't need him thinking I was throwing around conspiracy theories. Not yet, anyway.

"There's nothing to follow up on, Nate. And if there is anything to follow up on, it's a police matter, not something an EIS officer should play around with. Remember our mandate."

I wanted to remind him that our mandate was to identify and stop threats to public health, but I didn't.

"Also, I want you in Atlanta, ready to go down to Louisiana. There have been a few cases of West Nile reported. We're waiting to see how big it gets."

"So, which is it, Tim? Am I coming to Atlanta to coordinate lab work, or am I coming to hang out for West Nile to pop?"

"Both." Good old Tim Lancaster. Had an answer for everything. The real answer—that he wanted me out of this case—would never cross his lips. "You said the funeral was tomorrow? Okay, stay. But I want you in Atlanta by Saturday the latest. Give me a call when you get in."

"Okay," I said, though it would be impossible for me to button things up in California by then. And if I didn't button things up, I sure as hell wasn't going to leave for Atlanta. Il Duce would have to wait for that call.

"Well?" Brooke pushed a spoon into a bowl of some barnyard-looking mix.

"I still have a job. Until Saturday, at least."

"Good for you. What happens Saturday?"

"I have to be in Atlanta."

"That leaves us two days."

"*Us* two days? *Us?*"

"I didn't pull my first damned all-nighter since residency for nothing. This is important."

"What's important?"

"Nate . . ."

"I'm serious. What are we doing here? What's important?" My tone was sharp, and it occurred to me that I was being a real prick to this woman. Don't ask me why. Maybe because I was pissed off and unsettled at whatever weirdness was swirling around me. Maybe I was upset about Dr. Tobel being—what? Murdered? Involved in something that stank so much? Or maybe, just maybe, I was still miffed about Brooke leaving me a year before, and I wanted to punish her for it.

Anyway, whatever the reasons, I was being a jerk and I got a reaction. *Real mature, Nathaniel. Real mature.*

"Why are you on my case? I'm trying to help you out here."

"I'm not on your case. I'm just asking why you need to play the hero."

"What? Me, play the hero? I helped you out. Helped you do your fucking job, Doctor." Her eyes were blazing, real anger in them. "You know what, Nate? Fuck it."

"Brooke—"

"Take these two little shit dogs"—she gestured to the dachshunds, who were awake now, looking uncomfortably at the scene—"and go to a motel. Go poke around the city for whoever killed your beloved mentor. Because that's what it's really about now, isn't it? Not about some disease jumping around. It's personal now, isn't it, Nate?" Her voice got mean on that—*personal.*

"That's really wonderful, Brooke. Thanks for the sympathy."

"Or perhaps this is about Atlanta. Perhaps you needed to get one last jab in. Screw the best interests of the public health because of some misunderstanding a year ago."

How did she get to that? I was being so subtle.

"Oh, but no. Not you. You killed it off in Georgia. You're a real man, aren't you, Nate? An island. Totally in control of your emotions. Great. Really effective. You know what? Why don't you sit down and talk with your inner child for a while and figure out why you're really involved with this? And maybe, after that scintillating conversation, you'll realize maybe you should be in Atlanta, because you're so god-damned confused, you can't see the real situation out here."

"Confused? I'm confused? I thought *you* had a lock on confusion. Perhaps *you* need to figure out why you want to be deep into something that's not even your damn job. Work's not so interesting, so you need to step on my toes? You're still smarting from this blitzed marriage, so you want me to be your teddy bear? Your buddy? Is that it? I'm trying my damndest to make sure that what's in Baltimore stays there, that I find out what the hell's going on back there so I never have to worry about it again. And maybe I am wondering about why the only person who ever really loved me is stiff and cold at the ME's now. So crucify me for that, if you want. I don't care. I do not care, Brooke."

Screw her, I thought. *Screw her.* Screw her for not understanding where I was coming from, for not understanding her own motivations for being involved in this. Though she seemed kind, though she seemed to care about me, about Dr. Tobel, about this disease, she was a political animal—no better than anyone else. She was a budding Tim Lancaster with tits, great legs, and nice words.

I slammed into the bedroom to grab my things. I shouldered my two pieces of luggage and walked back into the living room. Brooke hadn't moved from the couch. Her jaw was set; she wouldn't look at me.

I said, "You can keep the goddamned dogs. Or take them to the pound. I don't care."

I left, marveling at how quickly things fall apart.

CHAPTER 58

So, two days. Two days to figure out who was the rapist, who was the raped, and how that meant anything to me. Two days to figure out how and if this played into the sickness in Baltimore, to figure out how Harriet Tobel was involved and if her death was tied to this. Two days to divine why I'd been such an ass to Brooke. Two days to wonder why I had to be the lone cowboy who fights his battles outside the system, who always gets the job done, who always gets the glory, who always gets the girl. Nate McCormick: Hero.

Except I wasn't getting the job done, I wasn't getting the girl. I was, however, fucking up. You would have thought I'd learned by now.

I headed north toward the university, toward another emotional vortex. The sad truth is I had to speak with Alaine Chen, who, as my luck would have it, was the person most likely to have some information about Harriet Tobel and a nondescript room number three somewhere in the hospital.

I felt sick to my stomach as I climbed the steps of the Heilmann Building. Going from a Brooke Michaels disagreement to an Alaine Chen summit would not have been my choice for a great afternoon. But heroes have to be courageous, right?

The Tobel lab buzzed with activity. Yonnick was there, as were the undergrad and some other students whom I didn't recognize. But something was missing, of course, though I couldn't tell if it was the actual zeitgeist in the lab or just in my head. The captain of the Tobel lab lay, at that moment, on an autopsy table. You could feel the lack of a presence. Still, I didn't know if anyone in the lab had learned of her death yet. Who would have told them? The police? Larry or Don? Probably not.

Then I saw Alaine and knew that she knew. She looked—well, stunned: her eyes were red, and her face looked ravaged. For a moment, I was touched. Alaine Chen, who'd been the coldest, most remote woman I'd ever known, could *feel*.

She caught my eye, forced a little smile, then motioned me into Dr. Tobel's office. I followed, and she closed the door behind me.

"Nate . . . I can't believe it."

"Neither can I," I said. Couldn't believe Dr. Tobel was dead. Couldn't believe two emotionally spent women in one day.

Though this would have been the moment to embrace, neither of us made the move. After a moment, we talked: about how sad we were, about how much of a surprise this was—all the requisite death stuff. I was feeling kind of close to her, though I couldn't tell if that was because we were both stricken with grief or whether it was genuine. Nevertheless, "close to Alaine Chen" wasn't a spot I wanted to be in.

No, that's not completely true. Actually, it's not true at all. As she went on about her feelings toward Dr. Tobel, about how lost she felt, I realized how desperately I *did* want to be close to her. I'd just lost my mentor and friend, Brooke Michaels hated me now and was probably sticking knitting needles into a little Nate doll, Tim Lancaster was ruing the day he hired me. I don't think I'd ace the emotional intelligence test, but I could see why I wanted to connect with Alaine. In that moment, it hit me how goddamned unhappy I was. Like Alaine. Would it be so dangerous to comfort each other? Would it be so bad to let gravity take over, let her fall against me, let her break down and feel her hot tears dampen my shirt, cup the back of her head in my hand, stroke her hair? To press my lips to her wet eyes, taste the salt? *It will be okay,* I imagined telling her. *It will be okay, Alaine. It will be okay.*

Alaine kept talking and I kept struggling. I leaned back against a lab bench, trying to keep myself steady and as far from her as I could. My hands were on the bench. *Keep them there,* I thought. *Make no gesture.* I could not afford once again to be in this woman's emotional orbit. I had a job to do. I had only two days.

"We have no idea what will happen to the lab," Alaine was saying. "Chimeragen and the FDA will want a big name to carry on the work. But we've done so much here, Nathaniel. We know the protocols better than anybody, and if they move everything to Duke or Yale . . ."

All right, Alaine, good. Break the spell by mentioning your career woes. This was the Alaine I wanted to remember—the ice queen, the self-obsessed. I did not want to see her feel. I did not want sympathy to wreck my defenses.

So, I didn't let it. I had walked away from Brooke Michaels that morning. I sure as hell could walk away from Alaine Chen.

"I need to show you something," I said abruptly. Alaine stopped her story, a little taken aback.

"There's a conference room on this floor, right? I need a VCR."

CHAPTER 59

I didn't give a lot of prelude to the tape, just said it had come from Dr. Tobel before she died. OK, I made it a little more pointed than that.

"Dr. Tobel called me to tell me where to find this. She left the message around nine o'clock. Three hours later, I found her dead."

I pushed Play and room number three swam into view. "You recognize the room?" I asked.

Alaine glanced at me, then back to the screen. Her mouth moved a little; then she said, "I don't know."

"Who is the woman?"

"I don't know."

"What do you mean, 'I don't know'?"

"How many interpretations of 'I don't know' are there, Nathaniel? *I don't know.*"

I shook my head. For what it's worth, I realized I was not wasting a lot of kindness or sensitivity on Dr. Chen. Chalk it up to my being an asshole or the lone hero Brooke Michaels took me for. Actually, chalk it up to that and to the fact that, minutes ago, I'd very nearly embraced the spider woman who'd caused me such pain. I felt like I'd narrowly missed a fatal car crash.

But there was something else at work here, too: Alaine's reaction to all of this bothered me.

"See if you recognize this person. Dr. Tobel probably knew who this is. I'm guessing you do, too."

The bath played out on the screen, then the masturbation, then the rape. Alaine's face slipped from a look I couldn't put my finger on to one of horror and disgust, to something like fear. I froze the tape on the man's exit. Alaine's eyes stayed locked on his image.

"Alaine?"

Her head jerked toward me. Her hand went halfway toward her mouth and hung there. It trembled.

"I . . . This is horrible."

"Do you know that man, Alaine?"

She stared at me for a second, as if she couldn't see me, then she looked back to the screen. "No. I can't see his face. Why would I know who this is?"

"You have any idea about this incident?"

She shook her head.

You goddamned liar, I thought. "Do you know where this room is?"

She didn't answer.

"Do you know where this room is?" I repeated sharply.

"Nathaniel, please—"

"Please what? The room is in this hospital, Alaine. Harriet Tobel had this tape. You're the head researcher in her lab. *Where is this room?*"

"I don't . . . I'm too upset. . . . Nate. Please. Please, Nate. I'm upset about Harriet's death. Then you . . . you show me this. What am I supposed to say?"

"You're supposed to say what you know, what Dr. Tobel told you. Why did she have this tape?" Alaine said nothing. "Why did she want me to have this? Why did she want to give it to me right after I told her about the outbreak in Baltimore?" Alaine's slicked eyes cut toward me, then away.

"Stop it, Nathaniel."

"Would Harriet Tobel have been killed because she had this?"

Nothing.

"Was Harriet killed because she wanted to tell me something?"

With that, Alaine Chen—soulless Alaine Chen—took a moment, put her head in her hands, and began to cry. And I—soulless Nathaniel McCormick—took a step toward her.

I said, "Alaine, please help me out here."

Nothing.

The idea of comforting her returned. Before me, there was no spider woman, just a sad, scared girl. The primordial, undefined warmth that I'd felt toward her years before and spent years trying to kill off returned. Before I could stop myself, I'd reached out and touched her shoulder. A small gesture, but it was enough. She rolled to my chest and began to sob. My arms closed around her. Her tears dampened my shirt. They were hot and wet. They felt just as I'd imagined.

So, the dangerous fantasy had become real. Standing there,

clutching this woman I'd loved, rocking her, whispering in her ear, I knew I had crossed a line. Crossed into what, however, I did not know.

On the VCR, the pause clicked off and the image of the rapist, of the comatose woman, of room number three, gave way to darkness.

Five minutes? Ten? I have no idea how long I stood in that ugly conference room, embracing my former lover. In the end, it was she, not I, who made the tiniest push to signify the end of things. Had she not done that, had it been up to me, we might have held the position for weeks, the two of us wasting away to nothing. I let go.

"You okay?" I asked.

"Yes," she said. She wiped at her eyes and forced a smile. "I'm sorry."

"No—"

"How are you?"

"I'm fine." I looked around the room. "There's a tissue here?"

She pointed to a roll of paper towels. I pulled off two sheets, handing one to her. I blew my nose in the stiff material. She followed suit, then tossed the paper towel, grabbed another. She began to dab at my chest, at the damp spot left by her tears. The tenderness of the act almost killed me. "Sorry about your shirt."

"I have others."

She stopped grooming me and we stood for a moment, looking at each other. The moment was over and I didn't know what to do. I nodded and said lamely, "I'll be going."

"Sure."

I nodded again, then crossed the room to eject the tape from the VCR. Another glance at Alaine Chen, and I left.

I was in danger of falling into a pit of nostalgia and what-ifs that couldn't benefit anybody, least of all me. Even so, I stood outside that conference room, waiting, I suppose, for Alaine to come out. I guess I wanted to see her vulnerable just one more time.

But she didn't appear. After a few minutes, I realized I was obsessing. I had more pressing business, I told myself. Six people had died. I left the Heilmann Building, a soundtrack of two words—*stupid, weak*—marking my steps.

Outside, I found a chair, a ratty discarded thing, under a couple of hemlocks. I set it upright, dusted the seat, and parked myself. I tried to think about things that had little to do with the sticky history between Alaine and Nathaniel.

A rape, Harriet Tobel, Alaine's supposed ignorance of the connection between the two. I didn't know much; that was clear. What I did know was that things—things about which I knew too damn little—were happening fast. Doors were closing, the wagons circling, all that. I didn't have much time.

"Damn it," I said. There was information I needed, information I failed to get because I'd run from Alaine like a kid running from a bully. I looked back at the Heilmann Building. Back in the lion's maw.

Upstairs again, I went to the conference room, half-hoping to find Alaine at the whiteboard, scrawling hearts shot through with arrows, *NM + AC* written inside in loopy girl-letters. But of course she wasn't scrawling anything; she wasn't there. I went to the lab.

Yonnick—bearded, Semitic, intense—fiddled with a small tray dotted with a hundred small wells.

"Is Dr. Chen here?" I asked.

He looked up briefly, then back to his tray. "Haven't seen her."

I watched him work for a moment, then asked, "ELISAs?"

He nodded.

"Fun, fun," I said. Running ELISAs was tedious. "What are you looking for?"

"Interleukins. Immune response."

ELISA is a test to see what proteins are present in whatever sample you chose to test. For example, if I became ill, my body would produce signaling proteins—cytokines—important for inflammation, which would help fight the disease. These would be picked up by ELISA.

"The Chimeragen project?"

Yonnick glanced at me suspiciously, then nodded.

"Anything else?"

"I work mostly on Chimeragen, some on HIV immunity."

"Okay," I said. "Where do the Chimeragen samples come from?"

He stopped working. "Who are you again?"

So, Yonnick was going to be a pain in the ass. I pulled out my badge. "I met you yesterday. Nathaniel McCormick from CDC."

"Yeah, I remember. You should talk to Dr. Tobel."

"Dr. Tobel died last night." Yonnick's face froze, mouth half-open, obviously disbelieving. A palpable quiet drifted through the lab as others stopped their work to listen in. "I'm sorry you had to find out this way," I said. "She died late last night of a heart attack. You'll want to talk to Dr. Chen about the details. But I need to ask you about your work here in the lab. So, let's start at the beginning. Again, where did the samples come from?"

"Talk to Dr. Chen about the details," Yonnick said, his voice impassive, and continued filling the wells on the ELISA tray. "We signed a nondisclosure agreement."

This guy was definitely pissing me off.

As I was about to rip into Yonnick, a voice came from behind me. "Dr. McCormick?"

Alaine. I turned.

"Why don't we talk outside?" she said, and, without waiting for me to agree, turned away. I followed her out into the hall to an office a few yards from the lab entrance. She opened the door, but didn't enter.

"You should go." Alaine's tone was chill and businesslike. Seems Dr. Chen did a better job of compartmentalizing than I did. It was like the embrace a quarter hour ago never happened for her.

"The room in the tape, Alaine—where was it?"

"Dr. McCormick . . ."

"It's Doctor now?"

"Nathaniel. We need to take care of some things here. I'll talk to you about it later."

"Tell me about Dr. Tobel's work. The Chimeragen work, the work with HIV."

"Please go."

"I need to find out everything she was working on. I need to know what's going on here. For the Chimeragen work, what tissue samples are you testing? Dr. Tobel said you were at the point of human trials, so I'm assuming the samples are human. Where are these people? Are they in the community?"

Her face stayed stony.

"I can call the FDA and get access to all this stuff anyway." That was a bluff. Though I could lean on the FDA to find out the protocols of Dr. Tobel's work, it would take days, if not weeks, to do so. And I would have to make a compelling case to them that I needed the information. Compelling wasn't necessarily what I had. . . .

I waited a moment for Dr. Chen to crack. She didn't; I shook my head. "Okay, Alaine. Thanks for your help."

I turned my back on her and walked down the hall. Before descending the steps, I turned to look at her. Our eyes met; hers betrayed nothing. A thick curtain had descended around Alaine and around the entire lab. It was impressive and creepy. And, to be totally honest, hurtful.

"I don't know what masters you're serving, Alaine. You're doing wrong, here. You know it and I know it."

But if her blank look was any indication, Alaine Chen did not give a shit.

CHAPTER 60

The car was baking hot. I sat with the door wide-open, one leg inside, one outside resting on the tire of the Porsche parked next to me. I'd just ended a call with Larry Tobel, who'd gotten into town a few hours earlier. He'd asked about the dogs, asked about the broken window at the Tobel house, and told me when and where the funeral was to be held.

After the call, I closed my eyes, felt the sweat leak from under my arms. I tried to piece together what the hell was going on here; I felt like I was working with fifty pieces in a thousand-piece jigsaw puzzle.

The medical library, for years one of the school's most acute embarrassments, was blissfully unchanged. The uncomfortable chairs, the two inadequate portable air conditioners, the god-awful study bins were exactly as I'd left them ten years before. Promises of a new facility—plans were drawn and redrawn—were still clearly only promises. I wondered how long until the student body would finally crack and make a run on the dean's office with torches, pitchforks, and malfunctioning copy cards.

I found a computer in what was called the research alcove, an ugly little room off to one side of the library. Computers sat on blond wood tables that looked like they'd been pilfered from an elementary school circa 1975. I pulled a chair to the computer and turned the monitor to the wall.

One of the portable air conditioners hummed away, creating an antarctic microclimate around me while the rest of the library fried.

At least it will keep me awake, I thought.

I wanted to begin my research at, well, the beginning. Luckily, the entire campus was networked to the same databases, so I was able to access Westlaw even from the medical library. I wanted to check on any court cases that might explain what I'd seen happening on the tape. I typed in *rape* and the name of the university. Six things came up: something about a junior baseball player who'd raped another student a couple years back; a number of cases of rapists who had taken degrees at the university. Nothing about a rape at the medical center.

Well, I wasn't comfortable with the law anyway. Back to medicine. I logged on to PubMed, typed in Harriet Tobel's name, and got a list of more than a hundred publications. A quick scan through the titles showed me none of them had anything to do with the Chimeragen project. Her most recent work was interesting, but probably not relevant: HIV vaccine work in collaboration with a researcher called Bonner at the University of California, San Francisco. I printed out the articles anyway and glanced through them. The thrust of the work involved mutating the HIV virus to a nonlethal strain and inoculating monkeys. The results, according to the articles, were promising but inconclusive.

Inconclusive, good word.

I Googled *Chimeragen* and cruised through its Web site. It was mostly marketing bullshit: an unending supply of organs for those in need, the dawning of "a new day in medicine" led by none other than Chimeragen, that sort of trash. The company, claimed the Web site, was backed by sterling venture capital. The market potential for "made-to-order" kidneys alone would be worth billions. Actually, it was pretty sexy stuff, the kind of revolutionary thing that made you want to throw in some disposable income, get your return, and buy that house in Martha's Vineyard you'd always wanted.

I went to the page that listed the officers of the company. Otto Falk—that eminent transplant surgeon—was there, of course, as Chief Science Officer. The name of the CEO, however, surprised me: Ian Carrington, Alaine's fiancé. I guessed Carrington was part of one of the venture groups backing Chimeragen and they wanted one of their own at the helm. Understandable, I guessed. But the connections jarred me.

Alaine Chen was second in command at the lab charged with independently validating the risks of the procedures financed by Chimeragen. Alaine and Ian Carrington, CEO of Chimeragen, were engaged. Conflict of interest here? Hmmm.

After a few more minutes, I found out just how far Chimeragen had progressed. Dr. Tobel had mentioned that the company was just about to enter Phase Three. Indeed, this was corroborated by the information on the Web site. Human trials for Chimeragen had been underway for over a year now, with "extremely promising preliminary results." I went on to the Web site's public relations area, filled with articles that, to put it lightly, gushed about the company's prospects. And I thought hyperbolic press coverage died with the dot-coms.

I printed out some of the juicier stuff.

By that time, the subzero temperatures were getting to me. But I still had some digging left to do on the Big Kahuna himself, Otto Falk, Chimeragen's Chief Science Officer. I went to the main section of the library, to actual print and paper, to where the air-conditioning couldn't reach. There, in the subtropical temperature, I found a few books that Falk had either written or edited. To say this guy was a leader in the field would be a disservice to him: Falk was *the* leader. One of the books I found had a time line of the man's accomplishments:

> 1969: Monkey-to-human kidney transplant. Patient lived five days.
> 1971: Porcine kidney transplants into two patients. One lived two weeks, the other for almost a month.
> 1979: Porcine pancreas transplant. Patient lived for eight days.
> 1986: Baboon heart transplant into infant. Patient lived two weeks.

And on and on. The procedures gradually became more complicated and the patients lived longer. It was truly amazing stuff.

> 1998: Porcine kidney transplant. Patient lived for three months.
> 1999: Porcine liver transplant. Patient lived for two months.
> 2001: Porcine kidney transplant. As of this printing, patient is still alive.

I stopped on a chapter, written by Falk, entitled: "The Case for Human Experimentation in Xenotransplantation." Fascinating. The intro to the piece said that the text was originally presented to a gathering of the American Society of Transplant Surgeons in the midnineties and that it generated a storm of controversy. When I read it, I understood why.

The gist of Falk's speech was that the time had come "truly to test, in a rigorous and controlled manner, the promise of xenotransplantation." For Falk, testing in a rigorous and controlled way involved putting animal organs into brain-dead individuals and observing them. He wrote: "Transplanting a porcine kidney into an otherwise healthy human and monitoring that individual for a day would yield more relevant data than performing a thousand transplants into primates and watching them for a year." He proposed asking the families of brain-dead individuals—those grievously injured in automobile crashes, for example—to allow him to use the bodies of their loved ones.

I thought about the woman who'd been raped. *My God,* I thought.

Back at the computer, I ran a PubMed search of Otto Falk's articles. I was looking for anything he'd published on clinical trials using xenotransplants. Not surprisingly, I found nothing; what I did find were the case reports on the one-offs he'd done with sick individuals and a bunch of animal studies. I wondered, though, if the human trials that Chimeragen was conducting had anything to do with brain-dead individuals. If Falk was conducting the studies with Chimeragen, it meant he could keep the progress under wraps with nondisclosure agreements. Even exchanges with the FDA could be corralled and controlled.

It was getting late and I wanted to do a little more digging in the hospital before everyone left for the day. Specifically, I wanted to talk to the functionary who would know about all goings-on in his or her domain, someone whose language I could speak.

CHAPTER 61

"Could you tell me where to find the hospital epidemiologist?" I was standing near the main entrance to the hospital, talking to an elderly black lady in a fantastic pink hat.

My question seemed to throw her for a second; the poor woman was probably wondering what kind of crackpot complaint I had that I needed an epidemiologist. She blinked twice, then fished a large book from under her table. It took her a few minutes to find the room and telephone numbers. She scribbled the digits on a small scrap of paper.

"G wing is down to the right. It's somewhere over there. I've never been there, so you'll have to ask around."

Okay, a medical truth: all hospitals are impossible to navigate. I've seen a lot of them and have come to the conclusion they were all designed by the same madman, or at least by his architectural firm. Add to this that I hadn't done my rotations at this medical school, in this hospital, so I didn't know the surgery wing from the medicine wing from my elbow.

It took me ten minutes and as many requests for directions to find the epidemiologist's office—off the main hallway, tucked deep in a warren of offices and narrow corridors. Surprisingly, the doctor was in, her door open. I knocked on the door frame and Elizabeth Perry, MD, spoke without looking up from her computer. "Yes?"

I introduced myself. "CDC" got her attention, and she stopped noodling away on the keyboard.

"Is there a problem?"

"No," I said. "At least I don't think so."

Perry, a large woman with glorious skin and a perfect coiffure, sat rigidly in the chair. Then she asked, "How can I help you?"

"I understand you house a few comatose or vegetative patients in the hospital . . ." I let the statement fade, hoping she'd fill in the details.

"Yes," Perry said, not filling in the details.

"Where are these patients located?"

That seemed to confuse her, not because she wasn't sharp but because my question was sort of asinine. "I'm not sure I follow you, Doctor. We have patients in the CCU and ICU in comas. On the medicine ward—"

"Any patients in a persistent vegetative state here?" PVS, as it's called, is different from a coma. Strictly defined, it is "wakefulness without awareness." In layman's terms, it means that almost all brain function has ceased except for the normal sleep cycle and basic reflexes.

"If they're in a PVS, we usually ship them to long-term care facilities."

"But do you have any patients here?"

"What's this about, Doctor . . . ?"

"McCormick."

"Dr. McCormick. I'm sorry I'm distracted. You caught me in the middle of dousing a small fire. We had a *Serratia* outbreak on the cardiac care unit last month and, well, you know the paperwork."

"That's what medicine is, right? Paperwork."

"Sad but true. Can you tell me why you're here?"

"Nothing official," I said, gearing up for another lie. "I went here for medical school and happened to be in the area. One of my pet interests at CDC is infection control measures for PVS patients. Just thought I'd pop in to see if you house any people here."

Dr. Perry looked doubtful.

"Like I said, this is for my own satisfaction," I blathered on. "Eventually, I might do a cross-institutional study on protocols and procedures"—lie—"but for now I just wanted a heads-up as to what was going on. I figured it was worth checking out my alma mater."

"Fair enough." She relaxed a bit and sat back into her chair, but I noticed she still hadn't invited me to sit. "Like I said, we usually ship patients to long-term care if they're in a PVS for longer than a few weeks. However"—she swiveled and batted a few things into the computer—"we do have some folks you might be interested in. It's not a normal situation, really, but it shows what we're doing with infection control." She was frowning slightly. "If you want to look at our protocol for the intensive care unit, where you'll find a lot of comatose patients, I can give you all our paperwork."

"Great," I enthused.

"And you're more than welcome to roam around up there if you like. I'll call and get you a visitor's pass."

"That's terrific," I said. "But I'm more interested in the situation you were telling me about before. The one that wasn't normal?"

"Well, I spoke too soon. There's relatively tight security down there. A faculty member here is conducting a study with a few PVS patients, and no one's allowed to see the patients but family and those involved with the study."

"What's the study about?"

"Oh." She shook her head. "The study. I would wash my hands of this, Dr. McCormick, except for the fact that it's in my hospital and I'm responsible for infection control. But I must tell you, I do not approve of what's going on here. The ethics are—how shall I say?—debatable, to say the least."

"So, why is the study continuing?"

"Money and glory, simple as that. And I don't like it." She narrowed her eyes and studied me. "Another reason I don't like it is that I'm worried I'm sitting on a bomb. May I see your CDC credentials, please?"

The non sequitur took me aback. But I managed to find my badge and hand it over. She perused it, looked hard at the picture, then hard at my face. As she handed it back, she said, "I was an EIS officer many moons ago."

"Where?"

"Austin, Texas, of all places. Where are you?"

"I'm in Atlanta. I'm Special Pathogens, so I get to go all over."

"You're out here for work?"

"Well, yes, but like I said, I'm here right now to satisfy my own curiosity." I just kept shoveling more of it. From her look, I could tell she didn't buy it.

"Well, that's too bad, actually. If you were here on official business, I would feel obliged to show you all you wanted to see. But if this is just personal . . ."

We stared at each other.

"But if it were official," I said, "it might alert some people who, at this time, I'd rather not alert."

"Then I wonder," she replied, "if it would be possible to make this an official visit only if we needed to."

"You mean . . . ?"

"I mean if any shit hits any fan, Dr. McCormick, I will be able to cover for myself and the hospital. Forgive the profanity."

"I have an amazing ability to draw shit in my direction," I said. "Forgive the image."

Elizabeth Perry laughed. "All right, then, Doctor, I think we understand each other. I want you to know that I don't believe anything untoward is going on; if it were, I'd scream bloody murder. But I also don't care for the secrecy surrounding this. Medicine should be an open book, and I figure the more people know, the better."

She picked up the telephone and dialed a number. "This is Dr. Perry. Who is this?" she asked. "Okay, Tom. I'm sending someone down to you. Dr. McCormick. He's just coming to look around." She paused.

"I don't know if he's cleared or not, but he's cleared by me, all right? Dr. McCormick's an epidemiologist checking out our stellar infection control down there." She listened for a moment. "Thanks. Oh, another thing, Tom—I don't want to deal with the darn paperwork, so do me a favor and don't tell anyone from the company or the Tobel or Falk labs that Dr. McCormick was there." Another pause. "Thanks." And she hung up the phone.

"Tobel or Falk labs?" I asked.

"Yes. You're familiar?"

"You could say that."

She scribbled something on a slip of paper. "Here's the suite number. It's in the basement, near the morgue. Fitting, no?"

Fitting or not, I didn't know, but some things were coming together for me. Though I thought I knew the answer to my question, I asked it anyway. "What is this ethically dubious study? You never told me."

Dr. Perry opened her arms in a mocking way, like she was presenting something grand to an audience. "Pigs, Dr. McCormick. They're putting pig parts into brain-dead people down there. In my hospital."

CHAPTER 62

In ten minutes, I was standing at what looked like a nurses' station. To the left were two double doors with a key card lock to the side.

The nurse, a big white guy in his forties who looked like he might moonlight as a heavy for the Corleones, was reading a book. He raised his eyes as I approached the desk.

"Dr. McCormick?" he asked. He smiled broadly; I immediately liked the guy.

"Tom?" He nodded. "Call me Nate."

"Call me Nurse Harrison," he said, laughing. "Dr. Perry said for me to let you look around. There's not much to see, but you can have your run."

"Thanks." His book, I noticed, was *Pragmatism*, by William James. "A little light reading?" I asked.

He stood. "Have a paper due on James next week. Gotta love the pragmatists. Philosophy that works. Not this BS Continental stuff where you read it and two hours later you want to put a bullet in your head because nothing means anything."

Nurse Tom Harrison walked around the nurses' station to the door and pressed his ID to the card lock. It beeped and clicked and he pushed open the door. "James, Dewey, all those pragmatists. Views you can use," he said.

I wondered where I could get some of those.

" 'Views you can use,' " I said. "That's good."

"That's a Tom Harrison original."

We moved into a short hallway flanked by three doors and three windows. At the end of the hall was a makeshift changing area, a screen pushed to one wall that could be moved across the hallway to block the view.

"Master's in bioethics," Tom said. "Been working on it for two years and will probably be working on it till the Second Coming. Which is a problem for me, since I'm agnostic."

"Well, it's the journey that counts, right?" He looked at me, and I could tell he was trying to size up whether I was pulling his leg or not. I wasn't.

"The journey. Right, Nate."

I stepped to one of the windows and peered inside. Though I'd half-suspected what I would see, I wasn't prepared for the wash of adrenaline through my body. My knees went weak. The room was identical to the one I'd seen on Dr. Tobel's videotape—comatose patient in a bed, surrounded by monitors. Room of the same dimensions. Of course, this could all be coincidence. . . .

"Are there cameras in the rooms?" I asked. "For security?"

"Sure."

"Could I see the monitors?"

Tom looked at me oddly. "Sure. Why?"

"No reason." To keep Tom Harrison from processing that, I continued. "So each of these people has some pig organ inside them."

"Yeah," Tom said.

I walked the length of the hallway, looking in on each of the patients. Three women and two men, every one spookily the same, lying like the dead on their pristine beds. Oddly, the last room on the left was dark. "Why is one of the rooms empty?"

"Oh, I don't really know. I just got here last year, after she was gone. They said she'd died from an unrelated infection. Unrelated to the new organs, at least."

"She?"

"Yeah. Originally there were four women, two men."

"They didn't say what she died of?"

"Not to me."

"Do you know her name?"

Tom smiled. "Can't tell you that, Doctor. Privacy rules."

I looked into the three rooms with the women, trying to recognize a face from the tape. But the woman's face in the security tape had been hazy and low resolution, and it had been hours—only hours?—since I'd last viewed the tape. I went back to the empty room.

"What room number is this?"

"Room three," he said. "Why?"

I didn't answer. Instead, I said, "Where do the pigs come from? The organ donors."

Tom was getting uneasy. He shrugged. "Doctor—Nate—I don't know why you're here. All I know is that Dr. Perry told me to let you look around. But I'm the wrong person to ask about any of this stuff. I just watch these poor blokes and give them their meds. You should talk to one of the company people or the lab people. There's Harriet Tobel, a man called Falk who heads this thing. And there's this very attractive doctor a young man like you should definitely meet. Dr. Chen—"

"I've talked to them," I said too sharply. "Is there anything you can tell me?"

"No. I've probably given you too much as it is. They made us all sign a nondisclosure agreement."

"They made everybody sign a nondisclosure. So much for open and free science." I rubbed at my face and decided I needed a shave. "So, what about infection control?"

"Pretty simple, really. Even though the patients are on minimal immunosuppressive drugs, we treat them as immunocompromised. But actually, the company people are pretty freaked about any bugs these guys might have, so we take universal precautions when dealing with them. You know, to protect us as well as protect them."

I thought of the man having sex with the vegetative woman, no condom—definitely not universal precautions.

I stood in front of one of the rooms occupied by a woman. There she lay, waxen and still, but otherwise looking pretty healthy. "What does the bioethicist in you say about what's going on here?"

"About what?"

"About this." I stretched my arm toward the motionless woman.

Tom laughed. "The work they're doing here has a great potential to save many lives. No more shortages of organs. Imagine that. Really wonderful. But I'm enough of a utilitarian to think that . . . well, they're not treating these people as *people.* These poor folks are a means to our ends. I wonder if that's right."

I turned away from the comatose woman and smiled. "Tom—Nurse Harrison—that was the most noncommittal answer I've ever heard. You'll make a great bioethicist."

He laughed again.

On the way out of the suite, Tom took me to the nurses' station. There, on the desk, were six monitors. One, labeled "3," was dark. In the others, I saw the exact same view I had on Dr. Tobel's tape.

Here, I thought. The rape happened here.

CHAPTER 63

Pig organs, a rape, a weird outbreak in Baltimore, Harriet Tobel's concern about the outbreak, her death. So, these things seemed to be connected, and it was worthwhile pursuing the connection. Well, *seemed to be connected* might be too strong. They possibly might have a chance of being connected.

I sat at the computer in the library, got to PubMed, and ran a search on PERV. A hundred and twenty papers came up. Despite the acronym, the authors of these papers were not interested in pedophiles. They were interested in something close to my heart and my career: viruses.

The PERV is the porcine endogenous retrovirus, a bug that lies dormant in pig cells. Most pigs carry a number of different variants incorporated somewhere in their genome, and at least three varieties have been shown to infect human cells. The PERVs—and I have to admit I love the name—are the little goblins of porcine xenotransplantation. The fear is, by introducing pig tissue into humans via grafts and transplantation, these viruses will jump the species barrier and infect the host. In the pig, PERVs are largely inert, due to thousands of years of coevolution. The two species, you could argue, learned how to get along, much like the cytomegalovirus, which infects well over half the human race and rarely has severe consequences. I mean, it's not in any parasite's interest to kill off its host, because that, in the end, kills the parasite, be it a virus, a bacterium, or a worm. However, you put a PERV in close contact with a new organism—people, in this instance—you run the risk of detonating some major biological fireworks. Think about HIV. Many theorize it grew up in monkeys and is relatively inert in them. But once HIV jumped to humans, to virgin territory that hadn't evolved adequate defenses . . . Well, everyone knows the rest of the story.

I blazed through a couple of papers to refresh my memory on the porcine retroviruses. Some elements didn't add up: retroviruses didn't make people bleed like what we were seeing in Baltimore. I might expect cancer, I might even expect an AIDS-like syndrome, but not the brutal picture painted by the dead Bethany Reginald and Deborah Fillmore.

I printed out a paper with the most recent information on detection and left.

Time to assess, to sit and try to figure out where I should be going. I needed somewhere quiet, away from the library and the med school and the possibility of another encounter with the past. And my car seemed like the place to be. In any investigation—I'm talking epidemiological here—there's a lot of sitting and thinking. Not really the stuff of action shows.

As it turned out, however, I did get something more exciting than a tranquil half hour to myself. It was getting late, and the ranks of the faculty's luxury cars and the students' decades-old beaters had thinned. From the outside, my rental looked fine, sitting, appropriately, between an old Toyota and the sparkling new Porsche. As I approached the car, though . . .

"Son of a bitch."

Something was missing. Hell, not *something*. Everything. All my things, which had been in the backseat, were gone. The bag with my clothes, gone. The bag with the video from Dr. Tobel, with Dr. Tobel's HIV vaccine work, gone. My goddamned toothbrush. Everything.

I swore a lot and I swore loudly. A couple of kids—undergrads, two Asian girls—glanced over at me and hurried away. I used the word *fuck* a few more times; the girls quickened their pace.

On the slim hope that the considerate thieves had placed my be-longings in the trunk, hoping to hide them from less considerate thieves, I popped the boot. Nada.

So, all I was left with were the clothes on me, my cell phone, pager, PDA, my notebook, and the printouts from the library. *Great,* I thought, *absolutely great.*

Now, I am not fucking stupid. Rash, maybe. Arrogant and inse-cure, sure. But not stupid. Car vandals don't case medical school parking lots in this part of California in the middle of the day; normal car thieves don't have the expertise to jimmy locks on a new-model Buick. And the coincidence of my showing Alaine Chen the videotape, of everything around me shutting down, and, then, of my only "evidence"—if you could call the tape evidence—disappearing . . . Well, now things did not seem on the up-and-up.

Without really thinking about it, I hustled up to Dr. Tobel's lab, in-tending to find Dr. Chen.

But no one was there. The lab doors were locked. I knocked and got no response, so I knocked some more. A guy walking down the hall saw me. "They're all gone," he said. "I heard Dr. Tobel died."

"Thanks," I said, and kept knocking. The guy looked at me quizzi-cally and I glowered at him; he scurried away.

Like I said, I wasn't really thinking, so my hand was red and smart-ing by the time I remembered that I had Dr. Tobel's ID badge in my pocket. I fished it out and swiped it across the black pad next to the door. The pad beeped and the door clicked. I pushed it open, stepped inside, and let the door swing shut behind me.

I guess you could say I was pretty pissed off about the car, and I in-dulged in a minute of vandal reverie—pictured myself smashing beakers and slide boxes, wiping out computers, leaving freezers open, torching lab notebooks. Feeling somewhat cleansed, I put on a pair of latex gloves and began to search.

I booted up all the computers, which, not surprisingly, were pass-word protected. I paged through lab notebooks, but because I was unfa-miliar with the protocols they described, what they contained meant little to me. Then I did what I'd planned to do in the car. I sat and thought.

Dr. Tobel's office, nerve center of this little empire.

I walked to the private office's door and tried the handle. Locked.

There was no card access here, just a plain old key, which I didn't have. There was, however, a window—a tall, narrow pane of glass above the doorknob.

Having broken a window in Dr. Tobel's house made it easier to break a window in her office. I was aware of the difference—one was a rescue situation, the other a true breaking-and-entering deal—but didn't really care. I figured it was payback for the car.

I lifted a fire extinguisher from the wall across the lab, heaved it back, and drove it through the window. The glass shattered and fell; then there was silence. I waited for the sirens, the rush of white-shirted security guys. More silence. I reached in through the broken window, unlocked the door, and entered.

So now I was a bona fide criminal. Tim Lancaster would not be pleased.

I booted the computer on the off chance it wasn't protected with a password. It was, so I turned it off and began looking through the files in the credenza. Déjà vu. In an exact replay of what Brooke and I had found in Dr. Tobel's study, the files had been cleared. More exactly, all documentation having to do with Chimeragen had been cleaned out. *Not surprising,* I thought, *but disturbing.*

I took the few files that were there—the current HIV work—and sat at her desk, paging through them. Just as in her office at home, there was a lot of chaff: old studies, the printouts from too many literature searches. At the back of one file, however, I found something that looked more interesting—"Human Trials." I began to read.

It was a grant proposal—actually, an incomplete grant proposal— for human trials for an experimental HIV vaccine. According to what I had in my hand, no trials had ever occurred, and, from the sketchy look of the application, no one had even applied for monies to conduct the trial.

Something jumped out at me. A computer printout of a long series of letters: AATGCCATATGCCT, and so on. A genetic code. I scanned across the letters and estimated it to be only a few thousand nucleotides long, meaning this was either a fragment of a larger string of DNA or a complete short piece. There was no identifying information on the sheet of paper to let me know what the code was, and the paper itself was loose, fitted just behind the aborted grant application. Weird. But at least it was something concrete. I closed the file.

Strange, Dr. Tobel. What the hell is going on here?

I walked out of the building. Still no security, so I was a free man for a while, at least. I dialed CDC and had them put me through to the lab. It was almost eleven East Coast time, but the CDC labs are often 24/7 affairs, or at least 18/7, and there was a good chance someone would be around. I didn't just need someone, however.

A woman answered the phone. "This is Dr. Nathaniel McCormick, Special Pathogens Branch. Is Dr. Vallo there?"

"No," she said.

"Do you know where he is?"

"Home, I'd guess."

"Then I need that number."

"We can't give that out."

"Of course you can. This is an emergency. I'll take the flak for it."

She sighed. "What's your name again?"

I told her, and could hear her flipping through pages, presumably to check that I actually worked at CDC. A moment later, she came back on the line. "Don't tell him who gave you this."

"I don't know who gave it to me. Thanks."

Repeating the number over to myself, I punched it into the cell phone. The phone rang until an answering machine picked it up. No way Ben Vallo would be out that night, just after a big blowup in Baltimore, just before a big blowup in Louisiana. In fact, I was surprised he wasn't at the lab. I redialed.

A sleepy man answered.

"Ben," I said.

"Who is this?"

"Nathaniel McCormick."

"Ah, Christ . . ."

"Listen, I need you to do something for me—"

He went from asleep to totally awake and ticked off in five seconds. "Nate, you know how much shit I went through for you? You sent down every goddamned thing in Baltimore. I'm surprised there's a city left. I figured I'd tested every last molecule in the whole damned place."

I heard another voice in the background and heard Vallo say, "Go back to sleep."

"This is different," I said.

"Sure it's different. You know, this is the first night in a week I've gotten to sleep before two?"

"That's why they pay you the big bucks—"

"Goddamn it, Nate, as soon as I get a promotion, I'm going to request a secretary whose only job is to tell you to go fuck yourself every time you ask me for something, but I don't know if we could afford the overtime."

Ben Vallo was a microbiologist a few years out of a postdoctoral gig at Duke. A year or two older than me, he had been at CDC since he finished his education. Because he was young and because, all appearances to the contrary, he liked me, Ben was the first person I called to do anything. And he never turned down the work. It was the fastest way to the top, and he wanted to get to the top fast. Why he chose to bottom-feed in governmental bureaucracy, I was still trying to figure out.

"You done?" I asked.

"I have a kid I haven't seen awake in three days. His first soccer season, and I've seen one game. One game, Nate."

"You done?" I asked again.

"No. I haven't eaten a meal at any place but the cafeteria on Clifton since you called the first time, and I've been farting like a wizard ever since. You give me rat piss, rat shit, rat cum, dust from kitchen site 1a behind the refrigerator, dust from kitchen site 1c behind the stove. I'm sick of it." There was a pause. "I'm done."

"Okay. Ben—Dr. Vallo—I want you to run RT-PCR on the samples you have from Deborah Fillmore and Bethany Reginald."

"I *have* run PCR on them, McCormick, for about a thousand different bugs."

"PERVs?"

"PERVs? The pig things?"

"Yeah."

"Why the hell would I do that?"

"You wouldn't. That's why I'm asking you now."

There was some harrumphing. "Let me get a pen." Again I heard Vallo say, "Go back to sleep."

"Okay," he said, "PERVs for Fillmore and Reginald. You going to make me look up the sequences for the primers, too?"

"No. I have them here. I'll e-mail them tonight."

"You're a goddamned saint."

"Tell that to Tim. I also have a sequence I'd love you to run against what we have down there. See if it matches anything in the database."

"That's it?"

"That's it. For now."

"For now? Jesus."

"I'll fax the sequence to you."

"E-mail's better."

"I only have a hard copy."

"Scan it."

"Okay, you win. Scan and e-mail," I said.

"Yeah, I win. I get you to do one ninetieth of the work I have to do—"

"Ben, one more thing. . . ."

"What?"

"I need this started tonight."

"No. No way."

To get the best deal, I started high with Vallo.

"I really need it, Ben."

"Best I can do is tomorrow morning. I'll go in early, but that's the best I can do. My wife is gonna kill me, as it is. Where are you?"

"California."

"I'll have your unknown sequence analyzed by the time you wake up. PCR will take until the end of the day at least."

"Fair enough. And one more thing."

"How many 'one more things' is it going to be tonight?"

"I don't want you to tell anyone about this. Not Tim or anyone."

"You running around on him?"

"No. Tim won't want to know about it yet. Trust me. If we get anything, I'll tell him."

"That's it?"

"That's it."

He banged down the phone without another word.

*   *   *

Back to the library. Before I e-mailed Vallo my sequences, there was something I needed to check. Something that, if it panned out, might strengthen the connections between Baltimore and California.

I scanned the sequence from Harriet Tobel's lab and converted it to text, then dumped the whole thing into a Word file. From the paper on PERVs, I copied the primer sequences, which were unique to the viruses and essentially defined the bugs. Then I put the PERV sequences into the "Find what" field in Word. I wanted to see whether what I found in the lab was a PERV genome. If so, well, that was something. It meant Dr. Tobel was concerned enough about PERVs to have the entire sequence on file.

I hit Enter on the computer. No match.

"Damn," I whispered. "Damn, damn, damn."

I e-mailed the sequences—the thousands of As, Ts, Gs, and Cs—to Ben Vallo, then returned to my violated car. On the way back to the vehicle, I passed the Heilmann Building. Still no security. At that point, it seemed I was going to get away with my brush with crime. Perhaps I'd missed my calling.

Anyway, I can't say I was in the best frame of mind. I knew I was falling apart a little—I was confused, operating on a few hours' sleep, scared. All bravado aside, I had just broken into an office. I mean, I was a goddamned doctor; I wasn't made for this.

So I dialed the number for the only person left on the planet who seemed to give a rat's ass about me, or, at least, who used to give a rat's ass about me.

"Go away, Nate," Brooke said.

"They broke into the car, took everything. They took the tape."

I could hear her breathing. "This afternoon. When I was in the hospital." Brooke didn't say anything. "They took the tape, Brooke."

"I heard you—"

"And my toothbrush. And all my clothes." There was a chill silence on the phone. "I'm really sorry about this morning. Really. I'm really, really sorry. . . ."

"Nathaniel . . ." She sighed. "I'm sorry, too. I guess we had to expect some sparks, right? Working this close after . . . well, you know."

"Par for the course, maybe."

"Probably. You were just being a prick, that's all." I suppose I should have hung up then, but I didn't.

"I know." I felt something like relief. "And you were kind of being a bitch."

"I only did it in the interest of team building. Prick and Bitch. The dynamic duo." She sighed again. "Okay, this is against my better judgment, but do you have a place to stay tonight? Do you *want* a place to stay?"

"No," I said, by which I meant yes. So I said, after a pause, "Yes."

"Well, come over, then. I have an extra toothbrush, and some of Jeff's clothes are here. Have you eaten?"

"No."

"There's a nice little jazz place around the corner from my apartment building. Let's meet there. OK? Nate? Are you all right?"

"Sure," I said. My throat was tight. "Thanks, Brooke. Really. Thank you."

CHAPTER 65

Toot's was a jazz club that didn't seem to feature much jazz—the stage had two tables on it, the piano was pushed to the wall and looked unloved and unused—but did feature cheap drinks and cheap food. So, in keeping with the mojo of the place, I ate and drank. Hamburger and gravy fries for me, salad with some sort of bean on it for Brooke. Chivas on the rocks with a beer chaser for me, six-dollar glass of chardonnay for Brooke.

"You found the most expensive thing in the bar," I said to her.

"I'm sipping."

"Come on. Don't make me drink alone."

"What's this?" She pointed at the glass of urine-colored liquid in front of her.

"You know what I mean."

I brought Brooke up to speed on the PERV situation.

"I don't know how much that tells us, Nate. Of course they would be concerned about PERVs."

"But if it's related to the rape. If it jumped species and got to Baltimore . . ."

"Then it probably wouldn't look like a hemorrhagic fever. It would be more . . . subtle."

"I know. But we could have a porcine-human chimera, right? The PERV picks up some genetic material from a human virus and goes wild."

"It doesn't make sense, biologically. And how does it get to Baltimore?" she argued. "I know you want to draw parallels here, but you can't force it. You're going to start seeing what you want to see, instead of what's really out there—"

"I'm not an idiot, Brooke. I've been trained in this."

She bit back. "Oh well, then, if you've been *trained*."

The snide remark notwithstanding, Brooke had a point. One of the pitfalls of any investigation, whether it be in the lab or in the community, is that you start to home in on something and strap on the blinders. You acknowledge that which supports your hypothesis and ignore that which doesn't. It was, goddamn it, a flaw of mine. I'd done it in Jurgen's lab a decade ago, and I might have done it again now.

"It's still a possibility," I said. "The PERV mutant. But we need to keep our minds open."

"Are you saying I'm right?"

"I'm saying your criticism may be valid."

"That's quite a concession, Nathaniel. Wow."

"Just part of my boyish charm."

"Yeah. Keep telling yourself that." She smiled.

Before long, it was obvious our gig at Toot's wouldn't last. I was fighting the spins by my third round. I was also fighting melancholy about Dr. Tobel's death and self-loathing about being so irresponsible as to get drunk when I had work to do, about fuzzy logic that was making me jump to conclusions. I was still pissed and unnerved about the car. Oh, and there was that little thing with Alaine.

"All my underwear, gone. I got this great blue tie and it's gone. They even got this Buddha eye I brought back from Nepal like ten years ago. You know, those necklaces with the bead? I never wore it, but still, I carried it in my luggage."

Brooke looked at me, nodding slightly; she'd finished her first glass of wine but hadn't really touched the second.

I continued, "I mean, who the hell would do that? Who'd break into a car in a med school in fucking richy-rich California in the middle of the day? Into a big American car, no less? I mean, that's weird, right?"

Brooke nodded.

"And they took the tape, Brooke. Why would they want that tape?"

"They took everything."

"Right. But they only took all that other stuff so they could take the tape."

"How did they know you had the tape?"

"Alaine told them."

"I see," she said. "Who's them, Nathaniel?"

"I don't know. Them. Whoever doesn't want us to know about this rape in the bowels of a prestigious hospital."

"And who would that be?"

I leaned forward on the table. "The people who run this study. Otto Falk, Alaine, the people at Chimeragen—"

"Nathaniel—"

"The same them who killed Gladys Thomas, who came over to Harriet Tobel's house the night she died. The same people who came over later that night and buzzed off before I could get their license—"

"Nathaniel!"

"What?"

"You're doing it now."

"What?"

"This loose-association flight-of-fancy thing."

"I'm just brainstorming."

"You're drunk."

"True. But, Brooke, there's a bug killing people back east. Harriet Tobel is dead. . . ."

I realized I was babbling a little. I gripped my drink and took a slug.

Brooke's face softened. "I know." She touched my hand. "Look, we don't have enough information, right? It's all very weird; you're right. It's odd that Dr. Tobel had this tape in the first place, that she didn't come forward with it earlier. She is—she was—highly involved in this project. Why didn't she come forward earlier if she knew?"

"Maybe she didn't know."

"And why wouldn't the investigators report the rape? It wouldn't have scuttled the entire experiment. The rapist would have gone to jail, and the investigators would have been able to come out of this pretty clean."

"You think the other families would have wanted their vegetative loved ones involved in an experiment where the overseers couldn't even prevent a rape?"

That stumped her, and she changed tack. "Maybe Harriet Tobel is the only one of the bosses who knew about it."

"And maybe you're totally full of shit."

"And maybe there's a perfectly reasonable explanation for all this," she shot back. "Come on, you and I both know how the FDA works on this. Everything would be documented. If there's anything fishy, especially a big conspiracy, they would know. I'll call them tomorrow, get you out of the loop here. They'll know about the death of this woman."

"They're not going to tell you anything. Everyone involved in the project signed a nondisclosure."

"I have friends at the FDA," she said.

"You really believe there's a perfectly reasonable explanation for this, Brooke?"

"Let's go," she said abruptly. "We'll piece this together tomorrow. I don't want to think about it now."

Dejected, nauseous, way too drunk, I followed Brooke to the car. Rape, Harriet Tobel, Chimeragen, Gladys Thomas, Bethany Reginald. All a big conspiracy. Right, Nathaniel. Right.

"I can't."

"Why?" I asked, trying to nuzzle Brooke's neck.

"Not like this. Not when you're drunk."

"I'm not drunk."

"Nate. Stop."

I pushed away from Brooke, slid to the far end of the couch.

"It's been a long day," she said.

"Sure."

"I don't want anything to start like this."

"Do you want anything to start at all?"

Brooke didn't answer. Instead, she stood and walked to the door to her room. Then she stopped.

I must have been a mess. I was wearing khakis that I'd had on for three days. My blue shirt and blue blazer had seen everything from Gladys Thomas's body to Harriet Tobel's body to Alaine Chen's tears.

All I wanted at that moment was for Brooke to be next to me. All

I wanted was to put my head in her lap, just for a few moments. Screw disease and sick people and dead mentors. Screw Alaine and her damn ambition. Screw Alaine for wanting a shoulder to cry on and nothing else. And fuck me for letting these thoughts run amok. I was pathetic.

Brooke said, "Good night, Nathaniel," and closed the door to her room.

Somewhere in the middle of feeling sorry for myself—so sorry for myself I wound up stroking the cat—I fell asleep.

CHAPTER 66

I woke early the next morning, sinuses swollen and draining, eyes feeling like they'd just been rubbed with poison ivy. Then there was the hangover, the splitting headache, the mouth that tasted like the cat had used it for a litter box.

There were blankets over me. Brooke.

I stumbled to the sink and gulped down a glass of water, rummaged in the cupboards for a multivitamin, something with B complex, something that might have a snowball's chance in hell to lift the pain. I found the vitamins and aspirin and swallowed a handful of pills. With a paper towel, I blew my nose hard, popping my ears, trying to core the mucus from my sinuses.

The dogs plodded around the room. I called them to the couch and they hopped up. The HIV files I'd taken from Dr. Tobel's office were on the coffee table in front of me. I cracked one open, trying to read.

From the bedroom, I heard Brooke's muffled voice. For a while, I sat on the couch, reading over the same paragraph on HIV resistance, not absorbing anything. My wheels spun like that for maybe fifteen minutes, until my cell rang.

"You sound like shit," Ben Vallo said.

"Thanks, man. You always know how to make me feel great."

"Then this will make you feel even better: I got no match on the big sequence you gave me."

"Not surprising, I guess," I said.

Vallo seemed to expect I would fill the pause with something, but I had nothing to say, so he spoke. "I made the primers for the PERVs. We should know if it's hiding out in the Fillmore and Reginald tissue later tonight. If it's there, we should have a screaming signal."

"Great."

"That's it?" he asked.

"Yes. That's it. Thanks, Ben."

"What's wrong?"

"Nothing's wrong. Thanks for your help."

"You're telling me all you wanted me to do was run this against a database? Do the PCR?"

"That's all."

"You going to call me back in half an hour and ask me to analyze the five hundred samples you just FedExed to me?"

"No."

"Okay, quit twisting my arm. Look, I'm going to run a Southern blot for the PERVs. The sensitivity won't be as good as PCR, but it'll be faster by a few hours. If there's enough there, we'll ID it, and I'll give you a call."

"Thanks."

Vallo, for all his bitching, loved the challenge of his work. And he loved to work. What I'd handed him the night before—running PCR on a few samples, bouncing Dr. Tobel's genetic code against our database of known pathogens—wasn't a challenge and it wasn't much work. "Tell me what the big sequence is," he said.

"I can't tell you. Sorry."

"Jesus, McCormick. You want to know about partial matches?"

"Okay, sure. Ben, did you get any partial matches?"

"It's a little weird. It looks like we have *env* and *pol* genes that are something like HIV. Not exactly, mind you, but something like it." *Env* genes coded for the protein envelope of a virus; *pol* genes, for the polymerase enzyme that enabled the viruses to replicate. "But we have a bunch of junk that I haven't seen. I got a partial hit for the *env* sequence of Junin, but I had to reduce the sensitivity a whole bunch. It's not like anything we have."

What Ben Vallo was telling me was that what we had looked like a mix of different bugs. This wasn't surprising, really. Nature is conservative, and when something works—a gene that codes for an effective protein coat, for example—she tends to riff on it. It's why humans share ninety-eight percent of their genome with chimpanzees. The old saw "If it ain't broke, don't fix it" is hard at work in biology. And what goes for people and chimps goes for viruses as well. That's why he got partial hits on a lot of the code. It crossed my mind that someone could have just cut and pasted genetic pieces from other bugs, though why Dr. Tobel would have such a sequence, I couldn't fathom.

"So, it looks like it's a virus?" I asked Ben.

"It looks like it might possibly be a virus."

"Way to be definitive."

"Hey, you want definitive, talk to God."

"He's next on my list. Anyway, thanks again, Ben."

"You're not going to tell me what this is about?"

"Maybe sometime over a beer. Not now."

"You're really working your way onto my good side," he said, and ended the call.

I looked up and saw Brooke leaning against the door jamb of her bedroom, that Penn sweatshirt brushing the tops of her thighs. "What was that, Nate?"

"Nothing," I said. "Dead lead."

"I talked to some people at the FDA. They wouldn't give me details—they wouldn't give me anything at first—but I pressed. They said everything with the Chimeragen trials was aboveboard."

"How hard did you press?"

"I've been on the phone for the last two hours, Nate. I talked to a friend, then a friend of a friend, then a friend again. She told me it was all okay."

"Crap." I slouched deep into the couch, threw my feet up on the coffee table.

"Poor Nathaniel. You hungover?"

"Exquisitely."

"Three drinks, by my count."

"They poured heavy." I eased further into the couch. "What can I say? I'm a cheap date. I ought to take myself out more often."

She laughed. "You look sort of cute in a roguish way."

I looked at her in that sweatshirt. "You look sort of hot in a porn star, college girl way."

She shook her head and smiled. "Just look roguish and don't speak, Nate. You're ruining the image."

"You have a cigarette?"

"Okay, the image is totally ruined."

She turned back to her bedroom.

"Don't tell me I just blew my chance," I said.

She made an exaggerated shrug, closed the door. I fantasized about her throwing open her bedroom door and standing there, stark naked. I heard the water run in her shower. Damn.

I was feeling sufficiently guilty about my performance with her the night before—well, about the night before and a bunch of other times—that I decided to perform a mea culpa and make breakfast. There were eggs in the refrigerator, some pancake mix in the cupboard. I set to work, aware enough then to know that I had less than twenty-four hours until I was supposed to be back in Atlanta. *I should really be moving,* I thought. *I should really get going.* Yet, moving and going where, I had no idea.

I beat the pancake mix with a fork and poured the batter into a heated pan. Orange juice went on to the table. In other circumstances, I would have taken some domestic pleasure in what I was doing. Now all I felt was hungover and confused.

Brooke stepped out from her room, hair wet, smelling good. "What's this?"

"I'm apologizing for last night with food. Well, your food." I shuffled some pancakes to her plate.

I sat; she sat. I glanced at the wall clock. Nine a.m. If memory served me correctly—and I wasn't entirely sure it did—Harriet's funeral was at eleven. "Harriet Tobel's funeral is in less than two hours."

"That will be hard," she said. She really was an intuitive and kind person.

"Would you like to come?"

"No," she said. Okay, scratch that; the woman was neither intuitive nor kind. "But I will if you want me to." She added, "I hate funerals."

"Not me. I love them. Go to as many of them as I can."

"Do you want me to come with you or not?" She wasn't making this easy.

The dogs were milling around our feet. Brooke looked at them, then stood up from the table. She took a bag of dog food from under the counter and poured it into two small bowls.

"I know I'm no cook," I said. "But come on, the pancakes aren't that bad." Brooke smiled wanly. It is possible she was growing weary of my a.m. wit. She placed the bowls on the floor; the dogs finished inhaling their breakfast even before she sat down.

"I can't eat when they're hungry. Makes me nervous."

I looked at the two little beasts, who were once again under the table, begging. These con artists were definitely not starved.

"Did Jeff leave a black suit here?" Maybe I wouldn't have to pull day four in my current threads.

"No," she said. "Jeff got rid of all his suits when he moved to California. He became all flip-flops, jeans, and old sweaters."

"Sounds like he became an idiot."

"That, too. But he's tenure-track, so it doesn't matter."

I could sense I was skating on thin ice there, so I skated away, which meant, at that moment, keeping my mouth shut.

Brooke said, "You should take the dogs for a walk after breakfast."

"Sure."

"So, when are you supposed to be in Atlanta?"

"Tomorrow morning. Tim wants me to take a red-eye."

"You're not going back, are you, Nate?"

A good question, actually. Though I kept telling myself I'd stay here until the bitter end, sacrificing career and, now, underwear and toiletries, I really wasn't sure about it. Maybe this was the hangover talking. Maybe.

"I don't know."

CHAPTER 67

Armed with two plastic bags, two squirmy dogs, and my cell phone, I stepped outside into another impossibly sunny day. The dogs strained happily against their leashes.

I had one unpleasant call I had to make, about a dozen other unpleasant calls I should make. As of that moment, I was committing to a life of efficiency, so screw the dozen calls.

The woman at the medical examiner's office directed my call to Luis Gonzales, the resident in pathology who'd done the autopsy on Gladys Thomas. He'd also done the autopsy, according to Brooke, on Harriet Tobel, as per her request. That's why I was calling.

Gonzales sounded rushed when he answered the phone. "Dr. McCormick, I have a double homicide coming in, so let's make this short, okay?"

I wanted to tell him his patients wouldn't mind a five-minute delay for their autopsies—they wouldn't care about a two-year delay—but instead I asked, "You performed the autopsy on Harriet Tobel?"

"Yes. Brooke told me you were close. I'm sorry about her death."

"What did you find?"

"It was an MI," Luis Gonzales, forensic pathologist extraordinaire, said. "No doubt. The left anterior descending artery was nearly seventy percent occluded. Right and left coronaries were about fifty percent."

"But that wouldn't have killed her," I said.

"No, it wouldn't have killed her by itself. It does account for the nitro you saw on the bed and we found in her mouth. This lady had a lot of trouble with angina."

"But angina didn't kill her. Did you find a blockage?"

"No. We think it was vasospasm. Her heart got a bit ischemic, then bam, her arteries spasm and she goes kap—she has an MI. A large part of the left anterior ventricle was necrotic."

"No trauma?"

"Nothing." He added gratuitously, "She died of a heart attack."

"That's it?"

"Yes."

"Brooke told you I was suspicious about her death?"

"Yeah. I took a long time with her, Doctor. But it was obvious. Large MI in the left ventricle."

My feelings at that moment were interesting. On the one hand, I was relieved; on the other, unsettled. Relieved because it looked like she really had died naturally, unsettled because I didn't fully believe it. I asked, "You sent off a tox screen?"

"Yes. It won't be back for a few days."

"No signs of trauma?"

"No. Look, Dr. McCormick, we covered—"

"And I thank you for that. You checked for small trauma? Injection marks?"

"We went over everything."

"What was in her stomach?"

"Dr. McCormick . . ." I heard him sigh, then heard the shuffle of papers. "All right, the autopsy report. She'd had partially digested chicken, green beans . . ."

"Okay, okay." I wanted to think of other questions, but I wasn't a pathologist, and it seemed these guys had asked all the right things. "Thanks for taking such care with this."

"No problem."

I hit End on the phone. So, I told myself, Harriet Tobel's death— the death that occurred when she wanted to tell me something, the death that occurred suspiciously close to when she gave me the videotape— wasn't murder. The experts said so.

So, why didn't I believe it?

CHAPTER 68

I hate funerals, especially those attended by a host of people from the darker corners of my past.

Until I walked into the chapel, Brooke next to me, I hadn't really thought of the social minefield I would be forced to navigate. First off, because Jeff, the ex-fiancé, had shed his old self back east, I was forced to wear what might soon be called "Nate McCormick Casual": khakis, blue button-down, blue blazer. I'm happy to report the natives of Northern California are observant, and I caught quite a few members of the old guard looking askance. I can only assume it was my clothes and not my gargantuan CDC reputation.

Anyway, I saw the old dean of the medical school, saw his eyes sweep the crowd. I wondered if he was still in power, and if that long look around was to note who attended the funeral and who didn't. Only fools or cavalier faculty with tenure would think about missing the funeral of such an icon.

Thankfully, the dean didn't recognize me, so I could stare at him a moment and have an unpleasant memory: his steely face when he informed me that my welcome at the medical school had worn out. I conjured up a more pleasant image: my hands around his neck, his eyes bulging, his arrogant face turning blue—

I felt a tap on my shoulder. "Nathaniel?"

I turned around and was looking at the top of a man's head, gray and black hair blown to a froth. It was Milo Shah, my old pathology professor.

"A terrible shame, this death," he said, and shook his head too vigorously, as if to get the dirty word out of the way quickly. "How are you, son?"

"Fine, all things considered."

"You have come back for the funeral?"

"Yes," I lied.

I could almost feel him gearing up for the big question. A medical student embroiled in multiple scandals lives on in many memories. People want updates. "What are you doing now?"

I told him, and to his credit, he seemed genuinely relieved. It was as if he expected me to tell him I'd started a career directing porn. "Very good," he said. "I'm very happy for you."

Brooke, sensitive to the sensitive situation, introduced herself. Dr. Shah nodded and beamed, drawing false conclusions about my romantic life. This was fine. Having an attractive woman on your arm goes a long way toward proclaiming how far you've come from the mess you'd made of your younger life. In some ways, it's better than a faculty appointment.

Dr. Shah shook both our hands and went off to intercept someone tanned and official-looking. As he left, I thought I saw the old lech give me a wink.

"This is hard." Brooke asked, linking her arm through mine. "I mean, the funeral, sure, but all the people from your past ... I can see they like you. They were worried about you." *Thanks, Brooke.* But maybe, just maybe, they're cursing my good luck and waiting for whatever character flaws that took me away from California to erupt and destroy me.

The chapel itself was the centerpiece of the campus, and sat like a crown at the head of the university's main quad. With its red-tiled roof and light sandstone arches, the chapel smacked of Córdoba, not Silicon Valley. This mix-and-match was intentional, I think, and fit with the ostensibly multidenominational vibe of the university. Southern Spain, that cauldron of religious conquest and appropriation, has its houses of worship alternately employed by Christians, Muslims, and Jews. The university managed to entertain all three faiths—as well as Buddhists, Hindus, Zoroastrians, et al.—simultaneously. The inside of the chapel was quasi–Greek Orthodox, with short transepts and a deep apse. I wondered how Harriet Tobel, whom I never knew to speak of religion, would feel about the heavy iconography. But as they say, funerals are for the living, not the dead. And Larry Tobel thought the university's chapel a particularly fitting place to lay his mother to rest, though I wondered about any tug-of-war between the rabbi and Larry over the appropriateness of the place.

Across the nave, I saw Alaine Chen, pale and puffy-eyed. She hung limply on the arm of a tall white man a few years older than me. My pulse quickened, and I tried to catch her eye. But it was futile; she looked shell-shocked and blank and never turned her head toward me.

"What?" Brooke asked.

"Nothing."

She tracked where my gaze had been. "Is that—?"

"It's nothing, Brooke."

I resolved never to feel any more kindness toward Alaine.

The ceremony was brief. The rabbi spoke with a practiced polish. Larry Tobel spoke, surprisingly eloquent and moving, with enough oratorical flare to pull the audience in but enough raw anger and grief to bring many of us to tears. I looked at Brooke sitting stoically next to me. Alaine had her face in her hands. The man she was with rubbed her shoulder possessively.

I didn't weep. I'd already done that.

CHAPTER 69

Just outside the chapel, in the sun-dappled courtyard, Alaine Chen finally looked at me. She forced what might have been a smile, but more closely resembled a grimace. She wiped at a tear, smearing a line of mascara across her cheek that stayed for a second before she got at it with her hand. Her emotion at that moment softened me, and my resolve crumbled. So I took the gesture as an invitation of sorts. "I need to talk to someone," I said to Brooke.

Brooke hesitated, unable, I assume, to interpret her role in that moment. Then she squeezed my elbow and stepped aside. I walked to Alaine. We embraced lightly; I kissed her cheek. Her body was limber and yielding. Her perfume smelled expensive.

"I still can't believe it," she said. "All these people . . . It makes it so final."

"But it's nice to see everyone come to . . . You're right. It is final. It sucks."

Alaine was staring up at me. This close, I could see the mascara rubbed into her pores.

"Yesterday . . . thanks," she said. "Harriet thought you're a good man, and so do I. I just wanted you to know that."

This was something for which I was *really* not prepared. Small talk, yes. Some bitching about how I wouldn't let her rest with my Chimeragen questions, sure. But not this. " 'To serve and protect and be a comfort to those in need'—that's my motto." I sounded bratty and I knew it.

"What I'm trying to say is that it might have been hard for you, considering—"

"Not hard at all. All in a day's work. Remember the motto."

I couldn't tell if she was hurt or annoyed or confused that I seemed not to be getting it. I could, however, feel invisible tentacles slithering around me. Why was she saying these things? Why was she trying to hook me again?

She pressed toward me. "Nathaniel, I need to tell you—"

I stepped back; I could feel those tentacles tightening. "What?"

"Nate—"

"You need to tell me what, Alaine? That you think I'm wonderful and couldn't we get together and talk about Dr. Tobel? Shoot the shit about the good old days? Weep on my shoulder again? Don't do this to me. Stop doing this."

I noticed Brooke had sidled up behind me, miffed, perhaps, that I'd abandoned her in unfamiliar territory to go talk to an old girlfriend. I guess I should have been grateful that she stopped what was most likely the beginning of some embarrassing monologue. But I wasn't. I was, actually, a little annoyed. Alaine seemed to be annoyed, too, and I saw the sweep of her eyes up and down over my companion, the flicker of a frown.

"Alaine," I said, "this is my friend Brooke Michaels."

They shook hands frostily.

I am no saint. Because I have no illusions about it, because Alaine was freaking me out a little, I feel free to confess I took great pleasure in

her pain at that moment. Not the pain about Dr. Tobel's death, God forbid, but the jealousy I saw painted on her face. Her guard must have
been down, or she never would have let me see how thrown she was by
Brooke's presence, by her athletic build and good looks. It was an illusion, for I placed the odds of Brooke and me falling into bed or, even less
likely, into a relationship at something less than the odds of Harriet
Tobel sitting up in her casket and asking for lunch. I mean, there was the
issue of our history—Brooke's and mine—and the unpleasant conversations of the past few days. Still, Dr. Michaels was a useful weapon in the
détente that existed between Alaine and me. As I was finding out, the
war between lovers never dies, just sits and waits to flare up again. Even
at inopportune times, even at funerals.

My dark pleasure, however, was short-lived; it was Dr. Chen's turn.

The tall fair-haired man walked up behind her, grabbed her elbow,
kissed her. "This is Ian Carrington. My fiancé." She threaded her hand
through his arm. For the first time, I noticed the rock on her finger. It
was the size of a quarter, and I wondered where she put it when she
worked in the lab. "This is Nathaniel McCormick, an old friend. And
Brooke Michaels." She forced a smile.

Right, the fiancé. Dr. Alaine Chen's arsenal was larger—magnitudes larger—than mine. If only, for that moment, Brooke was my wife,
was pregnant, had just won the Nobel.

I shook Ian Carrington's hand. His grip was firm, felt like money
and power and unlimited upside. I thought I caught a whiff of Choate
and Harvard, though it could have been his cologne. In any case, this guy
had probably never heard of Bondo; he was probably born knowing how
to pronounce "Goethe."

"A pleasure to meet you, Nathaniel," he said, "under the circumstances."

"Likewise," I lied.

Ian shook Brooke's hand. His eyes darted to her chest, then back to
her face. Oh, *come on,* man.

Alaine had disengaged some time ago. Boy, this woman could really turn it off when she wanted, fly to some remote emotional island
when things got too uncomfortable. It used to drive me nuts.

But then she swung her eyes to me. She was back. "I can't believe
this, Nathaniel. I really can't believe this. She was . . ."

Was what, Alaine? A stepping-stone? A way station on the journey to your own lab? Like me, a place to hitch when it made sense, then cast off when it didn't? I realized I wasn't being forgiving, but fuck that. I refused to believe that her relationship with Dr. Tobel had been anything more than rudimentary, employer-employee, each of them using the other.

"... she was the most important person in my life. Except for Ian." The last sentence seemed almost an afterthought.

Uncomfortable silence. Brooke jumped into the breach. "She certainly was admired and loved."

Alaine, Ian, and I mumbled our agreement. Noticing Ian was among the mumblers, I asked him a question to which I knew the answer. "You knew Dr. Tobel?"

"Yes. I work—worked, forgive me, this is still so new—worked with her. And with Alaine."

"Ian is the CEO of Chimeragen, the company I told you about, Nate. Harriet and I—"

"I know," I said. "Xenografts." I didn't like that Alaine used Dr. Tobel's first name all the time. *Harriet.*

"It's a great loss to us. A great loss." Ian looked lost in thought. Perhaps I should have slapped him to bring him back. "Thank God we have Alaine to carry on the work. If you'll excuse me ..."

I watched him cross the courtyard and begin to talk to a short, bullet-headed man.

"Who's that?" I asked.

"That's Otto Falk," Alaine said.

"He's shorter than his reputation suggests."

Alaine shook her head, disgusted with my peevishness.

"And balder," Brooke said. *Score one, Brooke.* We smiled at each other.

"I should be going," Alaine said abruptly. "With ... with the developments, there are going to be a lot of changes in the lab. If there is even a lab left ..."

"You're not going to the cemetery?"

"I need to get back to the lab."

"Why? The most important person in your life—"

"Nathaniel, come on. You haven't forgotten everything, have you? I'll be lucky if they haven't started planting flags in the space while I sat here crying."

Curtly, I said, "I wouldn't worry. At least your boyfriend controls your funding stream, right?"

"Not all of it."

"Maybe you can set up shop under Otto Falk's umbrella."

"Chimeragen wanted the work to be independent. The FDA wanted it to be independent, too."

Step one toward independence, Alaine, would be breaking the engagement with the Aryan prince.

We began our good-byes. Brooke and Alaine shook hands again. Surprisingly, Alaine embraced me hard, pulled me close. Her mouth was next to my ear; I felt her breath. "They know you broke in," she whispered. "Stop this."

CHAPTER 70

Alaine broke away from me and hurried across the courtyard in the direction of the medical campus. I shot a quick glance at Brooke, her eyebrows raised in question.

"I'll be back," I said, and hurried after Alaine. My pace fell in with hers. "Who knows I broke in?"

She didn't answer, just kept walking.

"What's going on?"

She kept her eyes on the ground. "Nathaniel, stop."

"What happened to Harriet Tobel?" I insisted.

"Stop!" She almost spat the word. She looked quickly back at the crowd, then continued her pace. I followed the look and saw Ian Carrington talking to Otto Falk. But he wasn't looking at the shorter man; he stared over his head, at us.

My last image of Alaine was dark hair, dark suit, as she disappeared around a yellow sandstone building.

Slowly, I made my way back to Brooke. Ian, I hoped, thought Alaine and I had just opened some old lovers' wounds, which wouldn't have been entirely untrue in my case, at least. But I could tell he was still looking at me, and I realized how stupid I'd been to pursue her like that.

By the time I reached Brooke, she was already talking to someone else. In almost any situation, a beautiful woman standing alone is like a hundred-dollar bill lying on a street in Manhattan: it's only a matter of time before someone picks her up.

The gentleman involved in this pickup looked to be about two hundred years old, so if it came to blows, I was relatively sure I could take him. Brooke introduced him as a former professor of classics. His time in the sun ended, the professor excused himself.

"What was that all about?" Brooke asked.

"Just fighting the last battles of our breakup." I could tell Brooke wasn't sure whether or not to buy it, but she kept quiet.

On our way off the quad back to the car, I scanned the dwindling crowd for any sign of Otto Falk and Ian Carrington. I didn't see them.

"She's very pretty," Brooke observed as we crossed in front of a patch of flowers near the parking area.

I didn't respond.

"The love of your life, right, Nathaniel?"

"I don't know," I said.

"She's a bit cold."

"For God's sake, Brooke."

"She's worried about getting back to the lab to protect her job."

"Wouldn't you be?"

"No. Not today."

We had taken Brooke's BMW to the ceremony and planned to take it to the burial itself. As she opened the car door, Brooke said, "You know, if you're still in love with her, you have to either admit it to yourself or get over it."

"I'm not in love with any—"

"In this case, I'd suggest you get over it."

She slammed the door and blazed the engine. I got in.

Okay, I admit I might have been defending Alaine Chen a little too much. But I appreciated that she warned me, and felt stupid about assuming that what she wanted to tell me had to do with the relationship.

To smooth Brooke's feathers, I said, "I'm not in love with her." I don't think she believed me, since she laid a little rubber tearing out of the parking lot.

"We had reconnected, Nate, come to some sort of friendship. At least I thought we had. God, I let myself get a little vulnerable with you, and you end up throwing it back in my face." By vulnerable, Brooke meant that she let me stay at her place, let me make her breakfast. This jealousy surprised me, though.

"It's not that," I said. I told her what Alaine had said, omitting, of course, any of the "You're a good man, Nate McCormick" talk.

She processed that for a moment. "I'm embarrassed." Then she changed the subject. "So Chimeragen is involved in something. It was either them or someone having to do with Dr. Tobel's HIV work. Who else would really care that you broke into the lab? Why else would Alaine know? Do you think the rape is the key?"

"A key. Yes."

"I do, too. I think they broke into your car to take the tape. Not for your couture."

I smiled at her. "Thanks."

By that time, we were well into the rolling hills surrounding the university. At this time of year, everything was dry, brushed an even amber. It was the grass—and the sunshine, and the metal—that gave California its moniker the Golden State.

"Why wasn't the rape reported?" Brooke mused.

"Well, if the study itself is not being protected, then some person is being protected. Maybe Otto Falk has a predilection for the brain-dead. Maybe Ian Carrington does. Do you remember the dimensions of the man in the tape?"

"No. The angle was weird. He could have been short, I guess."

I thought about that for a second. It still didn't add up. "These guys are smart. Why wouldn't they have turned off the camera? Or taken the tape out?"

"Maybe they didn't have time. Maybe they were surprised. Or someone was outside. Or someone who was in on the game wanted some blackmail material." She didn't have to say that someone might have been Harriet Tobel.

The cars ahead of us turned onto a side road toward the cemetery. We followed. "Besides, it wasn't Falk. It was an orderly. The guy who did this was an orderly."

"Or it was someone who wanted us to think he was an orderly."

CHAPTER 71

As we followed the cars down a small road shaded by eucalyptus trees, I thought about my last conversation with Harriet Tobel, trying to tease out anything useful. Chimeragen, the outbreak, her ragging on me about being too ambitious. Nothing jumped out at me. I played the conversation again. In the context of extraordinary circumstances, the exchange itself was pretty damned ordinary. All of it, except for . . .

"You moron," I said to myself.

Brooke heard. "What do you mean? I'm just following the cars in front—"

"No. Me. When I was talking to Dr. Tobel in the café, you know what set her off? What made her clam up and get weird on me, then just take off?"

"The outbreak?"

"No. It was when I mentioned Casey's name. A switch flipped. I can't believe I didn't think of it before."

For a moment, Brooke didn't seem to understand. Then, well, a switch flipped, and I saw recognition dawn on her. "There's someone we need to talk to," I said. "Someone, actually, *you* need to talk to."

CHAPTER 72

After the last symbolic handful of dirt was thrown onto Harriet Tobel's coffin, Brooke and I quickly left the cemetery. In the car, I dialed the national 411 directory and got a number and address I'd lost when my things were taken. Rosalinda Lopez.

The address wasn't immediately familiar to Brooke, but she thought she knew the general area, so it was my task to find it on a map. I paged through the atlas and finally came up with the street, which, according to my chauffeur, was in one of San Jose's less desirable neighborhoods.

We hurtled down the 280, Brooke's hair a golden halo in the sun and wind. If there hadn't been so much death around, I might actually have taken some pleasure in that trip. As it was, I couldn't shake the gnawing in my gut.

We discussed what Brooke was to say to the former employee of Santa Ana. I thought it would be better that she do the talking, since Rosalinda seemed to like me about as much as a root canal.

When we finally arrived in the neighborhood, I was surprised at how benign it looked. If this was poverty, it didn't look half-bad: nice little suburban places with yards, palm trees, an orange tree here and there. Sure, there were the houses with cushioned couches in the front yard, with cars up on blocks. But this place didn't hold a candle to poverty in Baltimore or Atlanta. Maybe it's an issue of space, which is at such a premium in eastern cities that all the crackheads and thugs get squeezed into the streets. Here, they could spread out a little.

6577 Urbani Road had a nice new Mazda in the driveway. Bad neighborhood indeed.

"Looks like she's home," Brooke said. She got out of the car, and I watched her walk to the door, slim and tanned in a black mourning outfit, and ring the bell. She stole a look at me and smiled. I smiled back and, for a flash, became very worried. So worried, in fact, that I had my hand on the door handle, ready to get out and grab Brooke, take her away from all this shit.

Before I could move, a shadow appeared behind the screen door. I saw Brooke talk, then stop talking. Then she disappeared inside.

I tried to relax, laid back my head, closed my eyes, and let the sunshine in to crack the DNA in the skin of my face. It didn't help: I was going out of my head with boredom and worry for Brooke. How these feelings are compatible, I don't know. All I know is that it's an unpleasant place to be.

I realized I had no idea what was happening back east, so I pulled out the cell phone, checked the battery power. It was low and I had no charger after my luggage was stolen. *Screw it,* I thought. I'd borrow Brooke's charger later.

I called my trusty public health doc in Baltimore. Herb Verlach picked up, which was a good indication that things were, for the moment, calm.

"Herb," I said. "Nathaniel McCormick."

"McCormick . . . McCormick. There was a guy I used to work with called McCormick. Went to California and opened a water bed outlet."

"The one and only."

"How's the water bed business?" *Okay, Herb, you're killing the joke.*
"What's going on?"

"All quiet on the Eastern Front. No new cases, and the cases we have in the hospital are recovering nicely. Except one. He looks like he might not make it. Twenty-six-year-old man from down in Laurel. Came in after you left."

"With Tinings, Reginald, and Fillmore, that will be four."

"So, they still teach addition in med school." Zinger. Still, it was good to hear he was in relatively high spirits.

I asked, "What's our case-fatality rate?"

"If this young man dies, about twenty-five percent."

"Pretty bad." By way of comparison, SARS had a case fatality rate of about ten percent in 2003.

"Yeah." He cleared his throat. "Tim pulled out. He left Beth and Andy here, but he's gone back to Atlanta with your division chief as of yesterday. There's been an outbreak of West Nile down in Louisiana. He headed out for that."

"He told me." It looked more and more likely that I would be called to Louisiana. As if it weren't bad enough to be yanked off this case, the last place I wanted to be in late July was Louisiana. The weather's so warm and humid, it feels like you're walking around in an overused kiddie pool. I asked, "What's the status of the Baltimore investigation?"

"We ripped apart the Jefferson homes, and Dan Miller's nursing homes. The labs here and in Atlanta are working twenty-four/seven, but we still don't have squat. It's weird, really weird, but it seems to have burned out. The attack rate is low now."

"We'll get it eventually."

"I hope." I considered telling Verlach about the PERVs, but decided I'd wait for the call from Ben Vallo. I asked him, "Are you guys cutting back?"

"Hell no. But the urgency's gone. FBI's involved now, in case it's a criminal matter, but even they're being half-assed about it. A few retarded folks die—big deal. I think they were waiting in the wings until it jumped to the population, then they'd come in and cherry-pick."

"Is it in the media yet?"

"About the FBI? Yeah. It's in the papers this morning, but everyone's downplaying it. The official line is that it doesn't look like bioterrorism, but we're investigating all possible causes."

"Read: covering our asses."

"Yeah. Anyway, it's become a jurisdictional mess. Your friend John Myers was screaming at the feds this morning. He stormed out of the building."

I laughed.

"Nate? It looks like your guy is the key."

"What guy?"

"You know, 'all roads lead to Rome'? Well, all roads are leading to Doug Buchanan. Or whatever his name is now."

"He's the only constant, hunh?"

"Yeah. Still no word on the murder yet."

I was a bit incredulous. "No word? The guy was gutted, Herb. His organs are floating out there somewhere. This was a big, sloppy murder and there's no progress?"

"Hey, I'm not the police. I only know what they tell me. Some fingers are pointing at Jefferson, but the doc has his alibis lined up. Anyway, I handed over your report to the FBI. They said they'd follow up with you and take it from there."

"Follow up out here?"

"I guess." He paused. "To be honest, I'd get out of there or at least avoid those guys. Who knows how ferocious they'll be?"

"I'll take it under advisement. Thanks, Herb."

I hung up the phone. Now, a good employee would call Tim and tell him he'd be on a plane that evening and be in Atlanta bright and early the following morning. He'd spend the rest of the day typing up a report on the past few days and e-mail it to him. But I was discovering just how poor an employee I was. I was also royally ticked about events back east. They were pulling everyone off the Baltimore outbreak, as if it didn't matter anymore. Maybe Verlach was right: a bunch of retarded people die, and no one cares. But if two rich suburbanites die of encephalitis outside of Shreveport, call in the troops. I was angry. Gladys Thomas and Bethany Reginald deserved better.

I waited. The boredom again, the worry. I seriously contemplated calling Tim just to have something to do, but stopped myself before doing something that insane.

I looked around the inside of the car. Brooke—lovely Brooke—had taken the keys, so I couldn't listen to the radio. I satisfied myself with the map.

By the time Brooke reappeared on the sidewalk outside the house, I'd managed to get myself a nice sunburn and had become an expert on the layout surrounding Rosalinda Lopez's house. As she slid into the car, I said, "Did you know that Mercado Street dead-ends, picks up, dead-ends again? It does it six times."

"Great, Nathaniel."

I didn't say anything, but let her sit in the car, start it, and decide when to speak to me. Ten seconds passed, and I couldn't hold out any longer. "Well?"

"You were right. Casey worked at a hospital."

CHAPTER 73

"She was really scared, Nate," Brooke said.

"Rosalinda?"

"Yes. Really scared. She made me swear not to tell anyone we talked."

"You told me."

"You know what I mean." Before going north to the hospital, we stopped at Brooke's place to let the dogs out and so Brooke could change clothes. Black is great for funerals, not so good for hospitals. It makes sick people nervous. "Somebody frightened her. It's why she quit the home after Gladys's death. She said she couldn't handle it anymore."

"Who was she scared of?"

"She definitely wouldn't tell me that. The only reason she let me know about Casey and where he worked is that she figured we could get that information anywhere. And I really rode her to do the right thing."

"Good work, Dr. Michaels."

"I feel guilty about it. If anything happens to her . . ."

She let the statement hang as she opened the door to the apartment. Inside, the dogs heard the lock turn and began to bark.

"Nothing's going to happen to her," I said.

"What makes you so sure?" she shot back.

Brooke went to the bedroom to change while I tried her cell phone charger in my phone. Got to hand it to the government for standardizing telecom contracts across the board. The charger fit.

"They're rolling back everything in Baltimore," I called to Brooke.

"What do you mean?" she called back.

"Verlach said they're working like mad, but that it's not a priority anymore. FBI's still involved, though."

"So it's not as hot. That's good."

"Doesn't mean it's not hot. It means it's not important to them."

She stuck her head out. "It's a good thing, Nathaniel. It gives us more freedom."

"More freedom to do what?"

She didn't answer.

While Brooke changed, I took the dogs outside. They performed, and busily sniffed their creations. I took the baggie and collected. I reflected on that: the world was falling apart, and I was scooping poop.

We were in the car, Brooke driving. Since it was getting late East Coast time and I still hadn't heard from Ben Vallo, I decided to bother the microbiologist.

"My favorite EIS officer," he said. "Hey, listen, I need to mark my calendar: when do you finish with CDC?"

Maybe sooner than you think, Ben. I said, "Funny."

"I know. I've been working on that one all day. Look, Southern blots are negative, so the PERVs aren't there in any great numbers."

"Which means it's probably not a PERV."

"Right. You'd think with such a massive hemorrhage we'd find the body swimming in virus. It's not. We checked five different tissue types." I looked at Brooke and shook my head. Vallo continued. "I got PCR data on kidney, liver, and lymph nodes, and that's negative. Still waiting on brain and endothelium."

"Thanks, Ben."

"Thanks is for the easily placated. A new driver, however—a Callaway Big Bertha Titanium, the new design—now, that shows gratitude."

"It'll be on your doorstep tomorrow."

"Right," he said sourly, and hung up.

Brooke merged onto the highway. "So, no PERV."

"No."

"But you're still thinking about the pigs, aren't you?"

"Pigs, sure. And other swine."

We arrived at the hospital around ten after four, still early enough to catch someone in the personnel office who could give us access, late enough that most of the worker bees there would have cleared out for the weekend. I still hadn't made flight arrangements back to Atlanta. Oh, well.

At the office, we showed our IDs to a woman who introduced herself as Mrs. Martle and who looked like she was ready to burst from the gates to her weekend. She sighed, asked how long we would be. I promised her we'd be no more than fifteen minutes, which, of course, was a lie. No use setting her off at the beginning of the search.

Security protocols wouldn't let us go through the computer records alone, so the dour Mrs. Martle sat at the keyboard with Brooke and me looking over her shoulder.

"Can you search by first name?" I asked.

"Yes."

"Casey." I spelled it for her.

The search went through. No hits. Fifteen minutes indeed.

We searched through about five different spellings of Casey, which, if you think about it, is kind of impressive. Still nothing.

I asked Brooke, "Do you remember the date on the tape?"

Mrs. Martle cocked her head, interested now.

"April, two years ago." We put in for all janitorial, housekeeping, and other low-level staff who had worked at the hospital during that year. Six hundred names.

"Can we print these out?" I asked.

Mrs. Martle made a big show of looking at her watch. "I need to call my supervisor to see if that's okay. I'll have to ask for overtime."

Well, you do that, Mrs. Martle.

She disappeared for a few minutes, then returned with some sheets of paper and a grimace. "You'll need to sign these," she informed us.

The papers were chock-full of legalese: about privacy, about prosecution if the contents were disclosed, blah, blah. I was happy I just had to sign the damned things and not to write them. I signed a copy and kept the other for myself; Brooke did the same.

"This will take about a half hour," Mrs. Martle said. She hit Print, and somewhere in the back of the office a machine began to whir.

Mrs. Martle was true to her word, and Brooke and I were out of the office about thirty minutes later. I wondered how much overtime that would add up to for the missus.

In truth, we probably should have headed straight to the hospital cafeteria and started combing through the records; if we found something, it would have been easier to go downstairs to where the Chimeragen patients were and pump the nurse there for any information. But I didn't want to spend any more time in the hospital that day, or any day, in fact. The whole place felt sinister.

Add to that that you couldn't use cell phones in the hospital and that I really needed to think about calling for a flight. We decided on a coffee shop near the campus.

In the car, I called the airline. They did indeed have a red-eye that evening to Atlanta. I hung up without making the reservation.

"You're not going?" Brooke said.

"Not tonight. I'll call Tim and tell him that in good conscience, I couldn't fly to Atlanta and be comatose tomorrow. The American taxpayer wouldn't be getting an alert EIS officer. The American taxpayer will thank him, and he'll thank me."

"You're doing the right thing, Nate."

"Make sure you put that in my personnel file," I grumbled.

CHAPTER 74

The two of us sat at the University Coffee House, each with a stack of paper two inches high in front of us. What we were looking for wasn't entirely clear. Our one toehold—the name Casey—didn't seem to exist here. Neither did Douglas Buchanan. My brilliant idea, that Casey or Douglas or whatever the hell his name is worked at that particular hospital and was our rapist, turned out not to be so brilliant after all. It didn't make much sense that Casey—if he was the rapist—would be protected by anyone. Not to be elitist or anything, but Casey wasn't an important player in the scheme of things. Still, we had "to leave no stone unturned," as Brooke so eloquently put it.

So, armed with two large cups of coffee, Dr. Michaels and I were going through the pages, looking for anything that might jump out at us: terminations, disciplinary actions, and so on. It was going to take hours, and twenty minutes into it, I found myself thinking about not taking the plane that evening, and about the hell I was going to pay with Tim Lancaster. I found myself getting tired of all this, of really wanting to take Alaine Chen's advice and "stop this." I mean, really, what was in it for me? Say I did crack open this case and find out that Otto Falk was a rapist and that Ian Carrington had covered up for him. Say I did find out where the nasty bugs in Baltimore came from. I'd have a lot of people pissed off at me, and I'd have to fill out a shitload of paperwork. And if Harriet Tobel's death was related to this? The police would be ticked that I'd interfered in their affairs. Like everybody said, she was old and had a bad heart.

Only in fairy tales are the renegades rewarded. Even so, idiot that I am, I pressed on.

One hour rolled by, then another. I began to wonder why Brooke was doing it. Instead of musing on it too long, I asked her. I needed a break anyway.

"Because this is important."

"Why?"

She looked up from her pages. "Because someone who couldn't even fight back was raped, Nathaniel. Because Gladys Thomas, who only wanted to be with her boyfriend, is dead. Because, like you said, a bunch of mentally disabled people are sick and dying in Baltimore and because we owe it to them to find out why. We're doctors, Nathaniel. This is what we do."

"But why? Why the hell didn't I go into plastic surgery? Work three days a week and drive a Porsche." She laughed. "I'm serious, Brooke."

"You didn't do it because it's not you. You're . . . you're better than that."

"Well, I'm sick of being better than that."

"No you're not. You're just tired and unsettled and a little scared."

"Ninety-nine percent of the planet doesn't care about this shit, and they're a hell of a lot happier than I am."

"You signed up for this."

"Not this." I pushed the stack of papers; some fluttered to the floor. That got her attention.

"Damn it, Nathaniel, what's going on?"

"What's going on is that I'm sick and tired of fighting the good fight. I want to get out of all this, have a little practice, a wife, a couple of kids. I want to mow my lawn on Saturdays and not worry about rapes and retards in Baltimore. The world is a bad place, Brooke. And it's going to be a bad place whether we figure out what the hell is going on or not. All I want is to relax a little, get my little piece, kick back, and watch the place burn."

"That's the shittiest attitude I've ever heard. Especially from you. You were the one pushing this so hard. Why?"

"That was before, Brooke. Going through all these fucking papers, I've seen the light."

We glared at each other. "You know what? You're like those CIA guys in the movies, the ones who see bad in everyone because they deal with the bad guys. They chose that life, and they forget there's a big world out there with a lot of good in it. They get swallowed up by their own tiny fraction of it."

I quoted: " 'When you look long into the abyss, the abyss also looks into you.' " I saw the confusion on her face. "Nietzsche."

"Deep, Nate, really deep. We need to go out more often. It's so much fun. You're a barrelful of laughs."

"You're the one who talked to Rosalinda Lopez, poor, scared Rosalinda Lopez. You saw Gladys. You hang out with AIDS and TB all day. All goodness and light, right?"

"There are some bad people in the world. And bad diseases. It doesn't mean the world's a bad place. It doesn't mean your old professor, who had a heart condition, did anything other than die in her sleep. You want darkness? Think about how terrible it is to have a heart attack and die alone. *That's* darkness." She looked down at her pile of papers, shuffled them. "You know what happens to those CIA guys? The ones who defended the free world against the bad guys for so long they forgot about anything else?"

"No. What happens to them, Brooke?"

"They become the bad guys."

" 'When you look long into the abyss—' "

"Oh, shut up."

"I think you need to work on your worldview. Too influenced by the media."

"And I think you need to work on your worldview, because it's fucked."

"Very eloquent, Doctor."

She pushed back from the table. "So, you want to give up? You want to go grab some sushi right now, call it a day, then head back to Atlanta tomorrow? I'll drive you to the airport."

I made a big show of looking at my watch. "Whoa. Let's go, then. Can't be too early nowadays. All that security."

She didn't find that funny. Seeing how enraged she was, neither did I, actually.

I began to restack my pages. "Let's finish this up."

I'm sure a thousand things ran through her head at that moment: what to say, whether to stand up and leave, whether to take my pages from me and say she'd do it all herself. But Brooke, ever full of nifty surprises, looked back down at her pages and began to read.

Over the next hour, I felt the burn in my head subside a little. I decided I would get on a plane to Atlanta the next day. First, though, I'd go to the police, tell them everything I knew. If they wanted to deal with a rape at this hospital, they could. If not . . . well, then, someone got off the hook. And it definitely wasn't the woman in room number three.

"Ah," Brooke said. "There's a Falk in the ranks of orderlies."

I kept on reading my files.

She continued. "He quit about a month after the rape."

"There're probably a lot of Falks in the world." She hovered over the file for a while. I made it through three more while she fixated. "You're stalling out," I said. "Keep reading."

"He worked at the hospital for four years before he left."

"Why did he leave?"

"Doesn't say." She turned the page over, then back to the front. "He's thirty-two now."

"Hmmm. Around my age. Maybe we're brothers. Maybe Otto Falk is our father." She kept on reading, not acknowledging me, so I had to guess she was really interested in this one. Most likely, she was interested because everything else was so goddamned uninteresting. "What's his first name?"

"Kincaid."

"Nice name. But it's not Casey."

She continued staring at the page. *Well,* I thought, *one of us has to make progress.* I went back to my files. After a few more minutes, I heard Brooke take a quick breath. "I knew it," she said, excited. "I knew this one was weird. Look."

She pushed the page across the table. It looked like all the others I'd seen over the last few hours: name at top, Social Security number, position, et cetera.

I read: "Kincaid Falk. 4566 Folkworth Way."

"Look at the name again."

"Kincaid Falk," I said.

"The whole name."

I read across the line. "Falk, Kincaid Charles." I glanced up and saw Brooke staring at me. She wasn't smiling, exactly, but I could tell she was excited.

"Read it again."

"Come on. What's up?"

"Read it. Normally: first, middle, last name."

"Kincaid Charles Falk."

"Again."

"Brooke . . ." I read it again out loud. "Kincaid Charles Falk." She mouthed it along with me. "This is stupid. Tell me what you saw." She didn't, so to get her off my back, I said it again. "Kincaid Charles Falk."

And then, out of nowhere, it hit me. Like the proverbial ton of bricks, it hit me.

"Kincaid Charles Falk. K. C. Falk. KC."

CHAPTER 75

I sat for a moment, processing this new bit of information. Brooke must have been processing, too, since she didn't speak or meet my eyes.

I swallowed some of my coffee. It was bitter, cold.

Brooke spoke slowly. "He worked there."

"We can assume that," I said. "It could be coincidence, though."

"He worked there. According to you, he was a sexual predator. And it looks like he might be related to the man who headed the whole damn thing. If the rapist was being protected, Nathaniel . . ." She wasn't finishing her thoughts. She didn't need to.

I began to dig into my pocket for my wallet.

Brooke said, "How could they let this happen? How many times did it happen? That poor woman . . ."

I opened my wallet on the table and began pulling out all the crap that had accumulated there over the past few months. Cards, slips of paper, pink dry-cleaning receipts, were spread in a pile in front of me. I grabbed one of the cards, took my phone, and dialed.

I got voice mail, then dialed the other number listed on the card. "Emily Walker."

"Detective Walker," I said, "it's Nate McCormick from CDC."

She took a second, during which, I assumed, she was trying to place me. Then she said, "I'm off duty, Doctor. This number is for emergencies only. Please call—"

"I need a small favor. It's kind of an emergency."

" 'Kind of an emergency'?"

"It's an emergency."

"Then call 911."

Why, I asked myself, *is everyone such a pain in the ass?* "I need to check on a missing person. It would have been about a year and a half ago."

"Call the police department. They can look it up for you."

"And how likely is it that I will get it done quickly on a Friday night?"

There was a pause; I thought I heard a child chattering in the background. Detective Walker said, "Mommy will be off the phone in a minute." She spoke into the phone, heavily and wearily. "Okay, Dr. McCormick. What's the name?"

"Kincaid Charles Falk. He would have disappeared—"

"—in the past year and a half. I heard you the first time. I'll get back to you later this evening." *What is it about detectives? John Myers and Emily Walker must have gone to the same hard-ass detective finishing school.*

"Thanks a million," I said. "I owe you."

"Oh, don't worry, Doctor. Next time my daughter is sick, you'll be getting a three a.m. phone call from me."

"Which I'll take. With pleasure."

"Right." I thought she hung up on me, when she said, "Does this have anything to do with Gladys Thomas's death?"

"I don't know," I said, which meant yes.

"Okay, Doc. I'll let you off the hook here. But you keep me informed of anything you find out. It kills me to say it, but you may have been right. I'm not sure it was suicide. That girl is really bothering me, you know."

Yes, I thought, *I do know.* I hit End on the cell.

"You think he disappeared?" Brooke asked.

"Yes."

"Why disappeared?"

"Because he took on a new identity back in Baltimore. Disappear as KC Falk, reappear as Douglas Buchanan." A few beats passed. "And then someone murdered him. I don't know. Maybe we won't find anything. Worth a try, though."

I finished off the acrid coffee.

Brooke looked at her watch, then said, "We need to take care of the dogs. Then you find Alaine Chen."

CHAPTER 76

While we rode south on the highway, the 101, my phone rang.

"Dr. McCormick, this is Detective Walker."

"That was fast," I said. She ignored the comment.

"I called the San Jose PD, and they did find something. A missing-persons report was filed early last year on a Kincaid Charles Falk." I looked at Brooke and gave her the thumbs-up.

"Who filed the report?"

"Let's see. I have the fax here." I could hear pages flipping. "Um, Otto Falk was the name."

"Father?"

"Yes."

"You have a home address for Kincaid?" I rummaged around the car seat for a pen and a piece of paper. Walker gave me an address in San Jose.

"Things falling into place for you, Doc?"

"Maybe."

"Well, you tell me ASAP when they do. I'm going to ride you on this one. You owe me."

"I know."

"And you're still going to get that three a.m. call." She laughed and hung up the phone.

I looked at Brooke, who was looking at me. I said to her, "We're on to something."

"We?" She laughed. "You've changed, Dr. McCormick." She edged the car up to ninety. "You back on the side of the good guys?"

I smiled and shook my head. "We'll see, won't we?"

The ride didn't take that long, despite it being a Friday evening. Most folks, I guessed, were in that place between Friday work and Friday play, which meant more people primping and fewer people driving. Also, Brooke kept our speed at well over eighty for the entire ride. I looked for a roll bar in the car, didn't see one, and resigned myself to a bloody demise on the highway.

Brooke parked the car in her carport and we made our way up to her place. On the way up the steps, I asked her, "How are you feeling?"

"The coffee was too big and pushed me into caffeine toxicity."

"Good one. You know what I mean."

"Kind of excited, kind of nervous. Probably more excited, though."

"More scintillating than HIV monitoring?"

"Almost anything is more scintillating than HIV monitoring." She hit the Up button on the elevator. "I should have been a cop."

"They don't get paid enough."

"*We* don't get paid enough. What do you think about all this?"

"I don't," I said.

"Bullshit, Nathaniel. An hour and a half ago you were spouting about becoming a plastic surgeon, quoting Nietzsche."

"See what happens when I think? I've stopped all reflection."

"You're impossible."

The elevator doors opened. "I have to ask," I said. "You wanted to be part of this from the beginning. How much of it was that you really thought it was important, how much of it was relief from boredom?"

"I don't know if I want to answer that."

"How much of it was that you wanted to work with me?"

"I definitely don't want to answer that."

I smiled. For the first time since I got that early-morning call from Verlach, I felt things were coming together. I felt . . . satisfied, I guess. Fulfilled. Maybe this was a game after all and damn it if we weren't winning. And, to be honest, I liked working with Brooke. I liked *her*. Before I could filter my next words, they were out of my mouth. "I think we make a good team," I said.

I half-expected Brooke to laugh at me, to chastise me for a lame come-on. Instead, she replied, "I do, too. I think we might even be a great team."

At that moment, I thought about kissing her. But I hadn't had any alcohol since the night before and my courage in these matters was down. So, brave man that I am, I followed Brooke down the hall to her apartment. She unlocked the door and entered. I hesitated for a moment, wondering if I could work in a kiss before striking out to question Alaine.

I didn't wonder long. I heard Brooke scream.

CHAPTER 77

Brooke was shaking, staring at the wall on which her road bike hung. Her eyes were wide, her mouth open and quivering. I rushed into the room and swung my head to follow her gaze. I felt my stomach clutch.

Wires ran downward from each hook that supported her bike. The wires stretched two feet. The ends were wrapped around the necks of the two dachshunds, so that the dogs looked like the weights at the end of the pendulum. The animals had been sliced through the belly and their entrails pulled out. The intestines hung another foot below the bodies. Blood dripped over the bookcase and the floor.

I grabbed her by the elbow and pulled her into the hallway. She was hyperventilating a little now. Down the hall, a few doors opened. Heads popped out. "Just a little scare," I said. "Cat got hold of a couple of mice." I did my best to smile.

The neighbors hesitated; then, one by one, they closed their doors. I leaned Brooke up against the wall. "Wait here. Okay? You wait here." She didn't respond, but she didn't move. I left her there and went back into the apartment.

"I'm calling the police now," I said to the room. A lie. I waited and heard nothing. Quickly, I stepped into Brooke's bedroom. I opened the closet door, checked in her bathroom. Nothing. I went back into the living space and checked the small bathroom near her office/guest room. Again, nothing. I opened the door to the guest room and walked inside. The sliding closet door was open a crack, and I ripped it open the rest of the way.

"Jesus!" I yelled. The cat bolted from the closet to the futon, looking freaked and ready to spring. I let myself calm down, then turned to the closet—except for the cat and collection of clothes and boxes, it was empty. I went back into the hall to Brooke.

"Get your things," I told her. She looked at me, still shaking, not comprehending. "Get some clothes. We're leaving here."

She nodded quickly. I walked her into the apartment. "You don't need to look at it." She didn't, and disappeared into the bedroom, keeping a wide distance between herself and the mutilated dogs.

I felt sick, but not as sick as I might have. It was possible, I thought glumly, that I was getting used to this shit. Even so, I couldn't take my eyes off the scene in front of me.

A few minutes later, Brooke came out of the bedroom with a duffel. "We need to clean—"

"No we don't," I said.

"Buddy—?"

"The cat is fine." Physically, I meant; there was nothing we could do about Buddy's state of mind at that moment. I moved to the door; Brooke didn't follow. "He's in the guest room." She still didn't move. "I'll leave him more food, okay?" This time, I pushed her out the door. I went to the kitchen, filled the cat's bowl with food. My hands were unsteady and I spilled kibble. I spilled the water as I filled up that bowl.

CHAPTER 7.8

Brooke and I drove separate cars to the motel, an antiseptic affair near the airport. When we pulled into the parking spaces there, I got out of my car. Brooke didn't. I walked over to her.

"I'll get two rooms," I said.

"Get one. Two beds."

She was looking straight ahead, so I had a little trouble seeing her face. I could, however, see tears dribbling down her cheek. I put my hand on her shoulder, held it there for a second, then went to the motel office.

Ten minutes later we were sitting on the stiff beds in the motel.

"It was a warning," I said.

"Oh, really?" Brooke's eyes were dry, a little puffy maybe, but she had pulled herself together. The sarcasm was back. "I thought it was my cat. Buddy always had an eye for the dramatic."

"I'm going to call the police; then I'll head back and clean up."

"What are the police going to do?"

"Nothing, probably."

"Then why call them?"

"I don't know," I said. Realistically, the cops would take down what happened and leave. I could tell them about the break-in to my car, too, and they could take that down. They could file reports, but then what? Tell them about a videotape I don't have? A rape that no one will talk about? A theory that involves the son of a prominent doctor, an outbreak in Baltimore, a dead man in Maryland, two dead women in California? Oh, sure, they'd listen. Then they'd call me a nut.

"At least we know we're on the right track," Brooke said.

I looked at her, surprised. I thought she'd want to get as far from this madness as she could. Now that it was real, now that there was a threat, I thought she'd decide HIV monitoring wasn't that bad after all.

"We're not safe, Brooke. Even though you might think we're un-touchable because of who we work for, we're not."

"I don't think we're untouchable. I think they don't want to touch us, but they will if we keep pushing."

"Then why should we keep pushing?"

"How many times do we have to go through this?"

"You're not understanding me here. *We* is the issue. *Us.* Look, I'm thirty-three years old, I've got no wife or girlfriend. I've got no kids. The plastics practice in LA isn't going to happen. I'm just me. If something happened to me, some people would be sad, but hell, some people would probably be happy. I've got nothing to lose."

"And," Brooke said, "I've got no boyfriend, no fiancé. No kids. The plastics practice was never going to happen for me anyway." She thought for a moment. "More people would be sad if something happened to me than if something happened to you, sure . . ." Her smile was crooked.

Okay, I thought, I needed to get moving. I really didn't want her to get involved in this any further. With the dogs, a line had been crossed. I was worried about her safety. Really, truly worried. I stood.

"Where are you going?"

"I told you. I'm going to clean up."

"Wait." She took my hand. She pulled me down to her and kissed me.

"What was that?" I asked.

"What was what?" She pulled me to the bed and kissed me again.

"I don't want you to get involved in this."

"Nate," she whispered, "I am involved in this. I want to be involved in this."

I was half on the bed, half off, looking, I'm sure, like some primate in midgait. I lowered myself to her. We kissed again. "These clothes—how many days have you worn them?"

"Less than ten, more than four."

"That's disgusting, Nathaniel. You need to get these off, off, off." She began to undo my shirt.

It had been a year since I'd last seen Brooke Michaels's naked body. A year, actually, since I'd seen any woman's naked body, at least the three-dimensional kind. But, as with riding a bicycle, old lovers never forget.

A few minutes later, both of us were entwined on the bed, naked, breathing fast. We made love, and it was like the intervening year and the distance between Atlanta and San Jose never existed. It was—and I know there were extenuating circumstances—perfect.

The postcoital conversation wasn't the one I'd choose, but considering the events of the past day, it was unavoidable.

Brooke was lying in the crook of my arm, talking. "So, say KC Falk rapes this woman; say she has some occult infection. So, it's not a PERV. At least we know that. But it could be something else. It's entirely possible that he picked it up from her and took it with him to Baltimore."

"True," I said, "but why would Falk let him go? It seems to me they would want to monitor him, keep him close."

"Maybe they just wanted him gone."

"Not these guys. Whatever they're doing, they don't want to introduce a new bug into the population."

"They also don't want to lose their work and money."

Things still didn't add up for me. "Harriet Tobel wouldn't have been involved in anything that had risks like this."

Brooke caressed my chest. "But she *was* involved, Nate."

I changed the subject. "We need something more than conjecture. You can be damn sure that no one's going to do anything—not Tim, not the police, not the FBI—unless we have a little more than employment records and a string of weird circumstances."

"But what? It's not like these people are going to keep a file on all this."

I reached over and set the alarm for four a.m. Five hours' sleep ought to do the trick. "I don't know what. But I think I might know where."

CHAPTER 79

I didn't, after all, get five hours' sleep. It was more like three, since Brooke and I still had some sex to work out of our systems. After we were finished, though, I slipped into the best 180 minutes of shut-eye I'd had for a month.

The alarm screeched for a while before I realized it wasn't part of a dream. I switched it off and pushed myself out of the bed. Brooke didn't move. I mean, she didn't stir at all, from the alarm, from me moving. I'd forgotten how hard this woman could sleep.

The shower brought me a small step closer to the land of the living. My clothes, however, took me a giant leap back toward the dead. Wish I'd had some deodorant.

Brooke still hadn't moved. I took the view in for a second. If I were sentimental, I'd say she looked angelic.

Okay, I *am* sentimental. But an angel like that didn't need to deal with dog carcasses. I found a piece of motel stationery and wrote a note asking Brooke to call me. From the table, I took her apartment key. Then I kissed her lightly—she didn't stir—and left.

The short ride on the highway to downtown was the fastest I'd ever made on a major Northern California artery. Four thirty on a Saturday morning. I almost wished I had farther to go, up to the city, maybe. Hell, if traffic stayed that light, I could be in LA in an hour. But as it was, I had two gutted dogs to dispose of.

Four weeks before, if I'd been shown what would happen to me, I'd have thought I would be frightened. Car broken into, *Godfather*-like animal mutilation. But I wasn't really scared. I was, mostly, angry. Angry that people had died violently. Angry that two little dogs had been killed to send a message. I mean, who does that shit? Mostly, I was angry that now, I was sure, doctors were involved. Say what you want about docs, but we're not supposed to be involved in this kind of harm. Sure, I know about Mengele and the freaks who poison their patients, but Jesus . . .

The apartment was, of course, dark. I turned on the lights, and the unsettling scene on the wall lit up like a theater piece. The blood was congealed and dried in places. I could smell death, a musty, organic odor, thick in the air.

Anticipating Brooke's call, I turned on my cell phone. Then I opened a window and began to clean.

An hour later, the dogs were double-bagged and the mess mopped up. I did the best I could, but there was still some blood encrusted in the gears and spokes of the bike. Brooke, I hoped, wouldn't notice.

I walked downstairs—I took the stairs on the off chance that someone was using the elevator—and threw the dogs and the bloodied towels into the Dumpster. The unceremonious burial made me a little sick.

Brooke still hadn't called, and I was thankful for that. At least one of us was getting some sleep. I really wanted a cigarette, but figured it was futile to go rummaging through Brooke's place, looking for cancer sticks. I actually contemplated going to the nearest convenience store and buying a pack. But time was short. I had other things to contend with.

As it was, the challenges started early.

The cell phone rang. Assuming it was Brooke, I picked it up without looking at the caller ID. Mistake.

"You're in Atlanta, I trust."

Mein Führer.

"No," I said.

"Oh, really?" Tim's voice was thick with sarcasm. "Because I just got a call from my boss here, who got a call from some guys at the FDA saying you're harassing some folks out there. Some pretty connected folks. And I wanted to say, 'Oh, don't worry about Dr. McCormick. He's

in Georgia now. No way he's harassing people in California.' But I can't
say that, can I, Nate?"

"I don't know. . . ."

"I can't say that because you're still in goddamned California."

So the swearing was back. Tim must have been very upset. I realized I was treading on dangerous ground here. To wit: Tim Lancaster's
career, not to mention my own, was feeling some heat.

"There have been developments," I said. I filled him in quickly on
what had happened, leaving out the bit about the dogs.

Except for the whistling from Tim's nose breathing, there was silence on the phone.

"File that in the report. We'll see it gets to the right people—"

"Tim—"

"And I want you on a flight today. Today. Saturday."

"I can't."

"What?"

"There's no time. These guys are closing ranks fast. I can't leave—"

"Wait. I don't think I heard you: you can't what?"

"I can't come back today."

Though I realized the gravity of the situation for the future
prospects of yours truly, I wished I could have seen the look on Tim
Lancaster's face at that moment. As it stood, the tone in his voice was
payoff enough.

"I'm placing you on administrative leave."

But I hadn't counted on that. I imagined the look on my face.

"Come on—"

"As of this moment."

"Tim, please—"

"Which means that any actions you take in the field under the aus-
pices of CDC are illegal. Which means your only legal place of employ is
at your desk in Atlanta."

"Well, an administrative hack has his administrative weekends. I'll
be in the office on Monday." I hung up the phone.

Almost immediately, it began to ring again. I turned the fucker off.

So, there goes the medical career of Dr. Nathaniel McCormick. I guess
I should have been surprised at how long it had lasted, how much good-
will I'd been able to squander before Tim finally gave up. Even so,

despite the circumstances, I felt okay. My tactics had been for shit—
though exactly how they'd been for shit I wouldn't know until I had
some time to reflect—but I was right about this. Damn it, I was *right*.

I went to Brooke's refrigerator, found a beer, and opened it. Not yet
six a.m. and I was sucking a beer. I couldn't tell if I was impressed with
myself or disgusted.

Since I had only two days left of my weekend, I needed to get to
work. So I went to the couch, pulled out the PalmPilot, located the Cs,
and took a swig of the beer. Then, from Brooke's phone, I called my former lady friend.

"Hello," she answered. Her words were crisp, telling me she
wasn't asleep. She wasn't, in fact, at home. I could hear ambient noise in
the background.

"Alaine, it's Nate McCormick."

She paused. "Hi. Hold on a second."

I heard her hand slide over the phone's mouthpiece, then heard
muffled words. After a moment, she said quietly, "Hello?"

"Six a.m. on a Saturday, Alaine? At the gym?"

"Working."

"Ah, well. Early bird catches the IPO."

"What do you want?"

"I want to know what's going on."

"I'm—" She stopped herself. "I'm trying to protect you, Nate."

"From whom?"

"Nate, please. Just go back to . . . back to Atlanta. That's where you
live, right? Forget all of this."

I wondered if she'd spoken to Tim Lancaster.

I said, "I don't know what exactly you're mixed up in, but it does
not look good. Not good, Alaine. I know some of what's happening, and
I know it's not going to end well for anyone involved. So my advice to
you is: don't be involved. Because I'm not going back to Atlanta. The
CDC is not sending me back to Atlanta." I hoped the lie sounded convincing. "Take a step back and ask yourself what the chances are of
things working out." I let that sink in, then said, "What is going on?"

Alaine said, "Moving."

"What?"

"Yeah, it's crazy here. It'll be crazy there, too, a little later in the
day."

She wasn't making sense. "What are you talking about?"

"The best way to get to Kings Canyon is to go down to Gilroy, then west." She paused. "Correct. Then head west on Fifty-six to the Five."

"Alaine, what—"

I heard her say something in the background. Someone was talking to her.

She said, back into the phone, "You have to make sure to check the farmland before you hit the reservoir in the Valley. It's very interesting."

I started to understand what she was doing. I scrabbled for a piece of paper and a pen.

She whispered, "Automatic gate, surveillance, thirteen miles from One-oh-one. Right side of the road." In a louder voice, she said, "Take a lot of water—the park is hot this time of year. Uh-hunh. Be careful. And I want you to think of me when you're there. Remember, I'm the one who suggested you go." She paused, as if waiting for an answer. I understood I wasn't to make one.

Even so, I said, "Thanks, Alaine."

"Kings Canyon will be gorgeous this time of year. Remember I told you about that wonderful place. You owe me one."

She hung up the phone.

For a moment, I sat with the phone in my lap, took a draft of the beer. *Okay, McCormick,* I thought, *your old girlfriend is feeding you information. She's telling you where to go. She's also asking you for help.*

I drained the rest of the beer. Then, to save batteries on my cell, I called in to the voice mail system from Brooke's phone. Two messages.

The first was from Brooke, asking where I was, sounding a little worried. The second, I assumed, would be from Brooke as well. It was received ten minutes after her call, just after six a.m.

A man's voice came over the line. "Dr. McCormick, this is Otto Falk. I apologize for the early call, but I wanted to arrange a meeting with you before you returned to the East Coast. I do hope we can meet. Please call me nevertheless." He left a telephone number.

"Are you going to meet him?"

"Of course."

Brooke let out a small breath into the phone. I could tell she was thinking. Finally, she said, "I'll come."

"No."

"I have to—"

"You have to come over here," I said, referring to her apartment. "We need someone to go through all these HIV files from Dr. Tobel. I don't know if it's connected in any way—"

"It's not connected."

"We don't know that."

"We *do* know that. It's the Chimeragen work that's important."

"We can't leave any stone unturned, honeybunch. Besides, you understand HIV. Retroviruses aren't my thing. But give me a good filovirus and a cup of coffee, and—"

"Nate . . ."

I guess she was tired of the joking. "What?"

"Be careful," she said.

CHAPTER 80

For all the hype and hoopla from the press and from Alaine Chen, the headquarters of Chimeragen looked pretty drab. Then again, in Silicon Valley all the architecture was pretty drab. People busy crafting the future have no time for silly aesthetics. People crafting the future need foosball tables and video games.

As it was, though, I was in postcrash California. There were no foosball tables, and the future-crafters had all gone back to consulting in Chicago or Boston. In fact, the entire office complex I now looked at was deserted except for the twenty percent occupied by Chimeragen. For Lease signs were posted on empty doors.

A few other cars dotted the parking lot: two junkers at the far end of the lot and a Mercedes and a BMW near the Chimeragen entrance. One of the German vehicles, I assumed, belonged to Otto Falk.

When I'd spoken to the man himself, he asked me to meet him at the Chimeragen offices. Normally, I wouldn't have thought twice about it, but I had just mopped up the carcasses of two gutted canines and was leery about meeting the man on his turf. I mean, I didn't think that Otto Falk had broken into Brooke's place with baling wire and a sharp knife, but I suspected he wasn't totally innocent, either.

I walked to the glass door emblazoned with the company logo, which involved a cometlike thing underlining the name and circling around the "n" in "Chimeragen." There was a buzzer next to the door. I rang.

A figure appeared in the reception room and walked to the door. The person was much taller than I remembered Otto Falk. Perhaps Chimeragen was also doing work on a growth serum that could give sixty-year-old scientists another five inches. If that were the case, I'd invest immediately. Hell, I'd down some of the elixir that morning. I'd always wanted to be six three.

But it wasn't Otto Falk. It was, to my chagrin, Ian Carrington—tall, blond, teeth so white it looked like he brushed with Clorox. He shined that smile at me through the glass. I shielded my eyes from the glare.

Mr. Carrington punched something into a keypad and manually unlatched a lock. "Dr. McCormick, good to see you again," he boomed, and thrust out his hand. As I shook it, I tried to imagine that hand pulling a knife through a dog, tried to imagine it pulling a rope around Gladys Thomas's neck. The grip was firm, but I still couldn't picture it.

"Likewise," I lied.

Carrington held the door open for me, and I entered into the nondescript reception room: a desk for the receptionist, a few chairs, a low table with some science and business publications.

"Welcome to our humble corporate offices," he said. I noticed that Carrington locked the dead bolt. The keypad beeped. Two locks. Bad sign.

Carrington led me through another door. This one had a biometric lock—he placed his hand on a pad; it scanned and beeped. *The only way for me to break in to this place,* I thought, *would be to lop off Ian Carrington's hand and hold it to the scanner.* All in all, not such a bad idea.

We walked down a carpeted hallway, white walls, brown wooden doors. Near the end of the corridor, one of the doors was open. Carrington went to it and ushered me into a conference room. I entered. Otto Falk stood. Ian Carrington closed the door.

Falk stuck out his hand and I shook it. "Dr. McCormick. So nice of you to come."

Well, I guessed I should feel good that everyone was so damned happy to see me.

"Sit," Falk said. "Please sit." And with a graciousness that is peculiar to dictators, Nazi generals, and power-drunk CEOs, Falk bowed slightly and waved his hand at the chair in front of me. I sat and waited for the bullet in the back of my head.

No gun went off and Falk and Carrington took their seats.

Now that I saw him up close, Otto Falk looked every inch the surgeon, despite his small stature: close-cropped thin gray hair, shiny pate, trimmed goatee. His glasses were too stylish for a physician his age, but then again, he was in California. And he was a businessman as well as a doctor.

No one spoke for a moment. After a good dose of uncomfortable silence, Otto Falk looked at me paternally and said, "We know you are upset by Dr. Tobel's passing."

"I sure as hell am upset."

"We all are. It was a great loss to us." He cleared his throat. "But I wonder if her death has—forgive me—somehow confused you as to the situation out here."

"I don't think I'm confused, Dr. Falk."

"Perhaps, then, *misguided* is a better word." That same paternal look—half smile, relaxed face. "Dr. McCormick, do you know how many people in this country are waiting for a kidney?"

The question seemed to come out of nowhere, but actually, I knew the answer, having read the prospectus for Chimeragen at the library the day before. "Fifty thousand."

"Fifty thousand eight hundred and ninety-eight as of last month." He let the exact number sink in. And when you think about it, it is an extraordinary number of people. More than the population of the small city in which I grew up. He said, "Sixty percent of them will die waiting for a suitable match. How many people are waiting for a liver?"

"Eighteen thousand," I said.

"Eighteen thousand seven hundred and fifty-two. Eighty percent of those people will die waiting." He leaned back in his chair. "You've been doing your homework, Dr. McCormick."

I waved my hand. "Nah. I have so much money left over from med school and residency, I don't know what to do with it, so I'm looking for investment ideas. Your company's prospects seem very promising."

Falk exchanged a look with Carrington and did not reply. The man was not averse to silences, and he let this one linger.

Eventually, he said, "I don't need to say more than that, do I, about how important it is what we're working on?" I guess he didn't need to say it, but he did anyway. "We're on the precipice, Dr. McCormick, of saving tens of thousands of lives a year. Tens of thousands! In this country alone. Can you imagine? You are a public health official, so you understand these numbers. But for you, tens of thousands of people are saved by building latrines and by antibiotics. Tens of thousands are not saved by high technology and by procedures. I know this. I know how public health looks at 'science.' Put more money toward education, you say! Toward prevention!"

Falk thumped his fist on the table. I could see where the unbridled enthusiasm came from, but I was not used to seeing it in academics. It was obvious, Otto Falk had been in quite a few venture capitalists' offices, bowling them over with juggernaut hyperbole, big hand gestures, and exclamation points. No wonder they'd given him millions to invest.

Even so, I wasn't a venture capitalist, and I was a little taken aback by this pitch. I mean, did these guys think they could dazzle me with pictures of a rosy future and make me forget about the dead dogs, about dead Douglas Buchanan and rape, about poor dead Gladys Thomas?

"Look at the numbers, Doctor. They don't lie. You saw the patients in the hospital. They don't lie." Falk studied me with a little half smile. "Oh, yes, Dr. McCormick, we know you went into the hospital to look at our facilities there. Were you impressed?"

"I guess you could say that."

"Good," he said. "You should be." He paused. "In the patients you saw, we have detected virtually no immunologic response, no rejection. And they are on very low doses of immunosuppressive drugs. Very low doses, Doctor."

"How did you do it?"

"Ah, the easiest question and the hardest one."

Spare me the zen bullshit, Otto.

"In the simplest terms, we stripped away all the markers that label these organs as foreign. We did this through tissue-engineering procedures developed by me and my colleagues. The animals from which these organs come lack all surface sugars and surface proteins that identify the tissue as other. These organs are blanks; they are universal spare parts." Falk grinned at me. "You see how monumental this is, Dr. McCormick. This is a revolution on par with the discovery of antibiotics. We have discovered . . . we have worked out how to make an organ that functions in almost anybody. The power of the technique is unparalleled. We start with kidneys and liver and we go to pancreas, to lungs, to heart."

Falk was a little red faced now. He must have felt he was about to blow a hose, because he took a breather. When he'd calmed down, he said, "I do not care about money, Dr. McCormick. I have enough to have a nice house and a nice car. I have enough for my family." I thought I heard him choke a little on the word *family,* but I might have imagined it. "There are those who care about money. Some of my staff, for example. My investors definitely." He looked at Ian Carrington, who just smiled blankly. "This venture will pay them handsomely. People will make tens of millions of dollars. Some may make hundreds of millions. You see, this country now relies on donations of organs. However, if we manufacture organs, we will be able to charge for them what the market will bear." He didn't have to tell me the market would bear astronomical prices. Your life or $50,000. Your life or $100,000. An easy choice.

"I myself have placed the stock I own in this company into a trust. It will go to support a foundation that will support research and also defray the cost of the organs for those who cannot afford them. Already, I have commitments from my staff and from some investors to place some of their stock in the trust as well."

He seemed to want me to say something, so I said, "That's very generous of you."

"Well, I am a doctor. And I have been called to this profession to do more than play golf every afternoon or to complain about what managed care has done to my practice." Falk then stood up to his full sixty-five inches and picked up a book that had been lying on the table. He walked over to me and opened it, it seemed, to a random page. It was a photo album, and I found myself staring at the picture of a little boy. "That's Daryl Tennenbaum. He's dead. Kidney failure after fighting off septicemia. On the page opposite him is Dody Fisk. Dead. Liver failure. We tried to transplant two years ago, but it was rejected." Falk flipped to a page deeper into the book. Four more pictures. "Kenneth Billings. Thirty and diabetic. Dead from kidney failure. We could not find a match. Geraldine Nieman. Thirty-four. Dead from an infection she picked up while on dialysis. It is an outrage that these people are dying, Dr. McCormick. An outrage. And we are close to being able to do something about it." He closed the photo album. "You understand the situation."

In fact, I didn't. This flurry of justification was unexpected. Though I didn't know exactly what would come of the meeting here, I'd been prepared for something a lot more sinister. Instead, what I got was some Holy Roller sermon on how much good he was doing.

"I understand."

"And we are very close to helping these people. We are extremely close to a book this thick with smiling faces with birth dates and no death dates. Do you see, now, the magnitude of what we're doing?"

"Yes," I said. I did see the magnitude. And as such, I saw how much these guys had to protect. So much that someone might be willing to take a few lives to save it. Kill a few to save thousands. On the surface, it seemed like a simple equation.

"If I may speak?" It was Ian Carrington, he of the gleaming teeth. Falk nodded.

"Dr. McCormick, I got into this on the business side," Carrington said, and I wondered which business side he meant—Chimeragen's or Alaine Chen's—"and I have to tell you that business has taken a backseat to the good we'll be able to do."

The bullshit was getting so deep, I almost had trouble seeing Carrington's face. Thank God for the teeth. I locked onto the shine.

"Sure, we all stand to make a lot of money, but the number of lives this will save . . . it almost made me want to be a doctor." *Right, Ian.* "It's offering me the chance to do some good in the world. I cut my teeth on tech companies—I took one public about five years ago, then led investments in a few small biotech firms—but this is the opportunity to be part of something much bigger than myself. The nobility of what we're doing—"

I couldn't take it anymore from this tool. He'd been speaking for less than two minutes and I still couldn't take it. "Shut up, Ian."

There was sort of a stunned silence. Carrington's smile flickered for a moment, I guess as he waited for me to let him know it was a joke. Finally, he got that it wasn't a joke, and the smile faded.

I turned to Falk. "Why did you ask me here?"

He forced a smile. "I wanted you to know what we're doing and why we're doing it."

"I knew what you were doing."

"I don't think so."

The timbre of our meeting had definitely taken a dark turn, but that was fine with me. This goody-good front was unexpected, bizarre, and though it might have been genuine at its core, there was so much shit covering it now I couldn't really see the nobility Otto Falk was spewing. It was like the surgeon's moral compass got broken somewhere along the way and, though he'd started out okay, he was now following an errant, fucked-up path. Plus, I was under no illusions about what these guys thought of me. If there were no laws against murder, I was sure I'd be pushing up daisies. Or, more likely, I'd be a brain-dead host for some pig lungs.

Anyway, I needed to fish for some answers and get the hell out of there. So I fished away. "What happened to the woman in Room Three in the hospital? Why is she gone?"

If these two were taken aback by my question, they didn't show it.

"You saw the empty room," Falk said.

I nodded. They must have known, too, that I'd seen the videotape.

Falk cleared his throat. "She died of a nosocomial staph infection."

A nosocomial infection is one picked up in the hospital. Staphylococcus is a common agent.

"That's it?" I asked.

"It's a tragedy," Falk replied, "but that is it."

I nodded. I could see the rest of this meeting wasn't going to get me very far, but I needed to know their motivation for asking me here, so I said, "This is all really super stuff, guys, but I have to ask: Why the hell did you ask me here?"

Again, the two men exchanged looks. Falk let Carrington speak. "Dr. McCormick, we wanted you to know what we are doing—"

"We've been through this," I cut in.

Carrington didn't acknowledge the interruption. "We wanted you to know that we are on your side. We know, too, that you've been concerned about certain . . . occurrences. But you're on the wrong track. That track—the wrong one—has consequences for us. And for all of the patients who could be helped by us."

Otto Falk was staring at the table, eyes half-closed. He looked up slowly. "We would be more than happy to work with the CDC, to show you all of our data on infection, on the porcine endogenous retroviruses and a hundred other infectious agents. But I assure you that you'll find nothing. The animals we use have been tested and tested by a scientist no less eminent than Harriet Tobel. The FDA has been scrutinizing us from the beginning, and they have found nothing."

"What about the patients you're monitoring in the hospital? Have they been tested?"

"Of course. That goes without saying."

"Does it?"

The silence again. The staccato pace of this meeting set me on edge, giving me the same tense feeling I had when I tried to sit through Beckett plays in college. The stakes now, of course, were a lot higher than a five-dollar admission fee and two hours of my time.

"Dr. McCormick," Carrington continued, "we feel your time is finished in California right now. We also know that your superiors feel your time is finished."

Okay, that surprised me. Though I suspected they had put some pressure on people in the FDA who put pressure on my bosses, I hadn't realized they'd gotten feedback about my conversation with Tim two hours before. These guys really were connected. I felt myself begin to get angry. *Reel it in, McCormick, reel it in.*

"We also acknowledge the good work you've done for your organization." Carrington looked at Otto Falk, who nodded slightly. "In light of that, we wish you to be a part of our organization. Now that the role Harriet Tobel occupied is vacant, we would like to offer you the position of consultant."

It was my turn to be stunned, actually flabbergasted. The men across the table from me must have seen the look on my face. Carrington smiled. "It will be virtually no work for you. You will still go back to Atlanta today. We simply want the opportunity to call on you for advice if we need it. For your troubles, we will give you a retainer. Say, four thousand shares of founders' stock?"

Otto Falk spoke. "I think that is only fair. In fact, in light of Dr. McCormick's expertise in microbiology, I would suggest we offer him five thousand shares, Ian. More, if his role expands."

I leaned back in my chair and laughed. "I can't accept that. You know that. I signed a contract with CDC—"

Carrington kept up with the smile. "We have very smart lawyers and accountants working for us, Dr. McCormick. No one would be the wiser. In fact, your tenure at the CDC ends in a year, correct?"

I didn't answer.

"That's perfect. We'll be able to make all official communication and transactions active as of the date of your departure. But don't worry, the contracts will be rock solid, so you will get what's due—"

"I don't think you get it. I don't care about CDC regulations. I'm not going to take the offer."

Otto Falk pointed his finger at me. "Dr. McCormick, this offer is best for all of us. You get to be a part of something much larger than yourself and much larger than the silly detective work you do for CDC. We gain access to a brain that can provide the necessary criticism—"

"You will not be allowed to involve me in schemes." I stood. "I cannot believe that you made such an offer to an officer of CDC."

"And how much longer do you think you'll be an officer at CDC?"

I stepped toward the door. "Good day, gentlemen."

"Dr. McCormick!" Falk shouted. "You must understand that our offer to you is your best path. Do not take the consultant position if you choose, but do not interfere."

"Nate," Carrington said. I was already furious, and his familiarity made me even more so. "Please. Think of all the kids in that book." He pointed to the album on the table. "Think of yourself, for God's sake. Think about your friend Dr. Michaels."

"You son of a bitch!"

I stood there, looking down at the two men, breathing heavily. High noon in the conference room.

Softly, Otto Falk said, "Do not make this mistake, Dr. McCormick."

"Watch me," I said. I walked to the door, then turned back. "Dr. Falk, where's Kincaid? Where is your son?"

Falk finally looked furious. It was nice to get a rise out of him, so I pushed it. "Did KC make the same mistake I'm about to make?"

"He made different ones, Dr. McCormick." Falk was struggling to get himself under control.

As I walked down the hall, I heard a fist hit the conference room table and heard a shouted "Goddamn."

I pushed into the reception room, went to the front door, and turned the dead bolt. The damned door wouldn't open, so I smacked the keypad lock. It beeped at me, but didn't open. Figuring I had nothing to lose, and that any delay in my getting out of the place was dangerous, I picked up a chair from the waiting room and hurled it at the door. Nate McCormick and chair–1; door–0.

I broke away fragments of shattered glass to let myself out. As I stepped through the hole in the door frame, I noticed that the Chimeragen logo was still largely intact on the ground, held together by the enamel or whatever it was that comprised the letters. I put my heel on the blue-and-green company name and broke it to pieces.

"Are you at the apartment?"

"Yes. I'm being your Girl Friday and staying where you—"

"Get out."

"I just got here—"

"Brooke, get out of the apartment now. Go anywhere—get a motel room or something. Go through those files, but don't do it at home. Get out."

"Why—?"

Her voice clipped out, then back in.

"Brooke, I'm going to lose you. You have to leave, okay?"

"Nate? What happ—" The signal on the cell phone died. I tossed the phone into the passenger's seat.

Okay, McCormick, the shit is definitely hitting the fan now, and, like you said to the hospital epidemiologist, you are a shit magnet. I just hoped some of my unique properties didn't rub off on Brooke Michaels. The gutted dogs were a blessing, in a way. They made Brooke wary.

Think, Doctor.

At that point, I had nothing but a bunch of assumptions about Falk, Carrington, and Chimeragen. I had nothing that would in any way entice the FBI or other law enforcement to tackle gentlemen who were so obviously well connected. To call in the troops now would do nothing more than sink my already listing career. Worse, these guys might be able to slap some slander or harassment suit on me. Then the courts could seize my old Corolla back in Atlanta. I loved that car.

I needed proof. And I thought I knew where to get it. Hadn't Alaine Chen told me as much? The iron was hot, and that iron was at a Chimeragen facility in Gilroy. I needed to strike.

Gilroy, California. The garlic capital. Cherries. And, it seemed, pigs.

I fired south of San Jose, the Buick cruising along on soft shocks, feeling like a luxury liner on a dead-calm sea. If I had taken my Corolla this fast, the thing would have protested and probably would have killed me.

As per Alaine's cryptic directions, I peeled off the highway onto Route 56 and marked the distance on the odometer. Thirteen miles. Electronic gate. Shouldn't be that hard to find.

It had always been a wonder to me that in the most populous state in the nation, one could be in such pristine farmland so close to a population center. California may be the seat of tech and entertainment, but it's also the agricultural capital of the country, and, therefore, of the world. At that time of year, the hills were covered in a fine grass, dry and gold, the fodder for livestock and poets and those spectacular brush fires. The valleys were irrigated and green, so that the place looked like a watercolorist's dream: all those vibrant hues drawn next to one another, the lines between them as crisp as the lines on a painting.

It seemed fitting that the organ farm—that's how I thought of it— would be located there. Just south of the tech hotbed, on the periphery of the agricultural hotbed, if there is such a thing. On this farm, the animals were not being cultivated for something so banal as their muscle tissue: their ribs, their loins, their shanks. They were cultivated for something much more exquisite and precious: their kidneys, their livers.

The odometer ticked twelve and I slowed, causing a backup of traffic behind me that my grandfather called a turtle. He loved to cause a turtle. I didn't, since it probably drew attention to me at that moment. As it was, I didn't really have a choice.

At 13.2 miles, I was already past the gate. I'd caught it out of the corner of my eye—a gunmetal-gray lattice set back from the road about ten yards. Having marked it, I sped up. The turtle crawled a little faster.

I didn't find a convenient turnout for a few miles. By the time I did, the hills had given way to a large body of water—the reservoir Alaine had mentioned. I pulled off into one of the parking lots and got out of the car to look around. Just a tourist from San Francisco, checking out the man-made natural beauty of San Luis Reservoir. Paranoid, I looked to see if any of the cars that had been backed up behind me pulled off, disgorging a few simian gentlemen with baseball bats and brass knuckles. None did.

After a few minutes, I strolled back to the car and went west on 56. A few miles later, I was stopped outside the nondescript gate. No name to the farm, only a number. A long dirt road ran from the gate, disap-pearing over a hill. A cattle guard lay like a huge automobile grille across the entrance. A few cattle grazed inside the fence. Just another California farm.

Right. What gave it away was the gate itself, disguised to look like a simple corrugated thing, like the ones that I'd seen from Maryland to Georgia to the West. But this gate wasn't hinged; it was on rollers. A small call box, camouflaged with morning glories climbing over it, sat off to the left. A tiny camera topped the box.

I was far enough from the entrance that I didn't think the camera caught me; even so, I wasn't going to park the car there. I backed out of the small road and drove slowly along the shoulder. After about a half mile, the shoulder flattened just enough that I could get the car off the road if I put most of it into the grass. I parked.

I made sure Dr. Tobel's ID cards were in my pocket, hoping that with my shirt and jacket and ID, I might actually be able to talk any rov-ing security guard into believing I was Harriet—call me Harry—Tobel. I took my jacket from the car and put it on, took the cell phone. As care-fully as I could, I climbed over the barbed wire fence. It wasn't careful enough, because I got a nice two-inch tear in the seat of my pants. Then I set out over the rise, hoping to God I wouldn't be picked up by maraud-ing security, wouldn't get lost, wouldn't die of dehydration.

Early afternoon in Gilroy was hot, and I'd sweated through my T-shirt and button-down before I was halfway up the hill. Depending on how long I needed to walk in this, dehydration would become a real risk. Once I actually got to the farm, I didn't imagine anyone would be wait-ing for me on the porch with a big glass of lemonade.

On the crest of the hill, I had a better view of what lay below. Unfortunately, the view did not include a farm of any sort, but I could see the dirt entrance road to my right and was able to follow it, keeping a good distance between me and it.

Down into a shallow valley, over another rise. I was burning through any excess body water I had and seriously considered calling it a day and heading back to the car. But, I hoped, they would still be moving things into the farm, still causing some sort of distraction. That was kind of a laugh, and I actually laughed out loud: distraction. As if I were a spy. I wasn't really sure what I would do with a "distraction."

Twenty minutes later, I saw it. I must have been a good two miles from the main road, and the collection of buildings I saw ahead of me was a half mile or more away. From that distance, I was impressed at how normal everything looked. I don't know what I was expecting—some glass-and-steel monstrosity, maybe—but what I saw looked like any other farm. A collection of white metal outbuildings, a few farm vehicles. Happily, a big white moving van was ass-end against one of the structures.

I sat, trying to recall every spy or war movie I'd ever seen, trying to figure out how to approach the place. I could wait for dark, but by then the movers would be gone. Hell, they were probably winding up as I watched, feeling my sweat dry, figuring out what to do. So, I stood and walked straight down the hill. There was a corral of sorts below me, and I walked toward it. I had my story ready: car out of gas, needed a phone. If they asked me why I'd walked for three miles instead of flagging a passing car . . . well, I suppose I could always turn on the tears.

I got to the fenced corral without being shot. The area was not the muddied flat you'd expect in a regular hog farm. From growing up in semi-rural Pennsylvania, I knew that hogs use mud to cool themselves off. But these weren't regular hogs, and so enjoyed a thickly sodded, well-tended pasture. Clean, if that term was appropriate for a farm. I wondered how the hogs felt about that.

. The split-rail fence was cosmetic—a weird nod to aesthetics—and was backed by an electrified grid. The hogs or other animals that frolicked in the area had no chance of escape. Extending into the larger fenced area were smaller pens, each about thirty feet square. For each pen, there was a door. These pigs were not allowed to mingle, after all. The long fence that ran around the whole area was redundant, perhaps to prevent escape.

The first thing I noticed about the building I now approached was its sheen. This wasn't some structure appropriated from an old working farm; it had been built in the past few years. The white paint was bright enough to have been applied in the past few months, after the winter rains. An air-conditioning unit hummed somewhere ahead of me.

I followed the sound to another building separated from the first by a paved pathway. Doors to both buildings gave out onto the path, each with a black security pad blinking with a red light. I waited for ten minutes and, seeing or hearing no one, walked along the path and around the corner of the second building. From there, I saw the white moving truck backed against yet another building, which looked like it was connected to the second. Unlike most science buildings I'd been to, this place was a jumble of small buildings connected by covered walkways. I guess that's how you build when efficiency of space isn't a consideration.

Men in blue coveralls were unloading the last of the boxes from the back of the truck into what had to be a laboratory. Among the burly men, I saw a flash of jet-black hair. Alaine. I pulled back behind the corner of the building.

Retracing my steps, I walked to the second building and fished Dr. Tobel's Chimeragen card from my pocket.

I should have waited, probably, until nightfall. I should have been dressed in black and armed with any number of high-tech gadgets. In fact, for this job, I should have been someone else, someone who'd done things like this before. As it was, I tucked in my shirt, then held the card to the black box next to the door. The lock beeped and clicked, and I walked inside.

The room was small, blank except for a door set into the opposite wall, a sink, a footbath, and a cart stacked with the usual protective stuff. And—oh, yes—a camera pointing straight at me. I grabbed a mask and gown and skullcap off the cart and quickly put them on—if anyone was watching, I didn't want to alert them by violating protocol. In the sink, I scrubbed my hands and stepped into the footbath. After that, I put my card next to another automatic lock.

A blast of air rushed out as I passed through the doorway into a much larger room. There was a single stainless steel mesh walkway down the center. Flanking the walkway were about ten pens, five on each side. I could hear grunting and the squeal of pigs. There were cameras everywhere—at either end of the walkway, looking down into the hogs' pens—but with my mask and gown, they didn't faze me.

The first pen was separated by a low metal gate. Its hinges were at the base, so it would fall forward—to the steel walkway—when unlocked, creating a ramp from the pen to the walkway; convenient, if you needed to pull Piggy from the pen and transport him to the OR. Speaking of the OR, the pen was as clean as many operating rooms I'd seen. The wood shavings at the bottom looked freshly changed. There was a spout running into the pen for water—no standing bowl of H_2O for these fellows—and another tubular device for depositing food. In the middle of the pen sat a medium-sized, impossibly clean and pink pig. He, or she, gazed up at me and grunted. Then, for whatever pig-reason, it jogged to the water tube and began sucking.

I walked between the pens, each identical, each holding a pig that looked exactly like the ones in the pens I'd passed. I pushed through the door at the end of the hallway.

I stood in a small antechamber. There were two computers here, a chair, a few environmental monitors (humidity, temperature), and security television screens that flipped back and forth between shots of the pigs and of the entrances to the buildings. The banks of screens were divided, it looked like, into "Bertha" and "Abby." As the images flipped, I could see that each of the pens was labeled with a number: Bertha 1, Bertha 2, and so on. Abby, however, showed a bunch of blank pens.

One of the Abby screens flipped to a screen called "Walkway 1"; on it, I saw a gowned individual striding along the stainless steel walkway.

"Shit," I breathed to myself.

CHAPTER 82

I heard a door open.

"Jesus!" a man's voice said.

I turned. *Gown and mask,* I told myself, *terrific disguise.* "Hi," I said.

"Hi," the man said. He wore glasses and I could see his eyes squinting behind them. "Who the hell are you?"

"I'm from Dr. Tobel's lab." I gave a little wave. You didn't shake hands in a sterile environment. "Yonnick . . . Gladwell," I said.

"Oh. You came in with the movers."

He offered; I took. "Yes. Just showing myself around. You don't mind?"

"Not at all. You wash up before you walked in?"

"Of course."

"Good. I'm Bill Dyson, staff veterinarian. I don't remember your name. You new?"

"Yes. Well, sort of. I worked in Dr. Tobel's other lab at the university. But came down here when . . . well, you know about Dr. Tobel. . . ."

"Yeah. A shame."

"Anyway, with the clinical trials about to rev up, they're reappropriating some of us. Or, actually, I wanted to be reappropriated."

"Who wouldn't?"

"I guess the pigs wouldn't."

Bill Dyson didn't seem to like that one too much; he sat down and glanced over the monitors. "This your first time here?"

"Yes."

"You want a tour?"

"Sure," I said.

Dyson clicked through the cameras angled on the pigs. This was going to be a video tour. "I don't know how much they told you yet."

"Not much. I've just been getting samples and testing them. Only for the past week, though. That's when I switched to microbiology."

"You said your name was Yonnick?"

"Yeah."

"Fun name. What is it?"

"Scandinavian." *Scandinavian?*

"Great girls up there."

"I wouldn't know. I'm from Wisconsin."

"Yeah. I dated this Norwegian girl. Six feet tall and lived for sex—"

"Great. The pigs all have the same name. They're clones?"

Dyson paused for a moment, put off, perhaps, that I'd switched the subject from his sexual conquest. He said, "Yeah. Well, Bertha is one line. Abby was another. We have two more buildings. Six lines in all."

"Where are the Abby pigs?"

"They, uh . . . they didn't tell you about Abby?"

"No."

"Well, suffice it to say, Abby was sick. So were all of her clones. We destroyed them."

"When?"

"About a year ago." He looked at me. "Man, they're really being tight about the info here. Don't tell anyone I told you about Abby. You're on the team and all, but . . ." His voice faded out.

"You only said they were sick."

"Yeah. Even that."

I changed the subject. "What's the building behind this one?"

"Oh. That's where the mamas are kept, before we impregnate them. They get to see the outside. These pigs, the ones we'll use for the organs, are kept in here. They don't get to see the sun. Too many contaminants out there."

"What's the procedure?"

"For what?"

"For making these guys." I pointed at the screen.

"Simple. You know about Falk's work, right?"

"More or less. Like I said, I just work on the diseases. They don't tell us much about what goes on on the other side of the wall."

"It's all coming out in a paper in *Nature* in the next year or so. That's what we hope, anyway. Shooting for *Nature*."

I decided to appeal to Dyson's vanity. "Why wait for *Nature*, when I can get it from one of the geniuses who helped do the work?"

He laughed. We were clearly bonding. "So, Falk discovered a way to strip the surface antigens off the porcine organs. Well, Falk discovered it with my help. These antigens are basically sugars on the pig's tissues that signal they are pig and not human. Falk finds the genes responsible for them and deletes those genes. Luckily, humans don't have a corresponding gene for these sugars, so he didn't need to insert a human gene where the pig gene was deleted."

"Lucky."

"Tell me about it. We get a fertilized egg, make sure the genes responsible for these surface antigens have been knocked out, and go about making a bunch of copies of the new oocyte. Normally, we let division progress to the sixteen-cell stage, before any differentiation has occurred. So we're left with sixteen stem cells."

"All of which can become a pig. And all of these pigs have organs with the surface antigens missing."

"Righto. But we need tons of cells. So we take these stem cells and put them into eggs from which we've removed the genetic material.

Then we give the eggs a little jolt of electricity and they begin to divide again."

"Like they did with Dolly." The cloned sheep.

"Yes. But we're not letting the eggs progress to embryo yet. We need to get as many copies as we can. When we get the eggs to the sixteen-cell stage, we separate the cells. Then we take those sixteen cells, place them in evacuated eggs, let them start to divide, and so on. Sixteen times sixteen times sixteen."

"How many times did you do this? Let the cells divide, stop division, put each of the cells in a new egg?"

"A bunch. We have about two thousand frozen blastocysts right now." The blastocyst is the early embryo. "That's for each line, each pig. The cloning process is real inefficient, so we need as many eggs as we can get." He played with the buttons on the video monitors. I could tell he was getting a little bored. "Then we did what any moron with the right tools can do."

"The cloning process."

"Yeah. We took the genetic material from these blastocysts, stuck it into an egg with its genetic material evacuated from it. This time, though, we didn't just keep the new fertilized eggs in a petri dish. We shocked them, then put them into surrogate mother hogs."

"Those are the surrogates out there? In the other building?"

"No. We kill the surrogates when the piglets come to term. We don't want to take any chances with a vaginal birth. You know, hogs are always rolling over on their babies. We deliver via cesarean section."

"Where are the genetic originals? The original pigs?"

"In another building. We keep them around just in case we need to go back and check the blueprints."

"Are all the pigs female?"

"Yeah. Easier to handle. And it doesn't make a difference for the organs."

"Mother Nature's not an equal opportunity employer."

"No, she's not. If we're not careful, we'll be lucky if there are any men left in a hundred years."

"What'll happen to *Monday Night Football*?"

I saw his eyes wrinkle in a smile. He tapped a few more times on the buttons near the video monitors. Images flipped on the screens.

"Pleasure talking to you," he said. "I have to go check on the other pigs. You want to come along?"

"Sure." I wondered at my newfound buddy, who seemed oddly forthcoming with his information. On second thought, it made sense. I was in the middle of nowhere; all the entrances were protected with key cards. Furthermore, chances were good that Falk and Carrington hadn't told the worker bees about any problems.

Dyson slid his card across the black panel. It clicked and we walked through Abby's wing, past the empty pens, which were free from any dirt or wood shavings. The entire place glistened.

I said, "Why are all these pens empty? You didn't start another line after Abby was . . . taken care of?"

"I guess someone's superstitious. Besides, we don't know where the infection came from, so they don't want any more animals in here."

"But we're walking through it."

"It's been completely disinfected about four times. It's clean. Dunno. I think it's fine. But like I said, they're superstitious."

We got to the end of the walkway. "Allow me," I said, and swiped my card against the black panel. I wanted Dyson to see that I had all the necessary cards for access. Gave me some cred. But the superior security of the place begged some questions. As we passed into another vestibule hung with sink, gowns, and masks, I asked him, "How do you get out if there's a fire?"

He began stripping off his gown. My gut clenched as I began to disrobe; I'd been taking a lot of comfort in my anonymity and didn't look forward to giving it up. But I didn't have much choice.

As Dyson pulled off his mask, I saw that the lower left side of his jaw, from the lip down, was deeply scarred. It didn't look like a burn, more like the flesh had been shredded and repaired. All of us, I guessed, had something to hide.

"If you're a hog, you don't get out. If you're human, the security system is supposed to disengage. I wouldn't trust it, though." He turned and looked at me. "The guys here are paranoid as hell. Glad I'm down here, away from HQ, but"—he canted his head toward the outside door—"it looks as if some of HQ is moving in." He put his hands in the sink and stepped on a foot pedal to start the water. "No big deal. I figure I wait two years, go through the IPO, then retire to Humboldt or something. Maybe open a tiny vet practice."

"Sounds good."

"Don't it, though?"

Dyson watched me as I washed my hands. He said, "Dog attack."

"What?"

"My face. Saw you looking at it. Pit bull attacked me when I was a kid. Nearly tore my chin off." Not knowing what to say, I focused on my hands. "And I decided to become a vet. Go figure."

Dyson put his card on the panel and opened the door to the outside. So many locks. I fingered the Chimeragen ID around my neck and began to worry. If anyone checked access records, they would see that the dead Harriet Tobel had been walking around, opening doors.

We walked across a small paved area. To the left, another long building jutted out into a grassy field. "That's the other holding pen?" I asked Dyson.

"Yes. And that one." He pointed to another building about thirty yards away, also thrusting into a pasture. To our right sat a larger, two-story square building, the three long hog pens radiating from it like petals from a flower. The square building, I recognized, was where the moving truck had been parked, though I couldn't see it from that angle.

"What's that?" I asked, pointing at the square building. Immediately, I realized my mistake.

"The labs and operating room. Offices, too. I thought you were in there already, helping with the move."

"Just the labs. They told me to take a tour, and I came to the pens first. Besides, this place is confusing. I'm getting all turned around."

"It happens," he said. He sounded unconvinced.

Suddenly, I heard a ringing. At first, I couldn't place the sound—a sort of techno trill—but I saw Dyson thrust a paw into his pants pocket.

"You get service here?"

"Only place in the Valley that does. I think that's why they picked it." He put the phone to his ear. "Yeah?" There was a pause, then, "I'll pick up some Chinese."

My cue. I tapped Dyson on the shoulder and waved. Distracted now by the phone call, he half-waved at me and turned his back. But as I walked away, toward the building that housed the offices and labs, I glanced over my shoulder: Dyson was watching me, scars glistening in the fading light.

CHAPTER 83

My back was against the cool metal of the building, and I looked out across the grounds of Chimeragen's farm. It was past seven, and the moving truck was gone, along with almost everyone else. And there, in the middle of hostile territory, I took a minute to figure out what the hell I was doing. Something—something useful to me—was close, but I had no idea what. That confusion—the confusion about what I was looking for—blossomed into real trepidation. I realized I had trusted Alaine Chen, but I now began to see the folly in that. What reason did she have to help me out? If things went well for me, and badly for the good people of Chimeragen, wouldn't that mean she'd go down with them? What reason did she have to help out an old boyfriend who, by all indications, meant nothing to her?

Video cameras dotted the corners of the buildings; I figured I looked a lot more suspicious slumped against the outer wall of a building than I would if I were walking around. So I walked. Set in the side of the building, twenty or so yards from the main loading dock, was a smaller dock, sort of like a garage door. Next to that was a regular door with the ubiquitous black panel beside it. Quickly, I swiped the card and stepped inside.

I was in a wide hallway with a concrete floor, spotless. Ahead of me was another goddamned door with another goddamned black pad on it, through which I thought I'd find the operating room. What I found instead was another vestibule with a scrub sink, more masks, more gowns. There were three doors in the room. One, I assumed, went to a changing room, another to the OR. There were no locks on these doors, and I assumed, finally, that I'd be finished with security for a little while. I pushed through the door directly in front of me.

The OR was on the other side of a large glass wall; the room I stood in had a few chairs in it, as well as a large video camera, which wasn't of the security type. Evidently, this was an observation room. I observed. The OR was clean and not fancy, just what you'd expect for the hogs. Basically, it looked like any old operating room in your local hospital. There was ventilation equipment, suture trays, and surgical paraphernalia. Pigs are almost as big as people, so the operating table was standard size.

I left the room through the opposite door and continued down a long hallway. A door to my right opened, and a young woman in a white lab coat stepped out. She muttered "hi," apparently not giving it a second thought that I was wandering around in the heart of Chimeragen. She moved away from me down the hall. "Excuse me," I said.

"Yes?" She was short, pretty face, too heavy. She carried a tray of test tubes.

"I'm from Dr. Tobel's lab and was helping with the move. I got a little lost. Can you direct me . . . ?"

"It's a maze, isn't it?"

I agreed it was.

"Just go down this hall, through the doors at the end. I think they've loaded everything into the pathology labs. It's the first door on your left after you go through the double doors."

I thanked her and followed the directions. The doors at the end of the hallway gave out to another, shorter hall, and one that ran transversely in front of me. There were a couple of doors here that could have been "the first door on my left," but I decided to go straight. On my left, I found a gray metal door marked with a big biohazard sign. A good omen. I pressed my ear to it and heard nothing. Opening it slowly, I saw that the lights were out but for a single bank of overheads. It gave the place a cold, ghostly cast.

There were five or six white boxes stacked along the wall, the only indication that a move had taken place. The rest of the lab was fully stocked, presumably set up long before the day's move. I walked around the microscopes and a relatively new videoscope, PCR machines, gas chromatographs. At the far end of the room, something caught my eye. It was another door, emblazoned with biohazard signs. I walked to the door and clicked the light switch next to it.

Through a small window in the door, I could see eight freezers pushed against the walls of a small room. A large sign said that all personnel must use universal precautions when entering. Another sign read: *Restricted. Authorized Personnel Only.* There was a unit for a key card next to the door. It was the first real security I'd seen since entering the heart of the building. Well, Dr. Tobel's card made me authorized personnel. I held it to the black box; it opened. Ignoring the entreaty for universal precautions, I went inside. Air rushed in with me, and the door shut with a wheeze and a clunk. I turned on the light.

Despite the ventilation, the air inside the room had a medicinal and yeasty smell, like so many other labs I'd been in. The difference here was its size—this room was ten feet by ten feet, just enough space to accommodate all the freezers around its perimeter. I walked to the first freezer, which blinked the temperature: −80 degrees Celsius. I opened the brushed steel door and saw a bunch of plastic trays with sealed plastic bags in them. The writing on the bags read "Corrine 3, Pancreas," "Corrine 3, liver," and so on and so forth. The bags were filled with organs, not just tissue samples. Evidently, Corrine 3 had been sacrificed for testing. Trays above and below were filled with small specimen jars for Corrines 1, 4, 5, and 6. Biopsy specimens—bits of flesh taken from the living—of the lucky Corrines that would walk God's green earth for a while longer. At least until called to duty.

The second freezer contained pieces of Bertha. Genius that I am, I picked up on the pattern here, and saw that each of the freezers was labeled with the name of one of the hogs; somebody had written the names on tiny pieces of tape at the very tops of the units.

To save myself time, I scanned across the remaining freezers. I stopped at the second-to-last one. The name on it was Abby, and the freezer was locked. Obviously, Abby was not being actively monitored. Either that, or someone was keeping Abby's tissue under lock and key.

I noticed something pushed to the side of Abby's freezer: two file boxes. Now, this was intriguing; one doesn't normally stack files in the freezer room of a laboratory, especially one in which universal precautions are recommended. It makes for contaminated paper, and no one flipping through a bunch of papers wants to pull on gloves to do so. I could only guess they'd stashed this stuff here to keep it safe.

I opened the first box and began leafing through the files. A good number of the tags on the manila folders were marked "Abby." A run of files called "Abby–Infectious-Monitoring" caught my eye. I paged through.

The first file contained blood and biopsy records, a listing of the organs from which the tissues were taken, and the date. The next few files listed the pathogens for which the tissues were tested: various viruses, parasites, bacteria, and rickettsial organisms. Negative, negative, negative. Except for one: the PERVs. Abby, it seemed, played host to four different PERV variants. Besides that, everything else was clean. *Odd,* I thought. Dyson had said she was sick, but most likely the PERVs wouldn't have made her so. Still, maybe someone was worried enough to kill off the line.

At the back of the box, there was a file called "Abby–Termination." I expected to find a load of papers detailing the reasons for the pig's euthanasia. You know, "Abby line terminated secondary to porcine endogenous retrovirus infection" or something like that. But the file was too thin; it contained only one record—dates and such—of the termination and body disposal. No reason given, no bugs highlighted.

I closed the box, moved it to the side, opened the one underneath.

The folders here were marked "JM," and stuffed with the same biopsy records, Southern blots, ELISAs, and PCR results I'd found in the box for Abby. No human pathogens detected. PERVs seemed to be a concern here as well, since there was a large sheaf of papers dedicated to locating the viruses. But no PERV was unearthed in JM. Perhaps that shouldn't have been a surprise to me, since JM was not a member of the family Suidae, but a bipedal sister in *Homo sapiens.* JM, a.k.a. Janet Margulies, was human.

At the bottom of each page was a signature, one I knew as well as my own. It consisted of little more than a looping A and C. Alaine Chen.

Damn it, Alaine, I thought.

The final file in the box was marked "JM–Termination." The first page contained in it was frightening for its simplicity: diagnosis was, as Falk had said, listed as a nosocomial staph infection. But it was the note at the bottom of the page that shocked me. "Discontinue antibiotic treatment as per protocol." The date listed was nearly a year before. The paper was signed by Otto Falk.

Janet Margulies. Most likely the patient from Room Three in the hospital, who, by all appearances, had died of a run-of-the mill staph infection. But then, why had they discontinued antibiotic treatment? And why had the file been marked "Termination"? You don't terminate a person with an infection.

An enormous red flag began to wave in my head. If you were intent on killing someone in the hospital, especially one who was brain-dead, introducing a staph infection might just be the way to do it. It would be expected that someone in Janet Margulies's condition could pick up the bug. Her dying of staph would not raise undue scrutiny.

But why would Otto Falk have wanted her dead?

I thought about that, playing things over in my head. They might want her dead if she was sick, but the surveillance seemed to indicate she was clean. So, what could have changed? There was the rape, of course. . . .

"Shit," I hissed.

Quickly, I rifled through the pages, through the catalog of Janet Margulies's biological history. I wanted lab tests this time, and someone had been kind enough to make a file called "JM–Labs." It was filled with a hundred pages of computer printouts detailing electrolytes, creatinine levels for kidney function, liver enzymes. I searched for dates near the one displayed on the videotape from Dr. Tobel. Finally, I found what I was looking for: a new test that had been added. Beta hCG, or beta human chorionic gonadotropin. The stuff of pregnancy tests.

Negative: 4/16, 4/23, 4/30, 5/7. Negative: 5/14, 5/21. Positive: 5/28.

Janet Margulies had become pregnant.

I cross-checked the dates. Four days after the first positive pregnancy test, Janet develops a nosocomial staph infection. Otto Falk decides not to treat, "as per protocol." Janet Margulies dies.

Gotcha.

CHAPTER 84

Okay, a glimmer of narrative began to shine. First, the rape. Following this sexual unpleasantness, the victim, Janet Margulies, becomes pregnant and is "terminated." Kincaid disappears; reappears as Douglas Buchanan. Buchanan dies, his organs stripped from him. And though I'm a consumer of sordid media just like any other good American, I did not think it was devil worshippers or psychos with a taste for human viscera who killed him. Nor did I think his murder was related to the pregnancy per se. I thought someone took his organs because they were looking for the same thing I was: whatever killed Debbie Fillmore, Bethany Reginald, Bryan Tinings.

But that means they thought Kincaid—a.k.a. Douglas Buchanan—was sick. And the most likely chain of infection—Abby the pig → Janet the brain-dead → Kincaid the naughty—was missing too many links.

For example, Janet Margulies was killed because she was pregnant, not because she was sick. Or was she sick? If so, why no documentation? If so, if they were worried that Kincaid had picked something up while raping the poor woman, then why let him go east?

Because they didn't think Janet was diseased, and therefore they didn't think Kincaid was diseased.

But they *did* think Kincaid was sick, ergo the missing innards. So let's assume that's true, let's assume it's a timing issue: sometime after the rape and before his murder, people became worried Kincaid carried a virus. If that's the case, then here's the big question: If it wasn't a PERV, if it wasn't one of the dozen bugs they were actively monitoring, then what the hell *was* it? And was this mysterious "it" the same thing that slaughtered poor Debbie Fillmore?

Damn it, I was missing something. Okay, maybe not something, maybe a lot of things. And I was getting tangled up in the logical inconsistencies. But despite the circumstances, I was in a glass-half-full mood then.

I realized that I had the first real evidence to interest law enforcement. Although feeble, it was my first toehold, and it would mean Messrs. Falk and Carrington would have a lot to explain. But I needed more, something admissible and truly damning. Another videotape would be nice. Maybe Falk and Carrington carrying on about how killing Janet Margulies and Kincaid Falk and Gladys Thomas was necessary because of all the good the docs were disgorging into the world. All this while they were snorting cocaine off the bare midriffs of ten-year-olds. That would be nice.

All right, fantasy time was over, and I had to admit I was freaked. It didn't take an MD to know that for people with so much at risk, one dead CDC officer was a small price to pay. These people had already proved what they were capable of, and I was down here alone—

Not alone.

I heard noises. They were faint at first—the click of a door, a few voices. Then, through the narrow window in the door to my small freezer room, I saw the lights flash full in the main lab. I cursed. The lights were like a goddamned beacon for anyone coming into the lab.

I shoved the files into the box and slammed it shut, dropped the Abby box back on top. There was a large freezer to the left of the door, so I skittered across to the door's right. Someone standing outside the window looking in wouldn't be able to see me, but if anyone so much as cracked the door, the jig would be up.

The voices. One female, at least. One male. Maybe two. Fuck it. I had no idea how many people were outside.

I was going to end up in a shallow grave somewhere near Salinas. I knew it.

With my knees pulled up to my chin, I waited. *Keep calm, McCormick.*

The electronic lock made a noise. My heart went crazy, and I could hear nothing but blood in my ears. I began to shake. So much for keeping calm.

The door cracked open two feet from me, and the dark eyes of Alaine Chen locked on mine. I heard her breath catch in her throat. Alaine Chen, whose name was on all those biopsy records. Alaine Chen, who—now it made sense—had given me the directions to this place, where I would be cut off from all help. I waited for her to call to whoever was with her, to sound the alarm. Instead, she stood there. She turned her head.

"Someone must have left the light on," she said. "There's no one here."

She pushed the door open further. I stopped breathing.

I heard a male voice I didn't recognize. "The computer said he used the card to get in."

Alaine said, "Maybe he did. Now he's gone."

"The cameras didn't catch him on the way out."

"He's a smart man."

The male voice got closer. "He was in the freezer, Dr. Chen. The computer said so."

"Well," she said, "he's not in here anymore." Then she closed the door. The lights in the freezer room went out.

So, Alaine Chen really was in my corner. Why she was, I couldn't say.

CHAPTER 85

Darkness. I sat in the room for a long time, put my hand up to my face, waited for my eyes to adjust. They never did. The only light I had was the illumination from my Timex. I held down the button for a moment, let it cast a green haze over the room, and let it go. Dark again. Dark was better. Safer.

Knowing I couldn't move for a while, and knowing that sitting still would just up my anxiety, I blazed up the Timex and located the file boxes. I put Abby's box on the floor, removed the top of JM's. The light on the watch was too dim, and kept going out five seconds after I turned it on, but it gave me an idea and I pulled out my cell phone. After scrolling through the menu for what seemed like ten minutes. I found the function that allowed me to turn on the screen backlight. The phone warned me about high battery consumption. Ignoring it, I turned on the light.

It was just enough to see. After a few awkward minutes of paging through JM's files with one hand, holding the phone with the other, I found it: the page mentioning termination. I pulled it, then pulled JM's pregnancy results. I folded both pages and put them into my pocket. Then I closed the boxes and restacked them, killed the light on my phone.

I sat.

And because I didn't have anything else to do—except to worry about how I was going to get out of here—I did my best to think.

One thing I couldn't figure was whether the good doctors at Chimeragen had identified a pathogen, so I tried to pump the whole factual soup of this investigation into an intellectual framework I knew pretty well: epidemiology. At first blush this might seem like something of a stretch, but take a step back. Unknowns are unknowns, and a bad guy's a bad guy, whether he's ten microns across or just slightly bigger, with weird glasses and a one-syllable German surname. Seriously, at its core, my training taught me how to look at the world in a certain way, how to analyze the movement of elements through a population. When you think about it this way, information is kind of like a disease. It's a discrete thing that you either have or don't have, it's passed from person to person, and it's relayed through some sort of contact. Information can be dangerous; ideas can be infectious. The metaphor, I think, is apt. And I really didn't have much of a choice but to see it this way, since epidemiology is the lens through which I viewed the world.

Okay, if information is our disease—specifically, information about whatever virus or pathogen I was looking for—then there would be someone close to its source, the person first infected. The source itself would be a test to find the pathogen, and the index case would be the person performing the test. Here, it would be the microbiologist brought on to monitor the disease.

Harriet Tobel.

And Harriet Tobel was dead.

I checked my phone. No signal.

The lights to the lab outside were still dark, and I figured—I hoped—that Alaine and her buddy would leave this place alone long enough for me to make a call.

The door had a glow-in-the-dark safety latch, meaning I didn't need a key card or a light to get out of the small room. Hunched over, I pushed the latch and opened the door a crack. For thirty seconds at least, I listened, and, hearing nothing but my own heart, I pushed the door the rest of the way open and skated to the far end of the room, behind a lab bench.

Two bars on the cell phone.

It was a long shot, sure, but I had an idea and needed to get things moving. I dialed.

"Vallo," I said. *Good,* I thought, *he's still in the lab.*

"Who is this?"

"Nate McCormick."

"Great. Why are you whispering?"

"Listen, I want you to make some primers from the long sequence I sent you. That Junin-HIV thing. And I want you to run Southern blot and PCR on Debbie Fillmore with it."

"Let me ask you a question: you know what time it is?"

"Late, I know."

"You're damned right it's late. I was walking out the door, just about to leave. But the freaking phone rings and, like Pavlov's dog, I pick it up. See what happens—?"

"Ben, cut it, okay? I don't have time to fuck around here."

There was a pause, Vallo shifting from the hale-fellow ball busting to something like concern. "Nate, everything all right?"

"I don't know. This is a long shot. A real long shot, but it's the best we have right now."

"What's going on?"

"Just run the tests. I'll call you later."

I hung up.

Okay, that was in motion.

In the silence, I sat and reflected and got scared again. On one hand, I'd found more than I ever thought I would. What seemed like unrelated events were coming together for me. This was good. On the other hand, it really seemed that there were a bunch of murderous scientists circling around me. Add to that that I had no idea in hell how I was going to get out of this mess. This was definitely bad.

I'd like to say I had a daring plan for escape, burrowing through the floor, cutting open one of the pigs and hiding in the carcass, dramatic things like that. I didn't. I figured the place was in some sort of lockdown, and I'd be found out as soon as I tried to leave. Obviously, they could follow the movements of Harriet Tobel's card, and follow those movements they would.

And I couldn't stay in this room forever. They'd be through there again; I was sure of that. Alaine might have a change of mind.

So, the only thing I could think of at that point was to call for help. My car might still be on the road. If Brooke called the police, it probably wouldn't be too difficult for them to find me. Too many ifs and mights, but it seemed like the only rational plan for a guy who definitely was not James Bond.

I dialed Brooke's number.

The phone rang and rang.

"Damn it," I cursed.

Just as I thought the voice mail was about to pick up, someone answered. "Hello?" Brooke said, her voice shaking.

"Brooke. Have the police come to where I am. I can get you near me. You can look for the car—"

"Get out of there—"

I heard some ruffling on the phone, Brooke saying "Get out, Nathaniel," then another voice: "Dr. McCormick?" a male voice asked.

"Who is this?"

"That doesn't matter."

"Like hell it doesn't—"

"Listen to me, Dr. McCormick. Your friend is with me now. She's safe. But how safe she stays depends on you."

I was very confused, so I said, "What are you talking about?"

"You know very well what I'm talking about. Who have you told?"

"Who have I told what?"

"Who have you called?"

"I haven't called anybody. Who the hell are you?"

"I hope you haven't. Listen to me, I want you in the front of the building at the farm—the main building—in fifteen minutes. If you're not there, if you're trying to run now, then go back."

"Tell me—"

"If you call the police—or call anyone, for that matter—your friend will disappear. Okay? I'm going to check your cell phone call history when I get there, Dr. McCormick. If I see there are any calls after this one, or if I see you've erased your call history, your friend will disappear. If I see you've received any calls, your friend will disappear. This is a promise."

CHAPTER 86

Stunned, I sat for a minute.

Brooke.

I backlit my cell again and fumbled around until I found the lab's phone. I trusted the bastard about my cell, but I didn't think they'd be able to track calls from the lab itself.

There was no dial tone, just a constant, oscillating loop of two tones. I jammed my finger on the nine. Still the two tones. I pressed various buttons for different lines. Nothing.

There was a computer in the room.

I hit the Power button and the thing whirred to life. Not fast enough, though. I checked my watch, saw that I had less than ten minutes left, and spent two of those ten cursing the slow IBM. A log-in screen appeared, asking me for username and password.

I wanted to pick up the keyboard and drive it through the flat screen, but checked myself.

So, someone had thought ahead and cut all communications. Whoever had orchestrated this was good, much better than I was. But if you thought about it, they were also much better than the Baltimore Police Department, the San Jose Police Department, the FBI. And who was I? A guy who tracked down pathogens, all of which were too small to have a cortex.

I began to open and close drawers, and eventually was able to find a small tray with what I was looking for. I dropped the disposable scalpel into my pocket and walked into the hallway.

The place looked deserted. This might have been a comfort if I hadn't suspected the bastard on Brooke's phone wanted the place to be deserted.

I turned down the hall, following the exit signs, passing a number of closed doors. Eventually, I came to a door at the end of the hallway. A black pad with a red light set in it was to the right, which was strange. One would think that people would be barred from getting in, not from getting out. Increasingly, though, everything about Chimeragen seemed strange.

I put the Chimeragen ID up to the pad. It beeped and continued to flash red. The handle, when I tried it, didn't move. Again, I faced the card to the black plastic. Again, a beep and the red light. I was locked in.

I thought of Brooke and the man with her. I didn't understand the angles here and didn't want to piss anyone off and risk hurting her—though, in truth, I knew she was already in grave danger. The image of Gladys Thomas's bloated face flashed through my mind. The gutted dogs. I pushed the pictures out of my head.

With the cell phone, I dialed Brooke's number. After a few rings, the voice mail picked up. I didn't leave a message. My watch said I still had two minutes until I was to be outside the building. I waited out the two minutes and called again. This time, someone answered the phone. It wasn't Brooke.

"Dr. McCormick. Where are you?"

"I'm locked in the fucking building." I tried to sound tough.

The man laughed. "They locked it down. Good for them. They're learning. Okay, Doc, I want you to go into the pathology lab, the one where you were before."

How does he know where I was before?

My cell phone chirped. Low battery.

The man said, "We'll be there in two minutes. I want you to be fifteen feet from the door, on the right side of the room, with your hands on the lab bench. You got me?"

"I got you." *Fucker.*

"If you don't do what I say, I will hurt Dr. Michaels. You understand me, Dr. McCormick?"

In the background I heard Brooke yell, "Get out, Nate! Don't listen—" Then the phone went dead. I checked my watch.

The pathology lab was as dark as I'd left it. I didn't need the lights to circle to the back side of the door, to snap off the plastic safety guard on the scalpel's blade. And there, behind the door, arm raised and quivering, I waited. Though it was clear to me that standing fifteen feet from the door with my arms spread on the counter was the wrong thing to do, it was not clear that planning to attack a man with a ten-gram scalpel was the right thing.

I listened and waited. I wanted to check my watch again, but didn't dare let my arm fall. So, I stood there, frozen, while the seconds stretched to minutes.

Then I heard footsteps, or, more exactly, shuffling and dragging sounds. The handle clicked and the door opened slowly. I stiffened my arm.

CHAPTER 87

Brooke stumbled into the room; she was backlit, two feet in front of me. The door opened wider, and I raised my arm, ready to stab down onto whoever was behind her.

I never got the chance.

Before I could react, the door swung open violently, knocking back my arm and crashing into my head and feet. Knocked off balance, I staggered backward. The scalpel was still in my hand, and I tried to orient myself toward the door. But then the lights were up and my vision flashed white. Next thing I knew, I was on the floor with someone's weight on top of me. Someone cranked my right arm behind me; a knee drove into the small of my back. Brooke croaked, "God, Nathaniel. Oh, God."

"We obviously have a misunderstanding about distance, Dr. McCormick," a man said. "This is *not* fifteen feet."

Across the floor, I saw the scalpel. I had no memory of its being knocked from my hand. I heard the ratchet of handcuffs and felt the metal bite into my wrists. The man—a man—pulled me roughly to my feet.

In front of me, Brooke wept quietly. Her hands, too, were behind her back. A fresh bruise, red and purple, darkened her left cheek.

From behind, hands fluttered over my body, emptying out my pockets. I felt the cell phone and my ID cards being pulled out. My car keys, my wallet. The folded papers with Janet Magulies's termination threat on them.

Powerful arms shoved me forward. Awkwardly, I stopped myself before knocking Brooke over. I turned and looked at my attacker, who, true to his word, scrolled down through the menus in my cell phone.

"What is this call? Four-oh-four number."

I was silent.

The man calmly walked toward me, put his hand between my shoulder and neck, and squeezed. A pain unlike anything I'd ever felt fired down my right side; my knees buckled.

"Stop!" Brooke yelled.

He did.

"What's the number, Dr. McCormick?"

I was trying to regain my footing. "A lab at CDC. Look at the goddamned time stamp. I called before I talked to you."

"Why?"

I didn't answer, expecting his claw to come down on my shoulder again. It didn't.

"Well, no matter. It just means we'll have to accelerate things on our end. Not good for you, I'm afraid."

Maybe he wasn't the last person on the face of the planet I thought would be so fast or so strong, but he certainly wouldn't be my top pick. The gent who'd slammed the door into me and disarmed me in less time than it took me to suck a breath was a good four inches taller than me, but probably outweighed me only by ten pounds or so. His shoulders caved slightly into his chest. He was balding, with dark, curly tufts sticking from the sides of his head. His eyes were sunken and tired looking, and fit in well with his pasty complexion. All in all, he looked like the attending doc on my surgery clerkship in med school. Maybe the guy was burped from the same ring of hell as Dr. Clement. Perhaps they shared the same rotten womb. If so, God help me. I hated Dr. Clement.

"Shall we?" he asked.

I looked at his hands and saw he held a small automatic pistol. He flicked the barrel toward the door. From just that motion, you could tell the man had spent a lot of quality time with guns.

Brooke and I walked into the hall. "To the right," the man whom I'd nicknamed the Surgeon said.

I glanced at Brooke. Her hands were bound behind her with metal cuffs. Quietly, I asked her, "What happened?"

She half-turned toward the Surgeon, but he didn't seem to care if we talked.

"He came to the apartment before I left. I don't know how he got in. And then we were in the car, coming here. I don't know what's happening."

We pushed through the doors to the OR's observation room. "Go through the doors," the Surgeon said. We went through the doors to the scrub room. He led us through two more sets of doors to the OR itself.

"All right, Doctors, you should be familiar with the surroundings. Sit." With the gun, he motioned to Brooke to sit down.

"Dr. McCormick, go over to the table and sit on the floor." I did so. He holstered his gun and pulled a cable tie from his pocket, the kind police use to round up protesters. With it, he cinched my ankles together. "Okay, Doctor, no funny stuff." He pulled me back against the table, undid the cuffs from one wrist, and reattached them around the leg of the table. Then he went around to all the wheels and made sure they were locked down.

The Surgeon went to Brooke. "Legs together," he said, which was marginally better than "Legs apart." At least he wasn't going to rape her. But no, not him. He was a professional.

Brooke slid her legs together and the Surgeon reached for his cable ties. As he pulled the tie from his pocket, Brooke kicked toward his face.

Her sneaker caught him on the tip of the chin. This seemed to piss him off, because even before his head had righted itself, his fist shot out like a rocket and smashed into her cheek. Brooke slumped backward and moaned; I yelled. The Surgeon didn't say anything, just grabbed her feet and zipped the tie closed.

"Why are you doing this?" I asked.

Ignoring my question, the Surgeon finished with Brooke and stood, surveying both of us. "All tidy," he said.

I asked again, "Why are you doing this to us?"

"Doctor, I think you don't know what you're doing."

"Of course I know what I'm doing," I said, though, of course, I hadn't a clue.

"No. You think you're doing a very good thing. But your actions would have hurt a lot of people."

"That's bullshit."

"I tried to tell them not to let it get this far. We should have cleaned house much earlier. But in some ways, they're just as blind as you are."

I didn't ask him what "cleaning house" meant.

"Now, unfortunately, you are the doctors who know too much."

"What do I know?"

"Don't be naïve. I don't know all of what you've found here, but that doesn't matter now. These"—he pulled out the papers with Margulies's pregnancy test and termination request—"as you probably knew, are valuable." He folded the papers tidily back into his pocket.

"You killed them, didn't you?"

"Who?" the Surgeon asked flatly.

"Of course he killed them," Brooke said.

"I didn't. Your brilliant doctor friends killed them, because they couldn't understand the situation. You see, I have experience in these matters. And they didn't bring me in until it was too late. Unfortunately, people had to be dealt with."

"Gladys Thomas?"

The Surgeon said nothing, just stared with drooping eyes.

"Dr. Tobel?"

"That was a tragedy."

I remembered the car speeding off that night at Dr. Tobel's house, the license plate I couldn't quite get. "You were at her house when I was there."

His silence told me he was.

"Where is everyone else?"

"They're with their alibis, Dr. McCormick."

Brooke groaned.

"Who the fuck are you?" I yelled. I saw what was coming and I was terrified.

"Dr. McCormick, Dr. Michaels, I know this is going to sound hollow. But I'm truly sorry for what's happened. If others hadn't made poor decisions—many, many poor decisions—we wouldn't be here now, but they have and . . ." The Surgeon trailed off, his eyes fixed on a point behind me. "I am being paid a king's ransom to fix their problems. At times I enjoy my . . . profession. For what it's worth, I'm not enjoying this."

Brooke, scared and angry, blurted, "Well, that's good to hear."

The Surgeon squatted on his haunches and looked at her sadly. "I can also see the big picture. I can see what your colleagues are trying to do, the people they want to help. It is one reason I chose to take this job."

"So you're a fucking saint," Brooke spat. The woman had guts.

"Of course not. A saint would let you go." The Surgeon stood. "The ends justify the means, Dr. Michaels. Don't fool yourself into thinking that's some trite sixteenth-century maxim. It's the way the world works. It's the way the world should work. It doesn't make it easy."

It sure as hell doesn't make it easy if you're the means, or rather, if your being dead is the means.

"You killed Kincaid Falk and Janet Margulies?"

"Janet Margulies was gone before I was in the picture. Kincaid Falk should have been dealt with long ago. Instead, things got messy." He stood. "Now, if you'll excuse me. You'll be happy to know you are in a very delicate situation. It's not clear what will be done."

I wasn't very happy to know that, but I was happy when he left the OR. A moment later, though, he was back.

He opened the drawers and the cupboards in a stainless steel cabinet. From it, he pulled out a box of disposable scalpels, a box of hemostats, a bunch of scissors, anything else that could be used to cut a cable tie. He threw everything into a tray.

"Almost forgot," he said. "Wouldn't want you to cut yourself on anything." Then he left with the tray.

I saw him through the glass in the observation room. He set the tray on a small table, then emptied his pockets of my belongings and pulled out a cell phone—his own, I assumed. I watched him as he hunted around the room, the phone in front of him like a divining rod. Maybe there was too much concrete in this part of the building for a signal. He looked at us through the glass, then disappeared through the door.

CHAPTER 88

So there we were. Me: feet bound, hands behind my back, cuffed to a metal table. Brooke: hands behind her back, feet bound together. All in all, not a real promising situation.

"He's gone," I reported to Brooke, who couldn't see the glass.

"I can't believe this, Nathaniel. I'm so sorry for pushing you into this. For getting both of us—"

"I got us into this." I yanked at the cuffs until my wrists felt like they were going to snap. I yanked again.

"Stop it," Brooke said. "You're going to break something."

I struggled more, but the flesh was beginning to tear. Pain seared around my wrist.

She said, "I can't believe people would do this. Goddamned physicians, of all people."

"They think they're saving humanity."

"They think they're going to get rich."

"That, too." I pulled at my wrists and yelped.

"What?"

"Nothing."

Brooke sighed and slumped against the wall.

I could feel the blood trickling down my hand. I scanned the OR, past the monitors, to the ransacked metal cabinet.

"Brooke," I said. She seemed not to hear. "Brooke." She looked up at me. "See if you can get to the cabinet and see what's in there."

"He took everything, Nathaniel. This guy thinks of every—"

"Do it. Now."

She glared at me a moment, then rolled to her side and wormed along the floor to the cabinet. With her hands still behind her back, she opened the door, then turned around so she could see. "Just chucks and Foleys in the bottom," she said.

"What's in the drawers?"

Brooke maneuvered herself to a sitting position. All those hours on her bike weren't wasted, and she pushed herself upright. She grabbed the drawer and hopped forward to open it a little. Then she turned around, hopping.

I wondered how many minutes had passed since the Surgeon had left us and how many minutes it would take to decide what to do about our delicate situation. "What's there?" I asked.

"Wait." She balanced and looked into the drawer. "Just some syringes."

"What meds?"

"I can't see— Oh, yeah. Just some lidocaine. A lot of lidocaine."

"Grab a syringe and a bunch of vials. They have two percent?"

"What? Yes."

"If you see any with epi, get it."

"What do you need lidocaine for?"

The question wasn't why I needed lidocaine, but why pigs needed it. But pigs feel pain, and the docs would probably use lido for any procedure, so as not to freak the hogs out too much. Also, they'd want lido on hand if there was any heart trouble—any arrhythmias—during the operation.

"Just get as much as you can hold and get over here."

Brooke backed against the drawer and squatted a few inches to let her hands drop down. I heard the sound of glass vials rubbing against one another.

"Hurry up, Brooke."

"Shut up, Nathaniel. What do you need this for?"

"I need you to block my hand."

She looked at me for a few long seconds. "How tight are the cuffs?"

"Tight."

"You can't do it—"

"Yes I can. Get over here." Another beat. "Brooke—"

"Okay, okay. Let me get a syringe filled." She fidgeted around. "I need a big one."

After a few more seconds, I heard her crack the top of one of the lidocaine vials, a pause as she filled the syringe, then another crack, and another. "You don't want to do this," she said.

"Of course I don't. Come over here."

She gathered a few more vials and pitched forward at me. Her body hit the floor hard; her head landed in my lap, but she still held the syringe and the vials. I moved to the side so my wrists were near her hands. Our backs were toward each other. I was still sitting; she was on her side. "Go for the left," I said.

"This one?" Her fingers brushed my right hand.

"No."

"Hold these." She passed the lidocaine vials into my right hand. "I'm going to use a lot."

"Good," I said.

She touched the left hand, and I felt her fingers move along the wrist. It hurt like a bitch to have her going over the ragged flesh, but not for much longer. Her fingers stopped along the outside of my wrist. "I'll hit the ulnar nerve first."

"Try to avoid the vessels."

"Thanks for the tip."

With the amount of lidocaine that Brooke was about to dump into my wrist, if she got a vein or an artery, there was a good chance that she could induce a fatal arrhythmia in my heart. Since our backs were to my hands, neither of us could see if she hit a vessel.

"You're sure?"

"Goddamn it, Brooke, just remember your anatomy."

She jammed the needle in. Not only was the needle she used large gauge and painful, the lidocaine she squeezed in felt like she was dumping acid into my wrist. I cursed.

She pulled out the needle. "Median nerve." She sank the needle directly into the center of my wrist. Pulling it out a bit, reangling, injecting again. I swore again.

"They let you graduate from med school?" I snarled.

She ignored me. "Let me have the other vials."

She took the vials from my right hand and cracked them. I could already feel the hand beginning to go numb. "Hurry," I said, glancing at the observation room door. Whatever discussion the Surgeon was having, thank God, seemed to be involved. Nearly five minutes must have passed since he'd left.

The needle plunged into my wrist just behind the thumb. "Radial nerve," she said. Again, I felt the in-and-out of the big needle. "I'm going to hit the ulnar again." She did.

I tried to work my fingers to move the lidocaine around. I felt pressure as the needle went again into the center of the wrist. "That's enough," I said.

"You're sure?"

"Yeah. Move back."

She slid away, then rolled 180 degrees so she could see me. I took a deep breath, worked the fingers of my left hand again, and pulled as hard as I could.

Even with the anesthetic, the pain lanced up my arm. A bone cracked as my hand compressed and pulled slowly through the small metal ring.

"Nathaniel. God, Nathaniel."

I arched my back against the OR table. The hand slid, too slowly. There was the snap of another bone. And another and another. I shifted the hand back and forth, trying to work it through the cuffs. The epinephrine in the lidocaine acted to constrict the blood vessels in the hand. In spite of it, blood ran across the floor to the drain. I felt bile rising in my throat and choked it down. As I slid the hand up toward the knuckles, there were more dislocations, more breaks. The hand seemed to be sliding easier; I guessed the bones had cracked and the blood had begun to flow and was slicking the skin.

I heaved once more against the hand. The OR table shifted, and, suddenly, I was free. My left hand popped from the cuffs, sending a spray of blood across the room.

CHAPTER 89

I looked at the appendage and vomited in my lap. Not only had many of the bones been broken and dislocated, but part of the hand had been what doctors call degloved, a particularly graphic and accurate description. The skin had been stripped from the wrist over the thumb and index finger, past the knuckles, and hung like, well, a half-removed glove, exposing the raw muscle beneath it. It bled, but because of the epi, it wasn't as bad as would have been expected. It throbbed dully.

There was pain in my shoulder, too. I must have torn a muscle as I pulled.

Brooke gaped at the damage. "Oh my God, Nathaniel."

"It's okay."

"Oh, honey . . ."

With my right hand, I pulled the skin back up along the hand and wrist. Bits of skin and blood clung to the cuffs dangling from my good hand. It struck me that if I survived this, my right would always be called that: my good hand.

I pulled myself to a standing position. The adrenaline and nausea made me unsteady, and I nearly fell as I hopped to the door of the OR.

As I staggered past her, Brooke gasped. "We need to get you to a hospital."

I opened the door to the OR and hopped through the small entryway to the observation room. I stumbled when I reached for the door, and fell heavily on my numb hand, smearing the tile floor with blood. With the handle in front of me, I was able to pull myself up. I got scissors and my wallet and cell phone from the observation room and cut the cable tie around my ankles. Quickly, I walked back to the OR and cut the ties that bound Brooke's feet. I helped her to stand.

"Let's go," I told her.

"Get gauze and bind that hand."

"We don't have—"

"*Now,* you asshole!" Her eyes were red and wet.

So, I went to the metal cabinet and found gauze. I wrapped the hand, the cuffs on my right hand looping widely as I twirled the gauze around my left. I pulled it tight to keep the skin near the blood vessels. There was a good chance I was trapping infection in there, but I wanted to keep the skin nourished so that maybe, just maybe, it would live for a few more hours. "There," I said.

We moved quickly through the scrub room. I turned toward the observation room when Brooke stopped me. "Where are you going?"

"We can't leave."

"What?"

"Just wait here." I walked into the observation room and pressed

my ear to the hallway door. I heard nothing, no heated conversation between the Surgeon and whomever.

"Let's go!" Brooke hissed.

I turned to her. "You go, then, Brooke. I need to get something. I
didn't tear all the fucking flesh off my hand just to walk out of here and
have nobody believe what I'm saying."

"They have to believe it."

"No they don't. You know that." I took a scalpel from the table and
broke off the plastic covering. The blade was polished, mirrorlike. Just
the thing. "Stay here if you want. Leave if you want."

Cautiously, I cracked the door to the hallway and slipped the
scalpel out. Maneuvering the blade up and down, I could catch a reflection of most of the hallway in front of me. I saw no one. I opened the
door.

Quickly, I walked toward the path labs. Brooke, her arms still
cuffed behind her, followed.

Every ten feet or so, I stopped and listened. Hearing nothing, I continued. Finally, I ended up at the door to the lab. No voices, no movement. I opened the door slowly.

The lights were on, and the door to the freezer room was propped
open. Again I listened and heard nothing. I made my way around the lab
tables to the small room, Brooke behind me.

"Nathaniel," Brooke said.

I stopped. She pointed her chin at a glass-faced cabinet of reagents
to my right. In it was, among other things, a bottle of concentrated nitric
acid. As carefully as I could, I opened the case and took out the small bottle. Still, I made a racket. "There's no one here," I said.

As I looked into the freezer room, I saw, indeed, there was no one
there.

"Oh, no," I said.

"What?"

The two file boxes with the biopsy reports on Abby the pig and
Janet the human were gone. And with them, any shred of evidence I
might have overlooked, any shred to help us out.

"It's gone," I said. "Everything is gone."

I put the nitric acid down on a lab bench.

"Take it," Brooke said. "Just in case."

CHAPTER 90

I led Brooke down the hall, back through the OR observation room, to the scrub room. A black plastic panel was next to the door. I tried the door. Locked. I swore.

We went back into the hallway, this time heading in the opposite direction. I saw a green exit sign ahead. We followed the signs until we came to another door. This one, too, was locked.

"No—" Brooke said. "No, no, no." She kicked at the door, sending herself off balance and almost into a fall. "No!" She kicked again.

"Stop," I said.

A few yards down the hall was a red fire alarm. I remembered what Bill Dyson, the vet, had said about the system; I hoped it wasn't overridden by the security.

I put the vial of nitric acid in my pocket and grabbed the lever on the alarm. The small glass rod in front of the lever broke, and, almost immediately, the cacophony began. A sharp buzzing sounded through the building as bright white strobes flashed up and down the hall. The sound was deafening.

"Let's hope—" I said as I tried the handle on the door and pushed. We were outside.

Though not as loud as inside the building, the alarm cut through the purple California evening. Strobes around the building blinked, their light dying in the gloaming.

I glanced around. There was an old outbuilding to the side of the far hog pen. From the look of it, this was one of the few structures that had survived Chimeragen's homestead—loose shingles, paint faded on the wooden planks that made up the walls. From my days growing up in Pennsylvania, I recalled that these buildings often housed vehicles, and most times, the vehicles had the keys in them. I hoped I wasn't fantasizing. I hoped the vehicle wasn't a tractor.

"Let's go," I said. We moved quickly toward the old structure.

Luck was with us, and there was an old pickup parked in front of the building. The keys were there. Contamination might have been a worry for Chimeragen, but not car thieves. I opened the door for Brooke and helped her into the cab as best I could. I circled to the driver's side and climbed in. The ancient Ford engine turned over.

I put the truck in gear and tore out of there.

"Nathaniel!" Brooke screamed.

Behind us, I heard the pops. They came fast, sounding almost like a single peal. The front and rear windows of the truck spidered as small holes appeared in the glass. Both of us ducked. There was a pause, and I raised my head to make sure we weren't headed for a wall or something. When I glanced around, I saw the Surgeon coming out of a shooter's stance and working with his gun. A clip fell to the ground. He slapped another into the pistol.

I braced for another explosion of gunfire, but there was none.

"You okay?" I shouted.

"Uh-hunh."

As we pulled onto the dirt road that led away from the buildings, I could see the strobes flash in a rhythmic pulse. Ahead of us, just off the side of the road, a small bonfire flickered.

Brooke craned her head backward. "He's walking away," she reported. Then, turning to the front, she said, "What's that?"

I didn't answer her, but I knew what it was: the last anyone would really know about Janet Margulies and the pig.

As we passed the fire, I saw something silhouetted against the flames. A white box.

CHAPTER 91

I swung the car toward the bonfire.

"What are you doing?" Brooke demanded. "Nathaniel? What the hell are you doing?"

I ignored her. To my left, I saw the Surgeon break into a run. He was at the far end of the building, a hundred yards away or more, moving fast.

"He's coming. He's coming! Get out of here! What the fuck are you doing?" It was a good thing that her arms were cuffed behind her back, or I bet she would have taken a swing at me.

In a few seconds, I'd brought the truck to a skid next to the white file box, putting the bulk of the vehicle between us and the Surgeon. The box was half-full. I opened the truck door.

Brooke continued to screech at me.

My hand looked and felt like a piece of meat at the end of my arm—flaccid, dead, heavy, soaked in blood—and every action took twice as long as it should have: opening the truck door, grabbing the box, heaving it into the cab, where it fell on top of Brooke, who was lying on the bench seat, cursing. Its contents spread across the floor, the pages streaked with blood from my hand.

Gunfire pealed, and I heard the bullets smashing into the back and side of the truck. I jumped into the cab, not bothering to close the door. Brooke yelped, a different sound from the obscenities pouring out of her mouth before. I slammed the truck in drive and pushed the accelerator to the ground.

"What happened? What happened?" I yelled.

In the rearview, I could see the Surgeon switch directions and head toward a waiting car.

"I'm shot," she said.

"Where?" Brooke didn't answer. "Brooke, damn it! Where are you shot?"

"I don't know." She groaned. "My ass, I think."

"Bullet hit an artery?"

"I don't know."

"Bone?"

"Jesus, Nate, *I don't know*."

I shut up.

Five minutes later, we were at the gate to the Chimeragen Farm, having bumped over a few miles of dirt road as fast as I dared go. Brooke had quieted down, now just gritting her teeth and letting out small grunts of pain as we vaulted over the old road. I didn't wait for the gate to open, and plowed through the thing as it began its slow trundle. It was getting darker; I saw that I'd managed to blow out one headlight.

We'd covered the distance from the Farm to the main road quickly, and I asked Brooke what kind of car the Surgeon had. She said some sort of rental, and I was relatively sure that we'd gained more than a few minutes on him with the truck.

"Where's the closest hospital?" I asked Brooke.

"I don't know," she said. As we passed under a lone streetlamp, I looked over at her. She was lying in a half-fetal position—her legs in the foot well, her torso stretched on the seat, facing the back of the truck. The passenger-side door had a few ragged holes in it. The inside of the door was slicked with blood. "There's one in Gilroy, just off the 101."

"We'll go there."

"He'll find us there," she said. "It's the most obvious place."

"We don't really have a choice."

"I'm fine."

"Right. There's a lot of blood, Brooke."

She sighed. "Okay. You'll see the hospital from the highway." She was quiet for a moment. "It hurts."

"You didn't get the lidocaine. Of course it does."

Wind from the broken windows stirred the papers that lay scattered in the cab. Brooke fidgeted.

As for me, well, if I didn't get pain medication soon—something that lasted longer than the lidocaine and adrenaline—let's just say I'd be bearing the pain with a lot less equanimity than Brooke Michaels.

After twenty minutes driving the truck as fast as I dared, I turned onto the 101 and pushed the pedal to the floor.

I saw the flashing lights before I heard the siren—they lit up the fractured back window in whites, blues, and reds.

"Oh, shit," I said.

CHAPTER 92

Brooke had been quiet, which worried me. She was losing too much blood, but managed a woozy "What?"

"Shit, shit, shit. Police."

"Good."

"Not good."

I didn't stop the truck as the police vehicle pulled close to my tail. A voice cracked over the cruiser's loudspeaker, but I couldn't make it out, because the holes all through the cab whistled. I assumed the officer wasn't telling me to keep up the good work.

Still, I didn't stop. He rode inches from my bumper for a few miles; then another cruiser joined the chase, pulling up along my left side. I looked into the police car and saw the cop's arm jutting out toward the shoulder, directing me to pull over.

"This is not good, Brooke," I said quietly. She didn't respond. "Brooke!"

"Yeah?" she said lazily.

"Stay with me. Please, okay? Just hang in there."

The situation with Brooke was decaying. I wasn't really worried yet, but if things continued to drag out . . .

I pulled the truck over to the side of the highway, the two police vehicles falling in behind me. I watched the cops get out of the cars in the side mirror. Their guns were drawn. Not a typical traffic stop, I guess.

One of the officers walked slowly toward the truck. The other stayed back, his pistol trained on the cab.

I noticed a lump in my right pocket. The bottle of nitric acid. I pulled it out and dropped it between my legs.

"This is definitely not good," I said quietly.

"Step out of the vehicle!" the policeman called.

"I'm injured," I called back. "I have an injured person here with me."

"I don't give a fuck! Step out of the vehicle!"

The cop from the first car, the profane one, walked an arc around the driver's side of the truck. He was almost on the highway, but still, that only put two feet between my head and the end of his pistol.

"Put your hands where I can see them, on the top of the steering wheel."

I did. He saw the bloody lump on the end of my left arm.

"What happened?" The guy was older—midforties, maybe. And he wasn't jumpy, which was a plus, all things considered. The last thing I needed now was a state-issued .38 slug through my head.

"Take us to a hospital now, and I'll tell you."

"Nathaniel?"

"There's someone in there with you?"

"I already said there was. She's injured."

"Ma'am," he shouted. "I want you to sit up and put your hands where I can see them."

"She can't sit up."

Confusion flashed across the officer's face. It was gone almost as soon as it appeared.

He yelled to the other policeman, "Robbins, we have an injured woman in the passenger side." The other policeman slowly rounded the truck, gun fixed on the cab.

I was beginning to get really anxious now, not about Brooke's losing blood, or about my losing blood, but about how long we were being delayed. I said, "Look, Officer, we are both injured. The man who—"

"Shut up." The other policeman was now near the passenger side. There was a sound to my right, and the door at Brooke's rump swung open. She let out a yelp.

"Jesus!" the second officer said. "Mike, we got a woman here, handcuffed and injured. It looks like she's—"

"I'm shot, you idiot," Brooke said. *That's my girl.*

The officer to my left began screaming at me, "Get out of the car! Keep your hands where I can see them!"

How I was supposed to open the door and keep my hands where he would see them I didn't know, but he solved that problem for me when he jerked his hand toward the door handle and pulled. I could hear the other officer calling for backup.

"Officer, with all due respect, we do not have time for—"

"Shut up!"

"The person who did this—"

"Shut up!" He was braced in a shooter's stance, finger on the trigger, ready to scramble my brains.

"I am a physician with the Centers for Disease—"

"I don't care if you're with the fucking White House. Shut up! I'm counting to three, and I want you out of the car by three or I will shoot you, motherfucker." Boy, such language.

The gentleman with the gun in my face began to count, "One." I looked to my right and saw the other cop with his gun on me, moving his eyes between Brooke and me. He was younger than the first cop and looked more agitated. Now, to put myself in the cops' place, I could see why they were nervous. A guy in an old truck riddled with bullet holes, he gives them a good little chase before pulling over; then there's this woman who's cuffed and hurt, lying on the seat with him. On the whole, it didn't seem totally benign.

"Two."

"Officers," Brooke said, "we are both physicians, working on a case. We—"

"Three."

I'd begun to move my legs out of the cab, hoping the guy wouldn't pop me if I showed I was beginning to comply. The bottle of nitric acid shifted and I was content to let it fall to the floor, when I noticed something. I stopped moving.

"Out of the car now, or I will—"

"Shit," I said.

The cop followed my eyes along the highway. A dark-blue sedan had pulled to the shoulder and was rapidly reversing toward us. As it got closer, I noticed the license plate began with a P. Though I'd suspected it, this was final confirmation that the Surgeon's car was the same one I'd seen, days before, scurrying away from Dr. Tobel's house.

"Get out of here now," I said to the officer. For the first time, I could see that the guy really didn't know what to do. "Get out of here! That's the guy who shot—"

"Robbins!" the older cop yelled. "Go deal with that. I'll take care of these two. You called backup?"

Robbins nodded and started to walk stiffly toward the blue car. His gun was drawn.

"Out—"

"Officer, please." I was getting desperate. "That is the man who attacked us."

I saw the door to the car open, and the Surgeon stepped out, his hands down at his sides.

"Put your hands in the air," Robbins said to him.

The Surgeon seemed not to understand. The older officer cut his eyes quickly from me to the scene in front of us, then back to me.

The Surgeon kept walking toward us.

"Hands in the air!" Robbins shouted.

The older officer backed up a step, and though his gun was still on me, his eyes kept cutting toward his partner and the Surgeon. Perhaps the guy was realizing I wasn't full of shit. Perhaps he thought the Surgeon and I were in cahoots.

"Stop right there!" Robbins shouted. Unfortunately for the young policeman, the Surgeon did.

The Surgeon paused on the shoulder; then, faster than I could follow, he dropped to his knee. As he did so, he produced a gun from somewhere. A shot rang out and Robbins fell. Half a second later, the gun was pointed at the officer next to me. Another shot, and the back of the cop's head exploded.

Brooke yelled.

I pulled my legs—now half out of the cab—back inside and began to unscrew the cap of the nitric acid. I was saying something—I don't know what—but it was probably something like "Holy shit, holy shit." Brooke kept asking what was happening.

The Surgeon walked toward the truck. A few cars slowed down along the highway, but no one stopped.

"Nate?" Brooke asked. "Nate?"

"Stay down there," I said, as if she had a choice.

The door to the truck was opened fully on Brooke's side, half-opened on mine. The Surgeon walked slowly along the driver's side, the gun down. He knew we didn't have any weapons, I suppose, and he knew that even if we did, he was faster than me.

He looked at the dead policeman on the ground below him. "A shame," he murmured. Then he raised those tired eyes to me. "Dr. McCormick, you're making this extremely messy."

I had the cap off the nitric acid and slowly—as slowly as I could—pulled the bottle from my crotch. "Don't you take any responsibility for anything?" I asked.

Brooke said, "You sick cocksucker." Where did women learn these words?

I saw him glance quickly into the cab, at Brooke, at the box of papers on the floor. "I know where my responsibility lies, Doctor. Goodbye." He began to raise the gun.

I swung my right arm toward the window and stopped fast. A spray of acid arced out, splashing across the Surgeon's face. I ducked down, anticipating that he would fire into the cab. He did, the shots splitting the air above me. With both my arms, I shoved the door of the truck—it swung into him, knocking him back. With the gun still in his hands, he began to claw at his eyes. A driver leaned on his horn and swerved to avoid him.

I turned the key in the ignition. The blessed old Ford started.

The Surgeon began to spray the side of the cab with the rest of his clip. I put the truck in drive and punched the accelerator to the floor. As

I sped along the shoulder, I managed to tag the tail end of the Surgeon's car. The force of the impact slammed Brooke's door shut. She yelped.

I hooked my dead arm through the window of my door and pulled it closed. As I did so, I looked into the side-view mirror. I saw the Surgeon raking at his face with both hands.

CHAPTER 93

"You're bleeding," Brooke said. Her head was resting against my thigh, her eyes focused up at me.

"I know. I have no skin left on my hand."

"No. Your shoulder. I think you were hit."

Only when she said it did I realize the pain and wetness on my back. I was still alive, I thought, and still breathing, so I assumed the bullet hadn't punctured a lung. I mean, I *had* to be alive. Heaven wasn't a nasty stretch of the 101, was it? Hell maybe, but come on, I was a good guy.

She closed her eyes.

"I'm losing a lot of blood, Nate."

"I know. Hang on." We drove for another eternity. "We're going to get stopped again. They'll think we shot the cops." Brooke didn't say anything, so I filled the silence with a quiet "Goddamn."

The wind was whistling through the bullet holes in the windshield and the doors. *How the hell did I get here?* I wondered. I was shot. Brooke was shot. Two weeks before, the worst thing I had to complain about was the heat and humidity in Baltimore. Now, if I were the betting type, I'd give two to one we wouldn't make it out of this alive.

Brooke, as if she'd been reading my thoughts, said softly, "It'll be okay."

"Will it?"

Rhetorical questions like that are nice, because they leave the field wide-open for answers of all types, open to all sorts of responses. And God, if He's actually up there, decided to answer. Ahead, off to the left, I saw a large building with green illuminated letters spelling out GILROY MERCY HOSPITAL.

"There it is," I said, and took the next exit.

CHAPTER 94

There wasn't much commotion in the ER when I arrived, but whatever noise there was ceased for a moment as I stumbled in. I could see the camera shot, long, from the point of view of the admitting nurse—bedraggled man in need of a shave, bloody lump of a left hand dangling at his side, blood slicking his back, yelling for a gurney.

I remember people surrounding me, trying to get me into a bed. I shoved them away and pushed back through the automatic doors to the truck, yelling the whole time about a gurney.

Outside, I opened the passenger-side door. Brooke's rump faced me, covered in blood. I looked, but couldn't really see where the bullet had entered. I put my hand on her hip and waited.

"It's okay, it's okay," I said.

Thirty seconds later, two guys came out, rolling a bed between them. A young doctor followed.

"What happened?" he asked me.

I told him Brooke had been shot. As the orderlies pulled Brooke onto the gurney, the doc looked at me. "You?"

"Shot, I think. Not too bad. And my hand . . ." I raised the thing to show him. He took it in for a second, then looked down at the gurney.

"Brooke?"

She looked up at the doctor and smiled like an angel. "Jaime."

Jaime glanced at me, then back to Brooke. "What the hell happened?"

The orderlies began to wheel Brooke inside; Jaime—who was annoyingly good-looking—followed. Nathaniel—with injuries almost as bad as Brooke's—was left alone.

"Hey," I called. "I need someone to help me with this." I pointed to the box of files.

Jaime looked over his shoulder. "Leave it. Come inside."

"No."

Jaime set his chiseled jaw, then told one of the orderlies to give me a hand. He took the orderly's place on the gurney.

"No police, okay?" I said.

"They've already been called."

That's it, then, I thought. I turned back to the truck to watch the orderly gather my files, then ran to help him get things in gear.

One of the nice things about a lot of blood is that it's dramatic, so we didn't have to wait for attention. Of course, at that point, I didn't know if we were being taken care of so quickly because of the blood or because Brooke and Jaime seemed to have, well, a history.

So, there they were, Brooke and Jaime, chatting comfortably. Or, more exactly, it was Jaime doing most of the talking. "You got shot in the butt?" I heard the scissors rip through the denim of Brooke's jeans. Jaime clucked his tongue. "What a shame. Like defacing Michelangelo's *David.*"

Brooke laughed, exhausted but genuine, charmed by the charming Dr. Munoz. Okay, it was an inappropriate feeling, I know, the jealousy that spiked through me. I mean, I had much bigger things to worry about—the police would be there any minute, asking questions about this mess and the mess on the highway ten miles south, I had to worry about the damage to my hand—but there it was. Jealousy.

Another doctor was tending to me. She was older, fifties maybe, and severe looking. She and I definitely hadn't slept together, so she didn't mention my beautiful butt, my beautiful shoulder, or my beautiful hand.

"Just wrap it, please," I told her. "Put a dressing on the shoulder."

She blinked when she finally pulled off the last of the gauze. "You need to go to surgery."

"Dress it. Quickly. I need to go. And get somebody down here with a bolt cutter."

"They've already been called. Dr. McCormick, I insist you—"

"Dress the goddamned hand."

The easy conversation in the next bay ceased. I reached up to the curtain and pulled it back. Jaime cranked his head around, furious at the intrusion. Brooke was draped in a sheet, which didn't hide her rear end, now bare, the jeans cut down the leg.

"I've seen her ass, too, Doctor," I told Jaime.

Brooke, to her credit, said nothing.

"I need to go, Brooke."

"Why?"

I glanced at Jaime and the doctor—Dr. Saxon, according to her hospital ID—who was caring for me. "I just need to go. I need to get something . . . before everything explodes."

Brooke seemed to get this, and she turned her head to look at me. "Be careful."

I said to Dr. Saxon, "Please wrap my hand and bandage the back as quickly as you can. If you don't, I'll leave."

"You have to sign—"

"I know. Bring me the papers."

Dr. Saxon called for the forms that would release the hospital of any liability for my checking myself out against medical advice.

Jaime Munoz pulled the curtain closed, but I stopped him.

"I need a car," I said, keeping my eyes on Brooke. She nodded slightly. *God bless this woman.*

"Jaime, give Dr. McCormick your keys," she said.

"What?" Munoz looked angry.

"He needs your car. Give him the keys."

Doctors Munoz and Saxon exchanged glances. "Why?" he asked.

"We can't tell you." The not-so-subtle subtext here was that it was very important. How could he refuse? His former lover had been shot; the guy with her was spattered with blood and mangled. They obviously weren't on the run, since Brooke would be left here to deal with the cops. Plus, I'm sure Dr. Munoz was thinking he might have another chance with the beautiful Brooke Michaels if he gave in.

I shouldn't have said anything about seeing her ass.

"Please, Jaime. It's very important." She put her hand on his arm.

Dr. Munoz huffed. Then he stripped off his gloves and dug into his pocket. He produced a key chain, took off a few keys, and pushed the rest into my good hand. "It's the black Mustang. In the lot right outside the ER." He began to draw closed the curtains, and I stopped him again. This guy was going to pop me if I didn't let up.

"Brooke, make sure the documents get to the police. Make sure they know how important they are. I don't know if there's anything important left, but . . ."

She nodded.

Jaime gave it a moment, then pulled the curtain fast. This time I didn't stop him. I heard Brooke say, "Thank you." I didn't hear any more conversation after that.

Dr. Saxon finished with my hand, then undid my shirt and pulled it off my shoulder.

"You're lucky," she said, poking around at the wound. "It just grazed you. It's already clotted. We'll just irrigate and get a couple of stitches—"

"Great. Then I don't need it dressed right now." I began to pull on my shirt. "Thanks," I said to Saxon.

She threw up her hands in a "whatever" gesture. By way of molli-fication, I said, "I just don't have time."

"No one ever has time, Dr. McCormick."

Not like me, lady, I thought.

A nurse brought the papers for my discharge, and I signed them. The cuffs were still dangling from my right hand, and I saw the nurse watching them make little loops as I signed; she looked hypnotized.

I heard a commotion at the end of the hallway. I stood and poked my head out of the curtain. Two policemen were talking to another nurse. I pulled back into the bay. "Is there another exit here?"

Saxon seemed confused. "Uh, the hallway curves around. There's an exit to the hospital proper in back."

"Tell the cops I went to surgery."

As I pulled the curtain to the empty bay next to me, I heard Brooke say, "Be careful, Nate."

I wished she were coming with me.

I made my way to the end of the hallway by crossing through each of the bays. Some were empty; others contained people—mostly of Mexican heritage, it looked like—who ogled me as I moved around past their beds. Eventually, I came out to the end of the hall. Quickly, I checked for the police, saw them talking to Jaime Munoz, who looked decidedly displeased.

Better him than me, I thought, then rounded the corner.

In the parking lot, I hit the Unlock button on the key chain and heard a double blip from my right. The Mustang was parked toward the back of the lot, stretched across two parking spaces. Poor Jaime, parking it back there to keep it safe. Now a guy with one hand was going to take it for a spin. He must have really been into Brooke.

I had to give it to him: it was a real car, only a year or so old. V-8, 300-plus horsepower. And, unfortunately for me, a five-speed. Good thing I knew how to drive with my knees.

I got in, turned on that four-and-a-half-liter, and put it into first. In a minute, I was on the highway, clicking along at ninety. *Who needs a left hand?*

After I passed San Jose, I pulled off the highway to a convenience market. My telephone still had a little juice—enough, probably, for one call.

"I need to see you. Where are you?"

There was a pause on the phone as decisions were being made and remade. She sighed, then told me to meet her at the university.

CHAPTER 95

I parked the Mustang in the med school's parking area, not far from where my car had been broken into the day before yesterday. Perhaps I should have opened up to the bad juju of the place, taken the cue, and gotten the hell out of there. In fact, in light of what would happen, there was no "perhaps" about it.

I got out of the car.

The buildings surrounding the parking area—which had been constructed with a lot of nouveau flair—looked different at night. Light blazed from within their exoskeletons, giving them the look of spaceships adrift in some cold corner of the galaxy. There was something very Arthur C. Clarke about the place.

Across the lot, I saw her—sitting on the trunk of her silver BMW, smoking, looking great in tight khakis and a black cashmere sweater. An expensive handbag sat next to her. The scene could have been an ad from a magazine, something touting female independence, contemplation, or whatever it was one exemplified while perched on the back of a Bimmer. In any case, I was surprised she still did that—smoked—but then remembered it was her answer to stress. A few during finals, a few when she and I split, that kind of thing. She tossed the cigarette as I approached.

"Don't mean to interrupt," I said.

She was silent for a moment, taking in my bandaged hand, bloodied shirt, and handcuffs. Then she shouldered the bag and said, "Let's walk."

So, we walked—across the medical campus to a path that snaked along Campus Drive. Only a few cars passed us along the road, cracking the darkness with their headlights. Alaine veered off the main path onto one of the smaller walkways that cut through the acres of trees that surrounded the campus. We had been this way many times before—Alaine and I—taking a break from study in the library to talk, hold hands, grope.

Everything was quiet, except for the wind moving through the large, spreading oaks and the occasional clink of the chains from the handcuffs dangling off my right wrist. I took the loose end of the cuffs into my hand.

"Alaine?"

Her eyes were on the ground.

"Alaine?"

"No one ever thought this would happen," she said quietly. "No one thought it would go this far."

"Then why didn't they stop?"

She looked at me for the first time in a while, but said nothing.

"Okay, what are we doing here?" Still she didn't respond. "The pig wasn't sick, was it?"

"No," she said.

"But I talked to one of the vets down in Gilroy. He said the Abby line was diseased."

"Because that's what we told him."

"Why?"

"Because that's what we thought at first. It was the most likely scenario."

We passed through a cactus garden tucked among the oaks—huge saguaro, prickly pear, yucca—and damn it if I didn't know where she was taking me.

The path opened to an asphalt expanse about half the size of a basketball court. At one end sat a building, a compact granite structure with big bronze doors and two white marble sphinxes perched beside the steps. It was a mausoleum, resting place of the earthly remains of the university's founder, his wife and son. During the school year, you could always find a few couples making out here, or a coven trying to raise some Wicca spirit. But it was summertime and deserted, though you could still see the wax stains on the stone steps.

Alaine and I used to come here. We sat on the steps.

She turned to me and crossed her legs. "So, indulge me, Nathaniel. Tell me what you think happened."

"Why?"

"Because I'll tell you what really did happen."

"I think I'm almost there."

"You probably are. You're a smart man, so nobody should be surprised."

"But you are," I pointed out cruelly.

"No. Other people were surprised."

"Otto and Ian."

"Yes."

I shook the feeling that it was ten years before and that we were here to neck.

Sucking deep some night air, I began. "Okay. I figure it starts with Dr. Falk, who comes out here and has a great idea, the idea he's worked with all of his life—to use animal organs in humans. He's on the cutting edge of xenotransplantation. The university loves it, the investment community loves it. He brings his kid, Kincaid Charles—KC—who is retarded and can't be too far from his family. He gets his son a job as an orderly in the hospital. Kincaid, somewhere along the way, finds a girlfriend—Gladys Thomas.

"Meanwhile, Falk is busy in the lab. He engineers pig organs that lack identifying sugars and proteins, making them invisible to the organ recipient. A paper comes out later that year. I assume it's around this time that things really begin to rev up with Chimeragen. Ian comes on board from one of the venture firms that backed the whole deal. You meet Ian, the world stops, the bells go off, an angelic host begins singing about true love amidst—"

"Nathaniel . . ."

"Wait, that's not how it happened?"

Alaine looked annoyed.

"Anyway, somehow Falk convinces the families of some brain-dead people to give their loved ones to medicine and science. He transplants these new, perfect organs into the patients. Not surprisingly, Kincaid is assigned to be an orderly or caretaker or whatever for the people. Everything is okay until KC rapes one of the women."

I looked for any sign of life in Alaine's eyes, but those black irises kept staring. The moonlight cast razor-sharp shadows across her face.

"Falk can't let the experiment go. I mean, at this point he has investment capital, he has his reputation tied up in this, and he thinks he's going to save the world. Risk everything because of a little rape? No way. Besides, the rapist is his own flesh and blood. Still, they can't keep a loose cannon like KC around, so Falk thinks a little and he remembers his buddy Randall Jefferson in Baltimore. The guy has a bunch of group homes for the retarded. Falk makes a discreet call. Jefferson is only too happy to oblige, since it won't be any skin off his nose to cloister a fugitive for a friend. He's been bilking the state out of funds for God knows how many people who've already died. Jefferson figures KC could just slip into the role of one of the deceased—Douglas Buchanan. He tells Falk to send him along, and KC is shipped to Baltimore.

"Around about now, something else happens: they find out Janet Margulies is pregnant."

I looked at Alaine for some positive feedback, but she just stared.

"Okay, Janet. Janet is with child. Now, this really would not have been good PR, so Falk has a little staph dropped into an IV. Janet dies. No one asks any questions. How many times did it happen, Alaine? The rapes?"

She finally broke, just a little. A tiny breath. "Five times, at least. We went back through the tapes. Thank God it was only with Janet. She was his . . . She was his favorite."

"Lucky girl. Anyway, they're worried that Douglas might have picked something up from sex with the woman. And they have to be worried that, given his proclivities, he's spreading it around. How am I doing so far?"

"Very well, Nathaniel."

"That's when the whole thing comes apart. About two weeks ago, there's an outbreak in the mentally handicapped community in Baltimore. The esteemed Dr. Jefferson tries to stymie the authorities back east—that's me and my colleagues—to give the folks here time to figure out what to do. They're not sure whether this has anything to do with Kincaid or not, but they're worried. When we—the authorities—begin to zero in on Kincaid, they freak out. Somebody kills Falk's son, strips the organs, and sends them back here for analysis."

I stopped for a moment. "Who killed KC Falk? Who stripped the organs?"

"A doctor back in Baltimore, I think."

"Randall Jefferson?"

"That would be a good guess. He'd been taking biopsies and doing routine physicals for months."

"Who received the biopsies?"

She didn't answer.

"Come on. This is important. It establishes who's involved." She looked away from me. And at that moment, I knew. "Oh, no, Alaine. Goddamn it. Why?"

"I didn't know what they were. I got some tissue and they told me to analyze it. I didn't *know*, Nate."

"You didn't know," I repeated. I also didn't know what to do now that Alaine Chen was intimately involved with this imbroglio. It was ugly.

I continued with my story. "Anyway, I get kicked out of Baltimore for ruffling too many feathers—mostly Randall Jefferson's—and am sent out here to follow up on a flimsy lead: Gladys Thomas. I talk to her, and she tells me she knows Kincaid. They were involved, in fact, though not sexually. People here get wind of it, they know that Gladys Thomas talked to me, and she dies. The lead, it seems, wasn't so flimsy after all."

Alaine was stony.

"And the rest, you probably know. The guy hired to do the heavy lifting—killing retarded folks, killing dogs—comes after me. But now, most likely, he's in a police station, unable to see his own nose, telling the police he was attacked by a mad Nathaniel McCormick."

We were quiet for a while, staring deeply into each other's eyes. If it had been a decade earlier, Alaine and I might well have been in this exact spot, our faces pressed together. I wished she hadn't taken me here.

"Are you in love with her?" Alaine asked, I guess picking up on the vibe.

"Who?"

She didn't answer, but said only, "She's very pretty."

And she has a bullet in her ass, Alaine.

"They killed Dr. Tobel," I said.

She smiled, a crooked, unhappy smile. "I thought you were never going to mention her. And the answer to your question is yes. They murdered Harriet."

"Why?"

"Because she was going to tell you just what you told me."

"So, it is the truth, isn't it?"

"It's what everyone else believes. Well, almost everyone."

"How did they do it?"

"I'm not sure. I think they gave her a shot of digoxin. I feel . . . They asked me about her health and I told them. They knew about her heart."

Digoxin—a drug used to flog a failing heart into beating stronger—is a great drug for folks suffering from congestive heart failure. Dr. Tobel had it in her medicine cabinet. But if you get too much, the heart beats too hard, it requires too much oxygen. Basically, that glorious pump burns through its fuel supply and you die of a heart attack.

I said, "I'll make sure the ME runs assays for digoxin."

"Yes," Alaine said.

At that point, I thought she was going to tell me what the truth was, what the kernel was that everyone else did not believe, or did not know. I mean, if there was ever an opportunity, this was it. Instead, she sighed and stood up. "I don't like this place anymore. I used to love it so much. I used to find it so peaceful, but now . . ."

She began to walk, and I followed. I didn't want to lose the thread of the conversation. So, to keep it going, I said, "Why did you help me?"

"Oh, Nathaniel. A thousand reasons." She gave me the sad smile again. "They killed Dr. Tobel. And . . . well, they were going to kill you. And Dr. Michaels, if you didn't stop."

"Really? Couldn't tell." She flinched. I asked, "How do you know about Harriet Tobel? I wouldn't think they'd say anything to you."

"I am getting married to Ian, remember?"

Right. Loose lips and such. "And you're willing to go to jail for this?"

She laughed, a real, warm laugh, the kind of laugh that used to make me melt. "Certainly not. I am leaving the country. With Ian." She smiled. "We're lucky he was rich before he got involved with this."

If I had felt any fondness or tenderness toward Alaine Chen—and I admit I had in the past few days and hours—it started to evaporate at that moment. Was she really as I'd come to see her over the past years—hardened at the core, wanting to do good, actually *doing* some good, but hard, hard, hard?

"But he was involved in all of this, with the deaths. . . ." I shook my head, frustrated. "What will he do when he finds out you—"

"Ian doesn't know, and at this point I don't know if he cares. He loves me, despite everything."

Like me, I thought. God, this woman was toxic. "Do you love him?"

"Do you really want to know?"

Yes, I goddamned do, I thought. But I said, "I couldn't care less, Alaine."

"Good for you. You're finally growing up."

Fuck you, I thought.

"So, what really happened? What's this thing that I got wrong and everybody else seemed to get wrong?"

We had broken from the darkness of the woods. Alaine paused under a streetlamp. "You know what it is. You stole it from Dr. Tobel's office."

I stopped walking for a moment, to think better. Maybe my coordination isn't as good as I thought it was. "The sequence. The Junin-HIV hybrid."

"Yes."

"I see. And it didn't come from the pig."

"That's correct."

"Well, you'll be happy to know we're confirming that now in Atlanta."

Alaine didn't flinch, nor did she make any move to fill me in. I'd had it with the game. "All right, sweetie, enough of this bullshit. Tell me what is going on."

"You sure you really want to know?"

"Don't fucking patronize me. Of course I want to know. Dr. Tobel knew, she found it, and that's why she was killed."

"She did more than find it, Nathaniel. She made it."

CHAPTER 96

Alaine took a large file from her handbag and handed it to me. She began to walk again and said, "Back in '96, Harriet was working on a vaccine for HIV—"

"She was working on it before then. I was in her lab for a while, remember?"

"In '96 she started making real progress in primate models," Alaine continued. "But she ran into obstacles. Consistently. It seemed she couldn't get a robust immune response from the hosts, who continued to develop a simian HIV infection despite the vaccinations.

"Harriet had this idea to combine some of the surface proteins from other viruses with certain elements of HIV to elicit a robust response. She experimented with a whole host of candidates, but she found the best response—"

"Oh, no," I said. Viruses were my life; I could see where this was going.

"The best responses were from some of the arenaviruses. Harriet settled on Junin, which we know from previous vaccine work elicits an effective immune response. She spliced the envelope gene for Junin into HIV, so that the new . . . organism . . . had both envelope proteins expressed.

"Well, the primate experiments went very well, but Harriet was having no luck getting any interest in a human vaccine trial, even though everyone was very excited about the prospect of an HIV vaccine."

"They still are, Alaine."

"Thanks for the public health angle. Anyway, people were nervous about introducing anything that caused a viral hemorrhagic fever into HIV."

"I wonder why."

"Are you going to let me finish?" she snapped. "Harriet abandons the project for a while; I come into her lab. Then we meet Otto Falk—or, more exactly, I meet Otto, since Harriet already knew him from Baltimore. Falk does his thing with the pigs, gets the organs in order, coauthors a paper in *Science* with some of his preliminary work. Then he approaches Harriet with his brilliant plan about the vegetative patients."

"You're lying, Alaine."

"It's in the file. Well, not all of it. But you can piece it together."

"I can't believe this." The file in my hand grew heavier and heavier.

"Harriet thought Falk's idea was a good one. She also saw the opportunities for her vaccine work. Otto really wanted her on board—they'd worked together before; she would bring enormous credibility to the project. She knew this, of course, so she told him the price for her involvement."

I waited for the other shoe to drop. But in this game we were playing in which Alaine would offer information, then not deliver, she said nothing.

In any case, I knew what Dr. Tobel's price was, and some part of me knew my old mentor was capable of something like this. Her argument would have been the same as Otto Falk's: one life to save a thousand, a million. With something like HIV, one could see how seductive the statistics were.

I said, "Janet Margulies. The woman KC raped. She was the price of involvement."

"Yes," Alaine said.

"What happened? Why the virulence?"

"I don't know. I was never part of Harriet's work on the vaccine. As far as I know, she did it all herself. I only found out about this because I found the files. Then I confronted Dr. Falk."

"What did he say?"

"Otto was, well, surprised."

"But he knew. From the beginning."

"Yes. He had to. He was the one who performed the sham surgery on Ms. Margulies. He cut her open, but left her liver intact. Falk told the team in the room that day that Janet Margulies was a negative control. No one but Falk knew the real name of the patient. Her face was obscured. All the records were sealed to ensure that no one would know who was the control and who wasn't. This way, no one would know Margulies didn't get the pig organs; they'd think she was part of the transplant experiment, just like everyone else."

"But she wasn't—"

"No."

"She wasn't a negative control—"

"Certainly not."

"She was part of a vaccine trial."

Alaine nodded.

"Why didn't they just come clean about the vaccine work? Separate it from the transplant experiment?"

Alaine laughed. "Can you imagine, Nate? This would have been much worse than something happening with the xenotransplants. We were prepared for something to happen with the transplants. We had mapped out the risks, gotten approval for every step of the protocol. But Harriet's study, if you can call it that, was never sanctioned by anybody. It wasn't well designed or controlled. She was doing it to test the most basic elements of her hypothesis, that's all. The results would never be published. She'd use them to confirm what she thought; then, later, she'd make a push for real trials. It was kept very quiet, as you can imagine. Even Ian doesn't know all of it. If any of this had gotten out . . ."

I filled in. "Then everything would have gone badly. But everything did go badly."

"True. Still, nobody saw how bad it was going to get."

"That's how these things go, isn't it?"

"I suppose so. I'm sorry, Nate. I know it's hard about Harriet. It was very hard for me, too."

"I'm having trouble taking this all in."

"I know."

"I'm having trouble believing this."

Alaine was quiet; so was I. But I was, as I said, having a good bit of difficulty. *Gutted* might be a good word to describe how I felt. Stunned, clobbered, eviscerated. Harriet Tobel, who'd been my staunch defender all those years, who I thought was holier than Jesus, had been no better than Otto Falk. No wonder, I guess, the two of them found their way into an unholy embrace.

I said, "I cannot believe Dr. Tobel would let Kincaid run wild."

"She didn't. She thought that when KC disappeared, he was truly gone; she thought the experiment had simply run aground. She never knew Janet Margulies had been killed on purpose. It was Falk who scuttled it. He, I assume, introduced the staph infection into Janet. He arranged for his son to disappear. He didn't trust Harriet."

"Which is why you, and not Dr. Tobel, were asked to monitor KC, to look at the biopsies."

"Yes."

"I'm sorry for that."

"So am I."

"You could have said no."

"Yes, I could have, Nathaniel. And I didn't. So, I'm paying for it."

And I guess she was, though whether a lifetime in exile was a fair price, that's for the Big Guy upstairs to determine.

I did my best to quiet my brain about Dr. Tobel, to focus on the information presented by the woman beside me. Things still didn't add up. "What I saw in Baltimore was not AIDS, Alaine. So unless the Junin-HIV virus mutated—"

"That's what I think. Or it picked up some replication machinery from another virus in Kincaid, something benign. And then it went to work."

"How?"

"Who knows, Nathaniel? Maybe the HIV part of the virus weakened the immune system and let the Junin part run wild. Who knows?"

I sat quietly for a moment, trying to make sense of all of this. "Kincaid was immune. But the women he infected weren't."

"Yes. I don't really know why. We looked at his tissue and found the virus, but it seemed benign in him. I don't know. . . . I must tell you that at the beginning, Harriet seemed very excited by this. Her guinea pigs—Janet Margulies and, unexpectedly, Kincaid Falk—were immune to the chimera virus. Even though they were out of the picture after a relatively short time, she felt the preliminary results were good. But when you came with the information about the outbreak in Baltimore, she must have known something went terribly wrong."

Alaine sighed and glanced up at the looming lab buildings. I looked at her looking at the buildings. She seemed very sad at that moment, and, again, I was confused about her, about who the hell she was. Was she an ice queen, or just a flawed, ambitious idiot like the rest of us? *God,* I thought, *I really don't understand people.* Scratch that. I really don't understand women. Men are simple ambitious idiots, present company included. Women—Alaine Chen, Harriet Tobel, even Brooke Michaels—are more nuanced. Infuriating for a guy who wants easy answers.

Alaine said, "It's horrible, utterly horrible, Nate. All of this."

I had another question, one that had been eating me alive for a few days. "What do you think Dr. Tobel wanted to tell me the night she died?"

"Maybe she wanted to come clean. Or maybe she wanted to pin everything on Otto Falk and the xenotransplants. We'll never know, will we?"

"I guess not."

"And now Otto will try to pin everything on Harriet. Ironic, isn't it?"

"What?" This was news. Silly me, thinking this whole mess was over.

"Don't be naïve about him. Otto has too much at stake; you can see that. His whole life is wrapped up in this work."

"How is he going to do it?"

"I don't know."

I thought about that, about how Otto would move the chess pieces to corner Harriet Tobel. Then I thought how I'd be able to checkmate the eminent transplant surgeon. I thought about what I had—basically some lab reports, little else. The only thing I had linking Otto Falk to the shenanigans of the past months was Janet Margulies's termination notice: "Discontinue antibiotic as per protocol." This wasn't really the stuff of ironclad prosecutions.

We were back at the parking lot, next to the Mustang and the silver BMW. The lights flashed on the BMW; the alarm chirped. Alaine walked to it. In the backseat I saw luggage, two overstuffed pieces that looked like they might be bound for points south or east or wherever they didn't have extradition treaties with the U.S.

"Wait. If you're so sure Falk is going to get away with this, why are you leaving the country? Why not let Harriet take the fall?"

"I'm not so sure Otto will get away with it."

"Why?"

"Don't be dense. You're here. You're talking to me."

I didn't really appreciate the "dense" jab, but she was probably right, and I let it go. She pointed to the file in my hand. "Use that information however you wish. And take these. I won't need them." She produced a clutch of IDs and keys: the university, Chimeragen, the Gilroy facility. She dropped the items onto the folder in my hand.

We waited a moment in the shadows, keenly aware, I guess, that this really was farewell. True finality—whether it's the finality of a marriage or the finality of a death, which this, in a sense, was—is a big deal and deserves some reverence.

She took in the building around us, then turned back to me and said, "I should be going. Good luck, Nathaniel."

I wondered, looking at her like that—resting with her back against the nice car, arms crossed in front of her, travel clothes on—whether there was some part of her contemplating what it would have been like if she had stayed with me. I mean, I wondered that all the time for the first few years: if she'd been with me, I wouldn't have socked Pablo in the coffeehouse and I wouldn't have been kicked out of school, I might have been a surgeon, I might have been a urologist. I certainly wouldn't have gone to Africa, then gone to CDC. And Alaine wouldn't have been with Ian, and she likely wouldn't be talking to me in this parking lot right now, getting ready to flee the country.

I wondered if she wondered. And I hoped she did.

But even as I was tracking through the myriad what-ifs of Nathaniel McCormick and Alaine Chen, I managed to get some clarity. In that moment, I felt I was finally free.

"It never would have worked out between us," I said.

A sad little smile pulled the corners of her mouth. "No," she agreed.

For all those years, I'd assumed it was I who had the problems, that I had derailed our relationship. Now I realized that Alaine was largely to blame. I might have fallen apart, sure, but she was the one who had bolted, who had left at the first sign of trouble. She was never in love with me, I think. She'd been in love with an idea of me, and when that fantasy started to crack, she was gone. In the same way, she was in love with the idea of Ian Carrington. But Ian was a murderer of sorts—not to mention a bland rube whose thoughts consisted only of where his business was going, whether he could save it, maybe whatever workout schedule he planned the next day—and I can't imagine that her fantasy of him was intact. At least he was rich, as she'd said. At least Alaine seemed to have come to terms with how important that was for her.

Anyway, I wondered how she would deal with a lifetime in Uruguay or in whatever backwater she was going to, how she would deal with Ian Carrington, the fugitive. Despite her game face that night, I didn't think she'd cope well.

And though I think I understood quite a lot about Alaine Chen in that moment, I still had trouble understanding why she'd helped me. I asked her.

"I told you," she said, "things were getting out of control."

"That's not it," I said.

"Well, I don't know, Nathaniel." Then she surprised me. Her eyes began to mist; the tears welled, then dribbled down her face. "I don't know anything anymore. I don't know who I am anymore."

And that, I think, was the most honest thing she'd ever said to me.

For the first time in a decade, I stopped hating Alaine Chen. I stopped loving her. I felt, simply, sorry for her.

She brushed away the tears and sighed. She was ready to go. I asked, "Anything I can do for you?"

"You can wait until tomorrow afternoon before you tell anyone I've gone. You owe me that."

And, in truth, I did.

I nodded. Alaine did, too, then stepped into the BMW. The engine turned over and the car slid quietly out of its parking space. I stood there, watching her go, the IDs and keys balanced on the thick folder. As she drove off, I raised my bandaged left hand. I saw her wave, a tiny flutter that seemed mockingly banal.

Good-bye, Alaine. Good-bye, good-bye, good-bye.

CHAPTER 97

I dropped my hand to my side, felt the blood rush into it, kick-starting the first, dull pulses of pain. The lidocaine was wearing off. It would not be too long before I'd be screaming for the damn thing to be removed. *No time for pain,* I thought. Easy to think, hard to endure.

My real problem was Harriet Tobel. More exactly, Harriet Tobel's legacy. She was being set up, right? I couldn't let that happen, correct? Less heroic thoughts began to creep in. To wit, I wanted to cleanse Dr. Tobel's file completely. Who needed to know she'd engineered a terrible virus? Her aims were good; her tactics and her morals were flawed. But we're all allowed one slipup in our lives, aren't we? Why allow decades of good work to be sullied by some bad decisions in the autumn of her life?

Besides, Dr. Tobel had scrubbed my file so I could return to medical school. I owed her this. I realized I was letting loyalty trump truth—I realized I was cutting Dr. Tobel a break where I wouldn't allow the same for Otto Falk—but screw it. I didn't allow myself to equivocate any longer.

So, now that the moral dialogue was over, I knew what I had to do. I just did not know where to do it.

What I couldn't figure was how and where Otto Falk was planning to set up Dr. Tobel. He'd need some evidence, something he could point out to law enforcement. I didn't think a smart guy like him would go in for hearsay. So, where would that evidence be? Falk's lab? The Gilroy facility? The Chimeragen offices?

No. Like the crooked cop dropping a bag of cocaine into an innocent's car, he'd plant the evidence where it counted most. The Tobel lab.

I opened Dr. Munoz's Mustang and dropped the file on the front seat. I gathered Alaine's IDs and walked to the Heilmann Building. There, I took the steps, the handcuffs adding a Quasimodo jingle to my journey upward.

The lights were on in Harriet Tobel's lab. *Shit,* I thought, and walked casually to the door. Just another overworked grad student out for a stroll, that's me. Bandaged and bloodstained hand? Handcuffs? Probably some sick psychiatry experiment.

I looked in the lab, half-expecting to see Dr. Falk himself: pitchfork leaned against a lab bench, barbed tail twirling, belching flames as he giggled to himself. I saw no one.

I was about to enter the lab when I heard something.

Doors from an elevator, opening somewhere up the hall. I managed to make it to a bend in the corridor before I heard voices. Then I peered around the corner. I saw two men whom I didn't recognize, dressed in jeans and T-shirts—working clothes—and carrying what looked like an ice chest. They stopped in front of the door to Dr. Tobel's lab, set the ice chest down. One of the men opened the door. They adjusted their load and disappeared into the lab.

What the hell is this?

As I waited for the men to exit, I found myself focusing on the pain in my left hand. How long, I wondered, before I would be willing to trade my kingdom for a couple of Vicodin?

More than five minutes, anyway, which is about how much time passed before I heard the men again. Their footsteps faded down the hallway, no talking this time. Elevator doors opened, then closed. I gave it a beat, then went to the lab.

The lights were off.

The door was, of course, locked, so I pushed Alaine's university ID to the black pad and waited. A red light flashed, then nothing.

Odd. I tried the card again. Still nothing. Alaine, it seemed, was being locked out. Why and when had this happened?

Before I started ramming the door with my wrecked hand or lacerated shoulder, I fished in my pocket for Harriet Tobel's old ID and used that. The light flashed green. I entered the lab, expecting the place to be cleaned out. But I was wrong. It looked like the movers I'd seen in Gilroy had taken only the clutter, less than half the equipment. Either that or these poor blokes were having a mother of a workday, moving items to Gilroy, then back to the university. Actually, on reflection, I suspected the latter might be the case.

Because the gentlemen had been carrying an ice chest, I used my amazing powers of deduction and figured they might have been toting something that needed to be kept cold. I went to the cold room, which, like the lab itself, was fashioned with an electronic lock. Again, Alaine's key card didn't work. Again, Dr. Tobel's did.

Christ, Alaine, why are you locked out?

The cold room was small, about ten by ten, with two upright freezers on opposite sides and one horizontal freezer directly across from me. Each had a small lock on the latch. I took the clutch of IDs and keys given to me by Alaine. I'd spent years getting into and out of freezers like this, and so I knew exactly what I was looking for. I found it: a small brass key.

Dropping the other items on the horizontal freezer, I went to the upright on my right, the LED on the front reading −80 degrees Celsius. I tried the key. Success. Evidently, it wasn't as easy to change physical locks as it was electronic ones. I turned the key, pulled the latch, and opened the door.

The freezer consisted of a stack of six shelves, each with a thin, frost-covered door in front of it. I went for the top shelf and pulled the door. A few racks of plastic Falcon tubes filled with a frozen pinkish substance. I moved to the next shelf and found the same. The next contained slide boxes. Nothing but tubes and slide boxes in the rest of the freezer.

I moved to the next upright. The same uninteresting stuff: slides, bags filled with microfuge tubes, racks of Falcon tubes.

"Come on," I scolded myself.

The next freezer was emblazoned with biohazard signs, those ugly crablike symbols that basically signify "Don't touch." Risk taker that I am, I jammed the key in the lock.

There was nothing in the top two shelves. On the third one down, however . . . Well, even for a guy who spends his life with germs, this was a shocker.

There was a tray filled with plastic bags and specimen containers. Innocent-looking stuff, really, except for what was written on the tray and the bags in big black indelible marker: BSL 3. BSL—biosafety level—was a series of protocols for dealing with microbes and graded on a scale of one to four. Very few bugs were BSL 4, a designation for only the most contagious pathogens—Russian spring-summer encephalitis and Ebola, for example—that could be spread through the air. BSL 3 was still bad, and encompassed many of the bacteria and viruses I feared most. Having BSL specimens sitting in a relatively unsecured freezer, in a room without proper ventilation and safety equipment, was a serious no-no. Maybe this was Falk's plan: get Harriet Tobel nabbed for hazardous-materials violations. In any case, it was pretty obvious this stuff had been moved here recently, say, in the previous ten minutes. Where it came from, I didn't know. It didn't really matter at that point, anyway.

I closed the door: this was BSL 3, after all, and I wanted some protection. I found a box of gloves and managed to squirm one on my right hand. I sure as hell couldn't pull on the left or get a mask on my face. Maybe I'd just hold my breath.

Slowly, so as not to suck more crap into the room than necessary, I opened the door. With my good hand, I took the tray from the middle shelf and set it on the floor, carefully removing one of the double-sealed plastic bags. You didn't need to go to medical school to know what I held in my hand. It was a heart. Human. I pawed through the other bags. Human liver, pancreas, spleen. I went back to the freezer. A small container was pushed to the back of the shelf: in it, double-bagged, were slices of a five-pound organ.

"Jesus," I said aloud.

On the bag was written a date not two weeks before, followed by another date two days later. These would be the harvest date and the date the specimen had been put into the freezer, respectively. The word *Brain* was written in small script. Behind that, three small letters in block capitals: KCF. Kincaid Charles Falk.

I put the bags with the liver and the kidneys back in the tray—threw them, actually. Besides being BSL 3 contaminants, these were from a guy who had been gutted and buried in the woods. Handling them like this had to be bad karma.

There were specimen containers—small plastic jars with screw caps—on the shelves below the organs, also a tray for Falcon tubes that looked like they were filled with blood. I pulled a tray that held about a dozen of the specimen jars. Again, "KCF" was written on each. And there was something else. A piece of paper enclosed in a plastic bag.

With some difficulty I managed to replace the tray and grab hold of the page. Through the frosted plastic, I could make out a standard contact page, who was responsible for the items in the freezer, how to get in touch with them in case of emergency, et cetera. *KCF organs and tissue* was written neatly in a space near the top. Underneath, next to the word *Contact,* was a name I did not want to see, along with cell phone and pager numbers. Her familiar signature graced the bottom of the page. Alaine Chen.

Suddenly, it made sense why Alaine's ID didn't work in the lab, why she was being locked out.

Harriet Tobel was not the only one who had been set up.

CHAPTER 98

I slammed the freezer door shut and ran into the lab, ran for Harriet Tobel's private office. This door wasn't locked. Not a surprise, considering Falk wanted this place to be open for the police the next morning. I was convinced Ian Carrington was in on it, too. Feeding Alaine the lines about Dr. Tobel's setup, letting Alaine think she had a confidant.

In the office, I opened the unlocked credenza. What had been empty two days ago was now half-full. I began tearing out hanging file folders, throwing them to the desk, opening them the best I could with my throbbing left hand and handcuffed right. Everything was here. Well, everything that could have directly linked Harriet Tobel and

Alaine Chen to the disasters of the past few weeks. There were biopsy records for Douglas Buchanan. The pages were signed by Randall Jefferson and stapled to FedEx airbills addressed to and countersigned by Alaine Chen. Medical records detailing physical exams for Douglas. Neurological exams. And that name—*Alaine, Alaine, Alaine*—on all of the receipts. God forgive her, because she knoweth not what she did. Alaine, who was always in control, who always made the calculated first move—whether it be to leave a young Nate McCormick or to leak information to an older Nate McCormick—had been duped.

Deeper into the files, I dug out a folder filled with bits and pieces of paper: telephone numbers, what looked like instructions for wiring money to a bank account. There was also a CV of sorts there: Richard Craw. Seems the guy worked for the CIA for a while, then for a bunch of private security firms. I guessed the Surgeon did have an actual name; he hadn't just crawled from the script of some straight-to-video thriller.

Richard Craw. Great name. Not great for Dr. Tobel's legacy or Alaine Chen's future. Though neither Dr. Tobel's nor Alaine's name appeared anywhere in this file, its placement in this lab sure as hell did not look good.

I spent a few more minutes blazing through what was left and, not finding anything good, stopped, feeling sick to my stomach. The desk, the top of the credenza, and the floor were all littered with paper. I gathered the incriminating things together in a clumsy stack and looked around for a bag or box to dump them in.

Back into the lab. On a bench I found a plastic box filled with bottles of ethanol and whatever other mix of flammable crap. I dumped the contents onto the bench, creating another hazardous-materials violation. Murder aside, if the university sent an inspection team in here, now *that* would be bad.

I put the files in the plastic box and I began to think.

Alaine was implicated by all of this, sure. I mean, her name was everywhere; the organs from the dead man in Baltimore were in the lab she ran with Dr. Tobel. A wee bit incriminating. But for her and Dr. Tobel to be responsible for everything—KC Falk, Gladys Thomas, the attacks on Brooke and me—well, that would be a stretch. Especially if she were able to defend herself, to implicate Ian and Otto. If it came to that, she would—I knew this much about the girl—bring down everyone and everything.

So, it wouldn't come to that. Otto and Ian wouldn't let her run to South America. They couldn't, I was sure, take a chance on her talking. "Otto has too much at stake," Alaine had told me. "Don't be naïve about him."

Well, I was becoming less and less naïve; I really began to panic.

I turned on my cell phone, got Alaine's number, and dialed out from a landline in the lab. No rings; voice mail picked up immediately.

"Come on, Alaine. . . ." I dialed again just in case and got the same.

I booted up the computer, hoping that in the new lax security of the Tobel lab, I wouldn't need a password. I needed Alaine's home address. If she wasn't there, I'd hit the Chimeragen offices, then—goddamn it— I suppose I'd come back here ag—

"Dr. McCormick."

I swung around and could not believe what I saw. Richard Craw. The Surgeon.

CHAPTER 99

He stood there, face alive with angry welts and blisters, tears slicking his cheeks. His skin was stained yellow from the acid and small burn holes pocked his shirt and jacket. The silencer on the gun in his hand extended from the barrel like a black roll of LifeSavers.

Not good.

He blinked twice, looked at me, then at the files spread all over the room, the box of files on the desk. "It seems we had the same idea." I didn't respond, so he offered, "We're both trying to clean house."

Grasping for the moral high ground, and white-lying a little to do so, I answered, "I'm not cleaning anything."

He cranked back the slide on the gun, chambering a bullet.

Okay, that was a nonstarter. I scrambled for something else to say, something to give me a little time to think. "How did you get off the highway?"

The corners of his mouth pulled to a smile; this guy obviously took some pride in his work. "Less than three minutes to get into my car and wash my eyes enough to drive. The police can't respond in three minutes."

"Wow."

The smile crumpled.

I sure didn't seem to be winning any points here. I said, "They're setting you up. You realize that. You and Alaine Chen and Harriet Tobel."

"I know."

"They're trying to link you to Dr. Tobel—"

"I know."

My face must have betrayed my confusion, and he went on to explain. "That is why I am here, Dr. McCormick. To clean house. Then I pay a visit to your friends. I will not become anyone's scapegoat."

Good for you, I thought. In any case, if he was going to pay *my friends* a visit, he must know where they are. In that, I thought I glimpsed an opportunity, though what good it could do me at that point, I didn't know. Truly. My superior powers of deduction told me that I was, to put it crassly, fucked. "Where are they?"

He didn't answer me, but said, "These doctors, they think they control everything. They don't. Nobody does. You don't control a virus, and you don't control a man, Dr. McCormick."

I thought that was a pretty philosophical statement from an assassin, but I guess this guy had a lot of opportunity to contemplate the bigger questions in life: power, influence, death.

He blinked again, squeezing out the tears. The scene was incongruous: the killer weeping, the gun pointed at my chest. I guessed he was having some trouble with the peepers. I began to raise my right hand slowly, elbow at my side, making sure to keep the cuffs from clinking.

"You don't have to do this. Tell me where Alaine is and I'll forget I ever saw you; I'll forget I know your name."

"You know my name?"

Oops.

My hand was now at about eight o'clock and rising.

"I thought you were different, Dr. McCormick. I thought you could see the angles."

He was getting very Chandleresque with all this "cleaning house" and "angles" talk. I was about to tell him I'd keep everything on the "quiet tip" and that he should "keep his shirt on," but his head jerked toward my hand before my big mouth got me in more trouble.

"Lower it," he snapped.

I obeyed, but I had the information I needed. To wit, the man was partially blind. Like me, he couldn't see all the angles anymore. He knew this, I guessed. He wanted to reduce the angles by one.

"I'm sorry," he said. The words sounded very final. I could feel my limbs going weak.

"So am I."

As the Surgeon raised the gun, I made my move: I grabbed the top file in the box and flung it at him, falling sideways as I did so. A jet of papers streamed toward him and fell across the desk a second later, but it was enough. Two dull thumps pulsed from the gun, and I heard the sound of breaking glass.

Then I scrambled for the door.

This move was a bit dicey, since the man stood between me and it. I rammed him with my shoulder as I passed, knocking him off balance. The gun spat again, and I felt a hand grab at my shirt.

In the lab. I dove for the light switch on the far wall, and though I never heard the shot, I felt something skip over my left arm. I yelped. At least he got the left, which was already useless. Like two flat tires on a car, the second one is just cosmetic. Well, cosmetic and painful.

My fingers slapped the wall and raked down. Except for the fluorescents from Dr. Tobel's office and the thin light seeping from the window in the main door, the lab fell to darkness. I keyed in to the square of light in the door and ran.

Another thump and something from the wall—plaster or wood chips—stung my face. Screw the door. I bolted for the far end of the room and rolled behind a lab bench.

Killing the lights did the trick. In the gloom, I could make out the Surgeon as he moved along the wall, left hand feeling the way, gun pointed in my general direction. The oddity of the situation struck me. If I hadn't been fearing for my life, it would have had comic potential: "One-Arm versus Blind Man." I could already see the Hollywood possibilities.

Blood from my left shoulder wet my arm. As the Surgeon groped toward the light switch, I fingered the wound, winced, and determined it was just a graze.

There was an old centrifuge on the lab bench in front of me. I cranked it to thirteen thousand rpms and turned it on. The Surgeon fired a shot in my direction; it slammed into something inches behind me. I turned on a suction hose, hoping the noise would drown out the sound of my movements.

I pawed along the lab bench, desperate for anything I could use. The best I found was a hemostat forceps, an odd hybrid that crossed scissors with tweezers. Not my choice of weaponry, but any port in a storm. I grabbed it.

The Surgeon was at the door, his hand sweeping up and down along the wall.

The lights blazed to full and I ran.

My left shoulder bit into his hips. I cried out as pain lanced through my fresh wound, but the impact knocked him against the wall and sent the gun sailing. Before I could drop the hemostat and grab for the door handle, I felt hands cup my head. A knee drove hard into my chin.

Contact, I realized too late, erased any advantage I'd had from his blindness. Not to mention that the last time I'd engaged in hand-to-hand combat was with an Xbox at a friend's place in Atlanta, and I lost against the computer every time. You'd think I'd learn.

My head kicked back and I fell hard on my ass. Somehow the hemostat didn't slip from my hand, but the mano a mano crap was truly working against me. The Surgeon gripped my left hand and twisted the gauze like he was cranking a motorcycle throttle. I screamed. The hemostat tumbled from my good hand.

He was on top of me now, hands moving incredibly fast, skating up my body, settling on my neck. He clamped down. I coughed, actually a squeak, because he was pressing so damned hard. In another few seconds, my trachea would be crushed and I'd be chatting it up with Dr. Tobel at the pearly gates.

Frantically, I began pawing the floor. My fingers brushed the stainless steel of the hemostat; I grabbed the handle and braced it on the meat of my palm. Then I drove it as hard as I could into the Surgeon's back.

It sank.

I must have missed the ribs, because the pointed end buried a good three inches into flesh. The Surgeon grunted, then clawed at his back. Fingers found the hemostat and he tore it from his body. Quickly—he was so goddamned fast—the instrument was across the room and his hands were back at my throat. I'd barely managed to bring my right hand up and get it between his hands and my neck.

Still, he pressed. Fingers slipped and slapped; I grappled, coughed, and gagged. But his grip was becoming weaker.

Finally, he slackened enough that I was able to break his grip. I shoved and kicked, and pushed the man off me. The pistol lay a few yards away. I crawled over to it, fumbled to get it situated in my hand, turned, and sat. The Surgeon was on his side now. My wounds throbbed.

Unsteadily, I got to my feet, stumbled over to the vacuum hose and centrifuge, and turned them off. The silence was nearly complete, except for the Surgeon's raspy breathing. I pulled down my jacket and looked at my left arm, where blood stained the shirt. Not too bad, actually. I tore open my shirt, popping a few buttons. Kimwipes, which I'd always used to clean slides and microscope lenses, would do a good job of stanching blood, I figured. I grabbed some and pressed them to the tear in my flesh.

Now that the adrenaline was gone, everything began to hurt—my hand, the old gunshot wound in my right deltoid, the new wound over my left acromion—it all really began to hurt.

Like the soundtrack to some B horror flick, the Surgeon's breathing became more and more labored.

"You need to get to a hospital," I said.

"You're a doctor."

I walked to a phone, slid the gun into my left armpit, and picked up the receiver.

"Don't do that," the Surgeon said.

"You need to be in a hospital."

"Do not touch the phone."

I held the phone for a moment, then placed it back in the cradle and edged closer to the Surgeon. His breathing was difficult, desperate almost. He sat up and hunched over his crossed legs, as if he'd just blasted through a hundred yards at top speed.

"Take off your jacket," I told him. He raised his head and glared at me. Many times, people have looked at me as though they wanted to kill me—patients whom I'm sticking for blood for the fourth time in a day, Brooke Michaels most of the time—but never as if they would actually follow through, never with such malevolence. Creepy.

Slowly, the Surgeon removed his sport coat and dropped it to the floor, revealing the crimson splotch on the back of his shirt below the shoulder blade. The bore of the hemostat was small, and the muscles between the ribs would have closed the tiny hole. Though this seems to be a good thing—this self-sealing of a chest wound—it was the worst of possibilities for the Surgeon.

He pushed himself to his knees, then pulled himself upright, heaving breath into his lungs.

"Stop." I raised the gun, gripped it tight.

He moved toward the door, little shuffling steps.

"Stop."

He kept moving. The bastard seemed to know I wouldn't shoot him, so I did the next-best thing. I put down the gun and again picked up the phone.

He heard me and, finally, stopped.

"Where are they?" I asked.

"You help me," he said weakly.

"Tell me where they are."

He said nothing, but braced himself on the lab bench. His breathing was becoming both shallower and more forced. It didn't take three years of residency to know the man had what's called a pneumothorax, literally, "air in the chest." I guessed the hemostat had pierced his lung. With each breath in, he filled the lung; with each breath out, the Surgeon was forcing air through that little tear, into the space between the lung and the chest wall. Since the hole in his back had closed, the air could not escape. One lung was collapsed from the puncture, and, with each breath, he was compressing the other. The air pressure would squeeze his heart, too, not allowing blood to fill it during relaxation. Too much air in the wrong places.

"You'll suffocate," I said. It wasn't a good way to die. The man standing before me had at most a few minutes. "Tell me where they are."

The Surgeon didn't respond. He placed both hands on the bench, blinking madly, the tears flowing out of his eyes. His face was a mask of wet, yellow, blistered skin. "You help me."

"Yes," I said.

"You . . . first."

I thought about that for a second, thought about the bargain we were negotiating with monosyllables. Being the good doctor I am, I chose the only viable option for me.

"Okay."

What I needed was a stiff tube: a ballpoint pen, maybe, a small-gauge pipe. Moving around the lab, opening drawers, tossing aside boxes, I found nothing useful. The plastic pipettes were too flimsy, Pasteur pipettes too thin. Not a goddamned ballpoint pen to be found. His breathing was becoming shallower and faster.

There was a small cell culture room across the lab. I glanced at the Surgeon, now sagging over on the lab bench and growing weaker by the moment. I walked the several yards to the space where Dr. Tobel's lab trolls grew their cells. Inside, I found what I was looking for: a box filled with thick glass cell culture pipettes. Ten-inch tubes that, unlike the thin Pasteurs, wouldn't shatter. Perfect. Wedging the gun under my left arm to free up my right, I took one and crossed back to the Surgeon.

"Don't move," I said, but he was too weak to respond.

I pulled his bloodied dress shirt over his head and, well, the surprises never end. On his left flank, running just below the twelfth rib, was a ten-inch horizontal scar. The only thing I could think of that would yield a scar like that was an open nephrectomy. It looked like the Surgeon, Mr. Richard Craw, killer of dogs and people, tormentor of the good guys, had donated a kidney.

To get a good point on the pipette, I smashed the end against the lab bench. The Surgeon jerked.

"What are you doing?"

"I need to let the air out of your chest."

He began to push himself up. "No."

"You'll suffocate."

He seemed not to care, and I spent the next ninety seconds watching a man die.

It was grueling to see. The whole scene had that sick rhythm I see in nature shows, where the wildebeest or elephant or whatever bleeds and struggles and dies over the course of what seems like hours. I am not good at this stuff, at just standing by. But I forced myself to wait; I stepped back and put the gun on the lab bench and watched the terrible show.

The Surgeon steadied himself on the lab bench and managed one step before having to rest. I suppose he was trying to get to the door, but he had to know he'd never make it. He took another step and another, but that seemed to be all he could do. Pressure was rising in his chest, squeezing air from his one good lung, squeezing blood from his heart. He placed both hands on the bench. For a moment, he held that position—a last stand—then collapsed to the floor.

Broken pipette in hand, I ran. His breathing was too shallow, too fast. He was hypoxic now and might have already lost consciousness; I couldn't tell. I yanked up the shirt. The hole from the hemostat was below and lateral to the scapula, where the muscle mass was lowest and where it would be easiest to gain access to the chest cavity. I'd been lucky on that first strike. And what worked once . . .

I raised the jagged glass tube, targeted the bloody dot, and stabbed.

Glass ripped through flesh, the Surgeon convulsed, and I heard the sweet sound of rushing air.

Strong work, Doctor.

Air continued to blow through the large-bore tube for a few seconds, reducing the pressure in the Surgeon's chest. A pause, then he heaved a great gulp of air into his good lung. Almost immediately, he began to squirm. Leaving the pipette in place, I scrambled off him and back to the gun.

"Don't move—you'll break the glass."

He didn't listen, and slowly got himself to a sitting position. His shirt caught on the glass and he winced; he reached around to his back. "Leave it there," I said.

He retracted his arm like some primordial sea beast slithering its tentacle. Then we sat in silence: I with the gun, the Surgeon with his ersatz chest tube.

Finally, I said, "You gave a kidney."

He nodded.

"Otto Falk did the work?"

"No," he breathed. "But it is why I took the job. That and the money."

"Who was the recipient?"

The Surgeon shook his head. "Why do you care, Dr. McCormick?"

I didn't know. Curiosity, maybe. Curiosity at the paradox of the man in front of me.

"My brother," he said haltingly. "He died anyway. Dead brother, and I have one kidney." The Surgeon paused, grabbing more air. "Too late for us, but it'd be nice if the pig thing worked out."

I asked, "Where are they?"

"I tell you, and we go our separate ways."

"Yes."

He took a few noisy breaths. Then he said, "The offices."

"The company? Chimeragen? Alaine is there?"

"That's what they told me. They wanted me to go there tonight."

To kill her, I thought.

So, now I had what I was looking for. Our pact was made. This was my cue to edge out of the room, let the guy get himself to a hospital or some ancient Nazi doctor refugee, wherever killers go to get fixed up. But I didn't move; I didn't know what to do.

"You need to go," the Surgeon said. "Your friends will wait for only so long before they do it themselves. They're scared. They're making bad decisions."

Well, I didn't want to place myself in their company, so I made a good decision. Bad for the Surgeon, sure. But screw him. I picked up the phone.

"What are you doing?" the Surgeon asked.

I dialed 911, gave the dispatcher the lowdown—that I had disabled the man who'd killed two police officers in Gilroy—along with location and my name.

"No—" the Surgeon said. He'd risen to his feet.

"Sit," I yelled.

The dispatcher asked what was going on. The Surgeon hobbled toward me. "You *liar*—"

I dropped the phone, grabbed the gun. And I did what I hoped I never would have to do, what I never envisioned myself doing.

I fired two shots.

One caught the Surgeon in the knee. He yelled as the bullet kicked his leg from under him and he went to the floor. Groaning, he began pulling himself toward me.

"Stop!"

He kept coming, and my hand, with gun and handcuffs, quivered like a fishtail. The grip was slippery with sweat. "Stop!" I fired a bullet into the floor in front of him.

He stopped.

The dispatcher on the other end of the line was squawking away— "Sir? Sir?" coming out of the receiver over and over again. I yelled for her to get someone over here immediately.

The Surgeon was splayed on the floor between the two benches, gasping, blood pouring from his shattered knee, tears pouring from his eyes. Quickly, I stepped past him. I found a roll of gauze and threw it to him.

"Put this on."

He just lay there, bleeding and weeping.

"Put it on!"

"We had a deal," he said.

"You should have checked my CV. I'm a cheat and a liar. They never told you that?"

Guess not.

As the Surgeon reached for gauze and began to bind his leg, I heard sirens. Nothing like gunfire and high-decibel dialogue to generate some get-up-and-go in the 911 system. I took another roll of gauze to wrap my arm.

"I'm going to kill you, Dr. McCormick."

Tires screeched.

"Looking forward to it." Another little lie, but I'd been lying all my life, right? It was easy at this point.

Having more pressing things to do than answer questions for the police and campus security, I left, the Surgeon's threats—"I'm going to kill you, Dr. McCormick, I'm going to kill you"—following me like a stench down the hallway.

CHAPTER 100

Avoiding the police on my way out the back door of the building, I'd like to say I was thinking about nothing but Alaine. Rescuing the damsel in distress, all that fairy-tale stuff. Truth is, I was pretty taken with slaying my own dragons. I'd nearly been killed, I'd just shot somebody, I was scared about what I'd find at Chimeragen. And I'd fucking lied—big, bald-faced, unabashed. We'd had a deal, the Surgeon and I. And I'd betrayed him.

The greater sin would have been to let the son of a bitch back into the world, but that betrayal seemed to shine a bright light on my deepest flaws. Maybe a moral man would have figured an honorable way out of the situation with the Surgeon. Maybe, as I said, I am a cheat and a liar. When the chips are down—when my career is on the line, when I want to protect a mentor's honor, when I want to save us from a murderer— maybe the only way I can do it is through obscuring and neglecting the truth. And if you examine the odds, you'll see I tend to screw up anyway: I wrecked on my career path; all the papers detailing Harriet Tobel's involvement with the Chimeragen fiasco would soon be in the hands of the police. At least the Surgeon would go to jail.

What a fantastic stand-up guy you are, Nate McCormick.

I pulled into the parking lot at Chimeragen. My head was really spinning now with pain and apprehension. Plywood covered the hole on the front door where I'd broken out the window. Guess scheming and double-crossing didn't give you time to call the glass company.

I popped the clip from the gun and counted four bullets, five with the one in the chamber.

Under the eaves of the building, a camera blinked. I didn't need my buddies inside to know that it was me, and not the Surgeon, come to pay them a visit. I steadied the gun on my left arm, aimed, and shot into the camera. Amazingly, I hit it. In its death throes, the thing threw out some sparks and smoke. Satisfying.

I pounded on the plywood with the butt of the gun.

After thirty seconds or so, I heard motion on the knob. I raised the pistol, stiffening my arm as much as I could, gripping the life out of the slippery handle. I would be goddamned if I'd let these guys see me shake.

The door opened.

"Hello, Ian," I said.

Carrington had a pistol in his hand, which he promptly dropped. Maybe it was the gun in my hand, maybe it was how I looked—bloodied, bandaged, the cuffs giving me an S & M flair. Whatever the cause, Carrington was more Nervous Nellie than I and lost his advantage.

Reflexively, he tried to regain advantage and reached down. But I was looped on pain and adrenaline and was feeling kind of Charles Bronson at the moment; I stepped forward, jabbing the gun into his chest. "Don't even think about it," I warned as I kicked the gun away from him. The Surgeon would have been proud.

Carrington stood straight and backed up a step, surprised, I suppose, at the hardass in front of him. The man looked as though he'd slept as little as I had; bags hung under his eyes, and the muscles on his face sagged. *Plotting to destroy your fiancée really takes it out of you,* I thought.

"You're making a mistake," he said.

"Where is she?"

Carrington didn't move. I jabbed the gun again, felt it bite into the flesh. "Stop that," he said.

"Where is she?"

Carrington kept his eyes on mine and backed up through the door. He looked at the gun on the floor, and I felt like he was considering another jump for it, but he managed some wisdom and turned slowly, led me through the inner door to the offices behind. A light was on in the conference room ahead where Otto Falk had given me his sermon and tried to involve me in his plan to save thousands, his plan to cover up the terrible costs.

"He's here?" I heard Falk say from the room ahead.

Quietly, Carrington answered, "Yes, he is."

I jammed the gun hard between Carrington's shoulder blades. He stumbled forward into the room, swearing. I followed.

The shock on Falk's face was, to say the least, gratifying. I could really get into this gun thing, except that firearms made me so anxious it was all I could do to keep mine from swinging back and forth like a blind man's cane. And there was the problem of the other guys' guns. Weapons were like rats—where there's one . . .

Anyway, Alaine was there and, thank God, not lying in a pool of blood on the floor. She sat in a chair at one end of the conference table, arms crossed in front of her. Same outfit I'd seen her in earlier. The gloss of tears was still on her cheeks. She seemed neither surprised nor happy to see me. She seemed already to have left for that South American beach.

Falk stood at the other end of the conference table from Alaine, holding, of course, a gun. He raised it inexpertly at me, elbow bent, pistol at waist level. Again, I was struck at how silly this was, all these guns in the hands of folks who'd probably never touched one before. I mean, Carrington dropped his at the first sign of trouble; Falk looked like he was holding a used air-sickness bag.

This was not our world. And we were all making a hash of things.

I suppose Falk was trying to think his way out of the hole he was in, and his lips pulled taut. "Dr. McCormick—"

"Stand over there," I snarled at Carrington, jerking the gun toward Falk, a move I'd learned from too many childhood hours in front of the TV. Ian shuffled over and stood next to the surgeon, the two of them in front of a rosewood magazine rack filled with business and medical journals.

"Richard Craw," I said.

"Who?" Falk asked, so obviously playing dumb it was embarrassing.

"Richard Craw is with the police now," I said. "Put the gun down, Dr. Falk."

"Why on earth would I do that?" His voice was steady, but I could see the end of his gun begin to jiggle. He gripped the butt with two hands.

"Because this is over." I took a step toward the older man. "Because Mr. Craw is going to help himself. He's going to tell them everything that will save his own skin. You know that. And you know what he says will not help you." I added, "He told me you were here."

I took another step. Falk raised the gun a few inches.

"The police are on their way here now." *Lies, lies, lies, McCormick.*

All was quiet for a moment, until Falk, suddenly furious, exploded. "You cannot do this," he said. "You cannot destroy everything I've accomplished. I will *not* allow you to do so."

"You've destroyed it yourself. I want to give you some advice: Save what you can. Accept responsibility. I will do what I can to see the research finds a home."

I glanced at Alaine. She watched the happenings with that same serene, detached look on her face. Eerie. She'd always been good at that, at shutting down in fraught situations. It had been her MO during our breakup. Christ, she'd done it only a few hours before, as we walked through the campus. Still, I couldn't help but wonder what was going on behind those eyes. Maybe she was thinking that despite being given something of a reprieve by her old boyfriend, she was going to spend a good amount of time in jail. Maybe she was thinking that betrayal is a bitch.

She shifted her eyes to her fiancé. Maybe she was thinking she'd like to cut the balls off the venture capitalist. If so, I'd pass her the scalpel.

"What do you want, Nate?" Ian Carrington said.

"What?"

"You want a million dollars? Two million?"

"Shut up," Falk said. My sentiments exactly. But Carrington plowed ahead.

"We can get you—let's see—probably two and a half million, maybe three. We can do that, can't we, Otto? We could do it tomorrow, first thing."

Alaine was looking now at Carrington; her face wasn't blank anymore, but settling somewhere between fury and disgust. *At least he's rich, right, Alaine?*

Anyway, the drama playing out between Ian and Alaine was not really my concern at that moment; ending the botched standoff was. "Alaine," I said. Her head swiveled slowly toward me. "There's a gun next to the receptionist's desk outside. Get it." Like a zombie, she rose from the chair and left the room.

All was silent but for the spinning of gears in Otto Falk's head.

Ian again, continuing some conversation in which he was the only active participant: "Three million. I can make some calls tomorrow and have three million dollars wired to your account—"

Falk sighed loudly. "It is over. You are right, Dr. McCormick." He placed the gun on the table.

"What are you doing?" Carrington squeaked.

Ignoring him, Falk said, "Work with me to see that what I've done is not lost."

"Of course," I said.

"It would be a tragedy if all this"—he waved his hand around—"if all of it were to be wasted." And like the air from the Surgeon's chest cavity, tension left the room. I couldn't help but admire this man—a man who'd both saved lives and taken them—just a little, just for a second.

"Bill Steadman at the University of Pittsburgh has been interested in this," he said.

"Bill Steadman. I will call him."

"Good."

Carrington made a move for the gun on the table. I raised mine. "Don't."

He froze. "What the hell is wrong with you?" he breathed. "Three million dollars. I can get more if you give me time."

I wanted to shoot the guy in the mouth just to get him to shut up. At that moment, though, I heard something behind me and turned. Alaine. She held the gun in front of her, more expertly than I would have thought. Perhaps we watched the same TV shows as kids.

"You can put the gun down," I said to her. "And get that one." I nodded toward the pistol on the table. She didn't lower her arm as she reached across the table and took Falk's weapon.

"Call the police, Alaine."

She didn't move.

"So, the police weren't on their way," Falk said.

I shrugged and he nodded. He seemed exhausted and—I might have been reading into things—relieved, as if finally all this was over and he could let events take their course. I repeated, "Alaine, call the police."

She stood next to me, one gun raised, the other dangling from her left hand.

"They were going to kill me," she whispered.

"Maybe," I said, "but now they're not. Get the phone." She didn't stir. "Alaine!"

Volume seemed to break the spell. She lowered the weapon and walked to the phone.

"Don't, Alaine." It was Carrington again. "What do you want, sweetie? All my money? Everything? You have the gun now, love. Make him let us go, and you can have everyth—"

"Shut up!" I yelled.

"Ian . . ." Falk said.

Alaine didn't even look up.

She dialed the phone, spoke with the 911 dispatcher. Too calmly, I thought. Like an android. I heard her replace the receiver.

"You bitch," Ian whispered.

"*Shut up,*" I said. I looked over my shoulder and saw Alaine held only one of the guns. "You can put that down," I said.

"Are we going to prison?" She asked it in a faint voice, as if she were very far away. In a way, she was.

"I don't know. You helped me. That will . . . I'm sure they'll take that into consideration."

She made no acknowledgment she'd heard me. She said, "My life is over."

"No it's not. Come on. Put down the gun."

"They were going to kill me, Nate."

"And now they can't touch you. Put the gun down."

"We were suppose to go away and he was going to kill me."

"Alaine, put down the goddamned gun."

"Why did he do this to me?" She brought her other hand to the handle of the gun. "They wanted to blame me for everything."

"What are you doing?" Carrington barked, adding to the poison in the room.

"Shut up! Alaine, put down the—"

"They wanted to kill me."

"Alaine!"

She pulled the trigger twice.

Ian Carrington's head jerked from the bullet's impact. I yelled, dropped my gun, and swung around.

Falk blurted, "Wha—?" as a bullet tore into his chest, knocking him into a chair.

"Alaine!" I swung around to see her staring at me, really staring, aware. Her eyes were wide; breath caught in her throat as she sucked air in tiny gasps. She looked terrified.

Things were happening too fast. I raised my arm, opened my palm, handcuffs swinging, trying to be as gentle as I could, trying to break through and stop her from doing what she was going to do. Nothing I'd ever learned—nothing in med school, nothing in residency, nothing in life—helped me out here. I stepped toward her. She drew up the gun, slid the barrel under her chin. "Nate . . ." she said.

I screamed "No!" and leapt at her.

The gun went off.

We landed in a tangle, like the lovers we'd once been, my body on top of hers. I felt the softness of her belly on my arm, the angle of her elbow in my gut. But we were no longer lovers; this was no longer that more innocent time. The woman underneath me betrayed no movement of breath, no life.

The bullet had ripped off the top of her head, leaving a mash of blood, brain matter, hair. The beautiful face was wide-eyed and staring, her pale skin spattered with crimson. The lips that I'd kissed a thousand times made small smacking motions, reflexes only. Her leg jerked with little spasms. Urine stained the khaki pants.

Otto Falk had been thrown back into a chair, slumped, his arms splayed wide in a mockery of a crucifixion pose, a red splash in the middle of his chest. Ian Carrington lay twisted on the floor. I couldn't see his wound, but I did see pieces of mortality sprayed across the magazine shelves, mixed with the glossy print.

The white ceiling above Alaine was red.

I sat, coughed, spit some bile onto my pants. I put my head into my hands to block out images I knew I'd see for the rest of my life. I breathed slowly, trying to get some control, but it was no use. I wept.

CHAPTER 101

Three funerals occurred over the next week. Otto Falk's in Pittsburgh, Ian Carrington's in Cambridge, and the last one in a tiny town between San Francisco and San Jose, where Alaine's family lived. I attended only the last.

It was a small affair in a Chinese Catholic church, understandably not well publicized. Alaine's parents, brother, and sister were there, but we didn't speak. They'd been suffering through questions from the FBI and the county detectives and anybody else who could get their hooks into such a sordid case. Perhaps they felt embarrassed. Perhaps they blamed me for their daughter's death. In any case, I didn't care. The Chen clan could deal with whatever emotional weather Alaine's suicide had churned up. They didn't need my help.

As it wasn't far to go for the funeral, and as we were now something of an item, Brooke Michaels accompanied me. We must have made quite a pair: Brooke on crutches, me with a lump of bandaged hand dangling at my side. I thought of those 1918 pics of wounded soldiers back from the trenches in France, parading.

Brooke swore as one of the crutches caught on a crack in the sidewalk. The bullet had cut an artery, but had missed major nerves, so her leg would return to one hundred percent after a few months and some hard therapy. I was happy about the leg and, well, about the surrounding regions.

Unfortunately for me, my situation was more uncertain; it wasn't clear if I'd regain full function of my left hand. The surgeon hadn't given the appendage a death sentence, nor could he say everything would be okay. Only the outcome of my reconstructive surgery and months of physical therapy would tell.

As for the organs of government, well, they can move fast when they want to. And in the few days after the bloodbath at Chimeragen, they wanted to. The night of Alaine's death, I had only a few moments to struggle with my grief before the fire hose of law enforcement was turned on Chimeragen, spraying what seemed like a thousand officers and techs into the building. I watched them like I'd watch a movie: camera dollies back, revealing Nate McCormick wrapped in a blanket, sitting in one of the offices, snot dripping from his nose, answering inane questions that really didn't matter anymore. Drifting through my fugue state, I wondered if this was how Alaine had felt that last night. Maybe. At least until the bullets had already torn through flesh and she looked at me with that last terrible, terrified face. But by then it was too late.

Goddamn you, Nate McCormick. If there is a Hell, you'll be in it, a special circle reserved for the stupid, for those who can't see "all the angles," for those who can't move fast enough, for those who try and fail to be the hero. When you need a rest, you'll vacation at a bubbling lake of lava reserved for liars.

Later that evening, I spent hours at the police station, giving my fiftieth account of the incidents. They asked me about the Surgeon, and I told them to ask the Surgeon. They asked me about Harriet Tobel and I told them to ask her. They either didn't get it or didn't appreciate my wit or both. I might have been shirking my civic duty by being a pain in the ass, but it really didn't matter, did it? Everyone was dead or in custody. Dead, mostly. Justice had been served in a perverse sort of way.

The FBI had split the seams of the Chimeragen corporate offices, the organ farm in Gilroy, the Tobel and Falk labs. The forensic geniuses from Quantico had managed to salvage quite a bit more than the scattering of papers I'd left in Dr. Tobel's office. Computers were pulled apart, hard drives anatomized. They even rescued some evidence from the Surgeon's bonfire. These guys—with their toothbrushes and X-rays—really were good. I only wished they'd been good a few days earlier; it might have spared some bloodshed. But I didn't know what the evidence would do for them. I mean, who was left to prosecute? Maybe Bill Dyson, the vet. I hoped not.

It turned out there were quite a few people left to prosecute. Randall Jefferson, for one. I'd gotten a call from Detective John Myers that the good doctor had been arrested and arraigned and was out on bail, contemplating life's big questions on his estate north of Baltimore. Myers assured me that the fraud case against him looked strong, and in perfect Myers-speak, he said the conspiracy and accessory-to-murder charges against Jefferson had "foundational promise to deliver." In any case, the state had stepped in to take over Jefferson's group homes.

A few bigwigs at the FDA had also taken hits. It wasn't until a few days later that we found out who, exactly, Otto Falk and Ian Carrington had been talking to. A number were on administrative leave while their comrades there figured out what to do with them and figured out who else would fall. The FBI knew damn well what to do with them: you could almost hear the sound of knives being sharpened in Washington.

So, while the forces of law enforcement whipped themselves into a frenzy, committed to taking down as many bureaucrats as possible, the forces of public health were finally able to take a breather. According to Dr. Verlach, the clampdown on group homes in Baltimore had effectively extinguished the miniepidemic there, though we ended up losing one more person to the disease. Ben Vallo—intrepid explorer of biology's terra incognita—left me a message that the Junin-HIV virus did, indeed, match virus in Debbie Fillmore's tissue, as well as virus in the tissues of all the other sick folks in Maryland. I didn't tell him that Alaine Chen had told me as much; I didn't want to hear the stream of profanity when Ben realized he'd pulled an all-nighter for nothing. In any case, we had an unfortunate new player on the viral scene. I prayed the genie was back in the bottle and would stay there, but as these things go, it was probably wishful thinking. For the time being, though, the genie was in an actual bottle, sitting in some BSL 3 freezer in Atlanta.

If there was any good that came out of this wreckage, it was that Bill Steadman, the transplant surgeon at Pitt, did indeed have interest in Dr. Falk's work. Steadman was shocked when I called him, of course, saddened that the transplant world had lost one of its luminaries under such circumstances. He must have known, too, that Dr. Falk's data would be political poison for a few years, so he really did shoulder a burden in taking responsibility for what was left. He told me he would talk with the FDA, gather the data, speak with the families, and see what could be salvaged. There was little upside for him in the near term, and a lot of headache and heartache. His selflessness and career-be-damned swagger led me to believe he was the perfect choice to direct the second act. I comforted myself with the thought that someday, some kid who'd been written off as hopeless would be peeing volumes with his brand-new porcine kidney.

Alaine's funeral service ended, and Brooke and I opted not to go to the interment. I didn't need to see Dr. Chen's coffin lowered into the ground. I'd seen quite enough for closure's sake.

So we dragged our sorry corpses to yet another rental car. Our wounds meant no stick shift for a while, so Brooke's BMW would get a good rest. The wounds—Brooke's, actually—meant that I would be driving for the foreseeable future. I climbed into the driver's seat. Brooke stretched out her legs and rested on her left hip. Her hand was on my leg.

"You okay?"

I wondered why she asked that, until I realized I'd been sitting, frozen, with my hand on the car keys for God knows how long.

"Sure," I said, but it was another lie. Though things had calmed down in the head, once in a while something would pop: snapshots of bodies draining blood onto a conference room floor, the sucking sound of the Surgeon's stab wound, worries about whether the Surgeon would somehow beat his prosecution and make good on his threats. And then there was Alaine: her face just before she blew out the top of her head, my impotence to stop her.

Anyway, I figured the best way to handle the meshugas was not to think about it. Let the shrink deal if it came to that. The tactic seemed to be for shit, though.

I started the car. "I'm fine. Really."

Brooke reached over and turned off the vehicle.

"What are you doing?"

She shushed me and kissed my cheek. She kissed my forehead, my nose, my eyes, my chin, my lips. A hundred tiny contacts covering my face like raindrops.

When she finished, she reached to the ignition and restarted the car.

"Where to now, Doc?" she asked.

Brooke and I had rented a small cottage a few hours north of San Francisco, near Eureka. There was a good small hospital there, with adjunct physical therapy. Actually, I didn't know if the hospital or the physical therapy was quality, but it was far from the Bay Area and far from any CDC outpost. That made it good. We'd put down money for a month's rental; one of my pet projects for the past few days was trying to figure out how to get reimbursed by my employer. Not much progress on that front.

Brooke asked, "No Tim Lancaster?"

"Tim who?"

She smiled and shook her head.

I was supposed to meet Tim in an hour at the Santa Clara Health Department, but had no intention of doing so. Surprisingly—or not so surprisingly, I suppose—my stock had risen at CDC. I have to admit, the rapidity with which I went from persona non grata to something of a company superstar was shocking. Brooke had always been a golden girl, so the events of the previous days just added to her shine at Santa Clara and at CDC. The folks in Atlanta are always thrilled when an alum makes good.

I'd called Tim Lancaster early on the day after Alaine was killed. The first words out of his mouth were "It hurts me to do this, Nate, but . . ." He said he'd already filed the necessary paperwork for a formal disciplinary hearing at the CDC home office. I should have hung up the telephone on him then, but I was sleep deprived and not thinking straight. Instead, I filled him in on what happened. After I'd finished, he said he needed to make a few calls. Most likely he was looking for corroboration of my story. Anyway, fifteen minutes later, he called back and said he'd be on the next flight to SFO.

For the next few days, I'd been pretty successful in avoiding the Commandant. He did intercept me a couple of times, but I was able to fake delirium twenty minutes into the meetings. I claimed it was the painkillers. Tim didn't believe me, but like I said, my rep was good and he let me off the hook. He was getting quite a boost, too, from my exploits and I think felt somewhat indebted. Maybe he even felt guilty for having put me on the block just a few days before, though that would be too human an emotion for the guy. In any case, I should have played him for more concessions, perks, or advancement, but what I wanted most of all was for him to leave me alone. He had my written reports and we could confer in Atlanta in a month. If he really wanted, he could go to the police and look at the reports there, he could go to the FBI and look at my reports there. There was no shortage of words from Dr. Nathaniel McCormick.

CHAPTER 102

I helped Brooke out of the car and we slowly made our way up to her apartment, to begin the task of packing for a month. The lease started that day, and I didn't want to lose any time. Packing for me was a cinch: the bloodied clothes I'd been wearing for a week were in a landfill somewhere, and I'd purchased exactly three new outfits for the trip. Five minutes, and I was finished, and that's with only one hand in action. Brooke, however, was another matter. If I'd had my druthers, she'd take a couple bikinis, a sundress, jeans, and maybe a sweater for the cool evenings. I didn't think she'd need a bra or panties. Brooke promptly nixed my overblown sexual fantasies, and we filled two suitcases with clothes and toiletries. Oh, yes, and a bag for all the dressings, gauze, pills, and salves we needed for recuperation.

The apartment phone rang as we were zipping the last of her suitcases. I answered, but no one was there.

Brooke, who was lying on the bed, asked who it was.

"A hang-up," I said.

She looked at me, worried.

"Just a hang-up," I said again.

In truth, though, I was worried, too, irrationally so. Though we both tried to shake it off, the subtext here was that our friend with the blistered face had somehow escaped, and was now checking to see if we were home so he could take care of unfinished business. I half-contemplated calling the cops to make sure the Surgeon was still in custody. But that would be silly, no? All my mental baggage was channeling itself into misplaced anxiety, right?

"Let's get some of this stuff in the car."

With one hand and aching shoulders, I couldn't haul much. I grabbed a suitcase and locked the door behind me. I was still nervous about Brooke, and the damned elevator was taking too long, so I opted for the steps. Hurrying the best I could, I shuffled to the carport and threw suitcase number one into the trunk, then sort of half-jogged back across the parking lot, up the stairs, and to the apartment.

I stopped at the door. I heard a voice, male. My heart began to thud.

I pictured the Surgeon in there, spewing his tough-guy talk before he put a bullet through Brooke's head. As quietly as I could, I put the key into the lock. Then I turned it fast and pushed open the door, rushing in.

I hit a body. The two of us stumbled across the room, striking the counter that separated the kitchen from the living room.

"What the—?"

The man was pinned between me and the counter. Not the Surgeon, but someone just as sinister. Tim Lancaster.

"What the F, Nate?" he said, brushing himself off and rubbing his hip where he'd collided with the Corian countertop. "I know you have an unabashed love for me, but come on."

Brooke was on the couch, smiling.

"What are you doing here?" I asked.

"I had to talk to you before you headed out to wherever you're heading. Why aren't you telling me where, by the way?"

"Because we don't want you to know."

"Right."

I looked at my boss, who, it seemed, hadn't done much sleeping in the past few days. I turned to Brooke, who still had the Cheshire cat smile plastered to her face. "He threaten you?"

She giggled.

Back to Tim. I asked, "Was it you who called and hung up?"

"Of course. I didn't want you running out on me."

"Nice move, Tim."

"It worked."

"You're lucky I didn't shoot you."

I let that one sink in, let Tim wonder whether I had a gun and whether I'd plug him if he ever sneaked up on us again.

"Here," he said, picking up a FedEx envelope from the floor and offering it to me. I waved my bandaged hand. "Oh. Forgot. Right." He ripped off the tab, pulled out a cream-colored piece of paper. The top heading read "Office of the Director." I glanced through the short letter. Basically, the director was commending me for my courage, resourcefulness, blah, blah, blah.

I looked at Brooke, who, I now noticed, also held a cream-colored piece of paper. "Congratulations," Tim said. "There's going to be a short ceremony in Atlanta later this week to honor you two. It won't be a big deal. Lunch with the director, a short speech by you."

"Great," I said. Two visions popped into my head. One: sitting on a porch, looking out over the Pacific, reading some thriller trash. Two: glad-handing in Atlanta, chatting with the giants of public health, choking down some government-issue coq au vin. Simple decision.

"Okay," I said, "we'll be there. Well, I can't speak for Dr. Michaels, but I'll be there, at least."

"Really?" Tim said.

"Of course. Just let me know when." I dropped the paper on a coffee table. "I'll have my cell on. I'm pretty sure we'll get reception where we're going, but if not, I'll call you with the landline number."

Tim nodded a few times. "Okay, okay." He clapped me on the back.

"Jesus—!" I yelped.

"Oh, sorry, Nate. Forgot. Okay," he said. "Well, Dr. McCormick, seems you're learning a few things about politicking. Good for you."

"I learned from the best." Though I couldn't be sure, I think Tim took that as a compliment.

"All right," he said. "That's all I wanted for now. Think about the offer, Brooke."

I looked at her. "They want me to come back to CDC," she told me.

Tim nodded in a paternal, giver-of-life way. I wanted to heave. I said to Brooke, "Just when you thought you were out, they pull you back in."

Tim laughed. "*The Sopranos,*" he said. "I *love* that show."

Yeah, that and . . . well, I wasn't going to give him a lesson in pop culture.

He opened the door. "Okay, I'll see you in Atlanta." I thought he was about to rip the cord and leave, but we weren't so lucky. "I'll call you later today or tomorrow with the details about the ceremony. Also, we're going to have some more questions about Tobel and Chen and their work with the bug. Take your computer—"

"Computer was stolen, Tim. When they broke into my car."

"I'm sure Brooke won't mind if you use her computer. I'll send you a few files today, which I'd like you to look over by tomorrow."

"Sure," I said.

"I'll let you go now. Enjoy yourselves, you two."

Brooke and I both said our thanks.

Tim almost closed the door, but stopped again. *It just never ends with this guy.* "Again, good work. Really good work. I have to apologize for . . . well, for throwing some obstacles in your way, but that was just . . ."

I waved him off. "Don't worry about it. You did what you had to do."

He nodded, pleased, and said, "Anyway, good job. You're both on the fast track now."

"I can feel the wind in my hair."

"Good. Well, enjoy the rest."

Bye-bye, Tim.

CHAPTER 103

A half hour later I had Brooke in the car, the front seat reclined the whole way so she could lie on her side. She had a map and a couple of Diet Cokes. We were ready. I pulled out of the parking area and pointed the car east to the highway, then north to Eureka.

On the 101, Brooke asked, "So, you're really going to go to this ceremony?"

"Aren't you?"

"I don't know. I don't want to. I don't know if I can sit on a plane for six hours."

"Be brave."

We crossed the Golden Gate Bridge, which, I have to admit, always makes me a little emotional. The whole experience is just so damned breathtaking: the russet bridge itself, the great expanse of the Pacific on your left, the sweeping expanse of North America on your right.

I was so overwhelmed, I pulled off at a parking lot at the northern side of the bridge. Well, maybe I had some other plans, too, besides taking in the vista.

"What are you doing?" Brooke pushed herself up and looked around.

"Nice view."

I reached into the backseat and fished around in my new shoulder bag.

"It's going to be dark by the time we get there, Nate."

"That's okay. There." I pulled out my cell phone and dropped it in my lap. I grabbed Brooke's computer bag and dropped that in my lap. "You have anything really valuable in here?"

She looked confused for a moment. Then, "No way. You're not taking the laptop."

"Come on."

She dropped onto her side so she could use her arms. She grabbed at the computer bag, laughing.

"No," she said through the giggles. "Give me that. Besides, I know there are no landlines where we're going." That was true. Drat: no file transfers from Tim Lancaster.

I put up a little more of a fight, then let her have the computer. She said, "I knew you weren't going, you asshole. Why'd you let Tim think you were going?"

"Asshole is as asshole does." I opened the car door. "You coming?"

"No. I think this is stupid. Besides, I'm comfortable."

I smiled at her and stepped out of the car, cell phone in hand. I rounded the car and opened her door and made another grab for the computer bag. She gripped it like a teddy bear. Women are so damn possessive.

The breeze was good, the air cool. I ambled to the walkway that would take me over the Golden Gate. The sun was falling in the west, electrifying all the colors around me. I passed tourists of all stripes: fat, skinny, European, Asian. Some smiled as they passed me. I wondered why until I realized I was wearing a grin from ear to ear. If I were a jumper, they'd tell the cops, "He just looked so happy. We never thought he'd . . ."

And I guess I was happy, for that moment at least. But I knew it was fleeting. I'd changed. All the bitching and cynicism aside, I'd always had faith that things would turn out okay in the end. That's the way in this country, right? Just on the other side of that new house, new job, new diet plan; just after med school, the Ivory Coast, or the next outbreak investigation, life would be better. There was that unshakable faith in perfectibility, in our power to make things right. I suppose I lost that. And somewhere in the previous few days, I lost, too, the illusion that I was the best guy for the job, that I was the most honorable, that I was the most competent. As Tim Lancaster and the rest of the world took their turns patting me on the back, I couldn't be sure who they were congratulating. Certainly not a savior; certainly not a rising star. Like Alaine Chen, I didn't know who I was anymore.

One thing I could be sure of: I was broken, as broken and empty as Kincaid Falk lying eviscerated in his earthen hole. I didn't know if the cracks would ever be repaired. But on my walk across that stunning bridge, looking forward to four weeks nuzzling a woman with whom I was probably falling in love, none of that seemed to matter. The tourists were right: I was, somehow, happy.

It took me ten minutes to walk to the middle of the Golden Gate. I stood there, gazing over the San Francisco Bay, at the white sailboats scattered across the indigo water. A man to my right asked me to take a shot of him and his family, thrusting a nice digital camera at me. I begged off and the gentleman seemed hurt until I waved my wrapped flipper at him. He got the picture, so to speak, and wisely took his electronica elsewhere.

Alone at last, I pulled out the cell phone. I really wished I had Brooke's computer, but this would have to do. I scrolled through the list of names until I got to *Lancaster*. I hit the Call button.

After three rings, Tim answered. "Dr. McCormick, what's up?" he asked, reading my number from his caller ID.

I walked to the guardrail. Then I pulled back my arm and let that thing sail.